**Praise for *USA TODAY* bestselling author
Debra Webb**

"Flawlessly combines action, adventure, mystery and romance."
—*RT Book Reviews* on *Colby Roundup*, Top Pick

"Colby action at its best, compressed into a tight timeline and with characters that tug at the heart."
—*RT Book Reviews* on *Colby Core*

"Fraught with intrigue...a tense and emotional nail-biter."
—*RT Book Reviews* on *Gunning for the Groom*

"The latest installment of the Colby Agency saga doesn't disappoint thanks to overlapping storylines, dark secrets and razor-thin tension."
—*RT Book Reviews* on *Broken*

**Praise for *USA TODAY* bestselling author
Victoria Pade**

"Victoria Pade's *Cowboy's Caress* keeps reader interest high with a charming cast of characters and a nice writing style..."
—*RT Book Reviews*

"Pade's couple is sweet, believable and heartbreaking as they work to clear the misdeeds of the past."
—*RT Book Reviews* on *A Baby in the Bargain*

"Ms. Pade has a special knack for creating fully developed, warmhearted characters that fit tightly together."
—*Rendezvous*

"Victoria Pade creates rich characters and a strong story about learning to forgive and love again."
—*RT Book Reviews* on *Cowboy's Love*

"Victoria Pade's *Cowboy's Baby* has a nice airy style that weaves a charming romantic tale.
—*RT Book Reviews*

Debra Webb born in Alabama, wrote her first story at age nine and her first romance at thirteen. It wasn't until after she spent three years working for the military behind the Iron Curtain—and a five-year stint with NASA—that she realized her true calling. Since then the *USA TODAY* bestselling author has penned more than one hundred novels, including her internationally bestselling Colby Agency series. Visit her at debrawebb.com.

Books by Debra Webb

Harlequin American Romance

Longwalker's Child
The Marriage Prescription
The Doctor Wore Boots

Harlequin Intrique

Safe by His Side
The Bodyguard's Baby
Protective Custody
Special Assignment: Baby
Solitary Soldier
Personal Protector
Physical Evidence
Contract Bride

Visit the Author Profile page at Harlequin.com for more titles.

HOME ON THE RANCH:
MONTANA
VOLUME 3

USA TODAY BESTSELLING AUTHORS
DEBRA WEBB
& VICTORIA PADE

HARLEQUIN® HOME ON THE RANCH

Recycling programs
for this product may
not exist in your area.

ISBN-13: 978-0-373-60311-4

Home on the Ranch: Montana Volume 3

Copyright © 2016 by Harlequin Books S.A.

The publisher acknowledges the copyright holders
of the individual works as follows:

The Doctor Wore Boots
Copyright © 2002 by Debra Webb

The Camden Cowboy
Copyright © 2012 by Victoria Pade

HARLEQUIN®
™ www.Harlequin.com

Printed in U.S.A.

CONTENTS

THE DOCTOR WORE BOOTS

Debra Webb

Special thanks to Alitza Wellstead
for always being there when I call.
This one is for you, Alitza!

Pre-Prologue

Once upon a time there was a beautiful young girl and a handsome young boy who fell deeply in love. But, alas, their families were at odds. So, determined to keep the two apart, the young boy's family took him and moved far, far away.

Many years later, when they were all grown up, the young man and the young woman found each other once more. Unwilling to risk separation again, they married swiftly before either of their families could object. As expected, many hurtful words were spoken, much damage was done, but love prevailed. Nothing could tear the loving couple apart.

To add to their happiness, less than one year later they were blessed with a perfect set of twin boys. The lovely young couple was so very happy at last. But that happiness was short-lived. Fate intervened in the form of a fatal car crash.

Both families were devastated. All that remained of their only children were the twin grandsons. A fierce custody battle ensued, widening the rift. Finally, a judge made the only fair decision he felt was possible; he gave each set of grandparents one of the twins. Due to the extreme hostility between the families, he ordered that all future contact be limited until they learned to get along. Taking the judge's words too much to heart, the estranged families, with their respective namesakes in tow, went their separate ways and never looked back.

Until now.

Prologue

O'Hare Airport

Dex Montgomery allowed his briefcase to collapse to the floor next to the only empty table in the crowded bar. He jerked at his tie and dropped into a chair, completely disgusted.

Two hours. His flight was delayed for *two hours*. What was he supposed to do for two hours?

"Are you ready to order, sir?"

Dex heaved a sigh fraught with equal measures of impatience and frustration and looked up at the waitress watching him expectantly.

"Scotch," he told her. "No water. And make it a double."

She nodded and headed in the direction of the bar, weaving her way through the throngs of occupied tables and pausing occasionally to take another customer's order.

Glancing at his watch, Dex considered whether or not to call in and inform his grandfather of the delay. He definitely wouldn't make this afternoon's meeting of the board. Dex frowned. Montgomery men had no tolerance for delays. There was little he could do about it, however. The old man would simply have to fend for himself. His frown relaxed a bit with that thought. Charles Dexter Montgomery, Senior, was getting a little soft anyway. Sparring with the sharks who made up the board of M3I would be good for him.

Considering the boring financial conference Dex had just endured, it was only fair. This was the third conference he'd attended in the last two months. He was sick of hearing how M3I could improve its profit margin. Dex clenched his jaw. Modern Medical Maintenance, Inc., affectionately known as M3I, maintained a very healthy profit margin. Dex and his grandfather saw to that. They'd started with a single facility in Atlanta and had built a medical empire. M3I now consisted of a chain of cutting-edge facilities throughout the Southeast. The business was focused on providing quality medical care and making a profit.

Not necessarily in that order.

"Anything else?" The waitress placed the drink in front of him and smiled. Not a thank-you-for-your-patronage kind of smile, but one that became a predatory gleam in her eyes. She was flirting.

"No, thank you." He paid the lady and turned his attention to his drink. He didn't need a flirtatious waitress and he damn sure didn't need two hours in a bar.

He needed work.

Dex almost laughed out loud at that one. What he did wasn't work, it was choreography. He led a well-rehearsed dance to the sound of money changing hands. The medical degree and license he held were mere icing on the cake of the distinguished position as chairman of the board. Dr. Dexter Montgomery. It had the right ring to it even if it wasn't for practicing medicine. No doctor with the Montgomery name would dare sully his hands treating patients. Not when there was money to be made.

Dex stopped himself. He always got this way when he spent any length of time away from the office. That's why he all but lived at the office. Work was his life. He knew nothing else, didn't even have a hobby. And why should he? He had plans. Plans that didn't include silly, sentimental musings.

"To profit margins," he muttered and downed a hefty gulp of Scotch.

The hair on the back of his neck suddenly stood on end. Frowning again, he tilted his head left then right, stretching to relieve some of the tension. But that little niggling sensation of being watched just wouldn't go away. He glanced around the room, then did a double-take. A couple of tables away a man, his cowboy hat on the table before him, sat, seemingly paralyzed, the glass in his hand halfway to his mouth.

Dex registered surprise first…then incredulity. The cowboy was dressed differently than he was, no Armani or Cardin, but he looked exactly the same. Same thick dark hair, cropped short. Maybe his was a fraction longer. Same dark eyes…same square jaw… same…everything.

Dex pushed to his feet, the legs of his chair scraping

across the tiled floor. Before he had the good sense to stop himself and think about what he was doing he'd crossed to the man's table, passed his drink to his left hand and extended his right. "Dex Montgomery," he said numbly.

Apparently shocked himself, the cowboy stared first at Dex's hand, then at him. "Ty Cooper," he responded stiffly. His callused hand closed over Dex's. The contact was brief but something passed between them. Some strange energy that felt alien but somehow oddly familiar.

Dex shook his head in question. "Who...? How...?" This was surreal. The man didn't just resemble him—he looked exactly like him.

Apparently at a loss himself, Ty gestured to the empty chair on the opposite side of the small table. "Maybe you'd better have a seat."

Dumbfounded, Dex complied. "This isn't possible. I mean..." He shook his head again. "I'm a doctor and even I'm at a loss for an explanation." This couldn't be. It was like looking into a mirror. It was bizarre.

The other man scrubbed a hand over his chin. "You're right, partner. It's a little weird looking at your reflection in another man's face. Maybe we're related somehow?" He laughed nervously. "You know, distantly. Identical cousins or something."

Dex lifted one shoulder, then let it fall. "That's possible, I suppose." A memory pinged him. "Did you say Cooper?" he asked, almost hesitantly.

Ty nodded. "Of Rolling Bend, Montana. We have a cattle ranch called the—"

"Rolling Bend, Montana?" A chunk of ice formed in Dex's stomach.

"Yeah." Ty swallowed hard. "You know the place?"

Dex's gaze settled fully onto his. *He* couldn't believe what he was about to say. "My mother's name was Tara Cooper. She was born in Rolling Bend."

Ty signaled the passing waitress. "Ma'am, we're gonna need another round here," he said, his voice hollow.

She glanced at Dex, then started visibly when her gaze landed back on Ty. "Doubles for doubles," she said with a giggle. "Are you guys twins or something?"

Dex glared at her and she scurried away. Ty leaned forward as if what he had to say was too unbelievable to utter out loud. "Tara Cooper was *my* mother."

A choked sound, not quite a laugh, burst from Dex. "But my mother died when I was three months old."

"My birth date is May 21, 1970," Ty countered. "My mother died in an accident with my father when I was three months old."

"Oh yeah? Well, so did mine. But I don't have any siblings," Dex argued, unable to comprehend what he could see with his own eyes.

"Neither do I—well, except for my adopted brothers."

Dex gestured vaguely. "Maybe there were two Tara Coopers in Rolling Bend?"

Ty moved his head slowly from side to side. "We're the only Cooper clan in that neck of the woods."

"I'm certain there's some reasonable explanation," Dex suggested. Adrenaline pulsed through his veins making his heart pound. This man couldn't be his brother. That was impossible.

"There's an explanation all right," Ty said flatly. "We've been had."

* * *

Three hours and too many drinks to remember later, Dex had concluded the only reasonable explanation. Ty Cooper was not only his brother, but his identical twin. They had both missed their scheduled flights home, but neither cared.

The stories of their parents' whirlwind courtship, marriage and tragic deaths matched down to the dates. Ty had been told, as had Dex, that he had no other family. Dex could just imagine the reaction of his grandfather when his only son had married a rancher's daughter. Dex had only been told his mother's name, little else.

"What I want to know," Ty said, his speech a little slower, thicker, "is how the hell did they decide who would take who?"

For one long moment the two just looked at each other. Dex wondered briefly what his life would have been like if he'd been chosen by the other set of grandparents, but he couldn't begin to imagine. Considering his grandfather Montgomery's penchant for absolute control, Dex couldn't help thinking how the old man would react when he found out that Dex had learned the truth. He had no doubt that his grandfather was the mastermind behind this whole scheme.

"We should show up together and stage a confrontation," Dex commented dryly before draining his glass.

Ty grinned. "You may have something there." Those unnervingly familiar dark eyes twinkled with mischief now. "I say we give 'em a taste of their own medicine."

A flash of concern found its way through the warm, Scotch-induced haze now cloaking Dex. "What do you have in mind?"

Ty motioned to the waitress and then pointed to their empty glasses once more. "I'm talking about trading places, brother. For just a little while," he added quickly. "Just long enough to teach our families a lesson."

Dex hesitated at first, then a smile slid across his face. "Oh, that's good. All we have to do is bring each other up to speed on how to act and what to do." He flared his hands and inclined his head in a gesture of nonchalance. "It's simple on my end. You leave the business decisions to the old man. I have a secretary and a financial advisor who take care of things at the office. They'll keep you straight on the day-to-day schedule." He paused, considering. "If a problem does come up and you need to make a financial decision on your own, use your own discretion. You *are* a Montgomery."

"Same here," Ty assured him. "I have two adopted brothers. Between them and the ranch hands, they can handle things at the Circle C. It'll be good for both of us. We can get to know the rest of our family."

Dex nodded, though he was more concerned at the moment with teaching his grandfather a lesson than anything else. He noted the time. "All right, then," he said. "We have ninety minutes before our flights leave for our respective destinations. Let's do it."

Ty folded his arms over his chest. "You go first. I have a feeling your folks are a lot more complicated than mine."

Dex didn't bother to tell him that *complicated* was not the word he was looking for, instead he told Ty Cooper everything he would need to know in order to play Dexter Montgomery for just a little while.

Chapter 1

What the devil had he done?

Reality crashed down around Dex Montgomery as he stood in the designated pick-up area at Gallatin Field Airport in Bozeman, Montana. Ty had told him where to wait for his ride, and someone from the Cooper clan would pick him up.

Dex swallowed hard, his head aching from one Scotch too many. It was the first time in his entire life he could recall having too much to drink and a hangover all in the same afternoon. But now, as the grim reality of his actions settled around him, he knew today was not like any other he'd experienced in his thirty-two years. He doubted his life would ever be the same again.

The Gucci briefcase, Louis Vuitton garment bag, and state-of-the-art cellular phone he'd left home with just four days ago were now in the possession of a virtual stranger. A stranger who was his twin brother, who, in another hour or so, would be climbing into *his* limo and riding to *his* home to meet *his* family.

What the hell was *he* doing here?

Dex dropped the army-style duffel bag belonging to Ty Cooper to the ground. He tugged at the collar of the unstarched shirt he now wore and attempted to straighten the off-the-rack jacket. It was very obvious to Dex that his brother had absolutely no taste in clothing. The jeans were criminally worn and far too tight for comfort. The boots—Dex shook his head—had definitely seen better days. Though he doubted that even in mint condition he would have cared for the unnaturally high-arched footwear. He tried not to think about the cowboy hat perched atop his head. The urge to remove it was almost more than he could restrain.

Didn't cowboys keep their hats on at all times?

What had possessed him to change clothes with another man, brother or not, in an airport restroom?

Temporary insanity. It was the only possible explanation. Stress had finally taken its toll. George, his valet, friend and confidant, had warned him that he was pushing too hard, working far too many hours. But Dex had refused to listen. He had to prove his worth, couldn't risk disappointing his grandfather. He was thirty-two, for Pete's sake. He had mountains to climb and oceans to cross. His mark to make.

He had lost his mind. Here he stood, in the middle of nowhere, when he should be dictating correspondence, crunching numbers, planning takeovers. His grandfather counted on him, trusted him unconditionally.

He couldn't do this.

One telephone call would end this ruse here and now.

Dex grabbed the bag he'd abandoned on the ground and pivoted toward the airport entrance. This was a bad idea. Surely there would be another flight out of here sometime tonight. At the moment he really didn't care where it was going, as long as it took him back to a more recognizable form of civilization.

"Ty!"

A vehicle screeched to a halt behind him.

"Ty! Over here!" a feminine voice shouted.

Dex froze. *Ty.* His transportation had arrived. Dex swore under his breath. He should just keep walking without looking back. But then he'd never know…

Slowly, his head throbbing with frustration and the lingering effects of alcohol, he turned and faced step two of his self-created nightmare.

A young woman waved from behind the wheel of an old pickup truck. "Sorry you had to wait!" she called. She leaned across the seat and opened the passenger-side door. "I didn't know until an hour ago that I would be coming to pick you up."

Blond hair, blue eyes—she was very young, twenty-two or -three maybe. Dex frowned, searching his memory banks for the name that went with the face. Leanne. Leanne Watley. Neighbor. Family friend. The kid-sister type, Ty had said.

"I got here as fast as I could," she hastened to add when he continued to simply stare at her. "Come on. Gran's holding supper until I get you home. They've got a big celebration planned for your return."

Somehow his feet moved. Dex wasn't exactly sure

how he managed the monumental task considering his brain felt paralyzed with uncertainty, but he took the necessary steps just the same.

He slid onto the ragged bench seat and awkwardly settled the big duffel onto his lap. He couldn't imagine what possessed people to drive vehicles like this. There was no place to put anything. And the seat was most uncomfortable.

Leanne laughed. "You can put that in the back. It's not raining."

The back. "Of course." His face heated. He wasn't usually so inept. As he climbed out of the vehicle, Dex hoped she couldn't see the level of disorientation afflicting him. His movements felt jerky, his ability to think nonexistent. He placed the worn bag into the bed of the truck and settled back into the passenger seat. He closed the door and offered her a strained smile. "Thank you."

She frowned, just the slightest creasing of her smooth brow. "I guess you're really tired. I'm sorry you had to wait for a ride."

"Your delayed arrival was completely understandable," he assured her. "Considering the unexpected change in my return itinerary, your reaction time was quite acceptable."

Her eyes widened with something that looked very much like worry. "Are you all right, Ty? You sound a little…strange."

Dex realized his mistake immediately. He was Ty Cooper now. Looking like him wasn't enough, he had to speak and act like him as well.

"Jet lag," he offered as much to his surprise as to

hers. Could one actually acquire jet lag on a short jaunt that only crossed one time zone?

She nodded. "Oh."

By the time they left Bozeman behind, the sick feeling in the pit of Dex's stomach had escalated to a near-intolerable level. He shifted restlessly, peering out the window. How long before they would reach the ranch? How could he possibly fool Ty's grandparents? This would never work. He should just demand that she turn around right now and take him back to the airport. Instead, he reviewed over and over again the information Ty had relayed to him regarding his family and the layout of the ranch. He reminded himself again to use his left hand as much as possible. Ty was a lefty.

"How'd the meeting with those investors go?" she asked, breaking the long, awkward silence.

Dex jerked back to attention. "Excuse me?"

"Are you sure you're feeling all right?" She looked at him with that genuine concern again.

"Yes, yes," he assured her. "I'm fine. The meeting went…was okay… I guess." He'd forgotten to ask Ty why he was in Chicago. She'd said investors. "I won't know anything for a few days," he added for good measure. That was typical. Investors made lots of promises, but the real story was revealed much more slowly. If Ty had begun some sort of deal, only time would tell if it was a good one or not.

Leanne sighed. "That's too bad. I know you were hoping to have news when you got back."

"Yes." He cleared his throat. "Yeah. I was."

He glanced at the young woman behind the wheel. What was she thinking? Had she seen through him already? Worry twisted inside him. If he couldn't get through a few simple questions from a neighbor without making her suspicious, how on earth would he fool the Coopers?

"I know how much this deal means to you, Ty," she went on, worry weighting her voice. "But maybe it's like your pa said. Maybe you'll just have to be happy with things the way they are. It's not like you don't have enough buyers to keep your ranch going. The Circle C has provided high-quality beef to its customers for three generations now."

The cattle market. So that was the kind of investors Ty had gone to the city to meet. Dex was somewhat familiar with the distressed American market. Foreign beef had made a big comeback in the United States recently, a huge surge from the past couple of years when disease had wrought such devastation for European countries. Was Ty trying to increase the reach of his own ranch's production? That sounded reasonable to Dex. He'd have to ask Ty about that or risk making a wrong step.

"I'd like to go to Chicago sometime," Leanne said wistfully, drawing Dex's attention in her direction. She huffed, her gaze steady on the endless ribbon of blacktop that lay before them. "I've never even been out of the state. I don't know why I'm fretting over Chicago. I doubt I'll ever be going there."

Dex looked at her then, really looked at her. She was quite attractive. She wore no makeup as far as he could tell, but she didn't need any. She looked vibrant, healthy. That notion sent the corners of his mouth tilting upward for some reason he couldn't understand. She was nothing like the women he knew. Oh, and young. He almost asked her age, but caught himself just in time. Ty would know how old she was. Young, that was certain. Too damned young.

"You should go sometime," he suggested. "Life is short, make the most of it."

"I don't see that happening," she said regretfully. Her gaze locked onto his as she slowed to make a right turn onto a gravel road. In that infinitesimal moment something electric passed between them. Startled, she looked away.

Startled himself, Dex gave his head a little shake. What the hell was that? He was disoriented, that's all. He'd be fine as soon as he—

As soon as he what? There was no way he was going to be fine. He was in the middle of nowhere with strangers. Worst of all he was pretending to be someone he'd only just met.

This whole idea had sounded much more doable before he'd sobered up.

Miles of nothing stretched before him as well as behind him. In the time since they'd left the city of Bozeman, they had encountered highway and mountains, nothing more.

A blue sky, fading slowly into dusk, looked almost low enough to touch. Dex couldn't recall ever feeling this close to the heavens before. He scrubbed a hand over his face. The disorientation was clearly turning to delusions. This was bad. Very bad.

She turned right again, this time onto a long winding dirt road. The sun barely hovered above the mountaintops in the distance. Acres and acres of fenced pasture yawned on either side of the rough road. Cattle grazed serenely on the lush carpet of green grass.

Around the next bend in the road, a sight that Dex would not soon forget appeared before him. A two-story sprawling ranch house stood against the breath-taking backdrop of majestic mountain ranges. A barn right off the pages of a New England calendar lay in the distance, as did other not-readily-identifiable structures. A corral he recognized from its circular design encompassed a large area near the barn. His gaze shifted back to the house. It was the house that held the place of honor among nature's and man's embellishments. With the authenticity of a perfect reproduction from the set of an old black-and-white Western movie, the house looked homey, inviting.

"Home sweet home," he murmured as his heart rate increased, sending adrenaline surging through his veins.

"Yessiree Bob," Leanne agreed.

She smiled, a gesture that sent a spear of heat straight through him. Were all the women out here so innocent-looking and apparently sweet?

"Come on, they'll be waiting."

She got out, skirted the hood and reached in back for his bag before he had the presence of mind to react.

Dex wrenched the door open and all but fell out of the truck. "I'll get that," he insisted, grappling for his equilibrium and at the same time reaching for the heavy duffel. She was certainly stronger than she looked.

"Gran fixed your favorite for supper," she told him with another of those wide, sincere smiles.

He nodded, but hoped to God he could bow out of dinner, er, supper. He wasn't ready to play Ty Cooper to a larger audience just yet. And he didn't have a clue what Ty's favorite meal was supposed to be. Surely the Coopers would understand that he was exhausted after his trip and required an early retirement this evening.

Dex followed Leanne up the steps to the wooden porch that spanned the front of the house. A low growl froze him in his tracks. His eyes widened when his gaze sought and found the source of the sound. A dog. A large, rather fierce-looking animal that appeared poised to lunge at him. Dex had no experience with dogs to call upon. Grandmother Montgomery had allergies. Pets had never been allowed in the Montgomery residence.

"Lady," Leanne scolded. "Why would you growl at Ty? Just because he took a trip without you?" she said in that childlike tone adults took when speaking affectionately to children or animals. "He's only been gone a week. Now you be a good girl. You know better than to misbehave." She scratched the big animal, which Dex now recognized as a golden retriever, behind the ears.

"You should recognize me, Lady," he put in when Leanne looked up at him as if she expected some sort of reaction. He certainly wasn't about to reach down and touch the animal.

Leanne gave Lady's head one final pat. The dog lumbered away, then dropped onto the porch as if too tired or disgusted to pursue the situation further.

"Looks like you're not the only one feeling out of sorts this evening."

Dex feigned a laugh. "Jet lag," he repeated.

Leanne stared at him for one long moment. "Yeah. Maybe I don't want to go to Chicago if flying is that tough on you." She opened the front door and entered the house as if she lived there.

No locked door. No knock first. Dex would have been appalled at the Coopers' lack of security measures had his heart not been pounding like a drum in his chest. He had to find a way out of this. He would never fool these people.

"We're here!" Leanne shouted as she wandered down the hall.

"Welcome home!"

Dex jerked to an abrupt stop in the middle of the hall. The duffel thunked to the hardwood floor. What looked like a dozen people, of varying sizes and ages, all beaming smiles, and heading for him, crowded into the entry hall. A big banner reading Welcome Home! draped from one wall to the other. One would think that Ty had been gone for months.

An older woman, her gray hair in a tight bun, her hazel eyes shining with emotion, threw her arms around him first. "It's good to have you back home, son."

His Grandmother Cooper.

Dex opened his mouth to speak but no words formed. He felt suddenly overwhelmed with unfamiliar emotions as those slim, frail arms tightened around him.

A strong hand clapped him on the back even before the older woman released him. "Take that hat off, young man."

Dex turned to greet the man who'd spoken. Tall, slim, thinning gray hair, brown eyes. Dex dragged the hat from his head and dropped it on a nearby table.

"Pa," he offered, the single-syllable word steeped in too many emotions to sort. This was his mother's father.

The older man slung an arm around his shoulder and started down the hall, Dex in tow. "Come on, boy, supper's waiting." He paused and beamed a proud smile in Dex's direction. "We're glad you're home, son."

Everyone started talking at once then. Dex lost track of the number of times his journey was halted so that he could be hugged and welcomed home. His Grandmother Cooper insisted that Leanne stay for supper. For some reason he couldn't begin to understand, he was glad she agreed to stay. He'd analyze that bit of irony later.

Right now it took all his powers of concentration to watch his step. Especially since three small children all but clung to his legs as he followed the crowd into the dining room. He felt certain his back would be bruised considering all the hearty poundings he'd taken from the male Coopers. For these people, outward displays of affection were apparently a way of life.

The dining table was long, like the one in his home back in Atlanta, only this one was a rustic country style, the tabletop scarred from years of everyday use. The heavy stoneware dishes bore the same worn appearance and spoke of both hard times and good times, neither of which were forgotten or taken for granted.

The elder Coopers occupied the head positions at the table. Leanne sat across from Dex next to Angelica, the five-year-old daughter of Ty's adopted brother Chad. Chad and his wife also sat on that side. Next to Dex was Chad's older brother, Court, his wife, and their four-year-old twin boys. At least he hoped he had the right name with the right brother.

Ty had explained that Court and Chad were the sons of Grandmother Cooper's younger sister who had died years ago, leaving the boys alone in the world since their father had already passed away. The Coopers had gladly taken in the boys, adopting them and rearing them as Ty's brothers. Dex suddenly wanted to know what that sort of love was like. That kind of family bond. Though he knew his grandparents in Atlanta loved him, it wasn't the same.

"So, did you have a pleasant trip?" Grandmother Cooper asked as she offered a platter of steaks to Dex.

Dex stared at the enormous platter as he accepted it. Big, thick, juicy cuts of beef. He selected the smallest portion then passed the platter to Court. "It was…" How the hell was it? he wondered. "…as well as can be expected, I suppose," he said noncommittally.

Grandfather Cooper snorted. "I told you not to get your hopes up, son. You're just like your mother, always dreaming big dreams. But sometimes you just have to be satisfied with the way things are."

Dex stared at the older man. *Just like his mother.* His mother'd had big dreams? What kind of dreams? He suddenly wanted to know.

"Enough of that," Grandmother Cooper scolded when Dex was relatively sure his grandfather would have gone on. "Ty's just gotten home. He can tell us about the business part of his trip tomorrow."

She smiled at Dex and he had the abrupt, overwhelming feeling that it was exactly like seeing his mother smile. Before he could dwell further on the gesture a bowl of green beans was thrust under his

chin. Dex peered down at the clearly overcooked veg-
etable. The whole meal was a ticket to an early grave.
Green beans, cooked with what appeared to be a
hunk of meat consisting totally of fat, steak, potatoes
brimming with golden butter, and a slab of cornbread
that looked as though it could keep them all fed for
a week. The kind of meal the Montgomerys avoided
at all costs.

Not a single lettuce leaf was in sight.

Dex surveyed the large group gathered around the
table. Hadn't any of them heard about eating healthy?
Without warning, something hit him square in the
chest. A green bean lay on the table, a greasy spot
just above the fourth button soiled the tan-colored
shirt he wore.

Across the wide expanse of worn, but well-polished
oak Angelica smiled innocently at him. Dex peered at
her in confusion for a moment, then at the bean once
more. Had she thrown it at him? He lifted his gaze
back to her just in time to see her use her spoon to
launch another one in his direction. This one hit high
on his right shoulder.

Dex frowned, uncertain of what course of action he should take, if any. He hadn't spent any time
around children. He only knew that they were messy
and cried a lot. This one appeared intent on the former. He scanned the other adult faces. All were engrossed in eating or some discussion about the ranch
he probably wouldn't have understood even if he'd
been listening.

Just when Angelica, an evil grin plastered across
her pretty little face, prepared to fire at him once more,

her father's hand closed over hers. "Stop that, young lady," he said firmly.

Relieved, Dex relaxed. "She's a pretty good shot, Court," he offered conversationally.

Everyone stopped talking and stared at him. What had he done? The sound of blood roaring through his ears made the silence deafening. Had he made a mistake already?

And then he knew.

"Chad," Dex amended, then shook his head. He'd called the man by the wrong name. Dex shrugged. "Jet lag," he offered in explanation.

All nodded, some even laughed and seemed to be satisfied with that excuse. All but Leanne, who studied him inquisitively. Flashing her a strained smile, Dex focused on the food on his plate. He'd have to be more careful. His head was throbbing, his heart pounding. But he was here now. He might as well give this trading places thing a shot. There was no reason he couldn't do it. He glanced at the child sitting across the table. She gave him one of those I'm-not-through-with-you-yet looks. Then again, maybe he couldn't do it.

Had he lost his mind entirely? Dex slowly studied the people seated around the table. Uncertainty undermined his newly found determination. How in the world was he supposed to fool all of them? When his gaze settled on his Grandmother Cooper again she chose that precise moment to turn toward him. Another of those heartwarming smiles spread across her lovely face. This was why he was here. *This* was his opportunity to learn what kind of person his mother had been. To see pictures…to learn about her past.

And maybe to somehow understand how a family as seemingly loving and generous as this one could take one child and turn their back on the other.

Chapter 2

Dex felt like a character from an episode of a reality TV show.

He was mentally and physically drained, but his first meal with the Coopers was nearing an end at last. The moment anyone seated around the large table made a move signaling the event was officially over, he intended to excuse himself for the evening. His senses were on overload. Too much conversation, too many different voices and personalities. He'd definitely taken for granted the experience of quiet dining. He doubted he would do that again anytime soon. This level of stimuli during a meal couldn't possibly bode well for the digestive system.

Not to mention he'd ingested more saturated fats in one sitting than he had in a lifetime of eating his usual cuisine. He had to admit, however, that the steak had been more than palatable…tasty even. If what he'd been served tonight was indicative of Cooper beef, then the quality was premium.

He could see now why Ty felt compelled to pursue larger markets. The product was certainly worth the extra effort.

"We'll clear, ladies," Chad, or at least Dex thought it was Chad, said as he pushed back his chair and stood.

At this point Dex wasn't sure of anything except that he had to be alone.

"Why, thank you, honey," Chad's wife—Jenny, if Dex remembered correctly—crooned with a wide smile.

Following the example of the other men, Dex stood as well. He knew a moment of panic as he considered what he should do next. He'd never had to clear a table before. How difficult could it be? Drawing on years of experience of eating at restaurants, he reached for his plate and glass like the waiters who'd served him in the past.

"No way, brother," Court said from beside him. "You've got the night off." Court winked. "Besides, you have company to see to."

Dex blinked, uncertain what the man meant. What company?

"Oh, don't be silly, Court," Leanne chided. She pushed to her feet. "I can see myself out. It's past time I got home." She leaned down and pressed a quick kiss to Grandmother Cooper's cheek. "Thank you for having me to supper."

"Anytime, dear," she returned. "Anytime. You tell your mama I said hello."

"I sure will." Leanne glanced at Dex. "Well, I guess I'll be going."

Court elbowed him. "I'll…ah…see you to the door," Dex offered, suddenly remembering his manners, and realizing, just as abruptly, that the rest of the family clearly considered Leanne his company.

Still trying to figure that one out, Dex followed her into the front hall. "Thank you again for picking me up at the airport," he offered for lack of anything else to say.

"I didn't mind," she said, turning back to him when she stopped at the door. "I hope something good comes of your trip, Ty. I do know how much it means to you."

The sincerity in her eyes was so genuine that it moved Dex. Or maybe it was just those big blue eyes that affected him. And all that silky blond hair. For the first time since he'd met Leanne, Dex took a moment to really look at her. She was of medium height, her figure curvy, voluptuous. Nothing like the waif-thin women he usually preferred. The well-worn jeans and button-up blouse were accessorized with scuffed boots and a leather belt that cinched her tiny waist. The smallness of her waist accentuated her womanly hips and particularly full breasts. Dex drew in a tight breath. She certainly had a nice set of…

"Are you sure you're all right, Ty?"

Her question jolted him to attention. He blinked and dragged his gaze back to hers. Though she looked concerned, he could well imagine what she must think at the moment. He'd blatantly stared at her breasts. Thoroughly measured her body with his eyes. He had no doubt he'd lost his mind. The chances of a speedy recovery looked dim at best.

"I'm fine...really," he insisted. "Fine."

She nodded, the doubt clear in her eyes. "Well, I'll see you around then."

He felt his head bob up and down though he couldn't recall issuing the necessary command. "Sure," he managed to choke out.

She hesitated when she would have opened the door, adding a new layer of tension to his already unbearable state. "I almost forgot." She stared up at him. "Are we still on for the dance Friday night?"

Dance? Ty hadn't mentioned any dance. Worry tightened around his throat like a noose. "Dance?" he echoed his bewildered thought.

"The annual barbecue and dance to raise money for the volunteer fire department. You haven't forgotten, have you?"

Faced with her expression of disappointment and maybe even a little hurt he heard himself say, "No, no. I haven't forgotten. I'm just too tired to think, that's all." He shrugged. "Sure, we're still on," he added, using her words.

Her face brightened. The smile with which she gifted him shifted something in his chest. How could a mere smile have such a mesmerizing effect?

"Good night," she murmured.

"Good night." Despite everything, he just couldn't help himself. He felt his lips curl upward as he stared deeply into those wide, blue eyes.

Before he could fathom her intent, she tiptoed and placed a chaste kiss on his jaw then rushed out the door.

Dex stared after her as she hurried away. He didn't close the door until the taillights of her truck had disappeared around the bend. He touched his jaw where she'd kissed him and he felt weak with something he couldn't name. What was it about this woman—this place—that made him feel so strange? He couldn't recall ever having felt so flustered, so uncertain of who he was.

"Dex Montgomery," he murmured. "You're Dex Montgomery." He had to remember that.

"Ty."

Dex turned to find Grandmother Cooper waiting near the bottom of the stairs. He smiled automatically, which was not his custom. He couldn't say for sure whether he intended the gesture or if he'd simply done it so she would smile back at him. There was something about her smile.

"I know you're worn out, son," she said kindly. "Why don't you call it a night? You can tell us all about your trip in your own time." She winked covertly. "I left a present for you in your room."

Dex felt weightless as he watched her walk away. His grandmother had gotten him a gift. Why that should give him such pleasure, he had no clue. But it waited for him in his room.

Dex stilled. No. It was waiting for him in Ty's room.

Where the hell was Ty's room?

How could she have kissed him?

Leanne slammed on her brakes and skidded to a frustrated halt a few feet from her own front porch. She shut off the lights and engine and heaved a disgusted sigh.

She'd kissed Ty. At least it had been only on the cheek, but she'd kissed him nonetheless.

She had undoubtedly lost her everloving mind. Why else would she have behaved so irrationally? Been so forward? There was no telling what he thought.

Depressed now more than disgusted, she laid her forehead against the steering wheel and considered how she would ever face him again.

Warmth spread through her as the brief meeting of her lips and his stubbled jaw played through her mind once more. Though always clean-shaven, Ty's dark features left him with a five o'clock shadow every evening. She'd always imagined that beneath that darkly handsome exterior beat the heart of a truly sinful lover. A man who could please a woman. The details of his muscular chest ran through her mind. Never had the idea of Ty's virility or masculinity intrigued her so.

Leanne straightened, frowning. She'd seen Ty shirtless hundreds of times. He was a strong, well-built man. She felt certain he would make some woman very happy some day. But not her. She loved him like a *brother*. Not once in her entire life had she felt even remotely sexually attracted to him.

Not once.

Until today.

The moment their gazes had locked at the airport she'd felt something…something different. She shook her head and climbed out of her old truck. The Coopers as well as her own mother had been trying to push the two of them together for as long as she could remember. She knew they meant well, wanted their children to be happy. But Leanne had other plans. She wanted to fall head over heels in love with a man who would sweep her off her feet. And she wanted to be financially independent.

"Yeah, right," she grumbled as she trudged up the steps to her house. Just how was she supposed to meet Mr. Right and be financially independent when she was barely keeping her head above water in more ways than one?

She unlocked the front door and went inside. Being careful not to make any more noise than necessary she closed and locked the door behind her. The stairs to the second floor proved a bit trickier when it came to her efforts to be soundless. But Leanne knew all the spots to avoid. She didn't want to wake her mother. Lord knew, sleep was the only peace she found.

Joanna Watley suffered with debilitating weakness and often a great deal of pain. Dr. Baker had done everything he could for her, to no avail. She needed further testing and a specialist or maybe even a team of specialists. But there was no money for such extravagances that would likely do no good, her mother insisted. Without medical insurance the burden of cost fell squarely on Leanne and her mother's shoulders. A burden Leanne was ready to accept if her mother would only allow it.

Leanne paused outside her mother's bedroom door. She slept soundly. Leanne eased into the room and sat down on the edge of the bed to watch her sleep. She was a truly beautiful woman. Long blond hair, peppered with a little gray, and blue eyes. The same blue eyes Leanne had inherited. Leanne's father used to say that she and her mother looked more like sisters than mother and daughter. He'd always known how to bring a smile to her mother's lips. It just didn't seem fair that he'd died four years ago, and then last year her mother's debilitating illness had struck. Leanne blinked back her tears. She loved her mother dearly and she would do whatever she could to help her.

Joanna Watley had a stubborn streak a mile wide, though. Leanne had begged her to sell the ranch and use the money for whatever medical treatment she needed. Joanna refused. She insisted that they hang on to the ranch no matter what. She'd be all right in time, she always said.

But that time never came. She only got worse. Leanne felt a burst of desperation in her chest. How would she ever convince her mother to listen to her? She probably couldn't, which left Leanne with only one choice. She had to make the money herself. She couldn't leave her mother alone all day to get a job in town. And anyway, Leanne had no real skills. With her father's ill health, then his death, and now her mother's illness, she'd been taking care of the ranch since she'd graduated high school. There'd been no time or money for college.

Instead, she spent every spare moment attempting to complete what her father had begun—turning their ranch into a dude ranch. Dude ranches were wildly popular, and this area of Montana was particularly attractive to tourists. No one else in the vicinity had one. It would be a gold mine, if only Leanne could finish the job.

The guest cabins had been constructed. The pool was pretty much complete. If Leanne worked hard enough, saved every cent possible, she could get it up and running. With the dozen horses they had kept and the guest cabins and pool ready, she could prepare to open this fall. She might not make much in the beginning, but her reputation would build. Then she would have the money to send her mother wherever she needed to go without selling the ranch.

But that seemed a lifetime away. Though Dr. Baker didn't feel her mother's symptoms were life-threatening, it was definitely debilitating, leaving her with a miserable existence.

Leanne blinked back a fresh wave of tears. She didn't want her mother to suffer like this. But she was an adult, Leanne couldn't make her go to a specialist.

"You home already?"

Leanne produced a smile at the weak sound of her mother's voice. "I didn't mean to wake you."

"I'm glad you came in to say good-night." Her mother frowned. "But you shouldn't have hurried home."

"I didn't want to stay out too late. You feeling all right?"

Her mother dredged up a smile from a source of strength Leanne could only imagine possessing. "I'm just fine. How did Ty's trip go?"

"He won't know for a while." Leanne looked away. She didn't want to get into a discussion of Ty with her mother. Not tonight.

"Is something wrong, Leanne?"

Her mother read her too well. "Oh no," she assured her. "Everything's fine." But it wasn't, she thought, remembering the way he'd looked at her in the truck on the way home and then at the door when they'd said good-night. Something was definitely different.

Her mama's hand closed over hers. "I wish I could make you see, child, what a good husband Ty would make. I don't know why you don't trust your mama's instincts."

Here they went again. Leanne sighed. "I know he'd make a fine husband, Mama, that's not the problem."

Joanna shook her head. "You've read too many of those paperbacks. You keep expecting some knight in shining armor to come take you away. Well, that ain't the way it works. You know Ty and his family. They're good folks. Marrying Ty is the right thing to do." She squeezed her daughter's hand. "It's the only way you'll ever save this ranch."

There it was, the bottom line. The weight of saving the family ranch fell squarely on Leanne's shoulders. "I know all that," she said. "It's just that I don't feel that way toward Ty." At least she hadn't until today. Maybe that was just a fluke.

Her mother sighed wearily. "You'll see, Leanne. Everything will be fine. You'll learn to love Ty that way. He's a good man. It's what we all want."

Leanne arched a skeptical brow. "You might be counting your chickens before they hatch considering he hasn't asked yet. Maybe he won't."

Joanna smiled. "Oh, he will. The Coopers have wanted to combine this land with their own for two generations." Her mother patted her hand. "He'll ask. It's just a matter of time."

Opting not to argue the issue further, Leanne kissed her mother's forehead. "Good night, Mama."

Leanne left her mother's room and headed toward her own. According to what her mother had told her eons ago, the Coopers had been disappointed when their only daughter, Tara, hadn't married the only Watley son, Leanne's father. Instead, she'd married the son of the Cooper family's archrivals, a Montgomery. Tara and her husband had died in a tragic accident just one year later, leaving their infant sons, one of which had died shortly thereafter.

Now, the sole Cooper heir and the Watley heiress were once more being groomed for merging the two properties.

But that wasn't the kind of merger Leanne was looking for.

After dragging off her boots, she stripped off her clothes and slipped into a warm flannel gown. It was May, not quite summer yet, and nights were still a bit chilly. She crawled beneath the covers and tried without success to block Ty Cooper's image from her mind.

Being Ty's wife wouldn't be such a chore, she admitted. He was handsome, broad-shouldered and a gentleman in the truest sense of the word. She remembered well her first day in kindergarten. The school bully had made fun of her on the playground. Ty had come to her rescue. Though nine years her senior, he seemed always to be there, taking care of her.

She heaved a weary breath and flopped over on her side. But she didn't love him, and she doubted he loved her. The Coopers already leased part of her grazing land. In fact, that lease money was all that stood between the Watleys and the poorhouse. Two or three times in the last year, they'd skated far too close to foreclosure for comfort.

No matter, Leanne didn't want to get married because it made financial sense. The lease appeared to be working for both families without a marriage to seal the deal. Why didn't they just leave it at that? Even if she somehow managed to bring life to her father's dream, it wouldn't prevent the Coopers from continuing to run cattle on her land. On the contrary, the cattle would add Western ambiance to her dude ranch. But her mother wouldn't hear of it. She intended Leanne to marry Ty.

Maybe Leanne could work up the nerve to talk it over with Ty. She couldn't imagine that he liked this matchmaking business any better than she did. Surely he would see reason. Then they would both be free to look for their own true loves.

That warm sensation that had bloomed in her middle when she'd kissed Ty suddenly swirled inside her once more. She remembered the searing heat in his eyes when he'd looked at her, as if for the first time, before she'd said good-night. She shook her head and hugged her pillow. It was ridiculous. He wouldn't be able to make her feel that way again. She was sure of it.

Spending time with him at the dance on Friday night would prove it.

The dance.

Leanne sat straight up. She had absolutely nothing to wear to the dance.

She mentally ticked off every dress in her closet. It didn't take long, she only owned three. She couldn't wear any of those old flour sacks. She chewed her lower lip. But she sure hated to spend the money to buy something new. Though she supposed that it was time she bought a new church dress. The whole congregation was likely tired of looking at the same old three over and over.

Funny, she mused with growing self-deprecation, she hadn't worried about anything new to wear to the dance until tonight. What was it about Ty this evening that made her suddenly feel so strangely attracted to him? What made this day any different from the thousands of others they'd shared in the past twenty years?

Leanne dropped back onto her pillows. She couldn't answer that question. She would just have to wait and see if that zing of desire happened again.

Probably not, she decided. Lightning never struck the same place twice.

Did it?

Dex had found Ty's room with only a couple of false starts. Fortunately no one had been around to see those blunders. The whole Cooper clan had gathered in the family room to watch television after he'd excused himself.

Dex felt immensely grateful for the reprieve. His feet were relieved as well. He simply couldn't imagine what made cowboys believe that boots were comfortable. Apparently their feet had been molded for the footwear since birth.

How would he endure the ill-fitting get-up he was supposed to wear for the duration of this ruse? He wondered then how Ty was faring in Atlanta. The notion that Grandfather Montgomery was probably completely fooled pleased Dex entirely too much. He knew he should feel some regret, but he didn't. Not in the proper sense anyway. He regretted wearing the boots. He didn't look forward to pretending to be someone he wasn't. Yet, he savored the idea of the discoveries he would make. He would learn about his mother and the people who'd turned their backs on him as a mere infant.

And he intended to teach the Montgomerys a little lesson as well. He and Ty were the victims here. No one could call any part of this entire sham fair. Their whole lives were based on one huge, bogus negotiation strategy.

Was Ty lying in Dex's bed in Atlanta and wondering how the Montgomerys could have chosen Dex over him?

It wasn't a good feeling. Dex knew firsthand.

He thought of his Grandmother Cooper and the way her smile did strange things to his heart. He glanced at the unopened gift waiting on the bureau. A part of him wanted desperately to open it, but it wasn't really for him. It was for Ty. Dex looked away. It was all for Ty. Even the smiles that made Dex feel as if he was looking into an expression his mother would have freely offered.

The bottom line was, he wanted to know more… to somehow understand. Besides, the elder Coopers intrigued him. He wanted to know what made them tick. What had precipitated the choices they'd made all those years ago? And before he returned to Atlanta, Dex would have the answers. He was very good at getting to the bottom of things.

Surviving in the shark-infested waters of HMOs and high finance had taught him a good many things. Not the least of which was survival of the fittest.

But nothing he'd ever learned or experienced had prepared him for the attraction brewing between Leanne Watley and him. Dex mentally reviewed every moment of the time they'd spent together. He decided it was her innocence, her naïveté that drew him. He'd never known a woman quite like her. She also intrigued him. Ty had likened her to a sister. But the vibes Dex had gotten from her were in no way sisterly.

He scowled as he considered the dance he was supposed to escort her to on Friday night. Had he imagined it or had she seemed excited at the prospect? Then again, it could have been him who was excited.

Dex closed his eyes and banished thoughts of Leanne.

He was a stranger in a strange place. He didn't know what he was feeling. If there was something between Leanne and Ty, Dex had no place in it. He'd have to ask Ty about her when they spoke. And he'd have to find a way to avoid her for the next few days. The last thing he needed was a case of lust for his brother's woman.

Brother. The word still felt alien, but it was an undeniable fact. He had a brother. He had another family. The question was, what on earth would he do with them when he had the answers he wanted?

Better yet, what would the Coopers do when they discovered he'd pulled the wool over their eyes?

He pounded his pillow with a fist and tried to get comfortable. Getting comfortable was as impossible as finding any kind of resolution to this quandary.

It was a lose-lose situation.

There would be no winner when he and Ty revealed their true identities and returned to their respective homes.

Maybe trading places hadn't been such a clever idea after all.

Chapter 3

It wasn't a dream.

Dex sat up in bed just as the rising sun spilled its warm glow across the aged hardwood floor. Morning had arrived with a good deal more pomp and circumstance than Dex was accustomed to. The crowing of a rooster and the clanging of pots were sounds he could have gone the rest of his life without hearing at the crack of dawn.

His valet George always greeted him promptly at 6:00 a.m. with a tray of steaming coffee and an array of newspapers. The day's wardrobe awaited him in the dressing room when he completed his morning workout and shower. By 9:00 a.m. he was at the office ready to work.

But not today.

Sometime during the night as he tossed and turned

he had made his decision. He would consider this a mini-vacation at a rather rustic resort. There was no reason not to relax and enjoy. He would have a much-needed, whether he chose to admit the need or not, break from the pressure of running a major medical corporation, and he would learn about the Coopers.

When he and Ty were ready they would go public. But not yet.

Dex threw the covers back and climbed out of bed. The wood floor felt cool beneath his feet, a definite contrast to the plush carpeting of his own bedroom. He strode over to a large armoire, which he had ascertained last night was in lieu of a closet. Scowling, he rifled through it. The shirts were all alike in design, the colors varied slightly.

Disgusted by the lack of selection, he dragged a shirt from its hanger and went to the bureau in search of pants. He found several pairs of scruffy-looking jeans and selected the least offensive pair. In another drawer he found white tube socks. For the boots, he supposed with a grimace.

From the duffel bag he retrieved a pair of his own underwear. He drew the line at wearing another man's shorts.

Since he found no robe, he tugged on the jeans and slipped into the hall, scanning warily for any of the Cooper clan. Silence ruled on the second floor. Everyone appeared to have gone downstairs already.

Good.

Dex padded down the hall to the communal bathroom. Though large and well stocked with linens and bath accessories, it was singular nonetheless. He lowered the toilet lid and placed his attire for the day there.

He tried locking the door but, after several frustrated failures, gave up. The latch wouldn't work. Everyone was downstairs anyway, why sweat it? He grabbed a towel from the linen closet and slung it over the shower curtain rod. After peeling off the jeans, he adjusted the water to an inviting temperature and then stepped beneath the hot spray.

His eyes closed in appreciation. Dex relaxed for the first time since this adventure had begun.

Despite his best intentions not to think about her again, the image of Leanne Watley filled his mind. Those big blue eyes and that silky blond hair. His gut clenched at the thought of threading his fingers in those lovely tresses. The feel of her lips against his jaw sent a stab of desire straight to his loins. His body reacted instantly and his mind conjured up Leanne's even more enticing assets.

He wasn't supposed to be thinking about her that way. Forcing his eyes open, he banished the image. If anything, she was Ty's girlfriend. He wasn't Ty. He couldn't allow this *thing* to progress.

"Fool," he muttered.

Dex grabbed the bar of soap and began soaping his body. He didn't need any complications during his stay here. He had to keep this simple.

For all parties concerned.

Rinsing his well-lathered body he frowned when his gaze halted at his feet. He cocked his head away from the spray and stared at the water swirling around his feet and then down the drain. He looked at the soap in his hand, it was blue. Then why was the water going down the drain tinted green?

An explosion of giggles launched him into action.

Dex jerked the shower curtain open. Court's sons, the four-year-old twins, stood next to the tub, an empty mouthwash bottle in their hands.

"What are you doing?" Dex demanded.

The two dark-haired boys looked first at each other, then at Dex. They dropped the plastic container and ran for their lives in a flash of Scooby-Doo pajamas, leaving the door wide open and shouting, "Mornin', Uncle Ty!"

Swearing under his breath, Dex stamped over to the door, leaving a trail of water on the tile floor, and slammed it shut. He whipped back around and almost fell in his haste. Catching himself, he retraced, much more slowly this time, his path. As soon as he'd washed his hair and rinsed the soap from his skin, he dried himself and the floor.

He thought about the bean-throwing incident and then the mouthwash. Didn't anyone discipline these children?

As a child he was never allowed to behave in such a manner. His grandparents had ensured his proper training from the age of four. Though he'd never had a nanny, at least not that he could recall. He remembered clearly the first day George, his valet, began his employment as Dex's teacher and mentor to the finer points of etiquette.

Dex stared at his reflection in the mirror and wondered what George would think of him now. Pretending to be someone else and wearing this getup. Give him Armani any day. George would likely shake his regal head and make that annoying tsking sound. Since he wasn't here, Dex didn't have to worry about that.

Back in Ty's room, Dex tugged on the cursed boots.

His feet ached even before he stood. The gift on the bureau snagged his attention again.

Would it be perceived as odd if he didn't open the present right away? Would his seeming indifference to the act of generosity hurt his grandmother's feelings? He sighed. He had no choice but to open it.

Dex placed his hands on either side of the box and hesitated still. His heart thundered in his chest. This was ridiculous. It was just a present. It wasn't even for him. Not really. The gesture meant nothing to him personally. He removed the lid, the scent of leather filling his nostrils, and studied the gift beneath. Leather chaps. The perfect gift for a cowboy, he supposed ruefully. He picked up the note from inside the box and read it.

> Ty, I knew you needed a new set of chaps but wouldn't buy any for yourself. Your old ones out in the tack room are being recycled. A welcome-home present seemed like a good enough reason to buy new ones for you.
> Love, Gran.

Dex closed his eyes and struggled with the emotions suddenly churning inside him. The Montgomerys never did little things like this for each other. He stared at the note once more. He couldn't even remember the last time he'd received a personal note from his grandparents. If either of them wanted to tell him anything they sent a message with a member of the household staff or his personal secretary. They didn't bother with personal notes.

But then, the Montgomerys had other assets. Just

because he was angry with them at the moment didn't mean he failed to recognize how much they loved him. Gifts such as this were never necessary. Dex always had everything he wanted given to him well before he needed it.

The Coopers had nothing on the Montgomerys on that score. Of course, he wasn't actually keeping score. Was he?

Twenty minutes and a half dozen false starts later, Dex made his grand entrance into the dining room. Donning the chaps hadn't been easy, but he was fully garbed now. From the hat to the boots.

"Good morning," he said cheerily to the rest of the group assembled around the table.

Grandfather Cooper choked on his coffee. Grandmother Cooper's eyes widened in a look of disbelief. The rest of the family burst into laughter. Dex frowned. What was so funny? He looked down at himself and then back at them. He looked exactly like the cowboys he'd seen in the movies.

What was the problem?

Maybe they'd all heard about the mouthwash episode. He narrowed his gaze in the direction of the twins.

"Planning on roping and branding cattle this morning, bro?" Chad suggested, barely restraining a new wave of laughter.

Dex didn't get the joke.

"Sorry to be the one to tell you," Court added between chuckles. "But today we're cleaning out the barn and surveying the pastures. You won't need your chaps today."

He was *over*dressed, he realized then. He opened

his mouth to explain, but then thought better of it. What could he say? That he was ignorant to the ways of cowboys?

Grandmother Cooper gestured to the vacant chair next to her. "Take your hat off, son, and have a seat. Your breakfast is getting cold."

Before taking his seat, Dex, determined to save face, leaned down and kissed his grandmother's lilac-scented cheek. "Thank you for the chaps, Gran. I wanted you to get the full effect," he told her as if he'd known exactly what he was doing when he put them on.

Court and Chad still looked amused. Grandfather Cooper had regained his composure with only a hint of a smile lingering about his expression.

Grandmother Cooper smiled kindly. "Well, you accomplished your mission, son." She patted his hand. "You look very handsome."

The telephone rang before Dex had a chance to sit down.

"Ty, would you get that since you're still up?" Grandfather Cooper asked.

"Then we can get the *going* effect as well," Chad teased, sending the younger Coopers into another fit of laughter.

Dex clenched his jaw long enough to restrain his temper. "Be happy to oblige," he drawled, doing his best imitation of John Wayne.

He straightened slowly, allowing the phone to ring once more in order to give him the general direction in which to look. The hall. He sauntered from the room, knowing full well Court and Chad were grinning behind his back. Judging by the way they were dressed, he definitely looked like the circus clown leaving center ring.

Annoyed more with himself than anyone else, he scooped up the receiver and barked a hello.

"Dex?"

"Ty?"

"Yeah, it's me."

Thank God.

Dex stretched the cord and got as far away from the dining-room door as possible. "Why the hell didn't you tell me about the investors and the chaps? And Leanne," he muttered hotly.

"Me? Why didn't you tell me about that piranha you've got working for you! And I think George is suspicious."

"What?" Dex was confused. What piranha?

"Bridget whatever-her-name-is," Ty snapped. "She won't leave me alone."

"Oh." Dex stroked his chin thoughtfully. Bridget could be relentless and territorial. Their physical relationship had always been convenient, nothing else. Not that she hadn't tried to make it more. "Tell her you want the monthly status reports early. That should keep her busy for a while. My best advice would be to avoid her if you can."

"What about George?" Ty demanded. "How do I handle him?"

"Tell him you're not in the mood to talk if he starts prying. That usually does the trick." It sounded as if Ty had the same problems Dex did. "What about your investment meeting?" he prodded.

"There's nothing to tell." Ty related what Dex already knew. "I'm trying to expand the Circle C's market and improve profit."

"I thought as much."

"You'll get an official response in a few days," Ty went on. "Let me know the moment you receive it. I'm anxious to know which way the wind is going to blow on my proposal."

Dex cocked an eyebrow. "All right. And you let me know how it goes there."

"Will do. Anything else? I don't know how much longer I can hide in this bathroom. George may be spying on me as we speak."

Dex chuckled. Yes, Ty was feeling the pressure too. "One more thing. About Leanne."

"What about her?"

"I thought you told me you were just friends."

"We are," Ty said flatly. "I guess I forgot to mention that our families would like it otherwise."

"I guess you did," Dex retorted dryly. "And this dance?"

"The one on Friday night? It's just a fund-raiser. I take Leanne every year just to keep the peace between the two families. A little bit of square dancing, foot stomping."

To keep the peace? Dex didn't even want to know what that meant. "Okay, I guess I can take her."

"You'd better be nice to Leanne and behave around her," Ty warned. "She's young and innocent and I don't want her hurt in all this."

"Neither do I," Dex said, surprised that his brother felt it necessary to warn him.

"Good. Now, how's my family?"

Dex heard the wistfulness in his voice. Ty missed

his family. Could Dex say the same? Maybe, he wasn't sure…yet. "The Coopers are fine. I have to go. They're waiting for me."

When Ty didn't respond, Dex added, "Ty, I have to go."

"Okay, but one more thing. What's between you and this Dr. Stovall?"

"Dr. Stovall?" Dex paused, searching his brain for recognition. "Nothing. She's a pediatrician, I believe, at the hospital. Sort of a do-gooder—"

"There's nothing wrong with that," Ty interjected sharply.

Dex sighed. This did not sound good. "Listen, Ty, watch your step. I have to come back there, remember?"

"Don't worry. Everything's under control."

"Good. I'll talk to you when I can. Gotta go."

Dex hung up the receiver. It took him three long beats to prepare himself to reenter the dining room.

"It was one of the people I met in Chicago," he announced to the expectant faces still gathered around the table. "I should have word in a few days."

Nods and sounds of acknowledgment echoed around the room. Grandfather Cooper maintained a solemn, clearly skeptical expression.

Dex pulled his chair out and sat down. He looked at his plate, laden with eggs, bacon and biscuits, just in time to see a Cheerio land in the middle of the two sunny-side up eggs. His gaze met the wicked one belonging to his five-year-old niece, who was sitting on the opposite side of the table eating dry cereal from a bowl.

"Morning, Uncle Ty. You're a sleepyhead this mornin'," she accused.

Before Dex could think of an appropriate response, the rest of the men stood.

"The day's a wastin'. We'd better get going," Court suggested.

Another Cheerio plopped into Dex's plate. "I'll just eat something later," he said as he pushed up from his chair.

Grandmother Cooper frowned. "Don't rush out without your breakfast. You can catch up with your brothers later."

"Really," Dex assured her. "I'm good."

He left the room amid a chorus of "Uncle Tys!" resounding behind him. The twins had joined his niece, whom Dex now mentally dubbed the princess, in her farewell dramatics. Dex was pretty sure he'd never faced an opponent in the boardroom as formidable as those three kids.

Considering he was staying for the next few days under the same roof with them, he couldn't see how things could get any worse.

Once in the yard, Court said, "Chad, you want to oversee the barn work while Ty and I check out the fencing?"

"Will do."

Check out the fencing? He could do that, Dex decided. He followed Court to the barn. He paused in front of two stalls where a couple of massive horses resided.

"Saddle up, bro." Court clapped Dex on the back. "We've got a long day ahead of us."

Dex stared at the horse eyeing him suspiciously. Things had just gotten worse.

When Court finally called it a day, Dex had a complete understanding of the phrase "too long in the saddle." Every part of his lower body ached.

Sliding off the horse proved almost as difficult as mounting the huge beast had. By the time Dex had gotten into the saddle, Court was convinced the whole routine was an act to make him laugh. He'd laughed so hard he'd nearly cried when he'd had to tighten the cinch. Dex had tried to emulate Court as he saddled his own horse, but obviously he hadn't gotten it exactly right.

Taking small careful steps now, Dex headed toward the house. He needed a long, hot soak in the tub. He needed food and drink. No. Strike that. What he really needed was a half dozen or so protein shakes and then a double Scotch to finish it off.

He winced with each step. How could anyone like this lifestyle?

"Ty!"

Dex looked in the direction of the driveway and the unexpected but welcome sound of Leanne's voice. Already he knew it by heart. He was far too exhausted to consider why.

"Leanne," he acknowledged. "How are you today?"

She frowned, the gesture deepening the worry already clouding her expression. "We need to talk."

Something was wrong. Dex could see it in her eyes. He had the sudden urge to put his arm around her slender shoulders and assure her that everything would be fine. He gave himself a mental shake. Slow down, he warned. This was a mistake he did not intend to make. He recalled Ty's warning, but the urge to reassure her still nagged at him.

"Okay," he said instead, tucking his hands into his back pockets as a precaution.

She glanced around. "Not here." Her too-serious gaze landed on his once more. "Do you mind taking a ride to my place?"

The thought of sitting down in anything other than hot water almost made him say no, but the need to put that smile back on her pretty face prevailed.

"Why not?" He offered his arm. "I'd be pleased to."

Looking even more worried, she placed her arm in his and walked with him to her old truck. He opened the door for her then hustled around to the passenger door as quickly as he dared. But lowering himself into the seat proved the most difficult task.

"Are you sure you're feeling all right, Ty?" she asked, her fingers poised on the key in the ignition.

"Fabulous," Dex returned. "Just fabulous."

Shaking her head she started the engine.

This young lady seemed to know Ty better than anyone else. At least, she appeared to be the only one suspicious of Dex. He studied her lovely profile as she drove away from the Circle C. His muscles tightened just looking at her, in spite of his numerous aches.

He definitely had to watch his step around her.

Leanne stood next to Ty on her back porch and surveyed the dream her father had started five years ago. Her mother was resting in her room. She wouldn't like it if she knew what Leanne was about to do. But she had to tell him before she lost her nerve. She had to be honest, especially in light of recent events. She'd thought about it all night.

"I know you remember my father dreamed of turning this place into a dude ranch." She looked up at Ty. He looked at a loss for a moment, then nodded. Leanne peered back out over the nearly finished guest cabins and the waiting pool. "I want to make it happen, Ty," she said quietly, bracing herself for his response.

A full minute ticked by in silence.

"It's not what either of our families wants," she hastened to add. "I know that. But it wouldn't affect the grazing land. The Circle C could continue to lease the grazing land, all of it if they want. That wouldn't be a problem."

He looked at her then. She couldn't read what he was thinking or feeling. *Please,* she prayed, *let him understand.*

"This is what you want?" he asked, his tone carefully measured.

She nodded. "Very much."

He took off his hat and threaded his fingers through his hair, then replaced the hat as if he weren't used to having to bother. Her frown deepened. What was it that made him seem so different since he'd come back from Chicago? Even the way he talked was wrong somehow.

He took the four steps down from the porch then turned back to her. "Do you mind if we walk?"

She shook her head and hurried down the steps after him.

"Is the wiring and plumbing for the guest cottages complete?" he asked as they crossed the yard.

"Yes," she answered, afraid to hope. "I still have

some painting and clean-up work to do. I'll have to buy furniture and pool chemicals. But I can be ready in a few months if I work on it every chance I get."

He paused near the pool and stared at her. "You're doing this alone?"

She sighed. "I didn't want to tell you." She hung her head. "I know what our families have always wanted." As difficult as it was, she met his gaze. "But *this* is what I want." How did she tell the man that she didn't want to spend the rest of her life as just his wife? She didn't want to hurt him. She cared about him. Deeply. She just wasn't in love with him. And she desperately wanted to see her father's wish come true.

"You could hire a contractor to finish up," he suggested, while studying the dark, mossy-green color of the pool water. It would take lots of chemicals to clear up that mess.

"That takes more money than I can afford to spend," she told him. It annoyed her because he of all people should know her circumstances. Well, at least, to a degree. She and her mother were too proud to tell the whole story. "I'd rather do the work myself anyway. That's what my father would have done."

He nodded. "Well, I think it's a great idea. Dude ranches are usually a big hit when operated properly. Are there—" He cut himself off abruptly. "Have you researched the probability of success?"

"If you're asking if I've done my homework, the answer is yes. There isn't one anywhere near here," she said, hardly believing he'd even asked. "Tourists love this part of the state, as you well know. I think it would be a tremendous success."

"All right, then." He braced his hands on his lean

hips and studied the guest cabins that circled the pool. "I'll help you."

Leanne felt a ripple of shock. "What did you say?"

He shrugged awkwardly. "I'll help you. Court and Chad have things at the Circle C under control. There's no reason I can't pitch in here." His gaze locked with hers, and heat roared straight through her. "Isn't it the neighborly thing to do?"

Leanne couldn't argue with that reasoning.

Truth be told, she didn't want to. Another little shock wave shook her.

"Well, then." He smiled, sending her heart into a wild tattoo. "Let's do it."

Before she could stop herself she'd thrown her arms around him. "Thank you for understanding, Ty," she murmured against his neck.

"It's nothing," he argued, his posture rigid.

Darn it. She didn't want to cry. But the tears came anyway. She held onto him with all her might and cried into his shirt. "I'm sorry," she muttered.

"It's all right." His arms closed around her waist sending a new shard of heat slicing through her. "I—" He let go a heavy breath. His arms tightened around her, drawing her nearer. "It's okay," he said softly, his breath whispering against her cheek.

And she knew it would be.

Because Ty had told her so. He'd never let her down before.

Chapter 4

For a long time after Leanne dropped Dex back at the Cooper ranch he just stood watching as the dust that had billowed from beneath her old truck settled. He thought about the day he'd spent on horseback with Court, touring the grazing pastures, surveying the fencing. The Cooper ranch was pretty spectacular. Dex couldn't recall spending that much time in such a wide-open space ever before. He couldn't think about that without remembering the ribbing he'd taken from Chad when it took him three tries to mount Ty's horse. None of it seemed quite real.

Outside the Cooper family and Leanne, he'd been introduced to two Circle C ranch hands, a neighbor searching for a missing bull, and the local veterinarian making a house call. Everyone had the same easygoing, laid-back way about them. No one was in a hurry.

Dex hadn't read the first hint of deception or ruthlessness in a single individual he'd met. It was completely unbelievable. And everyone helped everyone else. He and Court had spent an extra hour on horseback helping the neighbor look for his Brahman.

Dex, however, had balked at helping deliver a calf. He'd stood back and allowed Court and the vet to handle that one.

He turned toward the house and studied the massive structure as the sun set behind it. With the purple and gold hues fading around it, the house and its serene setting looked picturesque and inviting. Like the home, the people here were friendly and caring.

Lines of confusion furrowed across his brow. How had these people, the salt of the earth, pretended for over thirty long years that he didn't even exist?

Dex shook his head. He might never know without staging an outright confrontation and demanding the answer. And right now he was too tired and sore for battle. He strode slowly to the house, up the steps and across the porch. He'd never been so glad to see a day end. As he reached for the door, a low growl stopped him.

A few feet away Lady stood very still, watching him with wary eyes and emitting a long fierce rumble.

"Behave, Lady," he commanded, recalling Leanne's words and trying his level best to sound confident. He told himself that he wasn't actually afraid, just cautious. But the sweat that broke out across his upper lip betrayed him.

The standoff lasted about ten seconds, but it felt like an eternity. Finally Lady sauntered over to what he'd come to think of as her favorite spot and lay down.

She glared at him one last time as if she was still undecided as to whether he was worth any real effort.

Dex heaved a sigh of relief when she lowered her head to her front paws and closed her eyes. He'd made it past that barrier, he mused as he entered the house. Now if he could just make it up the stairs and to his room without being spotted, he'd be a happy man. He wanted a long, hot bath and a night of peace and quiet—alone. He had to think. To sort out all these confusing emotions.

The sound of feminine voices drifted to him from beyond the dining room. The women were likely preparing dinner, the men were probably still outside. The throaty laughter of his Grandmother Cooper stalled him at the bottom of the stairs. She sounded far younger than her years. He wondered if his mother had laughed like that, freely and with such heart.

Why did knowing more about his mother suddenly seem so important? He'd never suffered more than a fleeting moment of interest in the past. He had to remember what he'd come here for. To teach the Montgomerys a lesson and to show the Coopers what they'd missed all these years by turning their backs on him.

His jaw tightened. How had they chosen Ty over him? That was the million-dollar question. Had they simply flipped a coin? Who had made the first choice, a Cooper or a Montgomery? Was he taken only because the other child had already been selected?

Dex squared his shoulders and reminded himself he was Dex Montgomery, not Ty Cooper. This was not his home. These people weren't his family. Leanne was not his concern. Though he was sympathetic to her plight and had every intention of helping her while he was here, that was the extent of his plans where Leanne was concerned. The fact of the matter was, helping her would be to his benefit. It would get him away from the Coopers, the horses and that suspicious dog. Time away from the ranch would aid in retaining his cover. That was his only real motivation for offering her his assistance. In a couple of weeks this whole charade would be over and he'd be back in his own world.

Back where he belonged.

"Uncle Ty! Uncle Ty!"

Startled, Dex stared down at little Angelica tugging on his hand. "What is it?" he asked, more harshly than he'd intended. He wasn't accustomed to being accosted by little people.

"Hurry! Hurry!" she urged, pulling on his hand. "You have to come quick."

Reluctant, but uncertain what else to do, Dex allowed her to drag him along. "Where are we going?" he demanded.

"In here." She pointed to the family room. "The babies are causin' trouble."

A frown drew his eyebrows together as he attempted to decipher her panicked expression. "Trouble? What kind of trouble?"

"See." She paused in the open doorway of the family room and pointed. "If they fall, they gonna go *splat,*" she said, her eyes huge.

Dex followed her gesture and did a double take. The boys were, rather successfully, climbing a floor-to-ceiling bookcase. Books fluttered to the floor like injured birds in their wake.

What should he do? If he shouted for help or for

them to stop they might be startled and fall. His heart rate accelerated, making his chest tight. He had to rescue them before they hurt themselves. They were too young to realize the danger they were in, that much he knew.

Careful to be as quiet as possible, he rushed across the room, forgetting all about his numerous aches and pains, and grabbed the two boys, one in each arm, before they were even aware he was in the room. They squealed with what sounded like delight as he wagged them over to the sofa and plopped the two wriggling children down onto it. He stood there, glaring down at them, wondering how such small creatures could get into so much trouble.

"Do it again! Do it again!" they shouted in unison, bouncing on the overstuffed cushions like kangaroos.

Dex released the breath he'd been holding. Were kids always this much trouble? "Forget it," he told them when their chanting continued. He drew in another deep breath and let it out slowly to calm his racing heart.

"A story!" one countered. He couldn't say for sure if it was Danny or David. The two were identical.

"A story?" Only then did Dex notice the book one of the little devils held. "What about a story?" he grouched.

"Read it!" the two cried.

Dex harrumphed. "I don't think so."

"But, Uncle Ty, you always read us stories," Angelica chimed in, sidling up next to him. "Ever'day, almost."

Another thing Ty forgot to mention, Dex steamed.

"Maybe later," he suggested in hopes of getting himself off the hook. He didn't do stories.

Angelica pouted. "Later we'll be in bed."

Later he'd be in bed, too. Three sets of eyes peered up at him, expressions hopeful, almost pleading. One twin's lips quivered as if he might burst into tears. Oh no. If they all started to cry at once—

"Fine." He reached for the book. "One story and that's it."

His announcement was punctuated with exuberant cheers. The twins parted like the Red Sea, making space for him to sit on the sofa between them. The instant Dex sat down Angelica climbed onto his lap. A brief scuffle and heated debate ensued as the twins fought for their own section of territory. The threesome glared at each other when they were at last settled.

"Are we ready now?" Dex looked at Angelica and then at each of the boys.

All heads nodded.

Dex opened the book and read about Alice in Wonderland. The long version, apparently. By the time he finished, the twins and their tattling cousin were asleep.

Two little heads were snuggled against his chest, a third rested in the crook of his arm. He couldn't possibly move without waking one or all. Besides, he was totally exhausted. He needed to sleep himself. He'd tossed and turned most of last night. Tonight wasn't shaping up to be any better. One of the children sighed, and the sound was trusting, innocent and somehow mesmerizing to him.

He studied their little faces and tried to remember

what it had been like for him at that age. He'd never worn jeans and T-shirts, that much he remembered vividly. And he certainly hadn't climbed on any of the furniture. He frowned. He did remember a pony on his sixth birthday. A clown on his seventh. He was too tired to remember the rest.

Dex eased his head back on the sofa. What difference did it make anyway? He couldn't change the past. Didn't even want to.

The house was eerily quiet when Dex awoke. Quiet and dark, he noted as he rubbed his eyes. He sat up on the sofa, his arms and lap now empty. Where were the children? What time was it?

As if in answer to his unspoken question, the grandfather clock in the hall chimed the hour, falling silent after the eleventh resounding dong.

He switched on the table lamp at the end of the sofa and blinked to adjust to the light. How could he have slept through the children being taken from his arms? He obviously was more exhausted than he'd realized. He wondered, though, why no one had awakened him.

Dex stood and stretched. Since everyone else appeared to have gone to bed already, he might as well do the same. His stomach rumbled. He remembered then that he'd missed dinner. Surely he could find something in the kitchen. As he turned to leave the room something caught his eye. He turned back to the bookcases from which he'd rescued the twins and studied the fourth shelf of one in particular.

Photo albums.

A few steps later, he held two large albums in his hands. His heart started to pound again as he sat down and spread the albums on the coffee table before him. The first one held family photo after family photo. Pictures of the twins and the little princess. A smile stretched across his lips as he thought about their rapt attention as he'd read the story to them. He hadn't expected to feel that sense of protection, but he had. The idea that one of the boys could have been hurt climbing that bookcase had scared him witless. They weren't his children. He barely knew them. How could he feel that way?

Basic human compassion, he told himself, nothing more.

The next album he opened almost stopped his heart. Tara Cooper. Her Sweet Sixteen party. Dex swallowed tightly. She was beautiful. He touched the smiling face in the photograph. Blond hair fell around her shoulders. Bright hazel eyes flashed with happiness. The resemblance between her and his Grandmother Cooper was striking. And he'd been right about the smile. Their smiles were very similar, both wide, honest, heartfelt.

Dex turned the page and found a picture of Tara and a healthy-looking cow sporting a blue ribbon. He smiled. The next picture showed her winning yet another blue ribbon. This time from 4-H. He could barely make out the title of her poster: Better Nutrition, Eating Healthier and Leaner. He remembered then that Grandfather Cooper had said she'd wanted more, just like Ty.

He flipped another page. High-school graduation pictures. Visits home from college. Her twenty-first birthday. Her graduation from college. The elder Coopers looked so proud. He turned another page. A kind of shock rocked through him as his brain assimilated what his eyes saw next.

Tara Cooper and Charles Dexter Montgomery, Junior, together. So young…so happy. Dex was stunned at the smiling face of his father. Every single photo in the Montgomery house showed a solemn-looking young man. The man in these pictures laughed, hugged and played. Dex shook his head in bewilderment. Had his mother changed his father's life that much? Had she been the one thing that made him smile? Was that happiness what had distracted his father from the world the Montgomerys had so carefully constructed in Atlanta?

Why had no one told him how happy his father was during his brief marriage? Emotions twisting in his chest, Dex turned to the next page. His hand shook as he released it. His mother and father, tears of joy glistening in their eyes, holding two tiny babies, captured forever in that one frozen frame in time. This was his mother and father. He looked about the semi-dark room. This had been their home. They'd been happy here. And no one had ever told him that.

Unable to bear looking anymore, Dex closed the albums. How could the Montgomerys have not known how happy their son was here? Dex had always been led to believe that even if the tragedy had not occurred, his father would never have been happy with his mother. Could they really have been that blind?

Dex pushed to his feet and carried the albums back to the bookcase. Too many unanswered questions whirled in his head. If he confronted the Coopers, would they tell him the truth? Or would it merely be their version of the truth? But then, they did have photos to back them up. His father had been happy here. There was no denying that fact. Could the Montgomerys say the same?

As Dex turned to go, he hesitated. As an afterthought, he flipped through one of the albums again until he came to the photo of his mother and father holding their newborn twins. Glancing around the room first, he slipped the photo from beneath its protective cover and tucked it into his pocket. He wanted this picture. He wanted to understand how fate could have torn such a lovely little family apart.

When he put the album back on the shelf something else captured his attention. Tucked way back in the corner behind a couple of fallen books he found a bundle of old letters. The once-white envelopes were yellowed and bound together by a pink ribbon. The return address was his own back in Atlanta. His heart started to pound all over again. His father had written these letters. He decided to take the letters as well. He swallowed and struggled for composure. He would read them, just not tonight. He wasn't sure he could take any more revelations tonight.

Dex climbed the stairs still reeling with the emotions of his discovery. He was too tired and too disturbed to care about eating or that hot bath he'd promised himself. He hid the letters in the top drawer of the bureau, peeled off his clothes and slid between the cool sheets of his bed. He wondered briefly how Ty was doing in Atlanta. Though he'd rather deny it, he missed his grandparents. Slowly, but surely, one smiling face after another belonging to the Cooper clan flashed through his mind. He felt the peaceful silence of the big old house as the family slept, the whole ambiance of the ranch and its inhabitants. They were two different worlds, this one and the one in which he'd grown up.

With no place to meet in the middle.

Dex didn't want to think about any of this anymore. This wasn't home. These people were not his family.

There was nothing here he needed besides some answers.

The blue eyes and sweet smile of Leanne Watley protested his last thought. A warm, somehow softer feeling cloaked him. He told himself again that he didn't need her, either.

But she needed him.

Chapter 5

Leanne flipped through the rack of dresses once more. She didn't know why she tortured herself. She'd already selected the only one she even halfway liked that was in her price range. She might as well accept it as her dress for the dance. Mrs. Paula Beaumont, the owner and operator of Paula's Fashions, the only shop that sold anything besides denim and leather goods in Rolling Bend, had suggested it.

The pink color was pretty, though the design was a little plain. It fit a little too loosely, but Paula would make the necessary alterations. Leanne held the pink dress against herself once more and peered into the mirror. There had been a time when her mother could have made her a dress even prettier, but not now.

"That looks lovely, Leanne," Mrs. Paula said as she joined her near the mirror. "You can wear those white shoes you wore to church last Sunday with it."

Leanne frowned. She hadn't even thought about shoes. Her church shoes would have to do. She definitely couldn't buy new shoes, too. She wouldn't even be here looking at dresses if her mother hadn't insisted. She couldn't afford to buy a new dress. But her mother was right. She had nothing to wear.

"Don't you like it, dear?"

Leanne forced a smile. "Yes, ma'am," she said, dismissing her distracting thoughts. She hung the dress on the handy rack next to the mirror. "It's just that the blue one is so pretty." She glanced at the blue dress hanging alongside the pink one. A royal blue, the silky dress was beautiful.

Despite knowing she couldn't possibly afford a dress that cost more than a month's groceries, she'd tried it on anyway. The fabric had caressed her skin and hugged her figure in a most flattering way. The way the skirt swung about her legs when she moved made her giddy. Ty would like this dress. She was sure of it.

She sighed. Why on earth did it matter if he liked it or not? Why was she suddenly so concerned with looking good Friday night? Foolish, foolish, that's all.

"Oh, honey," Mrs. Paula offered with too much understanding in her eyes. "You're right, the blue dress is a pretty thing. But it's so expensive." She fingered the silken fabric. "And it really wouldn't be good for anything but the dance. It's a little too flamboyant for church, if you know what I mean."

It was true. The neckline of the blue dress was a little low, the shimmery material a little too flashy. Mrs. Paula was right. The dress was perfect for the dance. It would highlight Leanne's blue eyes. But it wasn't the sensible choice.

Mrs. Paula scooped up two handfuls of Leanne's hair and arranged it high on her head. "With that nice high collar on the pink dress it would look best to wear your hair up. And maybe a little flower right here." She gestured vaguely. "You'd look really nice," she added as she released Leanne's hair and stepped back slightly. "Pink is a good color on you, too."

"You're right." Leanne nodded. "I should stick with the pink one." Contrary to her words, she took the blue dress from the rack and held it against her one last time. It was so pretty. "But I do love this one," she said softly, wistfully.

Mrs. Paula nodded, another understanding gesture. "I'll ring the pink one up for you. I'm sure I can do the alterations this afternoon. I'll have Amos drop it by your house this evening. That okay?"

Leanne nodded without looking away from the mirror. When Mrs. Paula had left her alone, she turned side to side, swishing the material and taking in the look from every possible angle.

"I do love this dress," she murmured.

A long, low whistle sounded behind her, making Leanne jump. She whirled around to face the intrusion, the shimmering blue material swirling with her.

Ty.

Her breath caught. "Ty," she choked out. "What are you doing here? I thought your gran did all your Sunday-best shopping for you."

He smiled, a gesture that made her heart thump wildly in her chest. "I need a new shirt for Friday night."

She nodded mutely.

His gaze swept her from head to toe and back. She saw the masculine approval there when those dark eyes focused on hers once more. Another breath trapped in her lungs.

"Wow," he said softly. "You look…" He seemed suddenly at a loss for words.

Leanne quickly hung the blue dress back on the rack. "I should be going. I have chores to do."

He looked from the blue dress to her. "You don't want it?"

He knew she did, she could see it in his eyes. How long had he been listening before he made his presence known?

She didn't need Ty feeling sorry for her. "No," she lied. "I've already made my selection."

She'd be willing to bet he'd already forgotten about his promise to help her with her plans for the ranch, too. It was so easy to be gallant with words. It was still difficult for her to believe that he'd meant what he said.

"Oh," he said almost contritely.

Since Ty'd come back from the city, he didn't act like himself at all. Where was the decisive man she'd known her entire life? Ty never waffled about his thoughts. His assessment that her dude ranch was a good idea had out and out shocked her. Ty believed ranches were for one thing and one thing only, raising cattle. What had motivated this sudden change of heart? Was he hoping that her dream would somehow help him convince his family that the two of them weren't right for each other?

Well, good. Because she didn't want to marry him

anyway. Her temper flared. "Good day, Ty," she snapped as she started past him.

Strong fingers curled around one arm, effectively halting her and at the same time drawing her nearer to him. "Did I say something wrong?" he asked softly. "I only meant that you would look stunning in the blue dress, that's all. It wasn't my intent to make you angry."

She looked up at him. Those dark, analyzing eyes made her shiver. He had never looked at her that way before, not that she could recall. She was certain she would remember that look.

"I didn't mean to be short with you," she said, sounding breathless. She prayed he wouldn't notice. He was still looking at her so very intently. "I... I have a lot of work to do."

His fingers tightened around her arm at the same instant something new flickered in that dark gaze. He released her but not before Leanne recognized what she saw—desire. Another shiver rushed over her. She hadn't imagined it. It was there. She'd seen it clearly.

"Stop by the hardware before you leave town," he instructed, easing back a step, putting some distance between them. "Leave a list of the things you need for painting and the other repairs."

Leanne almost smiled. He hadn't forgotten his promise. Deep down she'd known he wouldn't. Ty never made a promise he didn't intend to keep. But thinking negative thoughts helped her stay focused where he was concerned. It would be far too easy to fall head over heels in love with such a caring, honest man. But it wasn't what she wanted—not with Ty. They didn't see eye to eye on a wife's role in marriage.

She knew what he wanted—a woman who would be happy at home raising his kids, and keeping house. She wanted more. Besides, she loved Ty like a brother.

Didn't she?

She suppressed the urge to shiver yet again. It was extremely difficult to think straight with him looking at her like that. She refused to call what she felt desire. It was probably just her subconscious reacting to the pressure of her mother's wish for her and Ty to marry. She'd spent a lifetime being an obedient daughter. Now she had no intention of doing anything except following her heart. As those dark eyes continued to peer deeply into hers, making her feel at once too warm and utterly restless, the only question that remained was, where was her heart taking her?

"All right," she finally said in response to his order to stop by the hardware. "I can't get it all at once, but I will give Mr. Dickson the list."

Ty nodded. "Good." He smiled again. Her pulse reacted. "How about helping me find something for the dance before you go? I wouldn't want to disappoint my date."

Date?

Leanne blinked. He considered Friday night's dance a date? "Well…ah…sure." She smoothed her suddenly damp palms over her denim-clad hips. "What did you have in mind?"

He shrugged. "I don't know. What would you suggest?"

"Well." Feeling suddenly bold, she took his hand in hers and dragged him toward the men's section. "Let's see what we can find."

When they reached a long rack of men's dress

shirts, Leanne shuffled through the offered selections. With his dark coloring she knew what she wanted.

"How about this one?" She held the long-sleeved white shirt against his broad chest.

Without even looking down, he said, "Perfect."

She blushed. "Don't you want to try it on? It might not fit."

He took the shirt from her and glanced around the store. "Sure, where's the dressing room?"

She angled her head toward the back of the store. "Back there, but there's someone using it right now. Mrs. Paula only has one dressing room, you know."

He thrust the shirt back at her. "No big deal. We'll just do as the Europeans do."

She frowned. "Europeans?" What in the world did that mean? Before Leanne could figure that one out, Ty had pulled his shirttail from his jeans and started unfastening the snaps. "What are you doing?"

He popped open the final snap of his shirt and dragged it off over impossibly wide shoulders. "I'm taking my shirt off," he said, nonchalantly.

Her eyes widened as all that sculpted terrain was bared before her. "I can see that." She glanced in Mrs. Paula's direction. The fiftyish, heavyset woman stood behind her counter, her mouth gaping. "Ty, you—"

He reached for the shirt she held, his fingers brushing hers as he took it from her. "You're sure this is the one you like best?"

She nodded, unable to speak or meet his eyes. She could only stare at that awesome chest. She'd seen him shirtless before. What made this time so different? He shouldered into the crisp white dress shirt and adjusted the collar. The stark contrast between his naturally tanned skin and the fresh white of the shirt took her breath away.

"It's…yes," she managed to say.

"What about a tie?" He reached behind her, making her heart stutter with his nearness. He dangled a black string tie near the hollow of his throat, drawing her rapt attention there. "What good's a white shirt without a black tie?"

She'd never known him to be so playful and talkative, not like this anyway. This was different. It was flirtatious. Sexy.

"You should definitely get the tie," she told him. His smile was contagious. She just couldn't help herself.

His expression grew serious. "You should do that more often. You have a beautiful smile."

She tried to think what to say, but no words would come. He felt closer suddenly, though she wasn't sure he'd moved.

"I have to go." The words had come from her, but she wasn't sure how she'd managed to say them.

He nodded. "Don't forget to stop by the hardware."

Before she could do something totally insane like kiss him again, Leanne rushed out of the shop. She didn't even stop at the counter to pay her bill.

Right now, she just had to get away from Ty. She told herself again that he was only a friend. One she'd known her whole life. He shouldn't be able to make her feel so flustered. So uncertain of what she really wanted.

Why would he? He'd never made her feel this attraction before. She'd always believed that he didn't want this arranged marriage any more than she did. So why was he suddenly behaving so strangely?

Leanne didn't understand it.

She wondered if Ty did.

Dex watched through the shop's plate-glass window as Leanne climbed into her old truck and drove away. A yearning so strong rose inside him that he couldn't take a breath for one long moment. He couldn't label it, didn't even understand it, but the feeling shook him as nothing else ever had. What was it about her that touched him so?

Deep in thought, he started to remove the shirt he'd tried on. A gasp startled him from his reverie. He stopped abruptly and turned to find the shop owner and another woman staring at him, wide-eyed, from their positions near the counter.

Knowing better, but suddenly not caring, Dex flagrantly, suggestively peeled off the white shirt, then took his time pulling on his own. One by one he fastened each snap, then tucked it into his waistband. When he'd finished, he winked at the ladies, earning himself another gasp from each.

He picked up the white shirt Leanne had selected and the black tie and headed for the cashier. One of the ladies grabbed her package and ran for the door. Dex grinned.

"Ty Cooper," Mrs. Paula scolded. "You did that on purpose. Your pa raised you better than that. Why, poor Mrs. Larkin will have to have one of her little nerve pills to calm down. I hope you think about that when you're sitting in church on Sunday and the reverend's talking about the evil sinners do."

Dex resisted the urge to tease her some more as he placed his selections on the counter. "I don't know what came over me," he offered contritely, with absolutely no sincerity. "I guess the devil made me do it."

The exasperation in the woman's voice when she spoke again was belied by the twinkle of mischief in her eyes. "I'm quite certain that you're right. It might promote business though. Perhaps you'd like to come by Saturday morning and model a few items." She cocked one eyebrow. "After all, if something good comes of the devil's work, the Lord might just overlook it."

"I'll check my calendar." Dex ran a hand through his hair, only then realizing he'd left his hat in his truck. He wondered if Ty would have been caught dead without it. Then again, he had a feeling Ty wouldn't have done a strip tease in the only fine clothing store in Rolling Bend.

Oh well. There was no telling what kind of fixes Ty was getting Dex into in Atlanta.

"Would you like me to put this on your account, Ty?" Mrs. Paula asked as she boxed his shirt and tie.

Dex considered that for a moment. He supposed that was the only way to go. He could reimburse Ty later. He definitely couldn't wear any of the shirts he'd found in Ty's closet to the dance. He'd found a pair of black jeans that would do.

As Dex signed Ty Cooper's name to the bill, he thought of the blue dress and the wistful sound of Leanne's voice when she'd said how much she loved it.

He hesitated only a split second. "What about that blue dress Leanne looked at?"

The lady shook her head. "Oh, it's far too expensive. Almost two hundred dollars. She's much better off with the pink one. What would Leanne do with a two-hundred-dollar dress?"

"But," Dex pressed, all business now, "it's the one she liked best, is it not?"

The shop owner looked taken aback. "Well, yes, but she has to be practical. The pink one will be good for church, too."

"The dress is for sale, isn't it?"

She nodded. "It's for sale, but…"

Dex looked her straight in the eye. "Put the blue one on my bill and deliver it to Leanne when you send her the pink one."

"Well… I…if you're sure that's what you want to do. It's an awful lot of money."

"I trust you'll take care of it?" he suggested.

"Of course." She passed him the package containing his purchases. "Anything else?"

"I think that takes care of everything." He winked at her. "Have a nice day."

She nodded uncertainly.

Dex pivoted and strode to the door. He suddenly wished he could be there to see the look on Leanne's face when the blue dress arrived. He smiled to himself. He could imagine just how pleased she would be. He frowned as he reached for the door handle. His actions this morning were so out of character. He couldn't say what had possessed him. If George were here perhaps he could explain what compelled Dex to make Leanne happy. He'd only known her for a few days, so why were her feelings so important to him?

Dex stepped back for two ladies to enter as he opened the door. They both stared at him, then giggled. He wondered what that was about. When the door closed behind him realization hit. The word of his little escapade was already spreading around town.

He slid into the seat behind the wheel of Ty's truck. His brother might not forgive him for tarnishing his stellar reputation. Dex grinned. Then again, the way he saw it, it would only add interest to a man who appeared to be far too reserved for his own good.

Dex considered that the same could be said about him. He was all business. Well, he amended, most of the time. He'd always been too busy for a real social life. Maybe he'd missed more than he realized. He'd certainly never dealt with everyday people as he had since his arrival here. He had a very efficient staff who took care of his needs. Maybe that was a mistake. Maybe he needed to be around people more.

Or maybe he just needed his head examined.

His Grandfather Montgomery would no doubt think so. Dex had been taught from a young age that appearances were everything. Power and respect could only be gained through the proper presentation.

It was about time he put that philosophy to the test.

Besides, it was all for naught. He was Ty Cooper right now.

Chapter 6

"All right, I'm giving you this one last chance." Dex looked the horse straight in the eye. "Don't push your luck. I'm out of patience."

Dex took the horse's silence as agreement. He walked around to the animal's left side as he had a half dozen times already, took a deep breath, placed his left foot in the stirrup and heaved himself upward the same way he'd watched Chad and Court do.

The horse sidestepped. Dex came down fast on his right foot, barely keeping his balance. He cursed loudly.

"Whatcha doing, Uncle Ty?"

He whipped around. Angelica stood near the barn door watching him. He'd have sworn the place was empty.

"I'm working with my horse."

Angelica studied him closely, as if trying to decide if he was telling the truth or not. "Why don't you call him Dodger no more? Did you decide to name him something else?"

Dodger. The horse's name was Dodger. That was helpful. Maybe this kid could be useful for something other than throwing green beans at him.

"No, I like his name." Dex pushed his hat up and scratched his forehead. "Dodger seems to be mad at me right now. He doesn't want me to take him for a ride."

"You ain't doing it right." Angelica took a few steps in his direction. "You gotta grab the saddle horn when you go up. That's what my daddy does."

Dex frowned. How had he missed that? He lifted a skeptical eyebrow. "You're sure about that?"

"'Course." She adopted an impish grin. "You know that."

"Just checking to make sure you do."

"Ever'body knows that," she told him.

Dex assumed the position, grabbing the saddle horn this time. He went all the way up and into the saddle with little effort. He grinned. He'd done it.

"Toldcha."

Dex nodded. "So you did."

"Are you gonna go for a ride, Uncle Ty?"

He considered it. "Yes, I think I will."

"Can I go, too? My momma says I can ride as long as I'm with a grown-up."

He supposed it was the least he could do since she'd helped him out. But then, how was he supposed to get her into the saddle with him?

She climbed up onto a bale of hay. "Please?"

Dex guided the horse close to the hay bale, then reached for the child, lifting her into the saddle in front of him. "You're sure your mother won't mind?"

"'Course not. She knows you'll take good care of me."

Dex made the clicking sound he'd heard the other men make and Dodger started forward. "Where are we going, Princess?"

"How'd you know I was a princess?" she asked, giggling.

"Just a good guess."

Angelica waved to her mom who had stepped out onto the back porch to check on her child, Dex presumed. He waved, too. Grandmother Cooper peeked out next, waving and smiling. The gesture made him feel warm inside. It was foolish he knew, but he just couldn't help himself.

For the rest of afternoon, Dex and the princess rode around the ranch with her explaining everything they saw, just the way her father had explained it to her. Dex found all this very helpful. Now he wouldn't be so lost. It almost felt as if the child realized he needed a lesson about the ranch. But how could she?

By the time the dinner bell rang, Angelica had grown tired and all but fallen asleep in his arms. After taking care of the horse as he'd seen his brothers do, he carried the child to the house. When he climbed onto the porch, Lady wagged her tail. Dex paused, surprised.

"Good dog," he commented. He supposed that Lady considered him harmless enough if he'd made friends with one of the children—especially the princess.

Inside, Jenny, Angelica's mother, waited to take

her daughter. "Let's get you washed up for supper, young lady."

As she ascended the stairs, the princess waved at Dex. He couldn't help a smile. He felt an unfamiliar shifting in his chest. He shook his head. A rugrat had stolen his heart. Unbelievable. Dex joined the men who were washing up in the kitchen. They'd been gone when he returned from town that morning. He wondered if they'd noticed he was missing.

"We missed you today, boy," his Grandfather Cooper said.

"I had some business in town," Dex offered, hoping that would be the end of it. Was he supposed to check in with his grandfather before leaving the ranch? Maybe there were certain tasks for which Ty was responsible.

"Mrs. Watley told your Gran that you'd offered to help Leanne get some work done over there." He clapped Dex on the back. "That's mighty good of you. We can handle things around here. You help Leanne out all you can. She's a good girl. The best."

Dex nodded, thankful for the reprieve. "I'll do that."

Court winked. "I think I hear wedding bells already," he teased.

"I know I do," Chad said as he dried his hands. "Guess Rolling Bend's about to lose its most eligible bachelor."

Dex felt heat rise up from his collar. "I just want to help her out," he assured Ty's brothers. "That's all."

"'Course you do," Court said with a laugh. "I saw the way you looked at her at dinner the other night. It was like you'd just laid eyes on her for the first time."

He had, but Dex didn't mention it.

"The next thing you know," Chad put in as they walked to the dining room, "you'll be hearing the pitter patter of little feet just like the rest of us."

The Coopers had him married and having children. Was this why Ty was all too willing to have some time away? The image of Leanne slipped into his head. The thought of her with Ty made his gut clench.

Dinner proved to be the usual Cooper clan experience. Lots of talk and laughter. Tonight's fare included fried pork chops, something the others called turnip greens, and baked beans. Like the green beans, the brown beans contained a large chunk of fatty meat. Seasoning, he'd determined.

"Did you have a nice ride with your Uncle Ty, Angel?" Chad asked his little girl.

Dex tensed. What if she told them about the episode in the barn or the fact that he'd gotten lost and she'd had to tell him the way back to the house?

She beamed a wide smile. "We had the bestest time. Uncle Ty promised to take me again real soon." She turned that mega-watt smile in his direction and gave him a little wink.

He'd promised her no such thing. The little blackmailer. "Anytime," he said, his smile matching her own.

The subject of the dance came up, then. The whole Cooper clan would be there. It was an annual tradition. Everyone sounded excited. The food was always great and the music loud, Dex learned.

He couldn't wait, he mused. It obviously took very little to excite these people.

"The dance is always a good time to make announcements," Grandfather Cooper commented aloud.

All eyes turned to Dex at the precise instant that a bean hit him in the chest.

Chad scolded his child while Dex grappled for something to say. "I'm not sure I'll know anything from the investors by then," he said, pretending to believe that's what the older man was talking about.

"Well, maybe something *else* will come up."

Dex smiled weakly at his grandfather. These people didn't give up. He wondered how Ty handled the situation.

"That was mighty generous of you to buy Leanne that nice dress," Grandmother Cooper said.

How did she know that? Dex swore silently. Small-town life. The whole place probably knew before sundown that he'd bought the dress. His mouth went dry at the thought that they might also know about his moment of temporary insanity.

"It was the one she wanted," he offered lamely.

Chad and Court hit a high five across the table. Dex felt like crawling under it.

"Agnes Washburn and Corine Miller said you put on quite a show in the shop," Brenda, Court's wife, suggested.

The brothers hee-hawed.

"Well, I…"

"You don't have to explain, son," Grandfather Cooper hastened to put in. "It's spring, you're in love."

"In heat," one of the brothers muttered.

Dex glared at both of them.

"That's enough of that," Grandmother Cooper

chided. She smiled at Dex. Her smile played havoc with his equilibrium.

Another bean flew in his direction, drawing Dex's attention back to the little princess.

He was in real trouble here, he admitted.

Ty would kill him when he came back. The whole family now believed him in love with Leanne. Angelica clearly suspected something. And the whole town was talking about his lack of modesty at the clothing store.

"I'm sorry just to barge in."

Dex looked up in time to see Leanne burst into the room. She looked angry—and beautiful.

"Join us," Grandmother Cooper offered. "You know you're always welcome here, dear."

Leanne shook her head. "I can't stay long. I just need to talk to Ty a moment." She glared at him. "Alone."

Bewildered and suddenly wary, Dex rose from the table. "Excuse me," he murmured out of habit.

He followed Leanne from the dining room, the sound of muffled laughter and throats clearing echoing behind him.

Outside on the porch she rounded on him. "How dare you," she demanded.

How dare he what? "Pardon me?"

She narrowed her gaze at him. "Don't play dumb with me, Ty Cooper. You know what you did."

He frowned, trying to figure out what she could possibly mean. "Would you like to let me in on exactly what you're accusing me of?"

She set her hands on her hips and glared up at him, fury snapping in those pretty blue eyes. "I bought the dress I wanted to wear to the dance. How dare you buy the blue one and send it to me!"

His confusion deepened. "I thought you liked the blue one."

She tossed her head, sending long blond tresses over her shoulder. "Of course I like it, but that's not the point. I bought the pink one. If I'd wanted the blue one I would have bought it. I don't need your charity."

Oh, so that's what this was about. "It wasn't charity," he said evenly.

"Then what was it?"

"It was a gift."

She huffed out a breath, but some of her fury had dissipated. "A gift? What for? It's not my birthday."

He crossed his arms over his chest. "For no special reason. I wanted you to have it."

Her temper flared again. "I don't need your sympathy, either."

He smiled. He couldn't help himself. She was truly gorgeous when her temper flared. "Do you know how beautiful you are when you're angry?" He shook his head, scarcely believing his own words. But they were true. He'd gone this far, he might as well finish what he'd started. "Your eyes light up and your cheeks flush." His gaze settled on that lush mouth. "It's amazing," he murmured.

She took a step closer to him and shook her finger in his face. "Are you trying to seduce me?"

That question sent a jolt of shock through him. "What? Seduce you? No. I…"

"Then what was all that about this morning, undressing in front of me?"

Was that going to haunt him forever? "I wasn't trying to seduce you," he protested. "I just didn't think. I—" He shrugged. "I don't know why I did it." Had he been trying to seduce her? He resisted the urge to shake his head again. That didn't make sense. Why would he—?

"Well, you shouldn't have behaved so...so forward," she said and sniffed as if incensed.

A theory nagged at Dex. "Methinks the lady doth protest too much," he said, the concept gaining momentum.

She shot him a seething gaze. "What does that mean?"

"It's simple," he said, leaning forward, going nose to nose with her. "I tried the shirt on because it was necessary. If the act turned you on—" He shrugged again. "Well, there's nothing I can do about that."

Fury blazed in those baby blues. "Don't flatter yourself. There's absolutely nothing about you that would turn me on."

His competitive nature stirred instantly. "Oh yeah?"

"Yeah."

"Then why is your heart beating so fast?" He had her there. He could see the pulse fluttering wildly at the base of her throat.

She didn't miss a beat. "Because I'm madder than hell, that's why, you...you jerk."

"And just a little turned on?" he insisted. *He* sure as hell was. His radar couldn't be that far off.

She surprised him. "So what if I am a little turned on? Big deal. It doesn't mean anything." She lifted her chin defiantly. She thought she had him there.

"Really?"

"That's right." She looked him up and down. "You're not exactly unaffected yourself."

She did have him there. It wasn't like he could hide it. "Prove it," he challenged.

Her gaze shot to his. "Prove what?" A good deal of her bravado dissolved right before his eyes.

"That it's nothing…that I only turn you on just a little." Oh, he was feeling really wicked now. Wicked and far too excited to think rationally.

She looked uncertain, but not quite ready to back down. "And just how am I supposed to do that?"

"Kiss me."

Her eyes widened. "What?"

"Kiss me. If it doesn't do anything for you, then you've proven your point."

"Good night," she said, her voice clipped as she brushed past him.

"Guess I was right, then," he said, smiling in triumph.

She whirled around, shooting him a drop-dead stare. "You are not right."

"Yes, I am."

Fury glittering in her eyes, she marched straight up to him, grabbed him by the shirt, jerked him down to her and kissed him hard on the mouth.

His mouth claimed hers. Her palms flattened against his chest. When she would have pushed him away, he drew her closer. His arms tightened around her tiny waist, aligning her body with his. She felt soft against him, and so very fragile. But her kiss was like fire. Her mouth full, soft, hungry. Her hands moved up and over his chest until her arms wrapped around his neck. She tiptoed then, pressing her hips more fully into his and creating a whirlwind of sensation inside him. He groaned.

The kiss went on forever. If he'd ever kissed a woman this innocent yet this eager, he had no recall of it. His body hardened to the point of pain. He wanted more than she would be willing to give, he was certain of that. But he would take this one moment.

She drew back, her face flushed, her eyes glazed with lust. "Stop," she whispered, breathless.

He couldn't help himself, and he kissed those full, wet lips once more. "Admit it," he murmured against her lips, "and I'll stop."

"You win." She stepped away from him, then swayed. He steadied her. "Satisfied?" Anger burned away the lust in her eyes.

"Not by a long shot." He cupped her face in his hands and kissed her once more before she could stop him. This time, he thrust his tongue inside that luscious mouth. She whimpered at the feel of him inside her. When he'd had his fill of exploring that hot little mouth, he drew back. "Now I'm satisfied."

She jerked from his grasp and rushed away before he could say good-night. The truck's engine roared to life and she spun away in a spray of dust and gravel.

Dex watched her go, his body still humming with desire. He'd made a mistake. He closed his eyes and shook his head. A huge mistake.

He'd tasted heaven and now he wanted it.

But he wasn't Ty Cooper.

He couldn't let lust sweep them away when she had no idea who he really was.

It wouldn't be right.

And no matter how many one-night stands he'd

had in the past without looking back, he had a feeling she wasn't the kind of woman a man walked away from so easily.

Even after a long hot bath Leanne couldn't relax enough to go to sleep. Instead she paced her room like a caged animal. She should never have allowed Ty to goad her into that first kiss. She closed her eyes and steadied herself when the flood of sensations that accompanied the memory overwhelmed her. The feel of his firm mouth on hers. The feel of his strong, lean body, hard with need for her, pressed against hers made her weak with want.

Leanne forced her eyes open, and thoughts of Ty away. She couldn't feel this way. She didn't want to marry him and be the kind of rancher's wife he wanted…needed. But she couldn't imagine why she suddenly had all these crazy mixed-up feelings for him. It didn't make sense. A week ago she'd felt nothing more than sisterly feelings for him. Now, suddenly, she couldn't sleep for thinking of him. Whenever he was near her heart raced, her pulse leapt. And after those kisses, she wasn't sure of anything anymore. She crossed her arms over her chest.

What had happened to her?

She stared at the shimmering blue dress hanging on her closet door. What had possessed him to buy it for her? Ty had never shown any interest like that for her in the past. They'd been friends, practically family. Now he was buying her fancy dresses and trying to seduce her. It just didn't make sense.

Leanne plopped down onto the bed. He had promised to help her with the guest cabins. Another unexpected gesture. Not that he wouldn't have helped in the past if she'd asked, but this was different. Somehow. God, it was just too confusing. She couldn't think straight.

What if he decided not to help her?

She chewed her lip. No, that couldn't be. Ty never went back on his word. But then, Ty never did any of these other things, either. Maybe he was going through some sort of change here. Maybe…

She'd just have to wait and see if he showed up tomorrow morning. If he did, she'd have to be careful to keep things platonic. No more hot kisses. No more touching.

She flopped over onto her side and pulled her knees to her chest. Getting the guest cabins and the pool ready to use were the most important things right now. She couldn't get caught up in anything else.

The dance.

How would she get through a whole night with him at the dance? Working together was one thing, but a date—and he'd called it a date—was entirely different.

The telephone rang. Leanne shot to her feet. She had to get to it before it woke her mother. She ran downstairs, two stairs at a time, not slowing to consider who would be calling her at this time of night. It was almost midnight.

She grabbed the receiver on the fourth ring. "Hello."

"Leanne?"

Ty.

She pressed her hand to her chest and tried to catch her breath despite the racing of her heart. "Yes."

"I know it's late but I felt compelled to call." Silence stretched for several seconds. "I wanted to apologize for antagonizing you tonight. I behaved despicably. I hope you'll forgive me."

She frowned. The voice was his, but the words were all wrong. "Ty?"

"Y-yes," he said hesitantly. "I didn't want you to be angry with me."

She shook her head. "I'm not angry with you." She hesitated. "Not really. I just don't understand what's happening," she said in all honesty.

"I'm sure it's nothing," he said, his words wielding a hurt she hadn't expected. "Why don't we forget the whole incident?"

She blinked furiously, surprised to find moisture gathering in her eyes. "It's forgotten already," she said hollowly.

"Good." He hesitated again. "I'll see you tomorrow, then."

"Tomorrow," she echoed, barely retraining the tears. This was crazy. She blinked some more.

"Good night, Leanne."

"Good night, Ty."

She hung up.

It was nothing.

Then why did it suddenly feel like everything?

Chapter 7

Dex parked in front of the Watley house the next morning at 8:00 a.m. Another sleepless night had left him with a less-than-amiable disposition. The kisses he'd stolen from Leanne had played havoc with his ability to relax. But with the phone call he'd made sure there was no misunderstanding. That was the last thing either of them needed. They could just start fresh today. He was here to help her, not seduce her. It had just happened. He was certain of it.

Today, like the days to follow, would be about work, about making her dream come true. Nothing else. Well, nothing else but keeping him off the Circle C.

At least here he was on steadier ground. He didn't know any more about painting than he did about running a ranch, but maybe he could do a better job of faking the former. Fighting his attraction to Leanne would certainly be simpler than enduring the Coopers' matchmaking schemes.

He remembered to retrieve his Stetson from the seat as he climbed out of the truck. Maybe painting would be a good excuse not to wear it. He could hope.

As he was about to climb the steps to the porch, Leanne came around the corner of the house. "Morning."

He nodded, instantly taking in the fit of her pink blouse and figure-forming jeans. "Good morning."

"My mother's resting. I don't want to disturb her, so if you don't mind I've already started around back."

"All right."

He settled the frustrating hat atop his head and followed her. Maybe he should be leading the way, he mused, since he couldn't keep his gaze off her swaying hips. Her long blond ponytail kept time with the rhythmic movement. He sighed, more loudly than he'd intended. She glanced over her shoulder, but didn't smile. He wondered if she could possibly know what he'd been thinking.

"I started on this one." She motioned to the cabin closest to the house.

When they entered the small cabin Dex was surprised that it was a good deal roomier inside than it looked. The one empty room was large enough to accommodate the appropriate living-room and bedroom furnishings. On the far wall was a small efficiency kitchen. On another wall there were two doors, one to a closet, one to a bathroom.

Dex's gaze settled on the two buckets of paint and the paint-filled pan sitting on the floor next to them. He frowned. "Did you pick up all the supplies we would need?"

"Two gallons of paint, one pan, a roller and handle and two paint brushes," she said triumphantly.

"What about the rest?" She would need a great deal more than that to complete all the work. He might not be a painter by trade, but even he recognized that much.

"I told you I couldn't get it all at once," she countered, an edge in her voice. "This should keep us plenty busy today."

The money thing again, he realized, annoyed. "Come with me." He walked outside, then retraced the path they'd taken around the house. Dex tried to tamp down his impatience, but the effort proved futile. He preferred that his orders were followed without question, but she couldn't know that. She thought he was Ty. Somehow that disturbed him even more, but he pushed the sensation away. He was here to help and to avoid making obvious mistakes on the Circle C, not to become infatuated with a woman who didn't even know him.

"Where are you going?" she asked, walking fast to match his stride.

"*We* are going into town to pick up the necessary materials to do the job properly."

"Wait."

He ignored her as his impatience quickly turned to irritation. He liked things done in an efficient manner. He hated wasting his time. He suppressed the urge to wonder what Ty was doing in *his* office. Grandfather Montgomery would never allow him to make a bad business maneuver. Dex could count on that. But he wasn't supposed to be thinking about any of that right now. He was supposed—

Leanne grabbed him by the arm and turned him around, effectively halting him and his thoughts. He wanted to be angry, but the electricity her touch generated startled him, reminding him of last night's kiss. Fortunately, he recovered swiftly enough. "What is it now?" he demanded.

"I told you I can't buy everything at once."

"I didn't ask you to," he said just as pointedly.

"Ty," she countered.

For the first time since his arrival, the urge to correct her was nearly overwhelming. Whenever a Montgomery made up his mind, he didn't like being detained.

"Get into the truck, Leanne. Don't argue. Just do it." When she hesitated, he added, "When you told me what you wanted to do, I got the impression this was really important to you. Was I wrong?"

The stand-off lasted about three seconds. "You weren't wrong."

"Then get in."

She rounded the hood and climbed into the truck. Dex breathed a sigh of relief. One hurdle down. He didn't want to consider how many more to go.

Mr. Dickson at the Rolling Bend hardware store was more than happy to help. The first order of business was getting Leanne out of the store. Dex needed to speak privately with Mr. Dickson as soon as he determined it was safe to do so.

"Haven't done much painting, have you, Ty?" Mr. Dickson commented, amusement twinkling in his eyes.

Dex shook his head. "Someone else usually takes care of that task."

Mr. Dickson nodded. "Yeah, I was thinking Court was the painter in the Cooper family. Could make a living at it if he had the time and the inclination to leave the cattle business."

Dex tried not to look too relieved that he wasn't expected to know more about this than he did. "This is everything we'll need?" he asked, determined to get on with it.

"That's it." Mr. Dickson crossed his arms and looked pleased with his large sale.

Dex glanced at the door to make sure Leanne wasn't back yet. "Can you give me a quick block of instruction?" He looked covertly from side to side. "I'd prefer not to look completely inept. Do you know what I mean?"

Mr. Dickson winked at him. "I understand completely. You don't want to look dumb in front of the little lady. I've impressed a few in my time."

Dex nodded slowly. "Right."

During the fifteen minutes that followed, Dex received a quick lesson in "do-it-yourself" painting. It sounded easy enough. Especially the rolling part. The edging part that needed to be done with a brush sounded a bit more complicated. He'd leave that to Leanne. She had surely done some sort of painting in the past. If she'd painted her nails, she had more experience with a brush than Dex.

Before Leanne returned from the bakery and the other errands Dex had sent her on, he'd loaded the truck with the supplies they needed to get the job done.

She stared, aghast, at his purchases stacked in the bed of the truck. She waved the white bag from the bakery, being careful not to tip the tray containing two cups of coffee in the other hand. "What is all this?"

Dex pushed up his hat and swiped his damp brow. He couldn't recall ever having perspired quite like this unless he was on a racquetball court. "What we'll need to complete the job," he told her bluntly.

She shook her head. "I can't afford all this."

He took the tray. "We'll work that out later. Right now we have to get down to business." Why did she always question his instructions? He was doing this to help her.

When he got into the truck she followed suit, still looking a bit dazed. He already knew from experience how she felt about charity. He wasn't about to tell her that he had no intention of accepting repayment. To his way of thinking, she was doing him a favor getting him away from the ranch, even if it did give the wrong impression to the Coopers. At least they weren't suspicious about his reasons for staying away.

"Ty, I can't do this," Leanne announced after a few minutes of riding in silence. "I don't know when I'll be able to repay you. It wouldn't be right not to tell you that up front."

He thought about that for a minute, then decided upon an idea he hoped would satisfy her. "I have a couple of friends who could use a few days away from the city. Maybe you'd let them be your first guests."

"As repayment for all this?" She held his gaze when he glanced in her direction, uncertainty in her own.

"If you feel that's right."

She considered his suggestion for a few moments. "Sounds fair." She stared straight ahead for a time, then asked the question he hadn't considered. "What friends? You've never mentioned any friends in the city before."

Dammit. He hadn't thought of that. "Just a couple of people I met when I went to Chicago," he said quickly. "No one I would have mentioned before."

"Oh."

Good save, he thought, relieved. Pretending to be someone else was a less than pleasant business.

"When would they want to come?" she continued, determined to nail him down on the details.

"Whenever you're ready to open for business."

"They could come, just like that?" She snapped her fingers. "Without notice?"

Dex couldn't tell her that it was two of his hospital administrators he had in mind, people who could adjust their schedules whenever he told them to.

"Sure." He left it at that in hopes she would leave it alone.

When he turned down the long drive that led to the Watley ranch and she hadn't asked any more questions, he decided she was satisfied.

Another hurdle behind him.

Who would have thought this Good Samaritan stuff was so complicated? Most women liked having money spent on them. The dress he'd bought Leanne, for example. He'd spent more than that on dinner and champagne for a date and never once had a complaint. He braked to a stop in front of her house and shoved the gear shift into Park. He just didn't get Leanne Watley. She wasn't like any woman he'd ever known. The memory of her taste broadsided him. His fingers tightened on the steering wheel. He had to stop allowing that to happen.

"Your *decaffeinated* coffee." She offered him a cup and smiled as he dragged his gaze in her direction.

His heart foolishly skipped a beat. "Thanks," he said, shaken.

"I didn't know you preferred decaf," she said, looking away.

Another misstep. "I guess I didn't know it either until I tried it while I was in Chicago."

"Seems like a lot of things changed while you were in Chicago," she said, the words almost too softly spoken to hear.

Dex tensed. Was she suspicious or simply surprised? He opened his mouth to offer an explanation but she spoke again before he could.

"I hope you know how much this means to me, Ty."

It was his turn to smile then, brittle though it might be. "I think I do. I have dreams, too."

"Like finding a larger market for selling your cattle?"

"That's one." He sipped the decaffeinated brew.

The bag rustled as she opened it and then offered him one of the pastries he'd asked her to pick up.

"Maybe later." He really wasn't hungry. Not for pastries, anyway. He forced his gaze straight ahead. No lustful thoughts, Montgomery, he reminded himself.

Looking thoughtful, she refolded the bag. "What's another one?"

He studied her for a moment, knowing full well it was a mistake. "Another what?" The thread of conversation had vacated his brain.

"Dream," she prodded.

Oh, yes. He'd stepped right into that one. But what could it hurt to tell her the truth? He exhaled a heavy breath and stared out at the wide-open Montana sky. He wondered how any sky could be that blue. Like her eyes, he thought, turning back to her. Like nothing else he'd ever seen. "Making my grandfather proud is one of my goals." He sipped his coffee. "Dream, if you'd prefer the term."

Her forehead lined with confusion. "But he is proud. He's about the proudest grandpa I know."

Well, that hadn't worked out as he'd thought it would. He scowled. How to get out of this one? He shrugged. "I guess I'm not as sure of that as you are."

"Ty, that's ridiculous." She opened the passenger-side door and scooted out. "You're being too hard on yourself."

He got out as well. That wasn't the first time he'd been accused of being too hard on himself. His valet, George told him that all the time. "Maybe so," he offered in hopes of ending the discussion.

"Do you ever wonder what life would be like if your mother and father were still alive?"

That question stopped him cold. He wasn't sure how to answer. He thought about the letters he'd found and the picture in his wallet. The one he looked at every chance he got when he was sure no one was watching. What if they had lived?

"I'm sorry." She placed a hand on his arm, sending another little zing of electricity through him. "I shouldn't have asked that. It was thoughtless."

"No, it wasn't thoughtless. I do wonder about that sometimes." He leaned against the front of the truck and stared at the cup in his hand as if it held all the answers. "I wonder how my life would have been different. Where I might be right now. If I'd have any brothers and sisters."

She nodded, those pretty blue eyes solemn. "It's so sad. They were such a beautiful couple. I've looked at their pictures a hundred times. But your grandparents have loved you as if you were their own," she offered. "Chad and Court have been like brothers to you."

He looked away. If only that were true. "Yeah, I know you're right. I should just be glad for what I have." Regret trickled through him. Maybe he was being too hard on his Grandfather Montgomery. Dex had no way of knowing how the decision had been made thirty-two years ago. This whole charade could be a huge mistake.

"I know you miss your twin brother," she said softly.

He frowned, uncertain of that ground. How was it that everyone else had known that there were two and he hadn't? Even Ty had known that part, even if he didn't know Dex was alive. Dex had been completely isolated from all this. The twinge of regret he'd felt faded instantly.

"I hadn't missed him until recently," he said in all honesty.

"It's a shame he was lost, too." She shook her head. "Mom said that when your folks came back from their visit down south they grieved for months over having lost your brother while they were away." Her brow lined thoughtfully. "I always wondered but didn't want to ask why they didn't bring him back here to be buried." She shrugged. "I guess the loss was too devastating."

Lost? He'd been lost all right. Ire rushed through him, scorching away all other emotion. And he had every intention of seeing that the people responsible for this ridiculous scheme answered for their manipulation.

"A real shame," he agreed. It seemed like a safe enough response and gave no hint of the emotions roiling inside him. He had somehow to sort them out. He didn't like how they made him feel.

"So," she said cheerily, "where do we start, boss?"

Now *there* was something he could do, give instructions. He'd always been good at that.

"Cabin One," he suggested, seeing that the cabins weren't numbered yet. "Or are you going to call them by names?"

"I haven't decided. But we'll go with numbers for the time being. This way," she said with a dramatic sweep of her arms. Another of those pulse-tripping smiles spread across her pretty face.

Dex had hoped she would lead the way again. He liked nothing better than watching that heart-shaped derriere sway from side to side. He'd never known a woman who walked quite like that. He was learning all kinds of new things from this sweet country girl.

He just had to remember one important point, the last thing she needed was a big, bad wolf like him. And right now he was definitely feeling wolfish.

Like a wolf who'd lied to her from the moment he'd laid eyes on her.

Leanne tried her best to stay focused on the painting, but she couldn't help stealing glances at Ty. She closed her eyes and shook her head. What was it that suddenly drew her so to him? Had the years of prodding from her mother and the Coopers finally kicked in?

Whatever the case, she was too close to seeing her dream come true to throw it away now. No matter how nice Ty was to help her, he would not want his wife running a dude ranch. He would want her at home having babies like Court's and Chad's wives. Not that Leanne didn't want her share of babies. She did. Just not right now. She had plenty of time to think about marriage and children. Plenty.

Her gaze stole over to Ty once more. He'd rolled up his shirtsleeves and was working diligently on his second wall. The first had been a little tough going. Leanne had kept her mouth shut, but she hadn't missed his irritation until he got the hang of things. The task appeared to be moving smoothly now. She smiled as she considered that he literally had paint all over him. He even had it in his hair.

But it in no way detracted from his good looks. The man was definitely fine. She sighed softly. Broad, broad shoulders. Those muscled arms. Oh, and gosh, that awesome chest. The ladies around town were probably still talking about how he had bared that spectacular chest in Mrs. Paula's shop.

She would never forget that little show, Leanne mused dreamily. She couldn't help but wonder if the rest of him looked that magnificent. She frowned, trying to remember the last time she'd seen him in swimming trunks or cutoffs. Oh, and the man could kiss as well. Despite being twenty-three, she'd only been kissed a couple of times, and chastely at that.

No one, *no one* had ever kissed her the way Ty had last night.

Another less pleasant memory, followed by an instant flash of fury chased away the tingling sensation the recall of his kisses evoked. He'd said it was nothing. So why should she tingle when she remembered it? She shouldn't. It was nothing.

She thunked her brush down onto the top of the paint can. It was almost noon. The least she could do was feed him. Of course, at the moment, she couldn't say if she cared whether he was hungry or not. "I'll get lunch," she announced without preamble or manners and started out of the room.

He placed his paint roller in its tray and turned to her before she could get away. "I should wash up."

There was no denying that. Despite her irritation, Leanne couldn't stop the grin that tickled her lips when she looked at him. His arms were sprinkled with white splotches. He'd smeared paint on his left cheek and there were at least two spots in his hair. His clothes would never be the same.

"You find this amusing?" He wasn't smiling, though she could see the amusement in his eyes.

Laughter bubbled into her throat. "I'm sorry. It's just that you look so funny."

One dark eyebrow arched, lending a devilish look to his handsome face. "Just point me in the direction of soap and water."

Ty followed her into the house. Leanne fully expected to find her mother waiting at the kitchen table. Instead she found lunch already prepared. Sandwiches and chips, even freshly made lemonade.

"Make yourself at home," she said to Ty. "I need to check on Mom."

He mumbled something but the spray of water from the faucet muffled his words. As she headed into the hall, Leanne resisted the impulse to look back and see if he would take off his shirt again.

Her mother watched television from a comfortable mound of pillows propped up on the couch. Her hands were busy with knitting needles. It was the first time her mother had bothered with her knitting in months.

"Thanks for making lunch, but you didn't have to do that." Leanne sat in the chair next to her.

"I feel pretty good today." Joanna smiled, another very rare thing these days.

Seeing that smile on her mother's face made Leanne feel lightheaded. "That's wonderful. Would you like to join us for lunch?"

"Oh, no. I've already eaten." She waggled her eyebrows. "Besides, the two of you don't need an old stick-in-the-mud like me intruding on your time together."

Leanne didn't bother telling her mother that it wasn't what she thought. She didn't dare do anything to bring those high spirits down.

"All right, then. If you need anything we'll be working in the cabin closest to the house today."

She nodded. "I know. I saw you through the kitchen window when you were unloading your supplies." She sighed. "I swear, that Ty gets more handsome every day."

Leanne kissed her mother on the cheek and took her time getting back to the kitchen. Why didn't she just go ahead and marry him? Being Ty's wife certainly wouldn't be a hardship. He might let her run the dude ranch. He certainly hadn't spoken against it when she'd told him about it.

She sighed. No, she wasn't in love with Ty. She wanted to be madly, truly, deeply in love with the man she spent the rest of her life with. Though she cared deeply for Ty, and even felt attracted to him lately, he just didn't make her heart flip-flop the way she'd dreamed her Prince Charming would.

Oh, he'd made it beat a little faster, that was true enough. But it just wasn't the way she knew it could be with the one man who was meant for her—with the man of her dreams, the one who had the power to make her forget all else.

Pushing the foolish thoughts away, she reentered the kitchen, producing a smile for her guest.

Ty stood before the sink, his back to her. Leanne stalled just inside the door.

He was naked from the waist up again. Shirtless and with his jeans riding low on his hips, his smooth skin glistened with water droplets. While she watched, he bent forward and splashed water on his face, then pushed his damp hands through his thick, dark hair. He straightened and turned away from the sink. Rivulets of water raced down his sculpted chest to soak into the waistband of his low-slung jeans.

Mesmerized, she watched as he dried his face and upper body. Her mouth went dry and her breath left her lungs with each stroke of the terry cloth. But it was her heart that reacted the strongest. It flip-flopped, hard, in her chest.

Just then Ty opened his eyes. He smiled at her. Not just any old kind of smile. But one that said, *I know*

*your heart just did a double somersault, and I'm about
to make it do the same thing all over again. And again
after that.*

Her heart did just that.

Just the way she'd dreamed it would.

Chapter 8

Dex jerked the tie loose and retied it. His fingers just didn't seem to want to do what he wanted them to. He stared at his seemingly useless hands and frowned. His skin was dry, callused almost. He'd had to scrub like hell to get all the paint off. His left arm ached from overuse. It just wasn't natural to him, but he'd had to keep up the act down to the last detail, just in case. He blew out a frustrated breath and dropped his hands to his sides. The whole week had been like this. Everything he did, everything he said, came out wrong. He'd never felt so clumsy in his whole life. It just didn't make sense.

Sure it did, a little voice told him. It made perfect sense. He was in lust with Leanne Watley.

"Dammit."

"I'm gonna tell," a little voice singsonged from the open bedroom doorway. "Uncle Ty said a bad word."

Dex glared down at Angelica. "Go away."

She hugged her doll and swished back and forth, apparently enjoying the sound of lace against the stiff fabric of her dress. "If you don't take me for 'nother ride on your horse, I'll tell," she warned, making a little song out of the threat.

The child had been blackmailing him all week. He'd been forced to submit to her every whim. But he'd had enough. He leaned down nose-to-nose with her. "So tell," he challenged. "See if I care."

Angelica harrumphed, then whirled in a flurry of white lace and taffeta. "Mommy!" she shouted as she ran down the hall. "Uncle Ty's been gotted by aliens!"

Dex heaved a disgusted sigh. "Great," he muttered. He and Angelica needed to have a talk.

The kid was entirely too much like him. She didn't quit until she got what she wanted.

A scream rent the air. Dex bolted in the direction of the sound. Surely a simple swear word didn't warrant that kind of reaction. He skidded to a halt outside the open bathroom door. Jenny, Chad's wife and Angelica's mother, stood in the middle of the room, something he couldn't identify in her hand, Angelica standing next to her, staring upward in confusion.

"Oh, God, Ty," Jenny cried, her eyes bright. "It turned blue!"

Dex frowned. "What turned blue?" he asked cautiously.

She waved the thing in her hand. "The stick!" She waved it again. "This! I'm pregnant!" She stared down at her little girl then. "We're going to have a baby!" She tossed the stick into the sink and grabbed Angelica in a big hug. "You'll have a little brother or sister."

Dex's frown slowly slipped upright into a smile. She was going to have a baby. "You're pregnant!" he said lamely.

Jenny nodded, tears rolling down her cheeks. "We've tried for so long." She let go of her daughter and rushed to hug him. "I'm so happy."

He hugged her back. "That's great." Something like pride or maybe happiness bloomed in his chest. "That's so great." He patted her awkwardly.

She drew back. "I have to find Chad!"

She rushed down the hall, leaving a stunned Dex and an equally stunned Angelica. When Jenny had disappeared down the staircase, he glanced down at the princess.

Her doll forgotten on the bathroom floor, she planted her little fists on her hips. "Well, what if I don't wanna baby brother or sister?" She made a face. "Got too many babies around here now."

Oh, this was good. The little princess was jealous. "Get used to it, kid. Once the stick turns blue there's no stopping it."

Dex pivoted and strode back to his room. He'd loved to hang around and see how the princess handled her dilemma, but he had other things to do.

Like picking up the prettiest girl in the whole state of Montana. He fiddled with his tie, finally accomplishing his goal of tying it this time. Working with Leanne for the last three days had done nothing to lessen his hunger for another taste of her. But she'd kept her distance. He hadn't missed the flicker of desire in her eyes once or twice, but she didn't get too close. That was a good thing, he decided.

He couldn't understand what precisely it was about

that sweet little country girl that drove him to distraction, but whatever it was, he couldn't get enough.

Dex stared at his reflection. The image of Ty Cooper stared back. The bottom dropped out of his stomach. No matter how much he wanted Leanne he couldn't allow their relationship to go beyond the kissing stage. Her desire was for Ty, not him. He had to remember that. The truth would soon come out. He didn't want to hurt Leanne.

He didn't want to hurt any of them.

He pulled his wallet from his jeans and slipped the photograph of his mother and father out of it. This family had opened their arms to his father, had loved his mother desperately. Whatever their reasons for allowing him and Ty to be separated, he couldn't permit his own actions to hurt them in any way. Make them regret, maybe, but that was the extent of the retribution he required from the Coopers. He still didn't know how he felt about his Grandfather Montgomery's deception. He would deal with that soon enough. But not tonight. Tonight he was going to relax and enjoy being a Cooper.

Who knew? His stay here could end at any time. If Ty was discovered or if *he* was, the gig would be up.

He glanced at the bureau drawer where he'd hidden the letters. A yearning welled inside him. Maybe they held the answers he sought. Soon. Very soon, he promised himself. He intended to open them and see. He'd struggled with the idea of breaching his father's privacy, but he had to know the truth.

A few minutes later Dex shook his Grandfather Cooper's hand and kissed his grandmother's cheek before leaving to pick up Leanne. The whole family would be at the dance, but he felt like showing them some affection. He almost laughed at the idea that maybe the Cooper way was rubbing off on him already.

But, he considered as he drove toward Leanne's, he couldn't quite dispel the hint of bitterness he felt over the choices they had made. He would clear the air on that score soon enough. Dex parked near the Watley house and dismissed that line of thinking. Tonight he was going to have some fun, Montana style. He forced away thoughts of his Grandfather Montgomery's constant warnings about money-hungry women. Leanne was about as far from that as a woman could get.

Leanne was out the door by the time he reached the top step. He'd known the blue dress would complement her angelic features and those big blue eyes, but he hadn't expected this. She was beautiful. Truly, extraordinarily beautiful.

Her thick blond tresses fell around her shoulders like shining silk. The dress clung to her womanly figure in all the right places. His entire body tensed as his gaze lingered on her full breasts. She was perfect.

"Stunning," he murmured, working hard to draw a breath into his lungs. "Absolutely stunning."

She smiled nervously. "Why, thank you, Mr. Cooper, you don't look so bad yourself."

Dex glanced down at his white shirt, black tie and jeans. Pretty simple, really. But the best he could do considering Ty was no clothes horse.

"Thank you, ma'am," he drawled, then offered his arm. "Shall we go?"

He walked her to the passenger side of the truck and opened the door. "Wait, I almost forgot something," he said as he reached inside. He withdrew the small box and offered it to her.

"What's this?" she asked, breathless.

"Open it," he urged. "You'll see."

Her hands shaking with impatience she quickly loosened the ribbon and removed the lid. "Oh, it's beautiful." She took the blue and white carnation wrist corsage from the box and smiled up at him, her eyes suspiciously bright. "Thank you, Ty. That was very sweet of you."

He slipped it onto her right wrist. "Can't take a lady to a dance without a corsage." He smiled, warmth filling his chest, reminding him of how sweet this particular lady was.

She pressed a quick kiss to his cheek, then shook her head. "I swear, Ty, it's like I don't even know you anymore."

He held out his hand to assist her into the vehicle. "Are you saying I'm not always this nice?"

"No, it's not that." She adjusted her dress, then looked at him. "But you took my idea of opening a dude ranch far better than I could have hoped." She lifted one slender shoulder in the barest of shrugs. "Now flowers." She reached up and felt his forehead. "It makes me wonder if you've come down with something."

What did Ty have against her opening a dude ranch? he wondered. Could he have overstepped his bounds there? They would have to discuss that as soon as Dex had a chance to call him, which had better be soon.

He gifted Leanne with a smile. "I've just decided that life's too short to sweat the small stuff. There's always a way to work anything out," he assured her, hoping like hell he was right.

When they arrived at the Rolling Bend community center the place was already packed. The band was loud, as Grandmother Cooper had said it would be, and the night was warm. Dex escorted Leanne to the door, but she stopped him when he would have opened it.

"Ty." She looked up at him, those pretty blue eyes far too serious. "Just for tonight could we pretend that we're not who we are?"

Confused, Dex tried to read her expression for some hint of what she was thinking. "I don't know what you mean."

She placed a soft hand on his arm, sending heat rushing through him. "Just for tonight, let's pretend you're not Ty Cooper, the rancher who loves nothing more than raising his cattle. That I'm not Leanne Watley, struggling dude rancher. And that our parents haven't tried to marry us off for years. Let's just be two people who want to have a nice time together for one evening. Just one night," she added softly.

The urge to take her in his arms and show her just what they could do together if they forgot for this one night was almost more than he could restrain.

"We can do that." He stared directly into her eyes, hunger roaring inside him. At that moment he would have given anything to *really* have her for one night. "Just for tonight."

He opened the door and they entered the loud, exuberant festivities. He wondered if Miss Leanne Watley had any idea how close to the edge she'd pushed him. It would take nothing short of a miracle to keep him from crossing the line tonight.

Before Ty could have the first dance with her, Leanne found herself whirled around the dance floor with half a dozen different young men. All single, all hoping she was looking for a husband. Did people around here think of nothing else?

Her gaze sought and found Ty. He looked so handsome. He'd abandoned his hat, leaving it on their table, but he looked even better without it. Why had she never noticed that before? She wanted desperately to run her fingers through that thick, dark hair. All week this crazy attraction had been building. She just couldn't get him off her mind. Finally, she'd decided there was only one way. She closed her eyes and wished they could really be together in the truest sense of the word for just this one night. Maybe she would realize it was nothing but raging hormones.

But Ty was too honorable for that. If they made love, especially under the circumstances, he would demand that they marry.

Sometimes being a virgin could be so annoying.

Ty looked up from his conversation with Mr. Dickson from the hardware. His gaze caught hers and he smiled. Her heart did that little acrobatic flip only he had the power to cause. The song ended and her dance partner thanked her. She wove her way around the fringes of the crowd. A fast, bluegrass tune started and the dancers still on the floor kicked their heels high and let go whoops of enthusiasm.

Earlier, Jenny Cooper had announced that she and Chad were expecting. Angelica, their little girl, looked downright miserable. Leanne was happy for Jenny and Chad, but she couldn't quite work up the proper enthusiasm. She told herself she wasn't jealous. She didn't even want to get married.

But part of her did, she admitted glumly, then chastised herself. Where on earth had that thought come from? She tried to understand it, rationalize it somehow, but she couldn't. It simply was. She *wanted* to be Mrs. Ty Cooper. Part of her wanted to have his babies. She shook her head and reached for a cup of punch. But a saner part of her wanted to do just what she was doing. None of this should be happening. It didn't make sense. Lord have mercy, she'd never been this confused in her life.

A wide palm settled against the small of her back and a familiar body, warm and muscular, moved in close to hers. "May I have this dance, pretty lady?"

Leanne sat her cup down and looked up into Ty's dark eyes. "I thought you'd never ask."

He smiled. Her heart flip-flopped. "I was waiting for the perfect moment."

Only then did she realize that a slow, aching love song had started to play. He led her to the dance floor, then drew her into his arms. As those strong arms closed around her, pulling her against the shelter of his lean body, everything else faded away. She inhaled the masculine scents of leather and spice, looked up into a face she knew as well as her own. But when she closed her eyes and laid her head against him, it was as if he were someone else.

She had danced with Ty many times before, but this time was different. The way he held her…the perfect rhythm of his movements…the feel of his hands as he traced her spine. The feel of his lips against her forehead. Her heart raced with anticipation, her pulse throbbed impatiently. This couldn't be real, she assured herself, but she clung to the moment with both hands. She wanted this one moment. Her fingers found their way into his hair. He reacted, pressing her more firmly against his hips, allowing her to feel how she moved him.

One song melded into another. It was as if the band knew they didn't want to part, so the slow, sensual music continued. She could feel the steady beating of his heart beneath her cheek, could feel each defined muscle of his lean body. She wanted to rip his shirt open and touch all that skin she'd seen the other day in her kitchen. She wanted him to kiss her again.

God, she wanted him to kiss her again.

Reacting on instinct, she turned her face up to his. A new rush of need flooded her when she saw her own desire mirrored in his eyes. He wanted her, too. Wanted her just as much as she wanted him. She could feel his breath on her skin, but he made no move to do what she wanted so badly.

She lifted her chin, putting her lips so close to his, close enough to feel the electricity sizzle between them. She felt his exhalation of frustration. He was holding back and she didn't want to hold back, not tonight. Tonight nothing else was supposed to matter. She stilled, then tiptoed, making the contact complete. He released her instantly, his hands going immediately to cup her face.

His mouth claimed hers with a gentle fierceness that made her knees go weak. On and on he caressed her lips with his own, tasting, teasing. Then he sealed his lips over hers completely, the move rougher, more frantic. This was the moment she'd waited for, she realized, as foolish as it was. His hot tongue thrust into her mouth. She whimpered, pulling him closer. His fingers threaded into her hair, angling her head to give him better access. His tongue glided along hers, sending fire straight to her center, then touched her so intimately, her feminine muscles clenched in response.

He drew back, his ragged breath fanning her sizzling lips. "If I don't stop now, I may not be able to," he murmured thickly.

She nodded, speech was impossible. They were no longer dancing, only holding each other in such an intimate embrace that it was impossible not to see the heat simmering between them. But she didn't care. She wanted this night. She wanted more. She wanted it now.

"Can we please leave?"

He looked startled.

"Please," she urged.

He searched her eyes for ten full seconds. She struggled not to show any doubt. This was what she wanted. Now.

He grabbed her hand and cut a path through the crowd, pulling her along behind him, and snagging his hat as they went. She focused her gaze on his broad shoulders rather than on the couples stopping to stare at them. She no longer cared what anyone thought. She simply wanted.

She wanted this man.

Tonight.

And for the first time in her life she was going to

take what she wanted with no thought to the consequences.

He kept walking. He didn't stop until he reached
the driver's side of his truck. Far enough, she decided
when he would have reached for the door. She pulled
him around to face her, the heat in those dark eyes
searing her.

"Kiss me again," she demanded, feeling even
bolder.

He did. Drew her hard against him, the fingers of
one hand kneading her buttocks, lifting her into him.
This was no sweet, tender kiss. This was rough and
hot, almost frightening.

He turned her loose long enough to open the door.
She climbed in at his ushering and scooted across
the bench seat, he slid in next to her, shoving his hat
onto the dash.

"Where are we going?" he asked, his voice as rough
as his kiss, the sound making her shiver.

"I don't care." She leaned toward him and kissed
his mouth again. "Anywhere."

He started the engine and spun out of the parking
lot. Leanne's heart was pounding so hard she could
scarcely draw a breath. Please don't let him change his
mind, she prayed. She knew Ty too well. If he thought
about it…if she really thought about it.

No.

She had to do something to keep up the momentum. But what? She had no experience with this kind
of situation. But she had seen lots of movies. She
scooted closer to him. He smiled at her, the expression strained.

Oh yes, she had to do something or he was going

to change his mind. She loosened the string tie and tugged it from his collar. He accelerated as if that simple move had somehow urged him on. Feeling empowered, she unfastened the button at his collar. His fingers tightened on the steering wheel. She smiled. This was really something. She opened another button, then another. With each move his breathing become more labored and a muscle flexed in his chiseled jaw. It was working, not to mention driving her wild.

She reached inside his shirt and touched him. She gasped at the feel of his skin. His right arm went around her and drew her closer. He pressed a kiss to her temple. She was breathing so hard and fast she felt lightheaded. She couldn't believe the way it made her feel just to touch his skin. It was so smooth, so hot. She wanted more. Another button, then another. Then she leaned between him and the steering wheel and tasted that amazing terrain.

He groaned, the sound savage, like an animal. She could hear him breathing…or was it her? Her lips brushed one flat male nipple. The fingers of his right hand fisted in her hair, telegraphing his approval of that move. She did it again, this time she lingered, touched it with the tip of her tongue. He made more sounds. She sucked. He swore. While she tortured that nipple, her palm slid instinctively down his flat belly. She tugged at his belt, then fumbled with the fly of his jeans.

He made a hard right, pulling the truck onto a side road, then ramming the gear shift into Park. The engine died. The lights went out and his hands were all over her at once.

He slid to the middle of the bench seat and pulled her astride his hips. He lowered her mouth to his and kissed her so hard it almost hurt. Her hands continued to explore his chest, teasing his nipples the way he liked, and molding to each contour of male muscle.

He tugged one thin strap from her shoulder, then lowered the bodice of her dress just far enough to expose one breast. For one long moment he only stared at the small, pale globe, his breathing so harsh the sound made her ache in a way she'd never known before. When his mouth closed over her breast, she screamed her pleasure. His hips rose from the seat, thrusting against her. She pushed down, reveling in the hard feel of him against the place that ached so for his touch.

Then he suddenly stopped. She moaned her displeasure. She didn't want him to stop.

"I can't do this." His words were barely audible above his ragged breathing.

"Please don't stop." She kissed his lips in hopes of changing his mind, at the same time pressing down against him. He groaned.

"Wait." He held her away from him and looked at her in the darkness. She could just make out his eyes, the grim set of his mouth. "We can't."

"I don't understand." She shook her head. "Don't you want me?"

"Oh, yes." He gently lifted her off him and settled her on the seat beside him. "But we can't do this." He shook his head. "It wouldn't be right for either of us."

She dropped her head back against the seat. "I can't believe this."

He slid behind the wheel once more and started the engine. "Neither can I."

He drove her home without another word.

Chapter 9

By the time Ty parked in front of her house Leanne was feeling more than a little embarrassed. What in the world had possessed her to behave so foolishly? Ty probably thought she'd lost her mind. She stole a glance at him. But he'd been a little out of control, too. She closed her eyes and shook her head. The truth was she'd pushed him into it. What man wouldn't react willingly with a woman practically taking advantage of him? She thought of that muscled, masculine frame, then of her own size and decided maybe *taking advantage* was a bit of an overstatement.

She'd just wanted this one night.

Just to see. To get this crazy thing settled once and for all. Then things could return to normal, she felt sure.

Without looking at her, Ty got out of the truck and

walked around to her door to see her out. When he opened it, she looked at him in the dim glow cast by the cab light. She saw the same confusion she felt and something else…regret?

Her heart sank, adding insult to injury. She slipped off the seat to stand directly in front of him. To her surprise he made no move to back away. He just waited. For her to say something, she supposed.

"I'm sorry," she said in a braver tone than she'd thought possible. "I don't know what came over me." She trembled but quickly crossed her arms over her chest to conceal the quaking.

He touched her cheek, those long fingers trailed along her jawline, making her shiver, before he dropped his hand back to his side. "You have nothing to be sorry for," he assured her, his voice as soft and gentle as his touch. "We both got a little carried away tonight." He smiled; her heart reacted. "The pressure has been on both of us and maybe we just needed to see what all the fuss was about."

He didn't sound convinced but his effort to make her feel better touched her. "Thanks, Ty." She peered up at him, once more amazed at how she could have known him all this time and not realized just how wonderful he was. "You're a good sport and I'm…" She shrugged. "I think I'm just confused."

"Let's forget about it, okay?" He ushered her away from the truck door so that he could close it, then toward her porch steps, his palm never leaving the small of her back.

Forget it. That was the way he handled everything lately. A jab of anger made her want to stop right there and tell him what she thought. It sure hadn't felt like he wanted to forget it when they were kissing. He'd been very aroused. She might not have any experience with men, but she knew when one was aroused. She'd read her share of romance novels and watched enough romantic movies. And now he wanted to act as if it had been nothing. This whole situation bordered on the ridiculous. All this time they'd been friends, now suddenly everything was spiraling out of control, and he wanted to pretend it all away.

Why couldn't she do the same? That was the truly frustrating part.

Leanne squared her shoulders and lifted her chin in defiance of her own doubts. Whatever was going on with her foolish heart, she'd get over it. Ty was right, they should simply forget the whole thing.

At her door, she turned back to him, head held high. "Good night, Ty. Thank you for taking me to the dance."

He moistened those full lips, causing a little hitch in her breathing. She swore silently. He appeared more uncertain now of what had happened than she did. He quickly, awkwardly pressed a chaste kiss to her cheek, lingering just long enough for her to be assaulted all over again by that tantalizing masculine scent.

"Good night," he murmured.

Leanne turned away from him, gave the doorknob a frantic twist and rushed into her living room. The urge to cry was nearly overwhelming. This was insane! Her emotions were on a roller-coaster ride. One minute she wanted to push him away, the next—

"Leanne?"

The weak sound of her mother's voice came from somewhere in the dark living room. "Mom?"

"I can't seem to get up."

Panic shot through Leanne. She felt for the light switch and snapped it on. Her mother lay in a crumpled heap on the floor, struggling hard to raise herself to a sitting position. "Mom!" Leanne rushed to her side. "Are you hurt?" Fear made her heart pound. She should have been at home tonight, not out misbehaving as she had. Guilt and worry swamped her. She should never have left her mother at home alone for so long.

"Is everything all right?"

When Leanne looked up Ty was striding into the room, concern marring his handsome face. He crouched next to her. "What happened?"

"She fell. Help me get her to her bed."

As Leanne tried to help her mother up, he halted her with a firm hand on her shoulder. "Wait. We can't move her yet." He eased closer to her mother, effectively nudging Leanne out of the way. "Mrs. Watley, are you in pain? Did you hurt yourself when you fell?"

Leanne's worry deepened into a frown as she watched him. He was examining her mother, checking her limbs, turning her head from side-to-side. A new surge of concern washed over her. What if her mother had broken something? A hip or her arm? Lord, she should have been here.

"No," her mother told him. "I don't think I'm hurt. Just gave myself a good fright." She smiled weakly. "Then I didn't have the strength to get up. But I'll be fine. I just need to get back to my room, that's all. I shouldn't have come downstairs without help."

Ty looked doubtful. He helped her mother into a sitting position, then studied her eyes. "Did you hit your head? Is your vision blurred? Do you feel dizzy or lightheaded?"

"I didn't hit my head, and I can see fine." Joanna patted Ty's arm. "Really. I'm fine. There's no need to fret so."

He assisted her to her feet while Leanne stood helplessly by, feeling like an outsider in her own home. "Let me help you to your room," she said quickly as Ty was about to speak again. She slid one arm around her mother's waist and led her slowly toward the staircase.

"I'm fine, really," her mother insisted. "I can manage. You should see to your company."

Leanne glanced over her shoulder at Ty, who appeared deep in thought as he watched their slow progress. "Ty'll be fine for a few minutes while I help you to your room."

"Take your time," he said, his tone somehow strained.

When Leanne had her mother safely back in bed, she asked, "Can I get you anything? Water? Milk?" Her mother shook her head. She looked so frail, so weary. Leanne wanted to cry. It just wasn't fair for her mother to suffer this way. Leanne sat down on her bedside. "I'm sorry I left you here alone," she murmured. "I shouldn't have."

Her mother reached up and stroked her cheek, affection shining in her eyes. "Don't be silly, child. I wanted you to go. I would have been fine if I hadn't gotten up to sit on the couch and wait for you." She shook her head. "It was foolish, but I wanted to be waiting for you when you got home like I used to do."

Leanne kissed her forehead, trying hard to restrain the tears burning in her eyes. "You rest now. I'll tell you all about the dance in the morning."

Her mother patted her hand. "You go on back down there and see to Ty. I think he's a little upset. I hope I didn't ruin your evening."

The concern in her eyes tugged at Leanne's heartstrings. She forced a smile. "'Course you didn't." She stood. "Good night, Mama."

"Night." Her mother closed her eyes and seemed to drift immediately to sleep.

Leanne watched a few moments longer just to be sure her mother was resting. As she left the room she turned out the light, then closed the door. She pressed her forehead against the cool wooden surface and fought the urge to weep. If only there was something she could do to make her mother well again. If she could just talk her into seeing that specialist Dr. Baker had suggested. But Joanna Watley could be as stubborn as a mule at times. She would not go to a specialist. Leanne knew it was the money and she hated the idea that her mother was suffering because Leanne couldn't work more quickly. Couldn't make things happen at a faster rate.

Another reason she should marry Ty. She shivered at the memory of how it felt to be in his arms. He'd made her heart flip-flop just like she'd known the only one for her would. She stilled. But she didn't love him…not like that, did she? And he hadn't wanted to make love to her. He'd stopped, called it a mistake.

Leanne sighed. God, she was hopeless. How could she have all these tangled feelings? This sudden attraction was most likely temporary. Maybe it was about sex. Maybe she'd simply outgrown her virginity. Maybe that was the whole problem.

She composed herself and headed back down to

the living room where Ty waited. That was it, she decided. This whole crazy week had been about nothing but hormones. It was a simple biological urge. It had nothing to do with love or Ty. He was just handy.

One look at the man waiting in her living room made a liar out of her where that last thought was concerned. The man standing there, his shirt wrinkled by her frantic hands, that thick, dark hair mussed by her urgent fingers, was more than just handy. He was good-looking, sexy and he made her tingle low in her belly. He made her want to finish what they'd started.

Those dark eyes connected with hers and the fierceness there brought her up short. "Tell me about your mother's health."

It wasn't a request. Leanne felt oddly off balance by the harsh demand. "It started last year." She frowned as she considered the question. "You know that. It seems to have gotten worse over the past couple of months. Doc—"

"What exactly is *it?*" Another demand. "There must be a diagnosis."

Leanne swallowed back the hurt that accompanied what she recognized as accusation in his eyes. "Dr. Baker isn't exactly sure. He's ruled out lupus and rheumatoid arthritis, but—"

"Has she seen an internist?"

"A what?"

Ty took a breath, clearly to slow his temper. He was angry. She could see it in his eyes, his posture. This didn't make sense.

"This Dr. Baker, he hasn't referred her to anyone else or requested any other specialized testing? There are literally hundreds of different tests that her symptoms might indicate."

Defensive now, Leanne crossed her arms over her chest and glared at him. She was too annoyed to care how he could know so much about medicine and suddenly seem to have forgotten all he'd known about her mother's illness. "Well, of course he has. You know how thorough Dr. Baker is. But she refuses to see anyone else. She thinks we can't afford a specialist. It—"

There was no mistaking the fury in those dark eyes now. "Money again?" he snapped. A muscle jumped in his tense jaw. "Did it never occur to you to simply ask for help? Your mother is ill. Not having the strength to pick herself up from the floor is not likely to be some simple, passing ailment that will go away by itself. She needs the proper treatment." He stepped nearer, that fierce gaze boring down on her. "But before she can get that, she has to have the proper diagnosis. There's no excuse for lack of appropriate health care."

He was accusing Leanne of failing somehow. "What do you think I've been doing? I've tried everything I know to make her go, but she won't. She thinks we can't afford it and she's right, but I can't convince her to go and that we'll make it somehow."

"She's your mother," he all but growled. "You shouldn't take no for an answer."

His words stabbed her like a knife. Maybe he was right. Maybe she hadn't taken a firm enough stand on the issue. But she had so much on her. The ranch. Taking care of everything. Finding a way to make every penny stretch as far as possible. Getting the guest cabins ready. A fresh wave of tears welled. But maybe it was her fault.

"I've done the best I could considering—"

"Obviously," he cut her off, "it hasn't been enough. You'll call her doctor first thing in the morning," he said sharply.

She could only nod. How could he think she didn't care? How could he believe she'd been negligent?

"Good," he said with a bit less ferocity, then looked away and took another of those deep breaths that did nothing to calm the outrage clear in his rigid posture. "I should go."

Leanne felt empty, hurt and too confused to know exactly why he'd lashed out at her this way or why it should wound her so deeply. "I'd like you to go."

He swallowed, hard, then started to say something else, but apparently changed his mind.

He walked out.

She locked the door behind him.

Taking a deep, bolstering breath she trudged across the room and sat down on the edge of the couch, suddenly exhausted. She stared down at the silky blue fabric puddled around her feet and thought of how Ty had wanted her to have this dress. She thought about how he'd kissed her…how he'd touched her…

And then she cried.

Cried for reasons she didn't even understand.

Cried so hard that her chest hurt.

Or maybe it was her heart. She wasn't sure she would ever be the same again.

He'd driven around for hours. Hell, he'd even gotten lost once. But he just couldn't go home.

Home?

Dex laughed, a humorless sound. The Circle C

wasn't his home, no matter how much it felt like home when he finally parked between the house and barn around 1:00 a.m. He stared at the big old farmhouse, noting that the front porch light had been left on, for him.

He'd never felt so disgusted or confused in his entire life. He got out of the truck and walked to the porch, his feet leaden, his chest even heavier. He'd been a real bastard tonight. Though he would never understand why anyone would allow their health problems to go unmonitored when good medical care was certainly available, even in the wilds of Montana, he shouldn't have taken his fury out on Leanne.

She hadn't deserved it.

But the idea that she would go along with her mother was simply beyond his comprehension.

Still not ready to go inside, Dex collapsed onto the porch swing. He'd hurt her. There was no way he could have missed the pain in her eyes or in her voice when she'd told him to go. She was so young and innocent, and he was such a fool.

"Idiot," he muttered. He leaned forward, braced his elbows on his knees and tunneled his fingers through his hair. He had absolutely no experience where these sorts of affairs were concerned. Briefly he wondered where he'd left Ty's hat. In the truck, he decided, trying to focus on anything else. But the echo of his own words kept replaying in his head, overriding all other thought. He was a complete fool. How could he have spoken to her like that? Now he'd have to find some way to make this up to her, to bring that smile back to her lips.

The thought of her lips made his stomach tighten

as he pictured every moment they'd shared tonight. Her eager kisses. The way she'd begged him not to stop. He'd wanted her more than he'd ever wanted any woman in his life.

But he couldn't do this. He would be leaving soon and he didn't want to hurt her. Besides, the whole town appeared to want Leanne and Ty to spend the rest of their lives together. Dex couldn't do anything to mess that up. For all he knew Ty was simply suffering from cold feet and might want Leanne when he returned. Dex couldn't risk hurting her or his brother.

He leaned back in the swing and shook his head. What a mess. He'd royally screwed up at every step. He couldn't understand or justify all the mixed-up emotions he felt. In Atlanta he made life-altering decisions every day regarding patient care, research, personnel. How could he feel so differently, so emotionally disabled here?

It just didn't make sense.

He closed his eyes and thought about the way Jenny had hugged him earlier tonight. She was so excited to learn that she was pregnant. Why had her news affected him on the level it had? He'd felt something, something he couldn't name. A fondness, pride. He shook his head. Something. Even Angelica and the twins had gotten to him.

Lady sauntered over to the swing, her tail wagging, then plopped down near his feet. He'd passed the final test, he mused, the family dog had grown to like him. Did all this mean he was a part of the Cooper family now?

He shook his head again. None of it counted. They all thought he was Ty. They would all be confused and hurt when it was over. Whatever had possessed him to believe that anything could be gained by this ruse?

Feeling too damned confused, he tugged out his wallet and removed the picture of his parents. He stared at the smiling couple in the photograph. They looked so happy, each holding a tiny bundle. Dex had no way of knowing which was him and which was Ty.

Why did his parents have to die?

Dex blinked back the uncharacteristic sting of tears. He was thirty-two years old. He was a doctor, for Christ's sake. He wasn't supposed to ask foolish questions like that.

The squeak of the screen door dragged him from his painful reverie. Grandmother Cooper, clad in a pale pink robe and matching fuzzy house slippers shuffled across the porch in his direction. This was the first time he'd seen her with her hair down. A long gray braid draped one shoulder. She smiled that smile that made him feel serene somehow.

"My, you did have a late night, didn't you, son?" She sat down beside him, her gaze going directly to the photograph in his hand.

Dex almost groaned. He'd forgotten about the picture. Now she would know. He returned her smile. "Yeah, I guess I did have a long night."

She nodded at the photograph in his hand. "I wondered where that picture had gotten to."

Surprised, Dex studied her for a long moment. "You knew it was missing?"

She leaned back against the polished wood slats, her gaze taking on a distant look. "There isn't a day goes by that I don't look at each and every one of those pictures."

It was difficult to breathe. Dex blinked at the emotion burning in his eyes yet again. He wanted desperately to know more, to ask her all the questions that twisted inside him. "You still miss them?" The one question was barely a whisper, but it brought another smile to her lips.

"More now than ever."

He needed so many answers but he couldn't bring himself to ask another single question. Rather, he nodded his head once in silent agreement.

She hugged him, then. Hugged him fiercely. The gentle fragrance of lilacs filled his nostrils. He closed his eyes and allowed himself to relax into the embrace of the woman who'd given birth to his mother. The woman whose smile opened a window to a past he hadn't known existed.

"I'm so glad you're home," she murmured. "I've missed you."

He was touched deeply and at the same time startled by her words. Sensing his tension, she drew back and pointed to the picture he still clutched in his hand.

"In that moment, your mother and father were the happiest of their entire lives. They were complete with each other." She leveled him with a watery gaze that left no question as to what she meant. "And with you and your brother."

A frown tugged at Dex's brow. He started to ask the one question that burned in his chest, but she spoke again before he could get the words out past the lump in his throat.

"It wasn't enough that we lost your mother and father, we had to lose one of the babies, too." Her gaze grew distant again, her tone wistful. "It was the hardest thing I've ever endured." She looked back at him. "But don't doubt for a second how much we loved you both." She placed a hand on his arm and squeezed gently. "We never stopped loving *both of you*."

She kissed his cheek, got up and went back into the house.

Dex watched her, too moved or too stunned to speak.

He looked down at the picture in his hand once more and thought of the things his grandmother had just said to him and suddenly he knew.

He scrubbed a hand across his damp face as a strained laugh burst out of him.

He wasn't sure how it could be possible, but he was relatively certain of one thing: she knew.

Grandmother Cooper knew his secret.

Chapter 10

By Monday morning Dex was certain he had things back under control. Despite what had happened between them on Friday night, he'd shown up at Leanne's house on Saturday morning, business as usual. He was dependable if nothing else. When a Montgomery gave his word, he didn't go back on it.

Staring at his reflection in the mirror, Dex fastened the last button of his shirt and finger-combed his hair. As one would suspect, things had been a little tense with Leanne. He felt like the jerk he was for being so hard on her about her mother. It was clear that she loved her and had done the best she could. She certainly couldn't force her to seek out additional medical attention.

In his heart he knew that Leanne had gone above and beyond her duty as a daughter. As far as he could tell she had no life outside of taking care of her mother and the ranch. He felt like kicking himself. As a physician, sometimes he failed to see that things weren't always black and white. Sometimes there were extenuating circumstances beyond one's control. He'd started to explain himself on several occasions, but she always changed the subject or insisted she had to go check on something. Finally, he'd given up.

Making amends wasn't his specialty. Besides, she seemed satisfied with leaving things the way they were. Why rock the boat? They had definitely needed something to extinguish the fire building between them. It was best for all concerned.

Neither of them needed that kind of complication.

He'd even spent Sunday afternoon at Leanne's. He'd had to do something to escape the family's scrutiny. It wasn't enough that he'd attended church services with the whole clan on Sunday morning and then endured endless matchmaking hints and suggestions during lunch—which the Coopers called dinner. Grandfather Cooper had suggested that after the meal of fried chicken, homemade rolls, peas, mashed potatoes and gravy, he and Dex should have a man-to-man talk about women and marriage.

Dex'd had no choice. He had to find a way to escape. Spending the afternoon *not talking* to Leanne while they painted yet another of the cabins was preferable to the "talk." If he could live through the fire-and-brimstone sermon the minister had delivered, Dex decided, he could do anything. Several times during the discourse he'd felt certain the man was speaking to him personally, but that was impossible. Wasn't it?

A wistful feeling surged through Dex. He did miss

his family. In spite of everything, he wondered how the Montgomerys were doing and if Ty had been accepted by them as he had been here.

Very soon he had to find a private moment to call Ty and find out how it was going in Atlanta. With a family this size it was almost impossible to find a second alone near the one telephone in the house. At this point he wasn't too worried. He assumed that since Ty had not made any frantic calls to him, all must be well.

Dex picked up his hat and slowly turned it in his hands as he considered that late-night conversation on the porch with his grandmother. He couldn't be absolutely certain, but he had a feeling she knew. His stomach tied up in knots every time he thought about how she'd hugged him and told him she'd always loved both of them, and that she was glad he was home. He ran an unsteady hand through his hair and swallowed with difficulty. Would all the Coopers be so accepting? Especially when they discovered that he'd lied to them, misled them for his own benefit?

The image of Leanne filled his mind. How would she feel? He sighed, anxiety nagging at him. He didn't want her to be hurt by any of this. Watching her this weekend, especially yesterday, had kept him breathless.

There was something about the fit of her jeans and the worn T-shirt that made her look vulnerable yet so seductive. His throat had gone dry every time their eyes met, but she'd turned away from him each time. She hadn't wanted to look him in the eye. And it was all his fault.

Now, the next day, Dex stared at the floor; even he was unable to look himself in the eye in the mirror. Life wasn't fair sometimes. He'd had everything he ever wanted. Leanne worked so hard, and yet she and her mother went without more often than not and were too proud to ask for help or even accept what was offered.

The inner strength of the people he'd met here amazed him. Would he be able to face such adversity so well? A frown inched across his brow. He didn't know. He'd never been faced with these kinds of sacrifices.

Dex squared his shoulders and glared at his reflection. He'd always been a man of action. There was no reason he couldn't be one now. Dex Montgomery wasn't down for the count just yet. He knew people, had connections. He could get things done that no one else could. The circumstances definitely called for action. Leanne's mother needed a specialist. Fine. He could take care of that. Ensuring that the dude ranch got off to a good start would be a simple matter as well. He'd find a way to see that she succeeded. The Coopers needed to improve the Circle C's cattle market. He could help with that, too. The first thing one did when seeking out new clients was to give off an appearance of quality and efficiency. Appearances were everything. Organization was the key.

And there was no better organizer on the planet than Dex Montgomery.

Thirty minutes later Dex met with Chad and Court outside the main barn.

"I want every single asset inventoried," he told the two men staring agog at him. "I've noticed that our two ranch hands aren't always occupied. I want the barns, the storage buildings and the equipment sheds reorganized ASAP." He handed Court the quick instructions he'd jotted down. "That should get them started. Feel free to add to or change the organization layout as necessary."

"But we've had things the same way for years," Chad protested, still looking a little startled by the orders.

Dex gave him an understanding pat on the back. "The future is about change, bro. The only businesses moving into the future are the ones willing to allow change." He gave the younger man a conspiratorial wink. "The Coopers are about to move into the twenty-first century."

With his instructions relayed, Dex headed back to the house. He wanted to take a quick look at the bookkeeping process and see how Ty and his grandfather handled that end of things. He would still make it to Leanne's that afternoon. They had almost finished the cabins anyway. But he had to find a way to get the cabins furnished without her going postal on him.

Dex paused in the kitchen long enough to pour himself a cup of coffee. He closed his eyes and enjoyed the full-flavored taste of Grandmother Cooper's own special blend. The woman knew how to mix her coffee beans. Decaffeinated or not, it was the best he'd ever had.

"I hear you're raising quite a ruckus with your brothers."

Dex opened his eyes and instantly smiled at his grandmother. She'd obviously been outside and overheard their conversation. The twinkle in her eyes told him that she wasn't bothered by his sudden attitude change.

"Sometimes things need to change," he offered, his words carrying a hidden meaning she would understand if, as he suspected, she knew.

She nodded, her gaze a bit more guarded now. "That's true enough."

He angled his head in the direction of the large walk-in pantry and grinned. "I couldn't help but notice that the pantry could use a little reorganizing as well."

She arched an eyebrow. "Don't even think about it," she warned. "The womenfolk will take care of the house."

His coffee in hand, still grinning from ear to ear, Dex sauntered into the downstairs room just off the family room that served as the office. His grandfather was busy at the calculator. Dex sat down at the other desk, the one Ty used, and started going through the files. His grandfather merely glanced at him over his bifocals, his fingers never letting up on the keypad.

Within a couple of hours Dex had a pretty good handle on the Coopers' finances. They had a good solid portfolio. Not great, but definitely good. He saw room for improvement in several areas.

Grandfather Cooper stood and stretched. "Well, I think I've done all the damage I can this morning." He scratched his chest. "Maybe I'll just go see if that heavenly smell coming from the kitchen is cookies."

Frowning, Dex looked up from his notes. He'd spent the last twenty or so minutes looking at ways to expand, or, at the very least, increase profits.

"One question," he said, before the older man could leave the room.

His grandfather turned back, his face expectant.

"Why is it we've never charged the bordering Mc-

Caleb ranch for water rights? The river is clearly on Cooper land which they have to cross to reach it." He pointed to the aerial photograph on the wall. "I'm quite certain that could be an additional source of revenue."

The older man's expression darkened. He strode over to where Dex sat and stared hard down at him. "Young man, I don't know what high-faluting ideas they put in your head in Chicago at that investors' meeting, but I can tell you one thing right now, we don't do business that way around here."

Surprised at his outrage, Dex flared his hands. "I'm only suggesting—"

"I know what you're suggesting," he said, cutting Dex off. His grandfather eased one hip onto the edge of the desk and visibly struggled for calm. "The Mc-Calebs are our neighbors. You don't charge neighbors when they share in the blessings you're fortunate enough to receive." When Dex would have offered an alternative perspective, Grandfather Cooper held up a hand, halting the interruption. "We've always helped our neighbors, son. That won't change in the future, investors or no investors. Furthermore, they've always helped us whenever we needed an extra hand. No suggestion from some fancy, shmancy restaurant chain is going to better what the Lord intended the day he handed down the law to Moses."

He'd lost Dex completely, but he tried not to show it.

"When the good Lord said to do unto others as you'd have them do unto you, he meant it." Grandfather Cooper pushed off the desk and clapped Dex on the back. "That includes neighbors. Don't you go forgetting the golden rule, boy. There's nothing in this life more important. Nothing."

Dex sat thinking for a long while after his grandfather had gone. *Golden rule.* Now he knew the one indisputable difference between the Coopers and the Montgomerys. The Montgomerys wanted to succeed. At all costs. The Coopers wanted to succeed in their business as well, except that they wanted everyone around them to succeed, too. Dex shook his head. It didn't make sense. In today's cutthroat marketplace it didn't pay to bleed when your neighbor was cut. But the Coopers did.

It went against every deeply ingrained business tactic Dex had ever been taught.

Maybe he'd been wrong about what the Coopers needed. All the reorganization in the world couldn't replace heart.

A new respect sprouted inside Dex. Hard work was what kept these people surviving one generation after the next, regardless of the obstacles life threw in their way.

Heart was what made them who they were.

An idea formed on the heels of that epiphany. There were lots of things one could do under the umbrella of being *neighborly*. Dex grinned. Lots and lots of things.

Leanne trudged up the back steps just as it was getting dark on Friday evening. She'd never been so tired in her whole life. At least all the painting was finished. She had Ty to thank for that. She paused on the top step and sat down to rest for a few moments.

Things had been strained between them all week. Not really unpleasant, just tense. He was careful what he said to her, she was careful what she said to him. They tiptoed around each other, not wanting to touch accidentally. As good as his word, he'd shown up every single day and worked hard to help her finish. Next week she would be ready to visit the bank president about a start-up loan. She'd keep the furnishings simple for the time being, and she could put the pool start-up costs off until she actually had bookings. She felt confident for the first time in a long time that she could actually do this. And she owed it all to Ty.

She'd never have gotten this far this quickly without his generosity. She still couldn't figure out why he'd gone along with her plan so easily. The fact of the matter was, there seemed to be a lot of things she couldn't quite figure out about him lately, not the least of which was this considerable attraction brewing between them.

She'd known Ty her entire life and now it was as if he was a stranger. He hadn't been the same since he returned from Chicago. She'd struggled the whole time he was gone to try and work up the courage to tell him about the dude ranch, had even offered to pick him up at the airport to give them some time alone together. But she'd lost her nerve, not to mention she'd been disconcerted by his peculiar behavior.

Strange behavior that entailed far more than this wild attraction between them. It was in everything he did and said—how he handled himself. His walk was even different. His touch. The way he looked at her. Maybe Angelica was right, maybe Ty had been taken over by aliens. Leanne smiled at the idea. She and Jenny had laughed until they both cried at the little girl's accusation. Leanne's smile faded as she considered the concept further. What if Angelica was simply noticing the same things Leanne had noticed…that Ty wasn't the same. Not the same at all.

She'd seen movies where people suddenly started to behave in bizarre manners, it usually involved drugs or some life-altering event. She frowned. But nothing like that had happened to Ty. She shrugged and pushed to her feet. Maybe it was just the strain of trying to venture into new markets. Maybe that's why he hadn't fussed when Leanne told him what she wanted to do.

She paused again at the door and allowed that now-familiar warmth to sear through her as she thought of the way it had felt to be held in his arms…to be kissed by him. It was magical and totally surprising. Who would've thought that she'd be feeling this way? She shook her head. Silly girl, she chastised. Ty had made it clear this week that he'd wanted to keep his distance. She should follow his example. Attraction wasn't enough. She wanted to be head over heels in love and she wasn't there.

She swallowed tightly.

Not yet anyway.

She opened the kitchen door and went inside. A long hot bath was what she needed now, not sinful thoughts of Ty Cooper.

A decidedly feminine and definitely unfamiliar voice stopped Leanne in her tracks. She froze, listening. Then she heard her mother's frail voice. Leanne relaxed. They apparently had company. Taking a breath, she headed for the living room to see who'd stopped by. They rarely had guests.

She was startled to find a woman, in her thirties maybe, dressed in a professional business suit, putting a bandage in the bend of her mother's elbow. Leanne stared at her, searching for any recognition. She was tall and thin, with dark hair. Leanne had no clue. Something in her peripheral vision grabbed her attention. A doctor's case.

"Is everything all right?" Surely nothing had happened while she was out at the barn.

Her mother smiled weakly. "Everything's fine, honey. Dr. Allen, this is my daughter, Leanne."

The doctor smiled, her hands busy putting away what looked like blood samples and medical paraphernalia. "It's a pleasure, Leanne. Your mother has been telling me all about the dude ranch you're going to open. That sounds very exciting."

She glanced at her mother, even more confused. "Did something happen while I was out?"

"Nothing happened. Dr. Allen needed blood samples for some tests."

"It wasn't easy convincing her, I can tell you," she said to Leanne, smiling. "I'm an internist. I'll be consulting with Dr. Baker."

Leanne stared at her in bewilderment. "Dr. Baker sent you here?" she asked, certain that couldn't be right. Dr. Baker would have told Leanne if an opportunity such as this had arisen.

Dr. Allen closed her case and straightened. "No, he didn't, but I will be sending him a full report on the results of these tests." She looked at Leanne's mother then. "I'll drop everything off at the lab in Bozeman. As soon as the results are in, Dr. Baker and I will determine the best way to proceed with your case."

"Thank you, Doctor," Joanna replied.

"Wait." Leanne moved between the woman and

the door as she was about to leave without further explanation. "I want to know who sent you here." This went beyond bizarre.

"I'm sorry but I'm not at liberty to say who sent me." She smiled again, not even a hint of impatience showing. "Suffice it to say that it was the neighborly thing to do."

Ty.

Leanne couldn't even remember if she said goodbye to the doctor or to her mother. Before she could think what she was doing she'd driven halfway to the Cooper house. Who did he think he was sneaking around behind her back? She was furious. After only a couple of kisses he was already running her life. Making decisions for her. Butting in where he wasn't needed.

She slowed as she turned down the long drive, her thoughts darting from Ty to her mother. They might know soon exactly what was taking such a toll on her health. Suddenly all the fight drained out of Leanne. Dr. Allen was a specialist. Ty had obviously talked her into making a house call at no telling what kind of expense. Leanne parked her truck and for a full thirty seconds rested her forehead against the steering wheel.

He wanted to help.

He really cared, deeply.

She squeezed her eyes shut and tried her level best not to cry. She loved him so much for all that he'd done. Another emotion swelled in her chest. If she admitted the truth, she loved him for a whole lot more than that. She straightened, staring out the windshield at nothing at all. How could she keep pretending he wasn't the one for her?

He made her heart do those strange little somersaults.

He made her laugh.

He made her want him so badly that she'd been willing to have a one-night stand without any regrets.

He'd done everything he could to help her.

God, she did love him.

Really loved him.

Leanne shivered.

She supposed it could still be all about sex, but she was a great deal less certain of that now.

But what if he didn't love her that way? What if he only felt sorry for her?

She lifted her chin and pushed open the door. It didn't matter. If that doctor could help her mother, Leanne didn't care what motivated Ty to send her. Love, sympathy or whatever.

She was just so thankful.

Leanne raced to the house. She opened the front door and called out, "Anybody home?"

"In here," Mrs. Cooper called from the kitchen.

Leanne rushed to the kitchen doorway and beamed a smile. "Is Ty home?"

"I believe he is," the older woman said without looking up from her breadmaking. "Upstairs, I think."

Leanne pecked her cheek and rushed in the direction of the stairs. Mrs. Cooper called out something else behind her but Leanne was already halfway up the stairs. She'd drop back by the kitchen before she left. Right now she had to find Ty.

"Ty!" she called as soon as she cleared the top tread. "Ty!"

The sound of his voice reverberated from somewhere a few doors down.

"I need to talk to you!" she called out.

"Leanne?"

She smiled, desire curling inside her at the sound of his voice. It had come from the next door on the right. Leanne opened the door and burst inside. "Ty, I wanted—" The words that followed died in her throat as her eyes widened in disbelief.

Ty was chest-deep in steaming bathwater. She had just burst into the bathroom. Her knees almost buckled beneath her. How could she have forgotten that this was the bathroom? She'd played in this house dozens of times as a child.

"I... I..." Speech, as well as rational thought, eluded her as her eyes took in the details. He was naked, of course, steaming water lapping against that perfect chest. Those sinfully dark brown eyes were staring directly at her, daring her to come closer. Oh, God. She felt lightheaded. There was an excellent chance she might just faint.

His dark hair damp and swept back from that handsome face, Ty just grinned at her. "Planning on joining me?"

His words jolting her into action, she spun around, giving him her back. "I'm... I'm sorry. I didn't realize..." Lord have mercy. She had the abrupt, overwhelming urge to grab the nearest magazine and fan herself. It was sweltering in here.

"It's all right. Was there something you needed?" he asked, that sexy, smooth-as-glass voice enveloping her in a new kind of warmth, one that spread like wildfire through her trembling limbs.

She swallowed, difficult as that proved. "I wanted to thank you for sending the specialist to see my mother," she managed to say, her voice breaking only slightly. Emotion gathered in her throat. "I don't know how you managed it, but it really meant a lot to me." She looked down, squeezing her eyes shut to block the flood that threatened to unleash.

"Well," Ty began, his tone light, teasing almost, "if you can't lead a horse to water, then you just have to take the water to the horse."

Leanne couldn't help herself, she laughed at his misuse of the adage. "Works for me."

The sound of water sloshing in the tub made her jump. She stiffened, uncertain what she should do now. Was he getting out? Did she need to—

Strong fingers curled around her arms. "Relax," he murmured close to her ear. She could feel his body radiating heat right behind hers. "I don't bite."

Her breath trapped in her lungs when he turned her around to face him. She knew he was watching her, but she just couldn't help herself. Her gaze roved over that amazing body. He'd wrapped a towel around his hips, its hold there precarious at best. Water glistened on his skin. Damp, silky hair covered those sculpted pecs. She shivered visibly as a fresh wave of desire swirled inside her. A dozen snippets of memory, the feel of his mouth on hers, his strong body pressed against hers, his hungry touch, flashed through her mind, flooded her senses with a need so strong she could barely restrain the urge to reach out and touch him.

He stared deeply into her eyes and said, "You don't have to thank me."

"Ty, I…" She couldn't think with him looking at her that way, with his voice so gentle yet so thick with what she recognized as desire.

He reached up, cupped her face in one hand and stroked her cheek with his thumb. "But if you insist on thanking me, I prefer my gratitude in a more tangible form."

Time seemed to lapse into slow motion as his mouth descended toward hers. Uncertain of her ability to stay vertical, she braced her hands against his chest. The feel of his hot, damp skin beneath her palms only made bad matters worse. But she no longer cared. She wanted this kiss, wanted his touch more than anything else in the world at the moment. She wanted to take up where they'd left off after the dance last Friday night.

The electrifying pull started the moment their lips were a hairbreadth apart and Leanne knew that this time was somehow different from the others…the barriers were falling.

His mouth settled onto hers as he tenderly cradled her face with both hands. The gesture was so endearing that she thought her heart might not survive this one kiss.

He was like fire pulsing into her, devouring her and she couldn't get close enough. She felt his arousal against her belly and moved closer still. Her arms slid up around his neck and she leaned into him. The moisture from his skin was absorbed into her T-shirt. Her nipples pebbled in reaction to the feel of him.

His tongue thrust into her mouth. She gasped. He didn't back down; he kissed her harder.

Their ragged breathing echoed in the silent room as his hand glided down her throat, his fingers caressing all that they encountered until he clutched her breast. She groaned, or maybe it was Ty…

He drew back abruptly.

Leanne's hopes plummeted. Was he going to push her away again? Had she misread what she'd seen in his eyes? What she'd felt in his body? This couldn't happen again. Weak with disappointment, she could only stare into his eyes, a plea in her own.

He was breathless when he spoke. "We have to…" He searched her eyes as if as uncertain of her as she was of him. "Go home. Wait for me." He kissed her lips one more time. "One way or the other, we're going to finish this tonight."

Leanne nodded, not sure whether his words were a promise or a threat.

She left the Cooper house and drove all the way home before she allowed herself to analyze what he'd said.

Tonight.

They would finish it tonight.

Chapter 11

Dex waited, none too patiently, until the family was gathered around the television preparing to watch the Friday evening lineup. All but Grandmother Cooper. Though she'd made herself comfortable along with the rest of the clan, she was deeply engrossed in her latest crocheting project. Dex had no idea what the bundles of yellow yarn would turn out to be when she finished, but he had a feeling it had something to do with her new grandchild on its way.

He couldn't help but smile at the sight of all of them together, munching on popcorn and waiting for the opening credits to pass. One big happy family. To the Montgomerys, family time consisted of going over stock reports. But, *this* kind of family time was kind of growing on him. His lips drew downward into a frown. But they weren't his family...not really. They treated him like family but that was only because they thought he was Ty.

How would this all turn out in the end? Would the Coopers be glad to find out who he really was? Would they accept him into their tight group as if he'd never left? Dex surveyed the big entry hall and considered that he'd spent the first few months of his life here. And no one suspected that he was back. Well, no one except Grandmother Cooper, and she hadn't mentioned it or behaved oddly, which led Dex to believe that perhaps he had misread her that night on the porch. Maybe she didn't know that he wasn't Ty.

Thoughts of Leanne intruded on his musings. He had to work this out somehow. She was driving him out of his mind. He wanted her more than he'd ever wanted anything before. *Anything.* And that was saying something. No woman had ever gotten to him like this.

He had to call Ty.

Dex picked up the telephone, and stretched the cord as far as it would go. He made it into the kitchen and barely far enough into the pantry to close the door. He listened for any sound coming from the family. He could vaguely make out the muffled voices from the television. Good. That meant that they couldn't overhear him as long as he didn't speak too loudly.

He quickly dialed the numbers. Now, if he could only fool whoever answered the phone.

"Montgomery residence," a soft feminine voice announced on the other end of the line.

His grandmother. A surge of emotion rendered Dex speechless for several seconds. He hadn't realized until that precise moment how much he'd missed her. Almost two weeks he'd been gone. Did she suspect that Ty wasn't the man she'd raised as her son? If he told her right now that he was Dex would she be glad to hear his voice? How were they getting along without him?

He let go a breath. Ty was there. He'd been there the whole time. They were obviously as fooled as the Coopers. They didn't miss Dex. They didn't even realize he was gone.

"Hello," she repeated. "Is anyone there?"

He quickly summoned a voice that in no way resembled his own. "Dex Montgomery, please," he told her, satisfied at how un-Dex he sounded.

To his utter relief she didn't ask who was calling. Instead, she asked him to hold and laid the telephone down. He heard the sound of her high-heeled shoes clicking on the marble floor of the foyer as she went in search of Ty. Another wave of emotion overtook him. He closed his eyes and envisioned the home in which he'd lived for as long as he could remember. And suddenly he wished he was there. He wanted to sit in his grandfather's study and discuss business while his grandfather nursed his favorite pipe, though he'd given up smoking it some time ago. Dex loved that pipe.

Or Dex could go out to the greenhouse and watch his Grandmother Montgomery with her roses and African violets. She had quite the green thumb. Grandmother Cooper tending her flowerbeds reminded him of home. At least the two women had one thing in common. Of course he couldn't see Grandmother Cooper going off to a friendly game of dice on Sunday nights. It was his Grandmother Montgomery's one vice.

"Hello."

The voice that echoed over the line this time was a carbon copy of Dex's, except for the slightest hint of a Western drawl. Dex grinned. He wondered how his brother had explained that slight change in inflection. Or maybe he'd carefully controlled his speech pattern and had only unknowingly dropped his guard for a moment.

"Ty, it's Dex."

"Thank God it's you." Ty sounded immensely relieved. "I was afraid it would be someone I should recognize and I wouldn't. Doggone if this trading places business isn't some flat-out nerve-rattling work."

"I know exactly how you feel."

"Is everything all right?" his brother wanted to know, a twinge of worry in his voice.

Dex gave him a quick rundown of how everyone was doing, including the news about Chad and Jenny's pregnancy. Ty followed suit, explaining that the Montgomerys were doing well and didn't appear to suspect a thing. George, however, was another story. Ty was pretty sure George knew he wasn't Dex.

"Don't admit anything," Dex warned him. "George always played those mind games to get the truth out of me when I was a teenager. If you give him an inch he'll take a mile. He's relentless like that." He sorely missed George. Missed them all, truth be told.

A stretch of silence lingered between them for a time.

"I think I've met someone," Ty finally said, quietly, solemnly.

Dex frowned. Surely Bridget hadn't gotten to him. Ty definitely was not in her league. She would eat him alive. "I thought you were going to keep Bridget busy with—"

"It's not Bridget. It's Jessica Stovall." It would have been impossible to miss the excitement in Ty's voice when he talked about her.

Uh-oh. "What about Leanne?" Dex felt compelled to demand. She was falling for Ty…well, for *him,* but she thought he was Ty. And here Ty was off falling for someone down in Atlanta. Anger twisted inside Dex. He didn't want Leanne hurt in all this. If Ty had ever made her believe for one moment…

"I told you," Ty interrupted Dex's runaway thoughts. "We're just friends. Leanne is like a sister to me. Nothing else."

His words stemmed the fury a bit. "So, there has never been anything between the two of you?" Dex persisted. He would have a definite answer. If there ever had been, then Ty would have to make it right. Dex would see to it.

"Never," Ty assured him. "Friends, that's all. Anything else you may have heard is only wishful thinking on our folks' part. I swear."

Another reign of silence stood between them for two long beats.

"Wait one cotton-picking minute," Ty said suddenly. "Are you and Leanne…?" He swore. A string of words that didn't bear repeating followed. "Don't even think about breaking that girl's heart. Do you hear me, Dex? I won't have it."

Dex's fury renewed itself. "I didn't come here to break any hearts," he said tightly.

"Then what the hell's going on? Why all the questions about me and Leanne?" Ty snapped right back.

"It's nothing for you to be concerned about. I won't do anything I can't *undo*." Dex prayed that was true. Hadn't he already done things he wouldn't be able to undo?

"I'm counting on that," Ty told him bluntly. "This isn't about revenge of any sort."

"You're right," Dex allowed. "It's about…" His brow lined in confusion. He didn't know what it was about. He'd lost all focus this past week. "It's about understanding the past," he finally said.

"Yeah," Ty agreed. "It's about the past."

"Call me if you need anything," Dex offered. "Or if you decide it's time to have our big announcement."

"I will." Ty cleared his throat. *"Soon."*

Dex sneaked out of the pantry and quietly replaced the phone on the hall table. He tried not to wonder what Ty had meant by *soon*. Was he weary of this ruse already? Or did he simply miss his family? Dex had no intention of setting a precise date until he'd learned all he wanted to know…satisfied his curiosity. And certainly not until he'd settled things with Leanne.

Dex retrieved his hat and keys. One thing was certain, he definitely missed his family, even if he hadn't actually realized it until he heard his Grandmother Montgomery's voice.

But for right now he couldn't think about any of that. He had to straighten this thing out with Leanne before they went too far. He had no intention of doing what she clearly wanted him to…what *he* wanted to.

He had to end this tonight.

After a quick good-night to the Coopers, he headed to Leanne's. Before he arrived he had to come up with a plausible excuse—one that wouldn't hurt her feelings—for putting the brakes on this thing between them.

She would understand.

He was certain of it.

Leanne had tried on everything she owned, which didn't take long, yet the decision as to what to wear seemed monumental. Finally she had picked the only dress besides the blue one that halfway complemented her figure, and made her feel feminine.

The white dress was old, but she'd always loved the fact that it buttoned up the front. It was long and filmy, with a hem that hit mid-calf and fabric that showed off her curves. Her skin was tanned just enough from working outside on the ranch to contrast nicely with the white. She'd left her hair down, but braided it in a long, loose style. Her old leather sandals were the only pair she owned, but they too were feminine looking. She smiled at her pink toenails. She'd even taken the time to do her nails. She flared her fingers and admired the short but freshly manicured tips. She didn't own any fancy jewelry or perfume, but she'd applied a smidgen of the strawberry-scented spray she saved for special occasions.

Now, Leanne stood back and studied her appearance. Her cheeks were flushed with anticipation, her eyes glistened with the desire she couldn't seem to hide. Even her mother had noticed the change. Was this what love was supposed to be like?

This overwhelming need to be with someone, that twist in her stomach each time she thought of him. She felt like such a child compared to Ty. He was thirty-two, and, considering his charming personality and handsome looks, she was certain he'd had his share of women. What on earth would a naive virgin have to offer him? She frowned. Yet he seemed interested enough. When he kissed her, touched her, it felt like he wanted her. Could she be reading too much into his reaction?

She let go a big breath. She was nearly certain that this was a mistake. She wasn't supposed to fall in love with Ty. She couldn't possibly be the kind of wife he wanted…she had other plans. Plans he now knew about.

Maybe he didn't want her for a wife.

Leanne chewed her lower lip and tried to rationalize that thought. He'd given absolutely no indication that he felt their folks were right and that they belonged together. In fact, he hadn't talked about the future at all.

Maybe he only wanted what she'd thought she wanted. Just to be with him. But she knew Ty better than that. He would never take advantage of her. Considering the vibes she'd been giving off lately, he most likely thought she was the one who wanted a future together or, at the very least, wanted to have sex with him.

What a predicament. She didn't know what she wanted. Should they just go with what their hearts told them and not question it? Would it be a mistake? It would. She was pretty sure of it. Ty would be extremely upset when he realized she hadn't been with anyone else. He would feel obligated to do the right thing…or stop.

Leanne moistened her lips. Then there was only one thing to do. She had to make him believe that she wasn't a virgin…at least until it was too late to change his mind. She would have this one night whatever the future held for the two of them. If this whole thing was simply about sex, then she would soon know it. She was through waiting for life to happen. Starting from this moment she was going to make it happen.

Her way.

Decision reached, Leanne made her way to the living room to check on her mother. Joanna was knitting a cap and sweater set for the coming addition to the Cooper family. Another twinge of anxiety plagued Leanne. What was it about babies lately that made her feel so anxious?

At least her mother was feeling well enough to expend a little energy. For that Leanne was extremely grateful. By next week Dr. Allen might even have some news or suggested treatment that could turn her mother's life around. That would make things perfect.

Just perfect.

"Can I get you anything, Mama?"

Joanna looked up. "I'm fine, child." Her eyebrows lifted a fraction. "My, don't you look lovely. Do you have another date with Ty?"

Leanne shook her head. "Not a date."

Joanna turned back to her knitting. "Um-hm."

Leanne started to insist that her mother was making something of nothing but a knock at the door stopped her. She gasped. Her mother eyed her even more suspiciously. Leanne marched to the door, cursing herself for being so transparent.

Ty stood in the open doorway looking more handsome than ever. Maybe it was the faded chambray shirt or the worn jeans that gloved his body so well. Whatever it was, he took her breath away.

The damp hair that had glistened when she'd walked in on his bath was now dry and combed neatly into place. But time and distance since their encounter had done nothing to lessen the intensity in those brown eyes. He looked every bit as hungry as she felt.

Then he smiled and her heart did one of those crazy flip-flops that sent warning bells off inside her head.

"Well, don't just stand there, Leanne," her mother scolded. "Ask him to come in."

If her mother only knew, Leanne thought. She planned to invite Ty a lot farther than simply inside her home.

"Come in," she murmured, stepping back to open the door wider.

Hat in hand, he came inside, and Leanne was struck all over again by how good he looked. Handsome as sin, with mile-wide shoulders. Why had she never noticed those wonderfully muscular thighs before or that equally well-formed behind?

He flashed a smile at her then turned to her mother. "How are you feeling this evening, Mrs. Watley?"

"Real fine, Ty." She literally beamed at him. "I'm mighty grateful for that fancy doc you sent out here to see me, but I'm awful worried that you shouldn't have done such a generous thing."

"Dr. Allen owed me a favor," he assured her. "She was happy to relieve herself of that debt."

Leanne frowned. How was it that Dr. Allen owed Ty a favor? He'd apparently made a lot more friends during his trip to the city than she could ever have imagined. She felt a stab of jealousy. What if the pretty doctor and Ty had...? She had no way of knowing for sure how Ty knew the doctor. It was pointless to get all worked up for no real reason. Ty was both charming and persuasive. He made friends easily. She couldn't know all his friends, she assured herself. And she would not let foolish thoughts ruin this evening.

He turned to Leanne then. "I thought we could take a drive." He shrugged, the gesture seeming as hopeful as nonchalant. "To talk."

A shiver trembled through her. "Sure."

Dex watched as Leanne kissed her mother and picked up her purse and then rejoined him at the door. "I'm driving," she said, then smiled, the expression tremulous. He suddenly wanted to hold her and tell her that everything would be all right. That *he* would make it so. But he wasn't at all sure he could do that.

Once in her truck, Leanne drove in virtual silence until they reached the destination she had in mind. For the first time since his arrival Dex longed for his Mercedes. He'd like to take her someplace special in real style.

The sun was beginning to melt along the top of the mountain ranges in the distance. For one long moment, he couldn't take his eyes off the view. They'd driven up a long, meandering slope until they reached a grassy plateau which overlooked the river that flowed across Cooper property. Dex felt reasonably sure its beauty rivaled any other place on earth he'd visited.

"This place is amazing," he murmured.

She nodded. "It's my favorite place in the whole world." She looked at him then. "I come here when I want to be alone to think."

At that moment he would have given any price to know what she thought about when she was all alone. "I can see why. It's…" He peered out over the natural beauty before him. "…perfect." And they didn't need a Mercedes to make it that way.

"Haven't you ever stopped on this ridge just to enjoy the view?"

He shook his head, hoping she'd take it as a no, he'd never taken the time, instead of the no he meant, which was he'd never been here before in his life.

"Come on."

As she opened her door she grabbed the blanket he'd noticed on the seat when he got into her truck. She'd insisted on driving. Since she knew where she wanted to go, that had been fine with him. Now he wondered if that had been a mistake. Leanne appeared to be a little too prepared.

No matter what else happened, he had to do this right.

He watched as she spread the blanket on the ground. The white dress she wore showed off her golden skin. The long, thick braid she'd twisted her hair into fell over her shoulder making him yearn to release it so that he could run his hands through all that silky hair. The dress buttoned up the front, but the top two buttons were unfastened leaving the barest peek at cleavage. His mouth went dust-dry.

After the blanket was smoothed to her satisfaction, she sat down and tossed her purse to the side. Hesitant but unsure what else he could do at this point, Dex joined her.

"This is nice," he commented, his attention focused once more on the sun as it slipped slowly behind the mountains.

"It sure is." She pulled her knees up to her chest,

the long dress cascading down to cover everything but her sandal-clad feet. She sighed contentedly.

Dex's gaze zeroed in on those sexy pink toenails and he suddenly wanted to kiss her there. He blinked, dispelling the arousing image of him kissing his way up her long, slender legs.

For several minutes they sat in complete silence. Dex tried desperately to keep his mind on the fact that he would be leaving soon and that he couldn't possibly do anything that couldn't be undone. *This* definitely couldn't be undone. He was certain of that, if nothing else. He would not hurt Leanne. He simply wouldn't do it.

Daylight faded little by little, taking the sun's warmth with it. Leanne chafed her arms with her hands.

"Are you cold?" Dammit, why hadn't he thought to bring a jacket or something?

She smiled, his pulse reacted. "No. I'm okay."

Oh no! He saw in her eyes the one thing he definitely hadn't wanted to see right now: desire.

"Leanne," he began, knowing he couldn't delay this any longer. He had to do something or risk making a terrible mistake. "There's something you have to know."

How was he supposed to tell her that he wanted her desperately but that it couldn't possibly work? He wasn't who she thought he was. He was an impostor. He flinched at the realization.

She held up a hand to stop him before he continued. "Wait." She quickly fished in her purse for something, palmed it before he could see what it was, then turned back to him. Too close…entirely too close, but he couldn't bring himself to move away. It was too much to ask.

"Leanne—"

"Don't say anything." She pressed her fingers to his lips. "I don't want this to be about talking."

She kissed him. He tensed, tried not to respond, but he was only human. A few seconds of that sweet mouth on his and he had to kiss her back. She rested her small hands against his chest, her touch made need surge hard and fast inside him. Slowly, her cool fingers trembling slightly, she released first one, then another of his shirt's buttons. Her efficient fingers moved lower, until she'd opened it to his waist. She reached inside and touched his bare skin. He groaned in spite of his promise to himself that he wouldn't let this happen.

He held back as long as he could, but she was pushing him harder and harder with that hot little mouth and those exploring fingers. His hands went to her face. He sagged with the relief of simply touching her soft skin. She ushered him down onto the blanket. He didn't resist. Couldn't have if he'd wanted to. Her tongue ventured into his mouth, then retreated. He did the same to her, daring her to come back for more. She grew bolder, straddling his waist, the long dress pushed up around her thighs now. She dragged his hands down to her breasts. He cupped them instinctively. She moaned and ground that fiery heat between her thighs into him. Any control he had left crumbled.

She quickly released several of her own buttons. His hands slid immediately inside her dress. He toyed with her nipples, awed at the tight little buds beneath his fingers. She broke the kiss, arched her back, pressing her breasts more firmly into his palms.

Dex watched her. Couldn't catch his breath at what he saw. She was beautiful sitting astride him, her head thrown back in ecstasy, her full breasts bared to him. She'd come here with the intention of offering herself to him. She wanted this. A new wave of desire roared through him. He wanted this.

But it was wrong.

She thought...

He rolled her over, putting himself in the dominant position in an attempt to regain control. His loins throbbed as his arousal pressed into her softness. He swallowed hard and forced himself to think. He had to think.

"Leanne, this would be a mistake for both of us," he said as calmly as he could, considering his voice was rough with need.

She shook her head. "No. We're adults. This doesn't have to be about the future or the family. It only has to be about here and now. About the need we have."

"You don't understand," he pleaded. She wasn't making this easy. "There are things you don't know. I can't—"

She shushed him with her fingers again. "I don't care. I want this. I know you do, too." She arched her hips against his. "I can feel how much you want this."

He closed his eyes for three long beats in an effort to slow his body's plunge toward the point of no return. It didn't work. When he looked at her again, he still wanted her with an intensity that shook him to the core of his being.

How could he say no?

He opened his mouth to try, but she stopped him with another of those hungry kisses. This time it went on and on until they were both gasping for breath.

A new reality peeked through the haze. He groaned. "But I don't have any protection," he whispered between her fevered kisses, disappointed rather than relieved as he should be.

Her mouth still taunting his, she groped around the blanket until she found what she searched for. She thrust the tiny packet into his hand.

"Here," she murmured, breathless. "I came prepared."

He looked at her for a time, unable to speak or move. She wanted him badly enough to make it happen. How could he disappoint her? How could he...

"Please don't make me wait any longer." The plea was punctuated by flames so hot in her eyes that they seared straight through him.

"You won't have to wait." He kissed her hard, with all the raging emotions bottled up inside him. He wanted her. He would have her. Now.

He kissed his way down her torso, opening more buttons as he went. She writhed and made tiny gasping sounds in his wake. He loved it. She only made him want to please her more. This would be about her, he decided then and there. All about her.

When her dress was open all the way down and her voluptuous body exposed fully to him, he sat back on his haunches and removed his shirt, all the while admiring every beautiful detail of her. She watched him, her eyes wide with anticipation and maybe a tiny bit of apprehension. When their gazes locked, she closed her eyes and took a deep breath, her perfect breasts rising and falling with the effort.

He unfastened his jeans, the sound of the zipper making her shiver and urging him on. He pushed his jeans and boxers down, the rasp of denim against flesh provoking another of those little shivers in her. He ripped the foil packet, and watched for the next reaction; she sucked in a sharp breath. Need pulsed through him, forcing him toward the edge of control. He slipped on the condom she'd given him and lowered his body over hers. She gasped, her warm breath eventually feathering across his jaw when she relaxed.

With painstaking slowness he kissed her lips, then made a path down her throat. Her fingers threaded into his hair and ushered him to her breasts. He took his time there, pleasuring her until she once more writhed beneath him, her breath so ragged he felt certain she might climax even before he entered her. Slowly he continued down to her hips. He dragged her panties along her legs, leaving a path of hot kisses, garnering more of those sweet little shivers. When he loomed over her once more, his arousal nestled against her mound. She arched upward, crying out with need.

When he would have reached for that place that ached so for him, she pushed his hand away and grasped the part of him that throbbed for her. She guided him to her entrance, too needy to bother with more foreplay.

"Now?" he murmured the question against her lips, then kissed them.

She nodded. "Hurry!"

He pushed inside only a fraction. He wanted this

tension to last…to mount until they both screamed with satisfaction.

Her expression taut with anticipation, she wriggled her hips, then locked her legs around his and arched upward forcing him inside one more hot, tight inch. She was so tight. It was all he could do not to thrust fully. The blood roared in his ears. His heart pounded so hard he could scarcely breathe, but he held back… making it last. His mouth found and melded with hers, his tongue thrust inside. He mimicked the move with his hips, withdrawing slightly then pushing deeper, just another inch, but he met with more resistance. Confusion buzzed into his thoughts. Desire pounded through his veins, making coherent thought impossible. He was on the brink of release and he wasn't even fully inside her yet. He was going crazy hovering somewhere between hesitation and desperation. But something was wrong.

He pulled back once more, pushed inside again. Realization crashed into his skull this time. He drew back from the kiss and stared into her startled gaze. He shook his head, unable to believe what his body was telling him.

"Don't stop," she urged, trying with all her might to pull him back down to her.

"You…this…" He shook his head again. "You're…"

He saw the determination in her eyes a split second before she acted on it. She surged upward with her hips, taking him past the barrier. They cried out together, the barrage of sensations overwhelming. Instinctively he plunged deeply inside her, then held perfectly still.

"I…shouldn't have…" he stammered, hardly believing what he'd allowed to happen. His whole body strummed with need. He wanted to drive toward release, but he had to hold back. Had to give her time…

She was breathing hard and fast, her eyes far too bright for his liking, even in the dwindling daylight.

"Are you all right?" he murmured.

She moved her head from side to side, her lips trembling.

Dex tensed. He swallowed with enormous difficulty. He was throbbing inside her. Her tight feminine muscles were pulsing around him, making him want to start that ancient rhythm without further delay. "I…" he began, uncertain of what to say or do. He'd damned sure never had this problem before. He wanted her so badly, but he had to be sure this was what she wanted.

She shifted her hips beneath him. "I'll be all right if you'll do what you're supposed to." She squirmed some more. "Please."

She looked so vulnerable, yet she wanted to be so brave. She'd allowed him to think she'd done this before…allowed him to fall into her tender trap. And he'd wanted to. Wanted to more than he'd wanted his next breath.

His lips found hers and then nothing else mattered. Slowly he found the pace that was exactly what they both needed. He would do what he'd intended only moments ago. He'd make this night about her.

Soon, too soon, they cried out together.

And no matter how wrong it was, it felt absolutely right.

Chapter 12

Leanne hefted the bags of groceries onto the passenger side of her truck seat. She let go a sigh of relief and closed the door. Thoughts of Ty suddenly making her step light, she quickly skirted the hood to reach the driver's-side door.

The last few days had been perfect. Her hand stilled on the door handle as a wave of warmth washed over her. She and Ty had made love several more times since the first time. He'd been so sweet and gentle with her, and yet, his tenderness had in no way lessened his amazing skill. Though she had no guide by which to judge, she was certain that Ty was a truly masterful lover. Her stomach quivered with memories from their first time. He'd regretted taking her virginity, at least at first. Then he'd turned extremely possessive. She smiled. She liked that part.

Caution had been his watchword ever since. She always had to initiate their lovemaking. He never pushed her in any way. He was so hesitant at times that she feared this whole thing between them was one-sided. But then he would prove her wrong with his wildly intense lovemaking. It was during those intimate sessions when his soul was bared to her and he was at his most vulnerable that she could see how deep his feelings were.

It scared her to death, only because she was so uncertain of her own ground. She'd been so sure for so long that she and Ty weren't right for each, this complete turnaround frightened her beyond reason.

It had to be right.

It felt right…most of the time, anyway.

Forcing her attention back to the present, Leanne reminded herself that she had to get home, because the doctor was supposed to call with news about her mother. Not to mention she had to put the groceries away and go over to the Coopers to visit Jenny. She felt guilty for not having dropped by already. They were neighbors and friends, after all. Leanne needed to congratulate her personally.

She pressed a hand to her stomach and wondered what it would be like to be carrying Ty's child. Butterflies took flight beneath her belly button, sending wispy sensations all through her. She shook herself. She was definitely moving too fast for comfort.

"Leanne!"

She turned at the sound of her name. Mrs. Paula waved from the door of her shop. Leanne threw up her hand and produced a smile. Lordy, what did she want? She'd never get home if she let herself be dragged into a conversation with the inquisitive, however well-meaning, woman.

"Come into the shop for a minute or two," Mrs. Paula insisted. "I have something to show you."

"Yes, ma'am," Leanne said, reluctance slowing her. Though she kept her smile in place, her pleasant mood wilted. She'd never get away.

"I got a new bridal catalog," the woman enthused as Leanne followed her into the shop. "You've just got to see the lovely dresses for this season."

Bridal catalog? Leanne's eyes went wide. Had word that she and Ty had…? Her stomach knotted with worry. Surely not. They'd been so discreet—for the most part anyway.

Mrs. Paula ushered her to the counter. "You know a June wedding is always the best. We've still got time to plan one if we start now." She patted Leanne on the arm. "Did you know that I'm a wedding planner, too?"

Leanne's stomach plunged for parts south. Oh, God. If Mrs. Paula thought she and Ty were a couple, the whole town must as well or would very soon.

"Mrs. Paula, I'm certain there's been some sort of mistake," she said, her voice strained with anxiety and a touch of embarrassment. "I haven't even been proposed to."

Mrs. Paula gave her another of those affectionate pats. "Not to worry, dear. The proposal's just a formality. We all know where the two of you are headed." She took Leanne's chin between her thumb and forefinger. "Why just look at that face," she cooed. "Anyone with eyes can see you're a woman in love. And the whole town knows how Ty has been wooing you."

She released Leanne and glanced covertly from side

to side. "I hear tell that he spends most of his time at your place." She winked. "Helping you out. And everybody saw the two of you on the dance floor last Friday night. Why, you couldn't have got a pin between y'uns without drawing blood. Gracious, I've never seen such a kiss."

Leanne had to get out of there. Anything she said at this point was only going to make bad matters worse.

"Now you come on over here, little miss, I have just the perfect dress in mind for you."

The bell on the shop entrance jingled. Leanne turned at the same time as a shrill feminine voice called, "Yoo-hoo!"

Agnes Washburn and Corine Miller scurried toward Leanne and Mrs. Paula, both outfitted in their Sunday clothes, hat and gloves included. Leanne suffered a moment of outright panic. If these two got wind—

"Paula called and told us you were right outside her shop. We came as fast as we could," Ms. Washburn exclaimed.

"Have you shown her the one we like yet, Paula?" Ms. Miller inquired. "It's on page hundred and fourteen."

"I was just getting to that," Paula assured her friend.

Too late…they knew.

Leanne had to warn Ty.

Dex was desperate to keep himself occupied, thus the rearranging of hay bales. He had already groomed Dodger and any other horse in the barn that would stand still for him. His efforts had been to no avail. He couldn't seem to work off the restless energy pumping through him.

He paused, grabbed the shirt he'd discarded and wiped his damp brow with it. There was no getting around it. He'd painted himself into a corner on this one—literally. Dex dropped onto a nearby bale and let go a weary breath. He'd only wanted to help make her dream of starting the dude ranch come true. He hadn't meant to complicate the issue. But complicated it was.

He couldn't sleep…he couldn't eat. All he thought about was Leanne. He didn't dare label the feelings she engendered in him, but he knew something special when he experienced it. Surrendering, he closed his eyes and allowed the memories that he'd worked so hard all morning to keep at bay to overtake him.

Making love to her had sealed his fate. He'd made love with lots of different women, but no one had made him feel this way.

Not even close.

With every fiber of his being he wanted to possess her completely…wanted to make her his. All that made him male roared with the need to claim her as his alone. It shook him as nothing else ever had.

He looked around the huge hayloft and tried to reconcile any part of this with who he was. It was impossible. Absolutely impossible.

He closed his eyes and unsuccessfully attempted to block the thought that always haunted him: what would she do when she discovered the truth?

He wasn't the man she thought he was. Dex, he reminded himself, not Ty. The very idea of seeing the pain in her eyes that reality would bring tore him apart inside. But how could he stop her from finding out? He couldn't. She would soon know the truth.

Soon. His conversation with Ty a few days ago echoed in his ears. It would all be over soon.

Dex swore softly. There was an ache building inside him that threatened to shatter all that he'd ever been or hoped to be. He didn't know what he wanted anymore...who he was. Not really. Helping Leanne's mother had made him realize how badly he missed practicing medicine as an intern. But his medical degree had never been about practicing medicine. Yet a part of him yearned to do just that, at least on some level.

His grandfather Montgomery would have a stroke if Dex even mentioned such a thing.

And what about the family here? How would the Coopers take his big announcement when the time came? Why hadn't he and Ty thought of all this before they set this charade into motion? He was a fool, that's what he was. He was supposed to have come here to find the truth about his parents and maybe show these people what a mistake they had made. He swore again. Where was the full measure of bitterness he'd anticipated feeling? Where were the ugly, hidden secrets he'd expected to uncover? Instead he'd found pictures of his father at a time when he had obviously been the happiest of his entire life.

Here...with these people.

And he'd found the letters.

It was time he looked at them. He wiped his hands on his denim-clad thighs and reached into his back pocket. He'd been carrying the small bundle around with him for days trying to work up the nerve to read them.

It was time.

He untied the delicate pink ribbon and opened the first envelope.

My dearest Tara…

By the time Dex finished the fourth and final letter his heart was aching as it never had before. His father had loved his mother more than Dex could ever have imagined. There had been some kind of rift between the families years ago. Something about money. Chuck had wanted to be with Tara anyway. Apparently they'd eventually found a way.

This had been their home.

Dex swiped the emotion from his eyes with the back of his hand. He retied the ribbon and tucked the letters back into his pocket until he could put the precious memories away where they belonged. His father had loved these people. And he was falling in love with them, too.

Love?

He laughed at the irony of it. Love. He was a businessman. He made business decisions on cold hard facts. He never relied on gut instinct alone. Emotion never entered into the equation. None of this was real.

He was simply playing a part. Getting into character. He was supposed to be Ty. He'd worked hard to fit in, master his role. All these confusing feelings would be expected from a man like Ty, he reasoned. Dex was only behaving as he believed his brother would. None of this was real.

That statement left a bad taste in his mouth. But it was true, wasn't it?

Soon he would be back in Atlanta and back to his old self.

He clenched his jaw hard.

But not today.

The memory of touching Leanne, tasting her… being inside her took his breath away, made him want to forget who he was for a little while longer.

Today he was Ty Cooper.

"Ty!"

Dex jerked from his troubling thoughts. Chad and Court had joined him in the loft. He stood and faced them. "What's up?" He knew a moment of disconcertion as their solemn gazes settled on him. Had he made a wrong step—one he didn't know about?

Chad shrugged, his expression suddenly sheepish. "Look, I wanted to apologize for ragging you so much about acting a little strange since you got back from your trip."

"We know you've had a lot on your mind," Court chimed in. "We just wanted you to know how proud of you we are."

Dex looked from one to the other and tried his level best to read between the lines. "Well…ah…thanks, guys."

"It was really something how you found that doctor for Mrs. Watley and all," Court continued. "Gran says she's going to fully recover."

"What?" This was news to Dex. Why hadn't Leanne told him?

Chad nodded. "Just before Gran left for town Mrs. Watley gave her the good news. I don't think Leanne even knows yet. Mrs. Watley thought she might be over here."

Relief and a kind of satisfaction, so profound, flooded Dex to the point that he thought he might have to sit down. "That's great," he managed to say.

Court hugged him suddenly. "You did good, brother. We're proud of you."

Chad took his turn with the bear-hug act. "Oh, yeah." He drew away and reached into his back pocket. "Something came in the mail for you." He handed Dex a business-size envelope. "I thought it might be from those investors."

Dex stared at the return address on the envelope, Dyson Brothers. He recognized the five-star restaurant chain. Ty had clearly been aiming high with his future plans. His lips formed a grim line as he ripped the envelope open. He knew what it contained before he opened it though. It would be a rejection. Accepted proposals didn't come in the form of a one-page letter.

He read the short, to-the-point letter, then blew out a heavy breath. Ty would be immensely disappointed. "They passed on the deal," he told his brothers.

While they were giving him sympathetic pats on the back and assuring him that something else would work out, Dex was stunned by his own mental slip. He'd just thought of Chad and Court as his brothers as if it was the most natural thing in the world.

And somehow, deep inside him, he knew it was.

His father would have wanted it that way.

Leanne parked in front of the Cooper house and just sat there for a few moments. Her mind still reeled with all that had taken place in Mrs. Paula's shop. She had to tell Ty. The whole thing had gotten out of hand.

She also needed to warn him that she was probably

falling in love with him and she had no idea how to stop it. She groaned. She couldn't tell him that…especially considering she couldn't be sure that he felt the same way. Leanne climbed out of the truck, disgusted with herself and the whole blooming town.

This wasn't supposed to happen.

She was so confused…so very confused.

Worry slowing her, she trudged up the steps and across the porch. Maybe things would work out somehow. Lord knew she wanted Ty. The thought of spending every night in his arms…of having his children, made her feel all warm and tingly inside. But there was so much to iron out before she could go there. Not the least of which was figuring out if he felt even remotely the same way.

She opened the front door and poked her head inside. "Anybody home?"

A glowing Jenny hurried from the family room to greet her. They hugged, tears filling Leanne's eyes. She was so happy for Jenny.

When at last they drew apart, Leanne said, "You look wonderful. I'm so proud for you and Chad."

"Visit with me awhile. Brenda and the kids are in the backyard." Jenny hooked her arm in Leanne's and led her to the dining room to sit down at the table. "We can't wait. Angelica's a little upset about it, but she'll come around."

"Sure she will," Leanne agreed. "She'll be a terrific big sister."

Jenny clutched Leanne's hand. "So tell me if there's any truth to all the rumors I'm hearing about you and Ty." She winked. "Ty won't say a word."

Leanne resisted the urge to sigh out loud. She'd

just bet Ty wouldn't. He most likely felt as trapped as she did…well maybe *trapped* wasn't the right word.

"I want to help plan the wedding," Jenny announced, bubbling with excitement. "We all do. Gran and Brenda are so excited, too. Gran's in town for a little shopping, otherwise she'd be in here."

How would Leanne ever get this runaway train back on track? "I think it's a little early to start planning a wedding," she suggested. "There hasn't been a proposal yet. To be honest I'm not sure there will be one."

Jenny dismissed that technicality with a wave of her hand. "You know how pig-headed Ty can be. He'll keep us all in suspense until he's good and ready to do it."

Leanne chewed her lower lip. "I think everyone has the wrong impression, Ty and I have been working together—"

"Oh, honey, *pleeeze.*" Jenny leaned across the table. "I don't think there's any way anyone could have gotten the wrong impression if they saw you two together at the dance."

Leanne forced her right leg to stop its sudden bouncing. "Well, that's not…" How did she explain?

Jenny shook her head. "I can tell you're in love. I can see it in your eyes." She grinned. "I can also tell that you've already been *together,* if you know what I mean."

Leanne blushed to the roots of her hair and maybe beyond. "I…we…" What could she say? It was true.

Jenny patted her hand. "Don't even try to deny it. Even if I couldn't see it written all over your face. I can see it on Ty's. Every time he looks at you or your name is mentioned, you can see the territorial gleam in his eyes."

Leanne managed a trembling smile. "That's good to know." At least Ty was as transparent as she was.

"Who knows?" Jenny offered cheerily. "There could be a little one on the way already."

Another rush of heat claimed Leanne's face. They'd only failed to use protection once. "Jenny—"

Again Jenny dismissed anything she would have said with a flippant wave of her hand. "Don't sweat it. Angelica was on the way when Chad and I got married. We haven't regretted it for a moment."

"We haven't talked about children yet," Leanne stammered. She'd never known that about Jenny and Chad. She frowned, mentally doing the math and finding herself shocked all over again.

"Well, you know the Cooper men. They love to breed." Jenny's eyes twinkled. "I'm definitely not complaining, mind you. Ty will want to start right away I'm sure."

Leanne squirmed in her seat, weighing the consequences of simply jumping up and running out of the house. "I have the dude ranch to get off the ground," she countered, suddenly feeling the precise definition of *trapped*.

"Oh, Ty will find someone to run that for you. Being Mrs. Ty Cooper will take up far too much of your time for you to worry about running anything. Once those babies start coming you won't have time to think of anything else."

A cold, hard knot formed in Leanne's stomach. Hyperventilation seemed a definite possibility. "Speaking of Ty." Leanne stood abruptly. "Do you know where he is? I need to talk to him."

"I think he's out in the barn." Jenny followed her to the back door, reluctant to let her go. "When you're through talking to your honey, come on back in here and let's map out that wedding."

Leanne only nodded.

Before the door closed behind her, she broke into a run. She ran all the way to the barn, skidding to a halt when she almost ran headlong into Court and Chad as they strolled through the double doors.

"Don't worry, Leanne," Chad teased with a wink. "He's still in there. We didn't let him get away."

The two laughed as they headed toward the house. Leanne felt suddenly sick to her stomach. Her hands shook as she tucked a loose strand of hair behind her ear. Her groceries would just have to wait. She had to straighten all this out first. Then she had to get home. She didn't want to miss the doctor's call.

Leanne found Ty just inside the barn door reading what appeared to be a crumpled letter. He stood as still as stone only a few feet away, his angled jaw rigid, his dark hair tousled. Her heart started to pound immediately. His hat was missing, which struck her once again as so unlike Ty. His shirt was completely unbuttoned and hanging open. As usual the fit of his jeans made her feel giddy. She fought for her next breath. Her chest ached with longing, but she pushed it away. She had to do this. She couldn't let things between them keep spiraling out of control. It had already gone way too far. And it was her fault. He'd tried to slow things down…to steer away from physical intimacy. But she'd forced the issue. She had to make it right now.

"Ty," she said, then paused to dredge up enough strength to keep the quiver out of her voice.

He turned toward her, a smile instantly lighting his handsome face. "Leanne, I was just thinking about you. Have you—"

"We need to talk," she cut him off. She moistened her lips and forced her feet to cover the distance between them.

Shoving the letter into his jeans pocket, he met her halfway. "Sure." As if it were as natural a reflex as breathing, he leaned down and kissed her. He didn't linger, just a quick, tender kiss that stirred that ache building inside her. It affected her so deeply she wasn't sure she would be able to do what she knew she had to.

"Before we talk about anything else, though." He took her hands. "There's something I want to ask you." His smile widened to a heart-wrenching grin. "I've been thinking about this for a couple of days now and I really feel it's the right thing to do."

Oh no. He couldn't.

No.

No matter how much she cared for him, this was wrong for both of them. Jenny's words had driven the point home. Ty would never be happy with her for a wife. He deserved someone who could be the kind of life partner he deserved.

And it wasn't her.

She wanted to do more than just be a stay-at-home wife.

She wouldn't put either of them through that.

She backed away from him, breaking the contact

of their hands. "I'm sorry, Ty." She shook her head, struggling to hold the tears back. "I can't do this."

His expression clouded for a moment, then cleared as if he'd just realized her hesitation. "Yes, you can," he insisted. "It won't be that difficult. I'll make it work if you'll just give me the chance. I promise."

Oh, God. He was going to ask her. She couldn't let him. It would only hurt them both in the long run.

He reached for her hand again. "No." She stumbled back a couple more steps. "Don't." He stilled, confused, concerned. "I can't do this," she explained, hysteria rising in her voice. "I can't say yes. Please don't ask me to marry you, Ty, because I can't."

The look on his face almost undid her. She shook her head, hot tears streaming down her cheeks. "I can't marry you," she repeated, her voice now scarcely above a whisper. Before he could say anything she ran out of the barn without looking back.

It was the best thing for both of them. When he'd had a chance to think about it he'd realize it, too.

Chapter 13

Stunned, Dex stared after Leanne. Marry him? She'd thought he was going to ask her to marry him? His intent had been to coax her into agreeing to his new plan for blasting her dude ranch into success. A friend of his in the travel business had agreed to include Leanne on his website. Dex had also managed to get a fantastic deal on furnishings for the guest cabins, furnishing he'd already taken the liberty of ordering.

Everything was set. All he'd had to do was talk Leanne into it.

I can't marry you.

Something shifted close to his heart and he felt an odd sense of panic. He shook his head, confused by his reaction to her totally unexpected words.

He'd had no intention of asking her to marry him. Had he?

The idea was preposterous.

Wasn't it?

Need, desire and an overwhelming urge to reclaim what was his only added to his mushrooming confusion. He'd made her his, on a physical level at least. Had those intense feelings somehow spilled over to something more?

Whatever it was, he had to do something. He couldn't just let her go.

Not like this.

There had to be a way to figure this out.

To make it right somehow.

Dex strode out of the barn and across the yard only to see the dust flying behind her as she sped away in her old truck.

Defeat weighed heavily on his shoulders. He'd done this all wrong. A sinking feeling accompanied the realization that he couldn't see any way to undo the damage. He'd messed up everything.

"She just needs some time."

Dex turned slowly to face his grandmother. "You don't understand…" He attempted to explain but couldn't find the right words. The weight on his shoulders suddenly dropped to his chest.

That steady, knowing gaze held his when he wanted to look away. "Yes, I do," she told him, her voice as steady as her gaze. "I'd just gotten out of my car when Leanne came flying out of that barn."

"She thought I was going to ask her to marry me," Dex admitted. He tried to drag a breath into his lungs, but the effort proved too monumental. "She said she can't marry me…but I…" He shook his head, uncertain of what to say or do. "She doesn't understand."

Grandmother Cooper patted his arm. "Come help me with my packages and I'll explain a few things to you."

Numbly, he followed her. She opened the back door of her car and hesitated. "We'd always thought it would happen, you know. Ty always…" She looked away a moment, as if catching herself before she said too much. "Ty and Leanne always seemed so close, such good friends. It was perfect. The ranches would be combined finally." She shrugged. "But the sparks just didn't come. The relationship never went beyond friends." Her gaze came back to rest upon his. "Not until now…until *you* came home."

Another surge of emotion shook him. She did know. "I didn't mean for it to happen. I don't even understand how it happened." He stared directly into the eyes analyzing him so closely. "I didn't come here to hurt anyone."

She nodded once. "I'm sure you'll explain everything when you're ready, but this isn't about how your being here came about. This is about Leanne. The whole town, the family, for that matter, thinks there's going to be a wedding. Whatever it takes, I know you'll make this right."

He massaged his forehead, only now aware that a piercing pain had begun there. "I will."

She reached into the back seat of her vehicle and retrieved a bag. "Leanne has been determined to make her father's dream come true for three years now. She's fiercely independent. She wants to make it on her own. Her mother's poor health is all that's stopped her." Grandmother Cooper thought for a moment before she spoke again. "It won't be easy to make her see that there's more to life than that ranch. That she doesn't have to be afraid of going out on a limb emotionally." She thrust the bag she held at Dex. "She has to understand that falling in love with you won't change who she is. This sudden about-face in what she's believed, what she's felt for years, has her running scared."

Dex laughed, a sound that held no humor. "I'm pretty damned scared myself. I've never been this confused before." He scrubbed his free hand over his face and sighed wearily. "I can't change what I've done. I wouldn't change any of it if I could," he said with complete conviction. "I know it's not going to be easy to make it right, but I'll face the consequences of my actions."

"Do I hear another 'but' in there?" she prodded, somehow reading the hesitation he'd hoped to conceal.

"But what if she refuses to understand why I've been less than honest?"

Grandmother Cooper passed another shopping bag to him, then smiled, her expression sage. "I have a feeling you haven't been yourself lately, son. Maybe you need to think long and hard about the future and what you really want…*who* you really want in it. You'll never straighten out this situation until you know what it is *you* want."

She was right. He had some thinking to do. Decisions to make. Damage to undo.

Soon, Ty had said.

Well, soon was today.

A bag of groceries in one arm, Leanne wiped her eyes with her free hand and took a couple of deep breaths before she faced her mother. The last thing she wanted to do was worry her. Leanne closed her eyes and pushed all thoughts of Ty away. Her heart ached unbearably. But she'd done the right thing. She knew she had. She couldn't possibly marry him. It would be a mistake.

It had all happened too fast. One month ago she and Ty had been nothing more than friends, close friends, but friends nonetheless. Then out of the blue things got all confused, turned upside down. It had started the day she picked him up from the airport. She remembered clearly feeling that uncharacteristic pull of attraction. He'd been behaving strangely as well, she'd noticed. Nothing about him felt the same. Leanne frowned. Between the changes in Ty, her own crazy hormones and the pressure from the whole community to get them together, it was no wonder they'd fallen into each other's arms.

They'd simply done what everyone had wanted all along. She took another deep breath. Though she loved him, there was no doubt about that, it didn't change the fact that she and Ty weren't right for each other. She obviously didn't love him the way she should or she wouldn't be having these second thoughts. She didn't want to be known only as Mrs. Ty Cooper. She closed her eyes and shook her head at that untruth. She did love him…completely. She wanted him desperately. Would like nothing more than to spend the rest of her life with him, making love the way they had this week. She just wasn't willing to sacrifice who she was—who she wanted to be—in order to make it happen.

Besides Ty hadn't said one thing about being in love with her. Though she could tell that he cared for her, that was clear. Had she given him the opportunity to propose, would he regret it when the heady rush of lust wore off? This wild attraction had come on so suddenly, so unexpectedly…putting much stock into it was simply too scary. What if it was only a passing fancy?

What if they both woke up six months down the road and realized they'd made a terrible mistake?

She couldn't take that chance.

Gathering her composure, she forced a smile and opened the door.

"I'm back," she called as she stepped into the quiet house. She frowned when a soft sound snagged her attention. Scanning the room, her heart dropped into her stomach when her gaze landed on her mother huddled on the couch sobbing.

The sack of groceries hit the floor. "Mama!" She fell to her knees next to the couch. "What's wrong? Did you hear from the doctor?"

Joanna looked up, her face damp with tears. She flung her arms around her daughter and hugged her tight. "Everything's going to be all right." Another sob wracked her frail form. "She called."

Leanne drew back, her own tears flowing now. "Tell me what she said." She hated that she'd missed that call. She forced away the thoughts of Ty that tried to surface.

Joanna shook her head. "It's so simple. My thyroid stopped working."

Confusion lined Leanne's brow. "But you had tests for that."

Her mother nodded. "I know. It's called a silent thyroid. It slows down, then completely stops, causing everything else to go haywire. The strange thing is it's very difficult to diagnose. The usual blood tests won't catch it, everything continues to appear normal."

"What does this mean? What can be done about it?" Leanne wanted to be thrilled, but she needed to know for sure that it could be fixed.

"Dr. Baker brought the medicine out to me a few minutes ago." She nodded to the red-and-white-striped bag on the sofa table. "I'll be taking a stimulant until it starts to work on its own again. He'll monitor the situation from here on out. He said I should see a noticeable difference right away."

Leanne sagged with relief. "Thank God," she murmured.

"And Ty," Joanna added. "He's a fine man, Leanne."

She could only nod. Tears had already sprung up to the point of spilling past her lashes.

"Whatever you do, don't ever let him go."

The ache in her chest sharpened, making it impossible to breathe and at the same time impossible not to weep.

Too late, she cried silently. *Too late*.

Dex had done just as his grandmother suggested, he'd thought long and hard about his future. He'd spent most of the afternoon walking the floor of his room, studying the picture of his parents, and considering all that he'd learned since coming to Montana. The truth had rattled him just a little.

These people were family to him, there was no denying that. He wanted them to be a part of his life even after he went back to Atlanta.

He just didn't know how he was going to break

the truth to any of them. His grandmother already knew, had known practically from the beginning. He sat down on the edge of the bed and contemplated the best course of action. Should he just wait until they were gathered around the dinner table and make an announcement? He shook his head. No, that would be too abrupt. A family meeting? The Montgomerys were famous for family meetings.

Dex wondered vaguely how Ty was making out at this point. Dex would have to inform him right away that he'd let the cat out of the bag, so to speak. He felt fairly confident that the Coopers would want to call Ty immediately to see that he was all right. Dex tried not to consider how his Atlanta family was going to take all this. It wouldn't be pleasant. Though Dex still knew little about what had precipitated this break between their families, he had a feeling that there was some really bad blood, otherwise there would have been no need for the secrecy all these years.

Maybe before he did anything else he would ask his grandmother to tell him the whole story. He knew from what Ty had told him and from Grandfather Montgomery's bluntness about his disappointment in his son's marriage, that the couple's coming together had not been accepted—at least not by the Montgomerys. But it went deeper than that.

Dex would have to have the answers before he came clean with the rest of the family.

But before he did anything else, he had to make things right with Leanne. He would not put her through any more unnecessary grief. She was his first order of business.

When he stood it took a moment to steady himself as memories and sensations toppled one over the other inside him. He couldn't imagine never being able to touch her again, never being able to kiss those sweet lips.

But did these feelings translate into the kind of love that led to a lifetime commitment? The kind of commitment Leanne deserved? Dex exhaled a heavy breath. He didn't know. He'd never been in love before, but every instinct told him that this was it. There were plenty of facts to go along with the instinct, too. Like the fact that he couldn't sleep or eat. And the fact that his every thought related to, began or ended with her.

Now he only had to figure out how he was going to make this right, make it work out, when she didn't even know who he was. He could just imagine the betrayal she would feel when she learned the truth. He tamped down the outright fear that accompanied that thought.

No point in putting off the inevitable. He had to do this. He had to do it now.

Dex picked up the ever-present, cursed hat from the dresser. That automatic action drew him up short. He almost laughed. Damn if he wasn't turning into a cowboy after all. Shaking his head he headed downstairs. Maybe, in time, she would forgive him for lying to her, misleading her and taking her innocence. Hell, he wasn't even sure he could forgive himself.

The twins sat on the last tread at the bottom of the staircase. "Excuse me, gentlemen," he said playfully. "I hope I don't need a special password to be allowed through."

The boys shook their heads simultaneously. "You

need money," one said, then held out his hand. "Lotsa money."

Dex frowned, trying to decide which was which. "Money, huh?"

"Yep," the other one said. "Angelica says we gotta give the new baby all our toys. We need money to buy new ones."

A grin eased across Dex's face. That was just like Angelica. Already planning a strategy so she didn't have to sacrifice for the new baby. Dex decided then and there that the little girl would make a great businesswoman when she grew up. "She told you that, huh?"

The boys nodded.

"Well," Dex said with finality. "You boys tell Angelica that if she insists on you giving the new baby all your toys that your Uncle De—Ty will just have to buy you new ones."

Their eyes went round. The two munchkins jumped up and raced away amid a chorus of yippees!

Dex took the last couple of steps and headed for the door. Kids. That was another thing he had to factor into his future. He paused, hand on the doorknob. Had he really just thought that? This place had obviously gotten to him even more than he'd realized.

"Do you have a minute, son?"

Dex turned to find his grandfather in the entry hall behind him. He looked solemn or weary, or maybe both. "Sure." Dex took the three steps that separated them.

Grandfather Cooper stared at the floor for a time, just long enough to make Dex uneasy. "I've been doing a lot of thinking since you got back from Chicago."

Dex went on instant alert. Had his grandmother told her husband who Dex really was?

He looked up at Dex then. "Since you've been back there's been times when you seemed almost like a stranger." He shrugged. "I know it sounds funny, but you just haven't acted like the Ty we know."

"I... I've been under a lot of stress," Dex offered hesitantly. He didn't want it to go down like this.

His grandfather nodded. "I know. And I feel like part of that is my fault."

Dex frowned. He opened his mouth to deny the assertion, but fell silent in anticipation of the older man's next words.

Grandfather Cooper released a breath wrought with anxiety. "I've made some mistakes in my life. Plenty." He shook his head. "But there are some I'm more ashamed of than others." He leveled that uncertain gaze on Dex's once more. "Your behavior the past few weeks has made me think how different things might have been if certain circumstances had been different. Made me wonder what I'd missed."

Another of those unfamiliar emotions, helplessness, washed over Dex.

That same helplessness was reflected in the older man's eyes. "I know I'm not making any sense, but it's been on my mind and I had to tell you how I feel. I should never have allowed anything to get in the way of what was right."

It made perfect sense to Dex. His grandfather regretted that the boys had been separated. Dex's un-Ty-like behavior had made him think and wonder about how the other twin, the one they'd given up, had turned out.

Grandfather Cooper's eyes brightened with emotion. "I just wish things had been different, that's all. We didn't want it this way. But, under the circumstances, it was the only way. Too much water had gone under the bridge."

Dex nodded. The bitterness he would have expected to feel a few weeks ago never appeared. He slung an arm around his grandfather's slumped shoulders. "Me, too."

His grandfather looked at him. "You're a good man, Ty. Like your father."

Dex wanted to thank him for saying so, even if he wasn't Ty, but if he spoke right now he would never be able to hold back the emotions pounding against his shaky facade of calm. Instead, he nodded again. There was so much that needed to be said, that needed to be done. He needed so many answers.

But not now. He had to work things out with Leanne first.

Distress claimed the older man's features. He opened his mouth to speak, but only uttered a gasping sound. He clutched at his chest, then crumpled in Dex's arms.

Startled, Dex lowered his grandfather to the floor. He recognized the signs instantly. A cold, hard knot of fear formed in his stomach. A cardiac episode. His grandfather gasping for breath, Dex ripped the man's shirt open and jerked it loose from his jeans.

Years of training overriding his fear, Dex shouted, "I need some help in here!" He checked his grandfather's carotid pulse. Thready, but there. Dex said a silent prayer of thanks, his finger still gauging the pitifully weak beat.

"Stay calm," Dex assured the older man. "Everything's going to be fine." God he hoped he was right. His grandfather struggled to drag air into his lungs. "I want you to try to relax. Don't be afraid. I'm here. I won't let anything happen to you." Another promise he hoped he could keep.

"Wayne!" Grandmother Cooper fell to her knees next to her husband.

Brenda and Jenny flocked around her.

"Call 911," Dex commanded. "Tell them—"

No pulse.

Dex swore. He leaned down, putting his cheek close to the man's mouth. He wasn't breathing. "Now!" Dex shouted when no one moved to make the call. He gave his grandfather two puffs of air and watched the fall of his chest as the air rushed out through his open mouth. Still no pulse.

"What's happening?" Grandmother Cooper cried.

Dex moved into position to do chest compressions. "Is he on any medication?"

His grandmother shook her head, fear shining in her eyes.

"Any heart problems?" One, two, three, he counted silently.

"No," she wailed. "What's happening?"

Another two puffs of air...more compressions. Ignoring the sounds and faces around him, Dex repeated the routine again and then again. He paused, watched for spontaneous breathing and checked the carotid pulse.

Faint, but it was back.

Thank God.

"Is he having a heart attack?" Jenny asked, her arms around the older woman now.

"He can't be having a heart attack," Grandmother Cooper argued, panic rising in her voice. "He doesn't have any heart problems."

Dex leveled the calmest gaze he could manage on his grandmother, his finger resting lightly on the weak pulse that told him his grandfather was hanging on… just barely. "We need help *fast*."

No further explanation was needed.

Brenda thrust the telephone at Dex. "She wants to talk to you," she said between sobs.

Dex took the phone.

"I'm going to get Chad and Court," Brenda called, near hysteria herself, as she rushed out the front door, leaving it standing wide open.

"Seventy-eight-year-old white male. Excellent physical condition, non-smoker, no history of cardiac disease, no meds," Dex told the 911 operator. "Complete cardiopulmonary arrest, but I have a faint rhythm going again. Pulse is thready. No way to gauge BP. What's your ETA?"

Fifteen minutes.

Dex breathed a curse. "Just hurry."

The pulse faded once more.

Dammit. "I've lost him again. Tell the EMT we're going to need full advanced cardiac life support. We need it *stat!*"

Dex allowed the phone to drop to the floor as he bent forward and forced another couple of quick breaths of life-giving oxygen into his grandfather's lungs. While he performed another set of chest compressions Jenny picked up the receiver and answered any other questions the operator had.

Dex leaned forward to issue another breath. "Don't you die on me," he murmured. "We have things to settle."

Chapter 14

By the time the ambulance arrived, Dex had again established and maintained a weak, but spontaneous rhythm. For the moment his grandfather was holding his own. Dex was exhausted and weak with relief when he finally relinquished care to the EMTs.

The rest of the family stood in a semi-circle around Dex, too stunned or too worried to utter the questions clear on their faces. Angelica and the twins sobbed in their mothers' arms.

Dex's entire body started to shake with the receding adrenaline. He'd forgotten how frightening a moment like this could be. He'd kept his grandfather alive long enough for prepared help to arrive. The likelihood of his survival had he not had immediate and expert attention would have been extremely slim.

Aboard the ambulance, one EMT hovered over his

grandfather's gurney, monitoring his vitals and adjusting the intravenous flow, the other assisted Grandmother Cooper inside. Once she was settled next to her husband, the young man turned to Dex. "You did a great job, Mr. Cooper."

Doctor Montgomery, Dex corrected silently. He was Dr. Montgomery, but he was too uncertain of his voice at this point to speak. What was he thinking? He couldn't have said that anyway.

Frowning thoughtfully, the man slammed the rear doors, closing off the worried face of Dex's grandmother. He hesitated before going to the cab. "Have you had medical training?" He studied Dex speculatively. "You seemed to know a whole lot more than your average CPR-certified civilian."

Dex couldn't answer. He was too emotionally drained to even attempt a response.

Everyone watched in expectant anticipation of some sort of plausible excuse for what they'd just witnessed first-hand.

The guy shrugged. "Too many episodes of *ER,* I guess." He clapped Dex on the shoulder. "We're taking him to Mercy. He's stable, so don't drive like a bat out of hell getting the rest of the family there."

Sirens blaring, lights flashing, the ambulance sped down the long drive, a cloud of dust billowing in its wake.

"Chad, you take Jenny, Brenda and the kids in the minivan." Court glanced at Dex, his expression as well as his tone brooking no argument. "Ty and I'll come in the truck."

Jenny straggled behind, reluctant to drag her gaze from Dex. He remembered the day she'd hugged him so fiercely and shared her life-altering news. The hurt and confusion was clear in her eyes now. Hurt Dex had put there. He'd lied to them all, and though they were too concerned about their grandfather at the moment to dwell on the matter, they knew something was very wrong.

Dex met Court's suspicious glare. "I know you want answers," he said, struggling for calm. "But now is not the time. We need to get to that hospital."

"You think I don't know that?" his brother demanded. "Let's go."

Neither of them spoke during the seemingly endless trip to Bozeman. Dex thanked God again for the emergency medical station in Rolling Bend. He wasn't sure he could have kept his grandfather going long enough for help to arrive all the way from Bozeman.

As they entered the city limits, Court finally broke the silence. "Who are you?"

Dex had known that was coming. He'd braced himself, considered his response. Still, he wasn't fully prepared for the question when it came. He took a heavy breath. Maybe it wasn't the question he wasn't ready for, maybe it was the anger and accusation he heard in Court's voice. Whichever it was, it struck a painful chord deep in Dex's chest.

For one long moment as he stared out at the traffic before them, Dex considered lying…keeping up the ruse. But it wouldn't be right. It hadn't been right from the beginning. He and Ty had made a mistake.

A mistake that would hurt the people they both cared about most.

Dex closed his eyes for a second to block the painful images of his grandfather…of Leanne. And then of the way Jenny had looked at him.

It was time to face the reality of what he'd done.

"My name is Dex Montgomery."

There was no way to miss Court's reaction. He knew the name. Ty had been a Montgomery until the Coopers had legally adopted him. The whole Cooper family knew who Charles Dexter Montgomery, Junior, was. He was Ty's father.

Dex's father.

Court glanced at him with something resembling uncertainty. "Where's Ty?"

"He's in Atlanta with my…with his other grandparents."

Court looked both ways at the intersection then sped through the red light to keep up with the ambulance. He took a left, then parked in the lot designated as E.R. parking.

He shut the engine off and looked at Dex before getting out. "I don't know how this can be possible. We thought…" Court shook his head. "But one thing I do know is that you lied to us." He shook his head. "I knew something was wrong but I never would have believed this. You had to know how this would affect all of us. What were you thinking? What was Ty thinking?"

Dex didn't blink under that hard stare. "We weren't."

Court clenched his jaw. He blinked then, but not before Dex saw the renewed anger in his eyes. "Why didn't you just tell us who you were?" he accused.

"We can talk about this later. Right now we have something much more important to do."

Court nodded. "You're right." He hesitated once more before getting out. "Later, I want the whole story. And I want to talk to my brother."

Dex followed Court through the automatic doors that slid open to admit them into the E.R. Court's words rang in his ears. *I want to talk to my brother.* That was the bottom line. Ty was Court's brother, not Dex.

Leanne's truck squealed to a stop in the parking lot outside the emergency room entrance of Mercy Hospital. She slammed the old gear shift into Park and burst out of her truck. Mr. Cooper'd had a heart attack according to Agnes Washburn, whose nephew worked as a paramedic in Rolling Bend.

Her heart pounding, she raced toward the entrance. Ty needed her. She had to be there for him. Nothing else mattered at the moment. She blinked back a fresh wave of tears. If his grandfather died… No! She would not think that way. Mr. Cooper had to be all right.

"Leanne?"

She stopped abruptly and looked around to find who'd spoken. Craig Washburn stood a few feet away, smoking a cigarette. Though she hadn't run into Craig in years, they had gone to school together, and he really hadn't changed much. His blue uniform was rumpled and he looked tired. A long shift, she supposed. He flipped the butt of his cigarette away and started in her direction.

"You here about Mr. Cooper?"

She nodded. "How is he?"

Craig blew out a mighty breath. "Very lucky."

Leanne frowned. "Lucky?"

"He's stable. According to the doc on call, if Ty hadn't done what he did his grandfather would have been DOA." He adopted a pointed look. "Dead on arrival."

Leanne knew what he meant. She moistened her lips. "Ty was able to help him?"

Craig made a sound, not quite a laugh. "Help him? Heck, he kept the old man alive." Craig shook his head. "I don't know where he took his training, but he not only performed the necessary CPR, he told us exactly what he needed. We were able to confirm medical orders from the doc on call while en route, based on the details Ty gave us over the phone."

An emotion akin to fear stole into Leanne's heart. She shook her head. "Ty's never had any medical training."

Craig shook another cigarette out of the pack he kept in his breast pocket. "That may be, but I know what I saw with my own eyes, what I heard with my own ears. I'm telling you the guy knows his stuff. Damned if he didn't sound and act just like a doctor." He flicked his lighter and inhaled deeply, then blew out a puff of gray smoke. "I've worked with enough of 'em to know one when I hear one. The way he started barking orders to us the second we arrived." Craig shrugged. "I'm just telling you how it happened." He angled his head toward the E.R. entrance. "The whole family's in there looking at him as if he's from outer space."

Every ounce of warmth in her body drained clean out of Leanne. Angelica's words about Ty having been abducted by aliens echoed in her mind. The dozens of small things she'd ignored over the past few weeks all flickered across her mind's eye. The way he talked... the way he moved. Her heart thundered in her chest. The way he touched her...her response to his touch.

Her body began to shake uncontrollably as the ice slowly slid through her veins. Now she knew why he'd behaved so strangely since coming back from Chicago... Ty wasn't himself.

He was someone else.

And whoever he was, he'd made her fall in love with him...he'd made love to her.

Craig steadied her when she would have dropped like a rock onto the sidewalk. "You all right, Leanne? Maybe you should come in and sit down. You look like you've just seen a ghost."

No ghost, she was too weak to protest, an impostor.

Dex stood on one side of the E.R. waiting room, which was empty except for the rest of the Cooper family, who were gathered on the opposite side as if they were afraid to get too close to him.

He forced himself not to dwell on what they clearly thought about him now. While he had relayed the details to the physician on call, Court had apparently filled the rest of the family in on who Dex really was. The suspicious looks cast his way by one member of the Cooper clan after the other made him want to lash out, to tell them that it wasn't his fault. He and Ty had done the only thing they could considering their circumstances.

He closed his eyes and mentally blocked out how he thought Leanne would react when she learned the truth. She would be hurt worst of all.

Dex ran a hand through his hair. They all hated him

now and he couldn't blame any of them. He'd lied to them. Used them for his own personal gain.

He had to call Ty. But he'd put off making that call until he had further word on his grandfather's condition. He didn't want to upset him unnecessarily.

The double doors that boasted Authorized Personnel Only suddenly opened. Grandmother Cooper, looking far too weary, emerged. The rest of the family crowded around her, launching a barrage of questions the moment the automatic doors slowly began to close behind her.

Dex kept his distance. He was an outsider. He might as well acknowledge his new standing with the other half of his family.

"Your grandfather is stable and conscious. He's resting comfortably now," she announced. Her words were punctuated by a collective sigh of relief. "They're going to keep him a couple of days to perform a few tests to assess any damage done by the heart attack and to determine the best way to make sure it doesn't happen again."

Tears and hugs filled the silence that followed. Dex watched, so relieved that his grandfather was going to be all right that he couldn't muster up any negative emotion regarding his new standing. He closed his eyes and silently thanked God, something he'd been doing a lot of lately.

He opened his eyes just in time to find his grandmother looking directly at him. She made her way through the loved ones gathered around her and walked straight up to him.

Dex squared his shoulders and braced himself for further rejection.

"I don't know quite what to say," she murmured, her voice strained. She blinked furiously, futilely attempting to hold back the tears spilling down her cheeks.

Dex wanted to tell her he was sorry, to beg her not to say anything. He wasn't sure his heart could take any more. He'd never felt this close to complete and utter desolation. But he couldn't, he couldn't say anything. They were right, he was wrong. He'd made a mistake.

She lifted her chin and stared straight at him. "There is nothing I can say, nothing I can do to show you how very grateful I am for what you did today." Her voice cracked just a little on the last word. "Despite knowing the personal repercussions of your actions, you saved my husband's life," she whispered. "You have no idea what that means to me. Thank you."

Dex didn't even try to stop the tears dampening his face. "I'm glad I was here to help."

She smiled. "Me, too." Grandmother Cooper hugged him close. His chest constricted. When at last she released him, she turned back to the rest of her family. "I have to get back to your grandfather soon. But first, there's something you all need to realize." She reached for Dex's hand and squeezed it. "This man saved your grandfather's life. Though we might not understand the circumstances that brought him back into our lives, the only thing we need to know is that he's family." She looked from one wary face to the other. "You treat him with the love and respect he deserves."

Dex stood very still, too uncertain…too undone even to guess what would happen next.

Jenny was the first to approach him. She smiled a watery smile up at him. "Welcome to the family—*Dex*."

She hugged him. "We're glad to have you home."

Dex trembled as his arms went around her. "Thank you," he managed to mutter.

One by one, the entire Cooper clan hugged him, more tears flowing. Angelica waited until next to last. She waltzed up to Dex and extended her arms upward. "Thank you, Uncle..." She scrunched her forehead in confusion. "Uncle Tex," she finished with a wide gap-toothed grin.

Dex felt a smile tug at his lips as he knelt in front of her and took the hug she offered.

"Listen, whoever you are," she whispered into his ear, "you'd better get them babies off my back. They keep dumpin' all their ol' yucky toys in my room."

He drew back and winked at her. "Don't worry, Princess, I'm sure it'll all work out."

She scowled her five-year-old best at him before trudging off to join her mother. Dex stood, painfully aware that Court had not made an effort as yet.

Before he'd scarcely completed the thought, Court took the two steps necessary to put himself within handshaking distance. He thrust out his right hand. "I want to thank you for what you did...Dex."

Dex accepted his hand and gave it one firm pump. "That's not necessary." He looked the other man straight in the eye. "He's my grandfather, too."

Court nodded solemnly. "You're right." He smiled then. "It's good to have you in the family." He pulled Dex into a heartfelt embrace.

When Court finally released him, he asked, "What are you, a doctor or something?"

Dex smiled, suddenly tired all over again. "Yeah. That's what I am." For the first time since his residency, he felt exactly like a doctor.

"Leanne, we didn't even see you over there," Brenda said suddenly, looking somewhere beyond Dex.

Time lapsed into slow motion then. Dex turned to face the only woman in this world who'd ever touched him deep inside. The hurt and confusion on her pretty face slammed into him like a blow to his abdomen.

She walked straight up to him and slapped him hard. He didn't blink, instead he allowed the sting to reverberate all the way to his heart. He deserved whatever she felt compelled to throw his way.

"I can't believe you lied to me." She shook her head slowly from side to side. "How could you pretend to be Ty…and do what you did?"

Dex felt unsteady on his feet. He'd never experienced this level of regret or pain before. "I didn't mean to hurt you. I only came here to get to know the other half of my family." He gestured vaguely. "It just happened," he explained softly.

She glowered at him, her fists clenched at her sides. "Were you just slumming, Doctor? Surely you didn't come here to stay?"

He closed his eyes against the anguish staring back at him…against the hurt throbbing in his chest.

"Answer me, dammit!" she demanded. "Did you come here to stay?"

It took all the courage he could dredge up to open

his eyes to her again. He shook his head, the gesture hardly more than a tic. "No."

The new flash of pain that flickered in those blue eyes ripped the heart right out of his chest.

"What was I?" she demanded, her voice faltering. "The entertainment?"

"Leanne, I—"

She took two stumbling steps backward, as if the mere sound of his voice had propelled her. "It doesn't matter. Just go back to wherever you came from and stay away from me."

She left him standing there, knowing for the first time in his life how it felt to have a broken heart.

"Dex."

He felt his grandmother's hand on his arm; slowly he turned to face her.

"You have to give her some more time," she offered kindly. "She feels betrayed."

He released a shaky breath. "I don't think there'll ever be enough time."

Grandmother Cooper took his hand in hers. "Come over here and sit down with me for a moment. We need to talk." She sent a pointed look across the waiting room.

"Let's go down to the cafeteria and get some coffee," Chad suggested a little more loudly than necessary.

The rest of the family looked startled for a moment, then realized what was going on. Sounds of agreement rumbled through the group.

"The babies can't have coffee, can they, Daddy?" Angelica announced as her father led her away.

Dex heard the patience in Chad's voice as he answered the princess. Dex found himself wondering what it would be like to have a child of his own, one completely unlike the princess, of course.

God, he had lost it.

Grandmother Cooper settled into a blue molded plastic chair and gestured to the one beside her. "There are a few things you need to think about before this goes any further."

Dex wasn't sure if he was up to this talk right now, but she appeared intent on giving it to him. "I'm listening."

"The history between the Montgomerys and the Coopers goes back a long ways. Back to when your father and mother were just children." She sighed, her gaze taking on that distant look he'd seen before when she talked about the past. "They were so different from us. They didn't want their Chuck being with Tara." She shook her head. "Your Grandfather Montgomery was president of the Rolling Bend Bank. He turned us down for a loan during a bad time. We barely survived. There were a lot of hard feelings."

Dex listened, a frown etching its way across his brow. It was hard to believe this whole cover-up went that far back. He found it even harder to believe his grandfather could have been so heartless. His lips formed a grim line. No, he didn't. If the Coopers were having a bad time of it and appeared to be a credit risk, he would have turned them down flat. It wouldn't have been personal, just business. Dex had made those same kinds of decisions himself. How could he have been so wrong? How could his grandfather have been so wrong?

"Anyway, the Montgomerys moved down to Atlanta when your father was still a boy. They knew even then that he loved our Tara. But they refused to allow it." She paused, a tiny smile playing about her lips. "Then, years later, when they were all grown up, Tara and your father met again." She looked directly at Dex then. "Completely by accident. Before any of us knew what was happening, they'd married. The Montgomerys would have none of it. Your Grandfather Montgomery threatened to disown your father if he didn't annul the marriage and return to Atlanta immediately. Of course, Chuck wouldn't do it. The next thing we knew, you boys were on the way."

Tears glistened in her eyes. "When you were only three months old…we lost them." She swiped at the tears determined to fall. "That's when things went to hell in a handbasket."

Dex couldn't speak, emotion had him by the throat. He could only sit there and wait for her to continue.

"The Montgomerys were determined to have the babies. We were just as determined to keep the two of you." She closed her eyes, visibly grappling for composure.

He knew there was something he should say or do, but the images her words evoked held him in a firm grip of silence.

"The legal battle went on for weeks, then months. Finally some hare-brained judge decided to do what he called the only fair thing to do, give one baby to us, one to them." She sighed again. "Because of the awful feud between the two families, the judge further ordered that there would be no communication between us unless it was a medical emergency until we learned to get along. By the time we got around to thinking how wrong the whole thing was, too much time had passed. It didn't seem right to disrupt your lives at that point."

Dex felt an odd sense of relief at the realization that his Grandfather Montgomery hadn't masterminded that whole plot.

Grandmother Cooper's gaze locked with his once more. "There have been far too many betrayals and lies in this family already," she said in earnest. "It's time we made this whole mess right."

"How do we do that?" Dex felt hopeless all over again.

"We have to call Ty and tell him what's happened. We have to find a way to bury the hatchet with the Montgomerys."

Dex lifted a skeptical brow. "After the way my grandfather disowned my father, I'm not sure I can make that happen," he said, feeling suddenly, completely empty.

"Your grandfather was hurting, Dex," she argued. "I'd be the last person on the earth to take his side, but the one thing I know for certain is how much he and your grandmother loved your father. They were hurt and lashed out."

Dex shook his head. "That still doesn't excuse his actions." Anger ignited, replacing the emptiness. "There's no excuse for that."

"You're right. It was the wrong thing to do, completely inexcusable." She placed her hand over his. "But I want you to think about the heavy price your grandparents have had to pay for that mistake."

Dex stilled at her words.

"Your father, their only child, died without their

being able to make amends with him." A lone tear trekked down her pale cheek. "There is no greater pain than the loss of a child, especially if that child is uncertain about how much you love him. I know, because I lost Tara. Your Grandfather Montgomery never got to make things right with his son."

Dex closed his eyes to block the sting of tears.

"I think they've paid enough."

Chapter 15

Dex wasn't exactly sure how long he'd sat in the deserted cafeteria before he made a decision, but it had been a considerable length of time. The fact that the rest of the Cooper clan, as well as the lunch crowd, had long since dispersed, made him reasonably sure that he'd been there two or three hours.

Long enough to know what he had to do. One way or another he had to make things right with Leanne. He would not leave Montana with this chasm between them. Right now, though, he couldn't do anything about that. He had to give her time to come to terms with what she'd learned about him today. Just as he'd had to accept this other part of who he was.

He would give her a few days, then he'd make her listen to reason. He was too good a negotiator even to think about defeat. Somehow he'd work this out.

But today, right now, he decided as he stood, he had a couple of things that he needed to attend to. As he exited the cafeteria he thought about all that his grandmother had told him. Once he'd assured her that he would call Ty, he'd come down here to think things through. He'd needed a little time to formulate a plan. And he'd done that.

Dex took the elevator back to the third floor, where his Grandfather Cooper had been admitted into the intensive care unit. At the nurses' desk, he paused to speak with the doctor who'd just made his afternoon rounds.

"Excuse me, Doctor…" Dex checked his nametag, "…Louden, I'm Dr. Montgomery. I'm here with the Coopers."

Dr. Louden looked up from the notes he'd been in the process of adding to a chart. "Yes." He extended his hand, which Dex promptly shook. "Chad Cooper went to school with my younger sister. I'm glad Mr. Cooper is doing well. Is there anything I can do for you, Dr. Montgomery?"

"Do you have a conference room available that I could use to consult with some of my colleagues in Atlanta?"

He nodded. "Certainly. It's on the first floor. Stop at the information desk. I'll call down and have someone waiting to show you the way."

"Thank you."

Less than ten minutes later Dex stood alone at a polished mahogany conference table, waiting for his personal secretary to put him through to the man she thought to be Dex Montgomery.

"Ty, it's me, Dex."

"Hey, what's going on there?"

Dex frowned. Ty sounded strange. Dex dreaded giving him this news. "I'm afraid Grandfather Cooper has had a heart attack."

"How—?"

"He's all right," Dex cut in, reassuring his brother. "We got him to the hospital and he's in stable condition."

"Are you sure—" his voice broke "—he's all right?"

Dex explained each procedure performed on his grandfather. Then the tests to assess his condition and the results. Finally he convinced Ty that he was stable and in no immediate danger. "He's strong, Ty. And the family's here with him."

"I'll be on the next flight out," Ty insisted, his voice strained with worry.

"I figured you would." Dex paused. "But we need to straighten out some things first."

"I know," Ty told him. "All hell broke out here this morning. I was getting ready to call you."

Dex frowned. "What's happened?"

A heavy sigh sounded on the other end of the line. "Bridget figured out I wasn't you. She announced it in front of the whole hospital board, including the Montgomerys."

"Damn." This was definitely not good.

"Grandfather Montgomery didn't take it well. He thinks I came here for the money." He fell silent for a long moment. "And he wanted to know what I'd done with you."

Dex hissed a curse. "Where is he now?"

"In a closed-door meeting with Bridget. They're

probably trying to figure out how to protect themselves from me."

Fury boiled up inside Dex. Money. It was always the bottom line. "I'll talk to him."

"There's something else we have to settle."

As Dex listened, Ty explained about a children's center he wanted to help Jessica Stovall build. It would mean a lot to her as well as the children of Atlanta. It sounded good to Dex. Then Ty told him about the possible embezzlements and the notations on the accounts.

"We'll fund the center," Dex told him without hesitation. It was past time the Montgomerys started giving something back. "I don't care what Grandfather said, you're part Montgomery, just like I'm part Cooper. I'll make good on whatever you promised the hospital."

"Thanks, man." Ty sounded relieved. "What about Bridget? She was pretty upset about using those two accounts I mentioned for the hospital fund."

Dex hesitated. "B & B," he said more to himself than Ty as he drummed his fingers on the conference table. "Dammit, I think I know what it stands for. The little backstabber," Dex growled. It made perfect sense… Bridget's Bonus… B & B. "She's skimming bonus money for herself from our accounts and we were too blind to see it."

Ty made a sound of agreement.

"I'll take care of her," Dex assured him. "Now, tell me, Ty. Did I hear a hint of something extra personal between you and this Dr. Stovall?"

"Yeah, but it's not going to happen." Sadness weighted his tone.

"Sorry." Dex knew how that felt. It looked as if they were both in the same boat where their love lives were concerned. "Listen, there's something else," Dex said, dreading this part too. "The company you met with in Chicago turned your proposal down. But I have an idea."

"I've already got a plan," Ty said, more enthusiastically than Dex would have expected. "In Mom's letters she talked about raising leaner—"

"Beef," Dex finished with a grin. He'd come up with the same idea after seeing the picture of her receiving the nutrition award. Obviously Ty had been doing the same investigating into the past that Dex had done. "We'll need more land—"

"And I'll have to invest in different feed—"

"The Watley ranch will be perfect," Dex said. "We can lease the rest of the grazing land and it'll benefit the Watleys as well as us." Had he just said we?

During the pause that followed Dex realized that they had been finishing each other's sentences. Great minds think alike, he mused.

"You said *we'll* need more land. Are you planning to stay there?" Ty wanted to know.

Dex considered that question, really considered it. Yes, he had every intention of making this his second home. "Not permanently. But I'll provide the money for the venture. You can run the day-to-day operations."

"I don't want Montgomery money," Ty said tightly.

Dex restrained a sigh. "Listen, Ty, I don't give a damn what my grandfather said. We're brothers, and if I want to be partners with you, that's my choice. The Coopers are my family, too."

When Ty remained silent, Dex said, "We can discuss it some more when you get here. Now, let me speak to Grandfather. Get him and Bridget in there and put me on speaker phone."

Dex listened as Ty buzzed his grandfather and waited.

"What the hell do you want?" Grandfather Montgomery thundered.

"Dex is on the phone," Ty said stiffly.

"Dex! Is that you, son?"

A surge of emotion made speech impossible for one long beat. "Yes," he finally said. "I'm here."

"What the Sam Hill is going on here?" the old man demanded. "I don't know what kind of nonsense those *people* have put in your head, but I want you back in Atlanta ASAP!"

Fury flared anew. "You have two options, Grandfather," Dex said bluntly. "You may—"

"Dex," Bridget cut in sharply. "I cannot believe you're talking to your grandfather in such a manner. What has happened to you? Who is this impostor posing as you?"

Dex settled into the closest chair and made himself comfortable. "Bridget—"

"Dex, darling," she purred. "How could you do this to us?"

"I haven't done anything yet," Dex said flatly.

"Please, Dex," Bridget hissed, "you must admit that this whole sham is incredibly bizarre. Perhaps you need an appointment with my therapist. He's—"

"Bridget," Dex interrupted smoothly, "you may leave now. You're fired."

"Y-you can't do that!" she stammered.

"I can and I am. And forget about taking those little bonuses with you."

Silence reigned for a few tense seconds before the sound of a slamming door announced what was no doubt her dramatic departure.

"I don't know what's gotten into you, son, but I'm warning you—" his grandfather began.

"No, Grandfather," Dex objected. "I'm warning you. On Saturday, if Grandfather Cooper is doing as well as expected, we're going to be having the mother of all barbecues at the Circle C."

"I'll be there," Ty stated for emphasis.

"By Saturday if you're not back in Atlanta—"

Dex again cut his grandfather off. "If you want me back in your life, you will accept Ty and the rest of the Coopers as family. This family feud has gone on too long. It's all or nothing, Grandfather. No compromises…no negotiations."

"How dare you issue me such an ultimatum!"

"If you're interested in remaining a part of *my* family," Dex informed him, "you'll be there on Saturday. Think about it this time. How much are you willing to lose before you realize that life is too short?"

Dex didn't give his grandfather time to argue further, he disconnected. There was nothing else to say. Ty would be flying in tonight or early tomorrow morning. Dex had done all he could from here.

Now it was time for stage two of his plan.

Winning back the woman who'd stolen his heart.

On Saturday morning Leanne returned home from the supply store to find a huge yellow rental truck, a moving van or something of that order parked in front of her house. Bewildered, she climbed out of her old truck and headed into the house. She could unload the horse feed later.

Inside she found her mother talking on the telephone while reviewing what appeared to be pamphlets spread out over the sofa table.

"That sounds wonderful," Joanna said. "My daughter will get back to you next week." She hung up.

Leanne hitched a thumb toward the front of the house. "What's going on? What's that truck doing here?"

"First," her mother beamed, "let me tell you about this." She thrust a colorful brochure at Leanne.

As Leanne studied the lovely travel pamphlet, her mother explained, "This is Stargazers Travel. They want to list us in their brochures and on their website. The president of the company thinks he can have us fully booked by next month."

Next month? "Whoa!" Leanne stared at her mother in disbelief. "How in the world do you think we can pull that off? We don't—"

"Come with me." Joanna grabbed her by the arm and tugged her through the house and in the direction of the back door. "You'll see," was all she would say.

Once outside, Leanne dug in her heels, slowing her mother's forward movement. Four men exited one guest cabin, two with moving dollies, and headed back toward their truck. "Mama, what is going on here?"

"You'll see," Joanna said cryptically.

Leanne had no choice, she had to go along.

It was amazing the difference in her mother after only one week of medication. She had more energy than she'd had in over a year. She was happy, always talking about the future and Dex.

Leanne pushed thoughts of him away. She would not think about him today.

Especially not today.

And now this.

Leanne tried to muster up some enthusiasm for her mother's benefit. She hated to be depressed when her mother was so obviously getting her life back. But she just couldn't help it.

"We are ready!" Joanna announced as she dragged Leanne into the first guest cabin.

Leanne gasped. The cabin was fully furnished with a queen-size bed, dresser and mirror, couch, two chairs, and a dinette set that seated four. It was beautiful. It was everything she'd dreamed it would be. But the bank had turned down her request for a start-up loan. How was this possible? How could this be?

Dex.

Leanne cried. She just couldn't help herself.

Her mother wrapped her arms around her. "Don't cry, child." She hugged her close. "He only did it because he loves you."

"He doesn't love me," Leanne wailed. "He lied to me!"

"Shhh. I know he didn't tell you the truth and he should have." She rubbed Leanne's back affectionately. "But deep down you knew all along."

She had known, Leanne admitted. She'd known he was different somehow…

"He's called you every day. Even come by a couple of times and you won't even hear him out."

Leanne swiped at her eyes. "How can I believe anything he says now?"

"Look at it from his point of view," her mother coaxed. "Look how much courage it took for him to come here and face the past…come to terms with who he is." She shook her head. "He didn't come here to hurt you—or to fall in love with you. But he did."

Leanne sniffed. "You don't know that he loves me."

Her mother smiled. "Yes, I do," Joanna said softly. "I'm not sure he fully understands exactly what he feels yet, but he loves you."

Leanne gathered her composure. "Well, he's got a funny way of showing it."

Her mother winked. "If my intuition is right, and it usually is, you ain't seen nothing yet. Now come along, we have to get all gussied up."

Leanne frowned. "What?"

Joanna curled her arm around Leanne's. "We're going to that shindig at the Circle C today."

Leanne stopped dead in her tracks. "I can't do that. I can't possibly face him."

"I've been cooped up in that house for over a year now. Would you begrudge your dear old mother a day of festivities?"

Leanne admitted defeat. How could she possibly deny her mother? She couldn't.

She would just have to face him. She prayed with all her heart that her mother was right—that Dex did love her. Because she was madly, foolishly in love with him.

Two hours later, her heart pounding like a drum, Leanne parked her old truck in the Coopers' crowded drive. It looked as if the whole community was there already. Anxiety threatened to shatter her bravado.

Firming her shaky resolve, Leanne walked to the backyard with her mother. Joanna was immediately swept into the crowd of friends and neighbors who were glad to see her out and about. Leanne waited on the fringes of the gathering, scanning faces for the person every fiber of her being ached to see.

Then she saw him.

Her gaze moved over him hungrily. The fit of his jeans, the way his broad shoulders filled out his white shirt. His wind-tousled hair. She smiled. He hated wearing a hat, she realized suddenly. That's why he was always forgetting it.

Dex was talking to his Grandfather Cooper, who'd been released from the hospital two days ago. Thankfully, Mr. Cooper was going to be fine. Medication and proper exercise were going to keep his condition under control.

Dex smiled at something his grandfather said. Leanne's heart reacted in its usual manner. How could she have thought that she could spend the rest of her life without ever seeing that smile again, without kissing those lips?

She couldn't. She simply couldn't.

Now, if only her mother's intuition would prove correct…

One-thirty. Dex's shoulders sagged. The Montgomerys weren't going to come.

He should have known. He'd expected too much too soon, he supposed. He shook his head. He just wanted his family together, where they belonged.

He'd been sure his ultimatum would work, but why

should it? It hadn't worked for his father more than thirty years ago.

A strong hand clapped Dex on the back. "Don't look so down and out, brother," Ty told him. "They could still come."

"I'm not so sure."

Ty squeezed his shoulder. "I am. I saw something change in the old man while I was there." He shrugged. "It was like all the little differences he noticed in me made him think about the grandchild he'd walked away from all those years ago."

Grandfather Cooper's words echoed in Dex's ears. He'd said virtually the same thing.

"I hope you're right," Dex offered.

"Boys." Grandmother Cooper hugged Dex, then Ty. "I just have to tell you one more time how proud I am to have you together at last."

Grandfather Cooper appeared and kissed his wife's cheek. "We're all proud." The happiness in his eyes punctuated his words. "We're finally complete now."

"Your mother and father would be proud of you both," Grandmother Cooper told them, emotion shining in her eyes.

"That means a great deal to me," Dex said humbly. This was as close as he would ever get to knowing what his mother was like.

Ty elbowed him and nodded toward the far end of the crowd. "You've got company, bro."

Dex followed his gaze.

Leanne.

She was beautiful. Wearing that same white dress she'd worn the first time they made love, she looked like an angel straight from heaven. At that instant

Dex knew that everything in his mixed-up life would be right if only he could convince her to forgive him.

Determined to make it happen, he excused himself and strode straight up to her. She looked ready to run. "Just give me three minutes." He took her by the arm, a jolt of awareness instantly searing him. "That's all I ask of you."

"All right," she said warily.

Dex led her away from the party. He paused a few feet from the barn, far enough away that they wouldn't be interrupted. He stared deeply into her eyes and told her the truth.

"When I came here it was more out of curiosity and maybe a little taste of revenge than anything else. I expected to resent these people, to be bitter about what they'd done to me." He slid his hand down her arm to grasp her hand. He didn't miss the little hitch the move elicited in her breathing. "But a couple of things happened while I was here. While I was pretending to be Ty I fell in love with these people."

Her big blue eyes peered up him, so full of hope yet still guarded. Though he could see the questions in her eyes, she waited for him to finish.

"The other thing is…" He squeezed her hand. "…Well, whether you can understand it or not, you saved me from the man I'd become. You showed me there was more to life than I ever imagined." He swallowed back the lump of emotion forming in his throat. "I fell in love with you. And if you can forgive me…"

She started to speak but he shushed her with a finger against those luscious lips. "I'd like very much if you'd agree to be my wife."

Leanne threw her arms around him. They held each other for awhile.

She finally drew back. "I love you, Dex," she said softly. "I love you so much. But I'm afraid that I won't fit into your world. We're so different…and I've got the dude ranch and my mother…" She shrugged. "I just don't see how it could work." She shrugged again, uncertain. "And…and I want more than just to be a wife. I want to make my father's dream come true in a big way."

He'd already thought of this. "We'll hire an assistant to help your mother run the dude ranch on a daily basis. We'll commute back and forth regularly." He smiled as he watched her eyes grow wider with hope. "Plus, I've talked to a friend of mine about forming a corporation that would set up dude ranches all over the state, maybe even in some others. You'll be the senior partner. You can run it any way you want." Before she could speak, he continued, "And you don't have to worry about fitting into my world." He cupped her face in his hands and kissed her, just the barest brushing of lips. "You *are* my world."

Tears slipped down her soft cheeks, but she smiled in spite of them. "In that case, then the answer is yes."

Dex escorted his bride-to-be over to his grandparents and made the formal announcement. He also introduced her to Ty's fiancée, Dr. Jessica Stovall from Atlanta. Everyone in the family had welcomed her with open arms when she arrived with Ty earlier in the week. Dex had never seen people go to such lengths to make another person feel wanted. They loved Jessica the moment they laid eyes on her. Since she had no family of her own, this was even more thrilling for Jessica. If only the Montgomerys would feel that way. Deliberately pushing that thought aside, happiness bloomed in Dex's chest as he watched Leanne welcoming Jessica into the family.

A hush abruptly fell over the crowd. The sound of a vehicle approaching drew his gaze to the driveway. A long black limousine parked only a few yards away. His heart skipped a beat when the door opened and his Grandfather Montgomery emerged from the elegant vehicle.

Grandfather Montgomery offered his hand to his wife as she emerged from the vehicle next, both of them looking the epitome of vogue and sorely out of place on this unpretentious Montana ranch. George, Dex's valet and confidant, climbed out next. They were all here.

Charles Montgomery, Senior, his wife on his arm, walked straight up to Wayne Cooper. For one long moment the two men simply stared at each other. Finally, Charles extended his hand and said so that all could hear, "I've been wrong about a lot of things for a very long time." He cleared his throat. "Worst of all, I hurt your family. I'd like to start fresh."

Wayne Cooper stood stock-still for three long beats, then he accepted the offered hand. "Nothing would please me more."

Grandmother Cooper hugged Grandmother Montgomery, tears of joy and relief flowing down their cheeks.

Dex hadn't realized until that moment that he was holding his breath. He exhaled raggedly. Finally, after all this time, things were right again.

"Holy smokes. Can you believe it?" Ty asked, stunned.

"I'm getting there," Dex murmured.

The Montgomerys approached Ty and Dex then. Dex found himself holding his breath all over again.

"Ty." Grandfather Montgomery nodded to Ty. "Dex." His gaze was bright with emotion. "I made a mistake thirty-three years ago. I was wrong and I've had to live with it all this time." He looked from Dex to Ty and back, then drew in a heavy breath. "I won't make the same mistake twice." He embraced each of his grandsons, then looked at them with pride beaming from his expression. "I can't believe the two of you are finally together." He shook his head. "I never allowed myself even to think this could happen." His voice wavered when he said, "Thank God I was wrong."

Dex hugged his Grandmother Montgomery as well. He was so glad to see them. She held on a moment longer when he would have pulled away.

She hugged Ty next, and murmured, "Thank you so much for having the courage to come to us." When she released him her own eyes were brimming with emotion. "And for making our family whole again."

Ty nodded, obviously too overcome to speak.

Dex put his arm around Leanne then. "This is Leanne Watley," he told the Montgomerys. "My fiancée." He wanted his family to love her as much as he did.

Another joyous round of hugs followed, accompanied by heartfelt congratulations. For the first time in his life, Dex felt right. Complete—whole, as his grandparents had said.

When the Coopers had ushered the Montgomerys over to meet some of their friends, George made his way to Dex.

"It's very good to see you, sir," George offered stiffly.

"Good to see you, too, George."

George looked him up and down. "I see you've been blending in with your environment."

Dex couldn't help a grin. "I have. Do you approve?"

A tiny smile twitched the reserved man's lips. "I most certainly do, sir. When in Rome…" He waggled his brows.

Dex, pride and love bursting inside him, ushered his fiancée forward a step. "This is Leanne Watley. We're getting married."

George gave her a thorough once over then gave Dex a nod of approval. "It's a pleasure, madam." He kissed Leanne's hand.

Before George could fathom her intent, she'd thrown her arms around him and hugged him. "Nice to meet you, too, George."

Startled, George cleared his throat when she released him. "Well, perhaps I should see to the Montgomerys' luggage."

Dex frowned. "Luggage?"

"According to their itinerary, they plan to stay the weekend." With that, George executed an about-face and went about his business.

"Dex."

He turned to Leanne, who made him want to take her in his arms just looking at her. "Hmmm?"

"Who's George?"

"I'll explain later. Right now—"

Dex's next words were interrupted by the easy bantering between the grandfathers over the best cut of beef.

"You might need this, brother." Ty paused beside him, offering a cold long-necked bottle of beer.

"I think you might be right," Dex agreed as he accepted the drink.

Ty held out his own bottle. "A toast," he suggested, "to the future."

"Hear, hear," Dex said as they clinked glass. He took a long swallow then turned to Leanne. "And to us," he murmured before kissing her lips.

Epilogue

One month later

Dex waited on the left side of the pulpit, Ty on the right. Both were dressed in similar black tuxedos, both waited expectantly to take the next step in the rest of their lives. Dex smiled when Ty's gaze caught his.

"Don't worry, she'll be here," Dex assured him upon noting the worry in his eyes.

Ty nodded. "I know."

Jessica had had to return to Atlanta to close down her practice and finalize other business affairs. Ty was scared to death that she was having second thoughts—especially after she'd called and said her flight had been delayed and she wouldn't be arriving until just before the wedding.

But she'd be here. Dex was sure of it. And, deep down, so was Ty.

A hush fell over the crowd assembled in the Rolling Bend Community Church as the wedding march sounded from the ancient organ. Angelica, looking like the princess she was, cantered down the aisle, throwing rose petals left and right. She paused at the pew where Jenny's twins sat then sprinkled the boys with pink petals. They giggled. Beaming, Angelica continued her enthusiastic journey toward the front of the church. When she stopped, she looked first at her Uncle Ty and grinned, then to her Uncle Dex and winked.

Dex felt sure she had some self-serving plan for him, but today he didn't care. He winked back. The little girl grinned.

Suddenly Leanne appeared at the far end of the long rows of polished wood pews. Pride filled him as Dex watched his bride, escorted by George, walk down the red-carpeted aisle toward him. The white wedding dress and veil only made her look more angelic, more beautiful. Dex wasn't sure his heart could tolerate the rush of emotions that surged through him.

Looking regal, George smiled as he left Leanne standing at Dex's side. They both looked back to see Jessica, accompanied by Dr. Baker, approach next.

Ty's sigh of relief was audible. Jessica looked stunning as well. Ty's eyes literally shone with the love burning inside him.

At last, Dex realized, everything was perfect.

The families were together with only the occasional colliding of egos. MOCO Enterprises, the name they'd given the Montgomery–Cooper beef venture, as well as the Wild W Dude Ranch Retreat, were off the ground and running.

And now, the icing on the cake… Leanne would be his.

It was all any man could hope for and more.

Before turning his attention to the minister, Dex quickly surveyed the faces of his and Ty's family. All seated together, all smiling.

It didn't get better than this.

"Dearly beloved," the minister began.

"Dex!" Leanne whispered, leaning slightly toward him.

He eased a bit closer to her, a question in his eyes as he searched her uncertain ones. "Yes?" he whispered back.

"The stick turned blue."

"What?"

The word echoed through the chapel, startling the minister into silence.

"We're pregnant," she murmured, then chewed her bottom lip as if she feared his reaction.

He was going to be a father.

He was going to be a father! His eyes widened in disbelief. Startled, confused, and humbled, Dex smiled down at his beautiful bride. "Are you sure?"

She nodded.

Dex pulled Leanne into his arms and kissed her for all she'd given him, for making his life complete.

"What's going on?" someone asked in a stage whisper.

"Didn't ya hear?" Angelica demanded, turning to those seated behind her. "She said the stick turned blue! Just what we need around here—more babies. Ain't the one Uncle Ty and Aunt Jessica's gonna adopt enough?"

Ty leaned toward Dex and offered his hand. "Congratulations, brother."

Dex pulled his brother into an embrace. "I couldn't let you get ahead of me."

Ty drew back. "Yeah." Emotion shimmered in his eyes. "I knew you'd catch up."

As the enthusiasm spread through the church, Jessica hugged Leanne. "I'm so glad we'll be doing the mommy brigade together."

"Thanks, sis," Leanne said tearfully.

Dex felt as if he might break down and cry himself. Neither Leanne nor Jessica had siblings of their own—and he definitely knew how that felt. The two were like sisters now. Life truly was perfect.

Once the cheers and applause had died down, the minister continued with the double wedding ceremony.

Dex kissed his bride.

So did Ty.

And they all lived happily ever after.

* * * * *

Victoria Pade is a *USA TODAY* bestselling author. A native of Colorado, she's lived there her entire life. She studied art before discovering her real passion was for writing. Even after over eighty books, she still loves it. When she isn't writing she's baking and worrying about how to work off the calories. She has better luck with the baking than with the calories. Readers can contact her on her Facebook page.

THE CAMDEN COWBOY

Victoria Pade

Chapter 1

Great—figures this would be a day I'm in a skirt and high heels...

Lacey Kincaid sighed as she pulled her sedan to the side of a dirt road and turned off the car's engine.

She'd been driving down one backcountry Montana road after another in search of Seth Camden for the last hour of her Wednesday afternoon. She'd found his house and was told that he was out fixing fences and how to find him. The man was not easy to get to even *with* directions.

And now that she'd made it to the part of the Camden ranch where she'd been told she could find him, he still wasn't going to be easy to get to. Particularly not when she was going to have to drop down about two feet from the roadside and cross several yards of field to actually reach him. And she was going to have to do it in a skirt and three-inch heels.

But today was the day Lacey needed to talk to him, and today—right now—was when she was going to talk to him.

This would, however, be the first time she'd met Seth Camden—or any member of the infamous Camden family. With that in mind, she wanted to be certain of her appearance, so she flipped down the visor that was just above her head and peered into it.

For work, she always wore her pale blond, shoulder-length hair swept back. She did it loosely and with a sporty look to it because she didn't want to appear stark or severe, but she was all business and she didn't want anyone thinking differently because of some unconscious hair toss that might give a different impression.

For the meeting to discuss financials that had taken up most of her second day in the small town of Northbridge, Montana, she'd twisted her hair into a knot and let some wispy ends cascade from the top. Checking it out in the visor mirror now she could tell that it was all still the way she'd done it that morning, so she didn't touch it.

She also avoided wearing too much makeup. A dusting of blush along the apples of her high cheekbones, a hint of lip gloss on her already rosy lips and a few swipes of mascara to color her lashes and accentuate her green eyes, and she was out the door in the morning. *Dolling* herself up—that's what her father would have called it if she did any more than that. And it would defeat her every purpose, because in Morgan Kincaid's view she would be just another ineffective woman more devoted to her vanity and nabbing a husband than to the job she'd been given.

Satisfied with her appearance, Lacey flipped the visor up again and got out of her car. She was wearing business clothes—a cotton blouse underneath a tailored coat that matched her straight, gray, knee-length skirt with its slit in the back to accommodate walking.

At least it accommodated walking anywhere but across the rutted dirt road to the other side, where she awkwardly hopped down the slope from the road to the field.

Teetering, she barely retained her footing as she got down into the gully. But once she was there, she did her best to walk with some semblance of dignity and headed for the man who didn't seem to have noticed he was no longer alone.

It didn't strike her as strange that he hadn't noticed her. He was replacing a section of fence that had collapsed somehow. His back was to her and to the road where she'd parked. Plus he was so far from the road that she doubted he'd even heard her car.

Lacey's right ankle buckled just then and she veered wildly to one side. She didn't fall, but it was close, and she checked to make sure she hadn't broken the heel off of her shoe.

She hadn't, so she continued on, focused on the man who was her goal.

A grayish-white cowboy hat was her only view of him from the neck up, but below that he was dressed in a white crewneck T-shirt, jeans and cowboy boots. Lacey could tell that he was tall even from where she was—over six feet tall, she judged. And he had broad, broad shoulders that she watched expand when his massively muscled arms rose in the air, lifting a posthole digger from out of the hole he was working on.

He gripped the handles of the X-shaped tool in his leather-work-gloved hands and he pivoted slightly to his left with it. He pressed the handles together to open the blue steel head at the opposite end, releasing the dirt he'd taken from the hole. Then he drew the handles apart, pivoted to his original stance and stabbed the closed head into the hole once more.

As she approached, he stood with his legs apart. Long legs that were thick enough to test the denim of his jeans. Even from a distance she could tell that the twin pockets of those jeans cupped a rear end that rivaled the best she'd ever seen. And being in contact with the players on her father's new football team—the Montana Monarchs—Lacey had seen some great ones.

Another near tumble almost landed her on her own rear end but she managed to keep herself upright, returning her gaze to Seth Camden as she continued on.

His back was straight and strong, and while the white T-shirt he was wearing wasn't tight, it was damp with the sweat of working in the sun on an August day and it clung to him like a second skin. It clung to back muscles that any athlete she knew would have envied. Well-honed muscles that narrowed gracefully to a taut waist. And that rear end again...

Okay, enough of that! she told herself, as she began to draw nearer. Near enough, she thought, to shout, "Excuse me..."

But either she wasn't near enough or her timing was bad because rather than respond, he again jabbed the posthole digger into the ground.

Feeling the August heat herself, Lacey paused long enough to remove her suit jacket, fold it neatly in half and place it over her arm. Thank goodness her cotton blouse was sleeveless because it was blazing hot out there.

Despite the heat and the terrain, when the daughter of football legend Morgan Kincaid set her mind to something, she followed through. So once she'd taken off her jacket, she forged ahead—this time keeping her gaze high enough to take in the man's substantial neck peeking from beneath the brim of the cowboy hat.

A Camden who was a cowboy—that seemed like a contradiction when the Camden family was renowned in the business world.

Lacey's own father had parlayed his professional football fame and fortune into an impressive empire that encompassed retail, rental and hotel properties, car dealerships and various other businesses along with his newest venture—owning an NFL expansion franchise.

But Camden Incorporated? If Camden was like a giant, lush bowl of fruit, the Kincaid Corporation would equal one small stem of grapes on a single cluster in the Camden bowl.

The stores that bore the Camden name were the superstores of all superstores. With multiple locations in every state and in several other countries, they had no equals. The Camden stores put under one roof almost every item and service the consumer wanted or needed at the lowest prices that could be had. They advertised that an entire house could be built, finished, furnished, landscaped and lived in for a lifetime without the owner ever needing to step foot in another store. Even banking, legal and health needs could be seen to there.

But behind the stores themselves, the Camdens

owned much of what supplied the products they sold—factories, manufacturers, farms, ranches, dairies, timberland, lumber mills, bottling plants, and numerous other production-level businesses and industries that facilitated their low prices. They also had a hand in distribution centers and had now added a network of medical, dental and vision clinics to each store to go along with pharmacies that offered low-cost prescriptions—because they even owned pharmaceutical companies and research facilities.

There just wasn't much the Camdens *didn't* have a hand in, so it was surprising to find one of the ten grandchildren who now ran Camden Incorporated acting like a small-town cowboy.

Not that she knew the intricacies of the family, because she didn't. An entire section of a course she'd taken in college had been devoted to studying the business model of Camden Incorporated, but when it came to the Camdens themselves, only H. J. Camden—Seth Camden's great-grandfather and the founder of the business—and H.J.'s son, Hank, who would have been Seth Camden's grandfather, had been discussed.

The present-day Camdens tended to crop up occasionally in the news in conjunction with charities they sponsored. But beyond that they kept a very low profile, and Lacey couldn't name them or what any of them did.

Still, it seemed strange that a member of a family like that would be out here working in the hot sun digging postholes.

"Excuse me…" she tried again.

But no sooner had the words come out of her mouth

than she raised one foot to take another step and lost her shoe completely, costing her precious balance.

In fact this time she pitched forward, her jacket went flying and only at the last second did she catch herself and somehow manage to keep from landing face-first in the dirt.

"Whoa! Nice save!"

Oh, sure, *now* he noticed her.

Lacey stood straight again, brushing her hands together to get the dirt off of them and retrieving her shoe with a yank to get the heel unstuck. Then she brushed the dirt off her bare foot, replaced her shoe and rubbed her hands together again.

When she was finally put back together she looked up to find that Seth Camden—if that was who he was—had abandoned his hole digger and gloves, and was picking up her jacket. It had flown off her arm and landed on the ground a few feet away.

He grabbed her jacket, shook the soil from it and then stood up to look in her direction.

The Camden blue eyes—Lacey did recall mention of those somewhere. Now she knew why they were noteworthy; when her gaze met his, the sight of bright, brilliant cobalt eyes staring quizzically back at her was something to see.

And since they went with a face that was drop-dead gorgeous enough to steal her breath, for a moment all Lacey could do was stare.

With his sharply drawn, chiseled features, the man before her couldn't have been more handsome if he'd tried. He had a squarish jaw and chin, a perfectly shaped mouth with lips that were full but not too full, a just-long-enough nose. And those eyes peering at her from beneath a straight, strong brow.

"Are you all right?" he asked in a deep voice that was so masculine it made very girly goose bumps erupt along the surface of her skin, even in the summer heat.

"Oh. Fine. I'm fine," Lacey said, coming to her senses. "Are you Seth Camden?"

"In the flesh."

Don't get me started thinking about that!

"Did you come all the way out here looking for me?" he asked, that brow furrowing from beneath his hat.

He took his hat off and ran the back of his hand across his forehead. There was an inexplicable sexiness to that gesture. His hair was the dark, rich color of espresso coffee beans, and was cropped short and close to his head on the sides, with the top left just long enough to be swept back in a careless mass of waves and spikes. And he didn't have hat-hair.

Then the Stetson went on again, and the blue eyes were once more leveled at her.

Just then she realized that he'd asked her a question and was probably waiting for an answer. She'd been so lost in gawking at him.

"I went to your house first. I found someone at one of your barns to tell me where you were and how to get to you. I needed to speak with you, so—"

"Here you are," he finished for her. "What can I do for you…? Or maybe you can tell me who you are first…?"

Another bit of negligence. Lacey wasn't ordinarily

so flustered, and she didn't understand why she was now. She just hoped it would stop.

"I'm sorry. I'm Lacey Kincaid—"

"I've met Morgan Kincaid—he and I did the closing on the property he just bought from us. And Ian and Hutch Kincaid—they've been around town—"

"Morgan is my father. Ian and Hutch are my older brothers. I don't know if my father told you or not, but the property he bought from you is to be used as the new training center for the Monarchs—"

"Right, your father's football team."

"And the project has been given to me to manage." Lacey hadn't intended to sound so proud of that fact, but it was such a big deal to her she couldn't ever seem to say it without sounding pleased with herself.

"And that's what you want to talk to *me* about?" he asked, handing her her jacket as he did.

Lacey accepted it and went on. "There are three things I wanted to talk to you about," she said in her best I'm-the-boss-and-this-is-all-business tone. "I just got into town yesterday and I'm staying in an apartment Hutch owns. But it's in Northbridge and it takes me fifteen minutes to get from there to the site—"

"Fifteen minutes is an eternity to you?"

That *was* the way she'd said it. "It would just be better if I could be closer, and I've been told that the nearest thing to the site is your place, and that you have a guesthouse. I was wondering if you might be interested in renting it?"

"To you? For you to live in?"

"It would just be me, yes. And I would hardly be there except to sleep because this project is going to keep me on-site the rest of the time. You probably wouldn't even know I was there."

"Oh, I think I would…"

Lacey had no idea what that meant but it had come with a hint of a smile that curled only the left side of his mouth. A smile that was even sexier than the brow wipe had been.

But why things like that were even occurring to her, she had no idea. She opted to ignore the phenomena and go on as if she hadn't heard his comment.

"I only need somewhere to sleep and shower and change clothes, really. And of course I'll pay rent—"

"You'd need a kitchen, too, wouldn't you? How else would you fix meals without a kitchen?" he asked, giving no indication whether or not the guesthouse *did* have a kitchen, merely seeming curious. In a laid-back, slightly amused way that was also sexy but still a little frustrating to Lacey.

"Okay, yes, a kitchen—or just a kitchenette where I could make coffee would be nice—but most days I eat whatever I can order in at the site," she answered, as if it were inconsequential. "And if you had some pressing need for your guesthouse while I'm using it, I could always spend a night or two with one of my brothers. If it was absolutely necessary—"

"And make that *looong* fifteen-minute commute?"

He was clearly teasing her because he'd said that with a full smile. A very engaging smile.

But Lacey was sweltering in that sun and didn't have time to waste admiring his smile, so she said, "Yes," as if his question had been serious. "The second thing I needed to talk to you about is the house and barn on the property we bought from you—"

"Yeah, we thought long and hard about getting rid of those. My great-grandfather was born in that house, his father used the barn as a lumber mill and that was where my great-grandfather started the business. As kids when we'd visit here we'd have sleepovers in the old place. But since nobody's used anything over there since we were all kids, and since the land is played out both for crops and for grazing, we decided to sell."

"Yes, well," Lacey said, impatient with the family history. "There are some things still in the attic in the house and in the barn—"

"There are? I thought we got everything out."

"Apparently not. Since they're your family's belongings, you should be the one to go through them, and throw them out or move them or whatever. And third," Lacey went on, "my father was… Well, let's say he wasn't happy with the way things worked out when he bought this land—"

"Your brother was supposed to get the Bowen farm for the training center but he ended up getting the girl instead and marrying her," Seth Camden said with more amusement. Then, apparently to explain how he knew that, he added, "Northbridge is a small town."

"Right. Well. Just when Ian thought they could pick up the McDoogal property instead—"

"I'd already bought it."

"Yes, you had." And Lacey couldn't be sure whether that had been because the Camdens had genuinely wanted the McDoogal place or if it had been a classic Camden move.

Buying the property out from under them had put the Kincaids in a position where they had needed to deal with the Camdens rather than the cash-strapped

McDoogals in order to get any land at all. They'd ended up paying more for less acreage—not the Mc-Doogal place, but the original Camden homestead.

It was the kind of situation that Lacey had learned about in her college class, the kind of situation in which the Camdens' gain was someone else's loss.

"At any rate," Lacey went on, lifting a hand to shade her face because she thought she could feel it beginning to sunburn, "when his temper is up, my father tends to act rashly. In his hurry to get the training center underway, he didn't wait for a complete report from our people, and now we know that to build the main road leading to the center, we need access to a section of land you still own."

"And you came all the way out here today to what? Negotiate?"

"It's simple access for a road. That's all I'm asking. We can buy that strip of land from you—"

"Or lease the land for the road and pay us a fee for it in perpetuity."

Was he just thinking on his feet or was this something he'd anticipated? Again Lacey wondered about the less-flattering things that were said about Camden business practices.

"It's hot out here, so let's see if I have everything straight so you can get out of this sun," he continued. "You want to live in my guesthouse, you want me to clear out the old attic and barn, and you want to put a road through Camden land for your training center."

"Yes."

"Yes, yes and no."

"Yes, yes and no…" Lacey repeated.

"Yeah, sure, you can use my guesthouse—which

does have a small kitchen, if you ever want to eat. Sure, I'll clear out the attic and the barn. But no way, here and now, am I giving the go-ahead to put a road anywhere on my property without a whole lot more information and…"

"Making sure that it's to the Camdens' advantage," Lacey muttered to herself.

"…without a whole lot more information and consideration of what all it would involve," he concluded. "At the time your father bought the property he was figuring the road that leads to the house and barn would work just fine. It isn't any of my doing if that's changed."

"It *was* your doing to buy the McDoogal place so we had to make so many changes," Lacey reminded him. She wanted him to know that she had no intention of letting a Camden get one over on her.

Seth Camden shrugged. "The McDoogal place was for sale, it connects to my place, I bought it. That's all there is to it."

And appearing innocent even when they weren't had been his great-grandfather and grandfather's trademark.

Still, Lacey knew she would get nowhere pushing him about the McDoogal place, and it was water under the bridge now, anyway. So she dropped it and concentrated on what she needed to accomplish.

"But yes, I can rent your guesthouse, and you *will* clear the attic and the barn?" she summarized.

"Absolutely."

"We should probably discuss rent," she suggested.

He shrugged again and Lacey couldn't help noticing that. Boy, oh, boy, were those nice shoulders….

Then he said, "You can just stay there. As my guest—it *is* a guesthouse, after all. Let's just consider it good relations between business associates."

Strings. That was part of what she'd learned about the early Camdens—there were always strings attached to what his forefathers did. She didn't think she could take the chance that Seth Camden might uphold the tradition.

"I'd prefer paying you," Lacey insisted.

"Okay, pay me whatever you think is fair, then. It really makes no difference to me. Just tell me when you want to move in."

"Tomorrow evening?"

"Okay. And then we can set a time for me to come out to the old house and see what was left behind. But for now I'm not kidding—you better either get out of this sun or use some of my sunblock." He nodded toward his tools and gear at the fence.

"I'll just go," Lacey said. "But we will need to talk more about the road."

"I'm sure we can work something out," he said, as if it meant nothing to him.

They could *work something out*...

Lacey didn't respond to that. Another of the things that she'd learned in the lectures about the Camdens was that H.J. and Hank had been very big into the you-scratch-my-back-I'll-scratch-yours mentality.

After saying her goodbye, she turned to make her way back to the road where she'd parked.

"Careful!" he cautioned when she came close to falling yet again.

Lacey righted herself and glanced back to find him still standing where she'd left him, watching her.

"I'm fine," she called over her shoulder, continuing the way she'd come but taking extra care not to stumble again while he looked on.

She got all the way back to the road before she stole another glance at Seth Camden.

He was still watching her, so she waved as if to tell him she didn't require any more of his supervision and got into her car.

But she couldn't help casting another glance out into the field. Seeing him finally return to his work, she inadvertently took in the sight of that amazing backside again.

No more! she ordered herself, forcing her eyes to the road and starting her engine.

But as she drove away she was thinking about the you-scratch-my-back-I'll-scratch-yours mentality.

And wishing that she wasn't imagining scratching that back of his quite so literally.

Or quite so vividly…

Chapter 2

"Hey, Cade, it's Seth."

"Oh, man, you gotta remember that I don't keep farmer's hours," Cade complained in a gravelly voice. Seth's call had obviously awakened him.

Seth laughed. It was only 7:00 a.m. on Thursday when he called his brother in Denver. Still he couldn't resist goading him. "I thought big businessmen had to rise and shine with the sun, too."

"No meetings today—I was going to get to sleep until seven-thirty, damn you."

"Them's the breaks, pal—I had to be up two hours ago to talk to our guy running the Kentucky farm, so now I'm headed out to finish fixing a fence and figured I'd get you before I left," Seth explained.

Despite the fact that Seth was the oldest of the Camden grandchildren and so had had the option of heading the operation, he'd instead chosen to handle the Northbridge ranch and oversee all the other agricultural aspects of Camden Incorporated, leaving the CEO and chairman of the board positions to brother Cade, who was a year younger.

All of the Camdens except Seth thrived in the city, in Denver, where they'd grown up. But Seth was the country boy of the bunch by choice. When it came to the business end of things, he oversaw the farms, ranches and dairies that Camden Inc. owned. He far preferred getting his hands dirty.

"Did we lose more cattle at the Kentucky place?" Cade asked. They'd been talking frequently about a vandalism problem that had been ongoing on the Kentucky farm.

"No, actually they caught the culprits—it was just kids," Seth said. "Kids whose family owned some of the land once upon a time and decided to make a statement—you know the song."

"Somebody has an old grudge against us and they passed it down," Cade said without surprise.

"That's the one," Seth confirmed.

"What are you doing about it?"

Since the agricultural portion of Camden Inc. was Seth's baby, he made any decisions that didn't require a vote by the entire board of directors—which was comprised of himself, Cade and their other eight siblings and cousins. Petty vandalism was not a matter for the board of directors; he was merely letting Cade in on how he was handling the situation.

"The kids are locals. It's a small town like Northbridge, and I don't want any more bad blood than we already have there. I'm having them work off the damages, and if they do that there won't be any charges filed against them, so they walk away with a clean slate. The guy I have managing the farm knows the kids. He's willing to put them to work so they don't end up with a record, and we'll just hope that takes care of it."

"Sounds good," Cade said.

Seth could tell by his brother's voice and the background sounds coming through the phone that Cade had gotten out of bed and was making coffee.

"You're coming for GiGi's birthday in three weeks, right?" Cade asked.

GiGi was what they called their grandmother—short for Grandma Georgianna. She'd raised them and their cousins after the death of their parents, and she was turning seventy-five.

"Wouldn't miss it," Seth assured.

"Anything else going on there?" Cade inquired conversationally.

And just like that the image of Lacey Kincaid came to mind. That had been happening on and off since she'd left him out in the field yesterday.

"I met Morgan Kincaid's daughter," Seth informed his brother. "I'm pretty sure she thinks we bought that last piece of property just to get one over on her old man."

"Same song, different verse," Cade said.

"Yep."

They were accustomed to the distrust that came with their last name.

"Did you tell her you just wanted the property?" Cade asked.

"Nah, it wasn't an overt accusation, just an attitude—you know it when you run into it."

"I do," Cade agreed.

"Now they need a road to come through here somewhere and I think that the fact that I didn't instantly buckle under made her more suspicious. As if I somehow knew they would need to build an access road there and positioned us so we could stick it to them."

"We're a cunning lot, we Camdens," Cade said facetiously. "So she's a ballbreaker, this Lacey Kincaid?"

Seth laughed. "No, I don't think so," he said, disabusing his brother of that unpleasant notion. He didn't like hearing Lacey Kincaid referred to that way, for some reason.

"I think she would have been a match for old H.J. and Granddad," Seth went on. "Drive, determination, all business—that seemed to be what she was about. She found me clear out at the north end and hiked from the road about a quarter mile to get to me. In the heat, in a suit, in high heels."

"Just to talk about a road?"

"That and to tell me we left some stuff in the attic and the barn over at the old place. And to ask if she could stay in the guesthouse so she doesn't have to waste fifteen minutes driving to her site."

Cade laughed. "Fifteen minutes is too much?"

"According to her. I know I haven't heard the last on the road issue, but I didn't come away feeling like she was trying to squeeze me. To tell you the truth, it was more like when the girls were little and they'd play dress-up and clomp around in GiGi's heels—seems like Lacey Kincaid might be trying to fill shoes her feet aren't big enough for."

But she had been a sight to see walking away from him across that field yesterday. At first he'd simply watched to make sure she didn't break her neck on her way back to her car, but then he'd found his eyes glued to a tight, round little butt that had nearly made him drool.

Of course that had only been the frosting on the cake because nothing about the front view of her had escaped him either...

"We left things at the old place?" Cade said, pulling Seth away from his wandering thoughts.

"That's what she claims. I thought everything was out of there, but apparently not. It can't be much, though. I'll take care of it."

"And what was that about her staying in the guesthouse?"

"She wants to rent it. I told her she could just use it, that I didn't care, but she's insisting on paying us something for it."

"You don't care if she stays in the guesthouse?" Cade said with an edge of suspicion to his tone. His curiosity was clearly piqued suddenly, because he added, "So somewhere between ballbreaker and little-girl-in-too-big-shoes—what's this Lacey Kincaid *really* like?"

"I only talked to her for about five minutes—just long enough for her to say what she wanted to say. I told you—she was all business. I can't tell you more than that."

"What's she look like?"

Oh yeah, Cade was suspicious, all right...

And what was Seth going to tell him? That Lacey Kincaid looked like a blonde goddess in a gray suit?

That she had hair that seemed to drink in the sunshine and reflect it back?

That he'd never seen eyes as sparkling a green—like twin emeralds sprinkled with stardust?

That she had smooth, creamy, flawless skin and a small, perfect nose?

That she had rose-petal lips that had looked too kissable to be talking business, and high cheekbones that had flushed adorably in the heat?

That she was only about five feet four inches tall but stood straight and compact with just enough peeking from beneath her white blouse to make him have to concentrate on not looking closer?

No way was he saying any of that to his brother.

So instead he said, "Blond hair, green eyes, fills out a skirt about as well as anybody I've ever seen—she looks like any don't-mess-with-me working girl."

"Who you won't mind seeing out your back window for some time to come if you told her it was okay for her to stay in the guesthouse," Cade goaded with a laugh.

"She's not hard on the eyes, no," Seth admitted. "But she swears I won't even know she's here because she'll be spending so much time working. And I believe that."

"Too bad…"

"Nah…" Seth said, even though he recognized that there was a part of him that wouldn't hate looking out the rear of his house and seeing Lacey Kincaid.

Still, looking was all he'd do, and he told his brother why. "You know how I feel about workaholics—in the short time we had with Dad we hardly ever saw him. Toss unbridled ambition into that pot, and Charlotte brought it home for me big-time how much I don't want any part of a woman with drive, drive, drive, who puts her goals ahead of everything else and has a problem with the fact that I don't. No thanks." The thought of his ex still rankled.

"Woo, still a sore subject," Cade said more to himself than to Seth. "Regardless, you're letting Lacey Kincaid use the guesthouse?"

"Like she said, I'll probably never see her. I'm just thinking public relations and not wanting bad blood again."

"Ah," Cade said, as if he didn't actually believe that but wasn't going to argue it.

And his brother wasn't too far off the mark in his suspicions, because even though Seth didn't want to admit it, lurking somewhere underneath everything he'd said was still a touch of eagerness to have Lacey Kincaid move in today.

But he definitely wasn't admitting it.

Instead he changed the subject to ask if Cade had gotten their grandmother a birthday gift yet.

That topic finished their early-morning conversation, yet Lacey Kincaid continued to be on Seth's mind long after he hung up.

Lacey Kincaid and all the reasons he *wouldn't* do anything more than enjoy an occasional glimpse of her from the distance.

He'd meant what he'd said to his brother—he wanted nothing to do with a workaholic or with someone who had the kind of drive he'd already seen in Lacey Kincaid.

Seth was the oldest of the kids in his family and the oldest of all the Camden grandchildren, so he'd had the most experience, and he had the most memory of his grandfather, his father and his uncle. And no memory of them *didn't* involve Camden Incorporated as their number one priority.

Yes, the intensity of their drive had built the Camden fortune. But that drive had meant that he'd had almost no relationship with a father who had sacrificed everything to his work. It was a drive that had caused no end of rumors that not all the means and methods used by the Camdens were something to be proud of.

Drive that intense rolled right over other people, and if Seth hadn't known before not to get in the way of it, he'd had it brought home to him by the last woman he'd had the misfortune of falling for.

So Lacey Kincaid might be lovely to look at, but that honestly wasn't why he'd said she could use the guesthouse. He was just being neighborly. Cultivating good relations with the new people in town. That was the reason.

But Lacey Kincaid was lovely to look at. And okay, that *might* have played an infinitesimally small role in granting her use of the place. But that still didn't mean he was interested in her. Or that he would let himself be interested in her.

And the fact that even at this early hour he'd already rearranged his schedule to make sure that by the time this day was done he would finish work good and early so he could be showered, shaved, ready and waiting for her when she got here?

That was just being a good host.

* * *

It was almost nine o'clock Thursday night before Lacey arrived at the Camden ranch. After turning off the highway she drove down a long road that ran between twin white-rail fences that bordered lush pastures where horses grazed at their leisure beneath tall oak trees.

At the far end the road circled an enormous fountain. Water cascaded down a rock waterfall into an octagonal-shaped pool encased in a stone wall that matched the stone of the Camden house.

The house itself was a sprawling two-story with a steeply sloped roof from which multiple chimneys rose. The windows all had earth-brown shutters, and the huge double door entrance sat atop a flight of five wide, semicircular steps.

Lacey had first seen the place the day before when she'd come to find Seth Camden, and while she hadn't been surprised that such a place belonged to the Camdens, she had been shocked to find it in the rustic countryside of Northbridge. Among English manor houses in the hills of Wales, or mansions in the most plush, elite estates of Connecticut, maybe, but not Northbridge.

Since there had been no answer to her knocks or to her ringing of the doorbell yesterday, she didn't know what the inside of the house looked like, and she didn't have any idea where the guesthouse she'd asked to use might be or what it might be like. She'd merely been told by one of the contractors for the training center that it existed. But she doubted it was a hovel.

In fact, she thought it was probably very nice. And maybe her excitement was over getting to see her new place of residence, she told herself. Not over getting to see Seth Camden again.

Lacey went halfway around the fountain and parked directly in front of the house, turning off her engine. She left her suitcases and the rest of her belongings in her car and went up to the front door.

A lengthy moment passed after she rang the door-bell and she checked the time on her cell phone. She'd fully intended to get here earlier, but work had kept her away. She hoped she wasn't so late that Seth had given up on her getting there at all and gone to bed.

Seth Camden in bed...

Why was she suddenly wondering what he slept in?

Then the front door opened and there he was, look-ing nothing at all like the Lord of the Manor.

He might not have been in a silk smoking jacket—in fact, he was wearing jeans and a simple white polo shirt—but the shirt showed hints of his muscu-lar chest, and the short sleeves were tight around his mouth-watering biceps. The man still looked good. Really, really good...

"I was beginning to wonder if you changed your mind about this," he said in greeting.

"No, I'm sorry I didn't get here earlier and I'm so glad you're up—I was afraid you might have gone to sleep," she answered.

"Oh, I was betting that *evening* to you was going to be later rather than earlier, so I was just waiting."

Why was he betting that? And why did he sound as if the worst had been confirmed?

"I got held up in meetings and then still had a dozen things that needed to be done before I could get back to Hutch's place to load my things, and I lost track of time. When I realized how late it had gotten I thought about calling, but I didn't have a number to reach you and it seemed like I'd just be wasting more time to try to find one. But I *am* sorry," she repeated.

"No big deal. Like I said, it's what I expected. I was just doing some paperwork myself."

"Paperwork? Did you want me to sign a lease? And we didn't talk about a damage deposit," Lacey said, just in case the *paperwork* he'd been doing had something to do with her using his guesthouse.

That put a curious frown on his brow, and from there Lacey's gaze went to his hair. No hat-hair tonight, either. The deep, dark, rich brown locks were neat and clean. There was a casualness to the style, as if all it needed in the way of combing was for him to drag his fingers through it.

Sexy. It was very sexy-looking.

And Lacey reprimanded herself for that thought.

"I honestly wish you'd just be my guest and forget the whole *renting* thing," Seth Camden said.

What might she owe a Camden if she *didn't* pay rent—that was what worried her.

"No, I insist. I did some research on what it would cost to rent a small house in town and came up with an amount—tell me if you don't think it's enough…" Lacey took a check she'd already written out of the pocket of her slacks.

Shaking his head to convey his disapproval, Seth nevertheless took the check, gave it a cursory glance and said, "Fine," before he jammed it into his own jean pocket as if it were scrap paper. "And no, I don't want a lease or a damage deposit."

He gave a slight roll of those amazing blue eyes

of his before he added, "Let's go through here—the guesthouse is out back. I'll show it to you and then we'll take your car around."

"Okay," Lacey agreed.

Seth stepped out of the doorway and motioned for her to come in. He was freshly shaven and smelled of a cologne that was reminiscent of the outdoors itself—woodsy and clear and crisp and clean. Lacey liked it so much she took a small, subtle deep breath as she crossed in front of him.

And then she was inside of the Camden house.

Wow! was her first thought as she went into the entryway. Lacey's father had money, and all the Kincaids lived very well. But it was nothing compared to this.

The place was as astonishing inside as it was outside. The entry was the size of a small house and reached up past the second floor to an enormous domed skylight that was like the ceiling of a planetarium, except that the stars glimmering beyond it were real.

Lacey glanced around in awe at this country mansion. Elegance and grandeur literally surrounded her in an opulent staircase that curved from one side of the entry all the way up to the second floor and swept around to the front again in the balustrade that bordered the staircase and the entire upper level.

From where she stood, Lacey could see a formal living room to the right, and a formal dining room beyond that. Straight ahead was a wide hallway with openings to the left and what she guessed was the kitchen at the opposite end.

"This place is… Wow," she said, at a loss for words. "You could probably put all of Northbridge in here."

"It's a little much for me. My great-grandfather had it built to show off. He grew up in Northbridge, got his start here. He wanted the people to know how well he'd done. I think it was an in-your-face kind of thing. I'm the only one here most of the time and I only use a handful of rooms on this floor, so the rest is just a waste unless the whole family comes out for some reason."

He didn't offer to show her any more of the place. Instead he pivoted on the heels of his cowboy boots and led her down the hallway. "I've actually considered moving out to the guesthouse myself, but my office would have to stay here so I just do, too."

Lacey stole glances into areas they passed along the way. There was a recreation room, a media room, and what she assumed was the office Seth Camden mentioned because an enormous desk was the centerpiece among shelves, file cabinets, three computer stations and various other office equipment.

"This is the kitchen," he announced, as they went into the restaurant-sized space that was well-appointed enough to excite a professional chef. But it also had a homey feel to it in the oak pedestal table and chairs that occupied an alcove, and in the six bar stools that lined the granite counter topping the U-shaped island in the center of the room.

The entire rear wall of the kitchen consisted of a series of French doors. Seth led Lacey through one of these to the outside onto a wide, covered terrace, which stood two steps above a tiled patio that was framed by lavish gardens and more tall trees.

In the far, far distance Lacey saw the three barns she'd discovered the previous day when she'd been looking for him, and an eight-bay garage. But closer in, just at the edge of the patio, was a swimming pool and a pool house. On the side of the pool was a small structure nestled in one of the stands of trees. It was single-storied and built of the same stone and in the same style as the main house, with identical windows and shutters.

"Your home away from home," he told Lacey, crossing the terrace and leading her down the steps onto the patio.

"It's so cute," Lacey said spontaneously, as she followed him around the pool to the little bungalow.

Seth opened the guesthouse door for her and flipped a switch to turn on the lights inside but waited for her to go in ahead of him.

Lacey did, entering a large, open space. A third of that space was taken up by a kitchenette complete with appliances and a round table with two chairs. The other two-thirds of the space accommodated the living room where a sofa, an easy chair, a coffee table, matching end tables and lamps faced a fireplace and an entertainment center.

"Those French doors open onto a little private patio in back," he informed her, raising his chin at the paned glass doors directly across from the front door. "The fridge has some staples in it that are yours for the using. There's coffee and tea and cereal in the pantry. The key to the lock is on the counter."

Then he pointed a thumb over his shoulder at an archway on the other side of the living room area. "There's one bedroom, one bath through there. The bedroom has a double bed, another television, and a couple of bureaus along with the closet. Sheets and towels are in the linen closet in the bathroom. You should find everything you need, but if you don't, just let me know."

And it was all spotlessly clean, which Lacey appreciated.

"It's perfect," she said truthfully. "Even more than I need."

"Great. Come on, then, we'll pull your car around to the garage and I'll help you carry stuff in."

"Oh, you don't have to play moving man—"

"Hey, if the service is good enough, I could get a big tip out of it," he joked.

Tipping a Camden—now that would be a novelty. Although the slightly flirtatious way he'd said that could mean he was expecting something other than money...

Or not. Her imagination was running away with her. And she needed to stop it!

Then Seth said, "Accept my lugging stuff in as compensation for the oversight of leaving old junk on the property we sold you."

Lacey considered arguing. But the tour had been brief, and if she convinced him not to help her, he could very well disappear into the main house and that would be the last she saw of him. So she just couldn't make herself deny his help.

They retraced their steps around the pool, through the house and out the front door, where Lacey got behind the wheel of her car and Seth slipped into the passenger side. He stretched a long arm across the back of her seat as if he'd been in her car a million times and pointed to where he wanted her to go with his other hand.

"Head a little ways farther around the fountain to that clearing in the trees—that's the drive that'll take you back to the garage."

Lacey did as he instructed without telling him that she'd done much the same thing the day before in her search for him. But when she reached the garage she refused his offer of access to one of the bays. "It's easier if I just park alongside of it—my hands and arms are usually full when I'm coming and when I'm going, and it's enough to maneuver the car door without dealing with a garage door, too."

"Sure," he said, as if that didn't surprise him, either. "But if you change your mind…"

"Thanks."

The man seemed so easygoing and laid-back. Where was that ruthlessness and relentlessness that her college professor had said marked the Camdens? That had given them such success? This guy seemed to take everything in stride.

Lacey parked and popped the trunk, and she and Seth got out of the car. It took multiple trips to unload her suitcases and two laptop computers, as well as a printer, a fax machine and several cardboard file boxes.

Seth volunteered to make the last trip alone for what remained of the file boxes while Lacey took her suitcases into the bedroom.

It was every bit as nice as the rest of the guesthouse; it had its own set of French doors that swung out onto the private patio, which was completely secluded by well-tended hedges and more shade trees.

After opening those doors to let in the cooler evening air, she went back into the living room just as

Seth returned with the file boxes. He held his power-ful arms straight out in front of him, biceps cut and bulging as they bore the weight of the boxes. The sight made Lacey's mouth go dry.

"Just set them down with the others. I'll organize at some point," she instructed in a quiet voice, as she tried to focus on the task and not the man perform-ing it.

"I shut your trunk and locked your car doors—al-though there isn't really a need around here," he in-formed her as he set the boxes atop some others. Then he faced her and slid a hand into one of his front jean pockets, and Lacey's gaze just followed without think-ing about where her eyes would end up.

When she realized that she was basically looking at his crotch, she yanked her head up in a hurry.

"You left these in the ignition," he said, pulling her car keys from his pocket.

He was being nice and considerate and thoughtful and conscientious, and her mind was in the gutter.

Even as she silently chastised herself, Lacey did a frantic search for something safe and bland to say to distract herself and make sure he didn't know she was thinking about him inappropriately. She settled on "So how is it that a Camden is a cowboy?"

Had that sounded sort of disapproving? She hadn't meant it that way.

Seth Camden arched one eyebrow. "Because the only jobs that matter are jobs that require suits and ties?"

So it had sounded disapproving.

"No!" Lacey was quick to respond. "It's just that the Camdens are...you know—*big business*. One of the *biggest* names in business—I even learned about your great-grandfather and grandfather in college. So I was surprised when my father said you had property in a place as small as Northbridge. And then to find you working the way you were yesterday..."

All sweaty and sun-drenched and sexy...

Lacey curbed those wandering thoughts, too. "I just didn't know that any of the Camdens *didn't* wear suits and ties on the job."

"Oh, it happens," he said, as if she were being shortsighted. But then he seemed to shrug off any offense he might have taken and answered her initial question. "We have old ties to Northbridge—"

"I remember that this is where your great-grandfather started out—"

"And where my grandmother was born and raised, where she and my grandfather met—"

"Really? Your grandmother was from Northbridge?"

"So was my mother—she met my father when he was here after he graduated high school. My grandmother converted pretty well to city girl, but my mother never did. She liked it here better, so when she was alive—and my father was busy working, which was most of the time—she would bring us kids to stay here. I guess country life just got into my blood. After we lost our folks, my grandmother would only bring us all here periodically, but it was still where I felt the most at home. So when I was old enough to make the choice, this was the life I opted for."

"Are you the hermit of the family?"

He laughed. Lacey wasn't sure whether she was relieved to hear it or if it was the sound of his laugh alone that she liked so much. But either way, she reveled in it.

"I'm not a hermit, no," he answered. "I just like country life, working the land, working with the animals. But we own over thirty farms, ranches and dairies across the country, and they're all my responsibility. I have managers at each place who report to me every day—sometimes more than once a day. I oversee things from here, then travel a few times a year for a closer look at what's going on. I keep a small plane on a strip at the Billings airport so I can get anywhere I need to be in a matter of hours if there's a problem."

Of course whatever a Camden had a hand in had to be on a grand scale. Lacey didn't know why she'd thought otherwise. Seth Camden might look like a cowboy, he might run a ranch and do the work of a cowboy, he might even have the cowboy's sense of decorum that had prompted him to help her move in, but she should have guessed that there would be more to him and to what he did than merely running a simple small-town ranch.

Before Lacey responded to what he'd said, he changed the subject.

"I think I can get out to your construction site tomorrow to take a look at what was left there. It probably won't be until late in the afternoon, so there won't be time to clear anything out, but it'll give me an idea of what's there and if I'll be able to do it all myself or if I'll need help or a dolly or a trailer or what."

"I'm not sure what you'll need, either. I do know that there's some sort of farm equipment thingy—"

He laughed. "Farm equipment *thingy?*"

"I don't know what else to call it—it's behind the

barn and it looks like it hooks up to a tractor or some-thing. But I couldn't begin to tell you what it is or what it does. So you're right that you probably need to get an idea of what there is to move before you try to do the moving."

"And tomorrow is okay?"

So she knew for sure that she'd get to see him again tomorrow…

She reminded herself once more that she shouldn't be thinking about such things.

"Tomorrow is fine," she said, as if it had no impact on her whatsoever. "Late afternoon is actually better for me because my meetings are all in the morning and early afternoon, and once the crew has left for the day I switch over to office work and that's the easiest for me to interrupt…"

That hadn't sounded good either…

"Not that you'll be an interruption. I just mean that's the best time for me to get away…"

Of course if she couldn't get away personally, there were other people who could show him what he needed to move. But somehow Lacey didn't want anyone else to do it…

"About four-thirty or five?" Seth said, not appear-ing to notice that she was flustered.

"Four-thirty or five is great," she agreed, deciding it might be better if she said less because every time she said more she seemed to put her foot in her mouth.

He headed for the door. "There's a landline on the wall in the kitchen—" He pointed to it. "My cell phone number and the number for my house are on a notepad next to the phone. If you need anything, just call. Try my cell first—that's the likeliest way to reach me."

"You don't have a housekeeper or staff who's over there even when you're not?" Her father had an assistant at work and a housekeeper at home who always knew how to reach him. It just seemed likely that a Camden would have at least that, too.

But something about the question made Seth Camden chuckle. "I have a lady who comes in once a week and cleans up the rooms I use. If family is due in for some reason she brings two of her friends to spruce up the whole place, but other than that everybody who works here works on the land."

Lacey nodded, realizing that again what she'd expected of him and the reality were two different things.

Seeing that his hand was on the doorknob, she said, "Thanks for the help tonight."

"Don't mention it." He opened the door to leave.

And for absolutely no reason, Lacey felt the urge to say something—anything—to keep him there even a moment longer.

So she said, "You know how to get to the site tomorrow?"

Dumb. There wasn't a single dumber thing she could have said.

Seth paused with his hand still on the doorknob to grin at her. "Uh... I do. I used to own the place, remember?"

Lacey grimaced. "Force of habit—I can't keep straight who's local and who's not, so I just automatically ask if anybody coming out to the site knows the way."

"Well, I do."

"Sure. Of course you do. I'll just see you tomorrow then."

"Right."

He stepped outside and closed the door behind him.

There was a big picture window not far from where Lacey was standing, and she instantly looked through it to watch Seth Camden walk around the pool and back to the main house.

With a cowboy's swagger that made her mouth go dry again.

Which was cause for her to command herself to look away, to put the image and every thought of the man out of her mind.

But still she went on watching until he disappeared inside the French door they'd come out of.

And as for thoughts of the man?

Even out of sight, he wasn't out of mind.

For the second night in a row.

Chapter 3

Lacey did not ordinarily go through her day watching the clock. Certainly since she'd been given the training center project, she'd been so swamped that she very often worked eighteen hours before exhaustion told her that it was well past quitting time. She'd always been shocked to realize just how late it was.

But on Friday, sitting at her desk in the original farmhouse that was being used as the construction site headquarters, she checked the time so often that it seemed as if she were aware of every minute that passed. Of how much longer it was until four-thirty. Until Seth Camden was due.

And that made her more disgusted and aggravated with herself than she'd ever been before.

What was wrong with her when it came to this guy? She was thinking about him every waking moment. She was dreaming about him when she finally could sleep. She was picturing him in her mind's eye. Ogling him when she did see him. She'd even spent this morning looking across the pool every chance she got, while she was getting ready for work, just in case she might catch a glimpse of him.

And this was all happening now, of all times. Just when she had the kind of chance she'd strived for since she was a little girl, the chance to prove herself once and for all, the chance to be a real part of her father's love of football, the chance to actually be on Team Kincaid and prove she could handle the responsibilities her father had previously thought only to entrust to a son.

Now of all times, when the last thing she needed was the slightest distraction, not only was she distracted but that distraction was coming in the form of a man—proving her father right...

Morgan Kincaid had always relegated his daughter to the sidelines—where women belonged, in his opinion. Women, he'd said frequently, didn't belong in seats of power in the business world and especially not in the world of football. Cheerleaders. Receptionists. Secretaries. Possibly assistants. Decorators. Event planners. Morgan Kincaid had a very limited vision of the role of women anywhere. But in the Kincaid Corporation and when it came to football, those were the best positions that could be hoped for.

A woman, he insisted, would always eventually meet a man, and focus on getting him to marry her. Then, when she did succeed in marrying and having a family, that family would be more important to her than a job.

To Morgan Kincaid, that was just the way it was.

He was sexist, old-fashioned and downright silly. Lacey had argued with him again and again, citing any number of women for whom his theory didn't hold true. But her father was a stubborn, hardheaded person and there had been no telling him differently. Especially when it came to his daughter. Who he was convinced would ultimately end up a wife and mother.

Yes, Morgan Kincaid employed Lacey—after battles and battles to convince him that she wanted to work, that she could work, that she should be allowed to work. But until now, the best Lacey had accomplished within the Kincaid Corporation was to oversee the remodeling of new office space, the hiring of office and restaurant staff, discussing menus with the chefs, working in public relations and marketing.

But to play a role in any important project—particularly when it came to football? No way.

Until now.

Now, when—even though it was by default—Lacey had been given the opportunity to oversee the building of the Monarch's training center. The Monarchs—the NFL's newest expansion football team. Owned by her father. His dream come true.

But Lacey *had* gotten the job purely by default.

It was her twin older brothers who Morgan Kincaid had been convinced would carry on his legacy—both in football and in business. But long ago her brother Hutch had turned his back on the game, disappointing and alienating himself from their father because of it. Hutch had only recently returned to the family fold but not to the Kincaid Corporation—Hutch owned his own very successful chain of sporting goods stores, and it was clear he had no desire whatsoever to have anything to do with the Kincaid Corporation or working for their father.

Hutch's twin, Ian, had also had a period of alienation from the family, but had come back to the position of second-in-command at the Kincaid Corporation. Even now Ian was the chief operating officer of the Monarchs—a position he retained because he was needed there.

But as Seth had said, Ian had gotten the girl rather than the property. In the midst of acquiring the land for the training facility, Ian had met and fallen in love with Jenna Bowen. He and Jenna had ended up engaged, and Ian had been instrumental in helping her retain her family farm rather than purchasing it from her because it was the originally approved site for the training center. That had stirred Morgan's ire.

Then, to make matters worse, the McDoogal property that Ian had been confident they could get had instead been sold out from under them to the Camdens. And Morgan Kincaid had lost his second choice, as well.

Their father had been livid.

Morgan had tempered his anger enough not to out-and-out fire Ian and enter into another of the rifts that had cost him both of his sons for a while. But there had still been consequences for Ian. Morgan had punished him by taking the entire training center project away from him.

And because Morgan was determined that the project be overseen by a member of his family, by someone he was convinced had an unwavering loyalty to him, he'd reluctantly turned to Lacey. But not without letting her know that he would be watching her very, very closely.

Ian seemed to be taking his punishment in stride. He was currently far more focused on his bride and on his new life. Not only had Ian become Jenna Bowen's husband, he'd also taken on the role of father to Abby, Jenna's orphaned niece. They had adopted her as their own daughter. Ian had assured Lacey that he wasn't holding it against her that she'd been granted the project and had offered her whatever services or advice she might want.

But what Lacey wanted was to do this on her own. And to do it so well that she could finally carve out a niche for herself in the Kincaid Corporation and in her father's eyes. She'd fought tooth and nail for even small jobs on important projects in the past, and her father had left no doubt that it was only his deep desire to keep the business in the family that had garnered this opportunity for her. That this was her greatest test.

But Lacey didn't care how she'd come to have the project, and she didn't care how much pressure she was under to succeed. She was still determined to show her father that she was as much a value as his sons.

And nowhere, nowhere, nowhere in any of that did she have even a split second to be attracted to someone. She couldn't risk taking her eye off the ball.

Not even to look at Seth Camden's fabulous rear end.

Or any other part of him.

This was her moment. And she couldn't blow it. She wouldn't blow it. She was going to make the Monarchs' training center a crowning jewel. She was going to do this job so well that her father would wonder why he'd ever put so much stock in his sons and discounted her.

And she was *not* going to get distracted by anything or anyone. Certainly not by a man.

Even if that man was great-looking.

It was just that thinking about Seth Camden seemed to have become second nature to her. And trying not to think about him was distracting on its own.

Those blue eyes. That slow smile. That tight backside and those thick thighs. Those massive shoulders and muscles rippling in the summer sunshine that first day, flexing under the weight of file boxes last night...

The image of him haunted her, and she just couldn't seem to shake it.

But she was going to! she swore to herself. She was going to right now!

Except that at that exact same moment she glanced at the clock in the corner of her computer screen, registered that it was nearly four-thirty and—without another thought—saved her work, put her computer on standby and headed for the bathroom.

If Seth Camden was going to be there any minute now, she had to make sure her upswept hair hadn't wilted, that her silver-white blouse wasn't too wrinkled and was still neatly tucked into her gray slacks, and that her mascara hadn't smudged. And she wanted to put on a little lip gloss...

"He'd say he was right..." she muttered to her reflection in the cloudy old mirror that hung above the rusty bathroom sink.

Her father would say he was right, that here she

was, finally in a seat of power, important responsibilities bestowed upon her, and what was she doing? She was thinking about a man. She was worrying about how she looked for that man rather than working. She was suspending work in order to be with that man…

Delegate, Lacey told herself.

Someone else could show Seth Camden what his family had left in the attic and the barn. That was definitely not a job she needed to do.

But then she wouldn't get to see him…

Oh, but she hated that the thought had voiced itself.

She told herself to go with delegation. To return to the farmhouse's dining room that she was using as her office, go back to what she'd been doing—to what she should have finished hours ago except that her attention had lapsed so many times into thoughts of Seth Camden—and not so much as leave her desk to deal with him or with the issue of the things his family had left behind.

That was what she told herself all right.

But when the sound of wheels on gravel announced that someone had just driven up to the front of the house, she did a quick swipe of the lip gloss, judged her appearance satisfactory, and left that bathroom to turn toward the old house's entrance and not in the opposite direction to her office.

And when she caught her first glimpse of Seth Camden getting out of his big white truck, dressed in cowboy boots, jeans and a Western shirt, and looking even better than he did in her mind's eye?

She knew there was no way she was getting anyone else to show him around.

And she merely went outside to meet and greet him.

* * *

"As far back as when I was a kid, this place was only used for storage and for a few meetings my great-grandfather and grandfather had out here," Seth was saying as he and Lacey walked to the barn.

Meetings for some of the under-the-table deals the old-school Camdens were suspected of? Lacey wondered. But of course she didn't ask that.

She'd gone out to meet Seth at his truck the minute he'd arrived. She didn't even want anyone else to incidentally encounter him and suggest that they show him what he needed to see. Now she had him all to herself. Which made her inordinately happy...

"My brothers and sister and cousins and I all played in the barn and pretended the house was haunted," he went on. "When it sold, I came out here for the first time in about a year. There was hardly anything left and I needed to leave town on business, so I sent a couple of my guys to deal with what needed to be dealt with. I'm sorry they missed things, but now that I think of it, I didn't say anything about getting up into the attic or looking behind the barn."

"There's also a desk in what I'm told is the tack-room, too," Lacey said, as they reached the old barn. "I'm using the house as the construction office and the barn for construction supplies and equipment. I'm not really sure how anyone realized there was anything in the attic, but my crew is all over the barn and they thought the tackroom would be a good place to store screws and nails and hardware—the smaller supplies. They'll be putting up some shelves, but I don't want them to do that until the desk is out of there so

I can be sure they don't damage it in case it has some value to you."

"I'll be surprised if it does, but thanks for the consideration."

There was lumber already stacked in different sections of the barn, and Lacey led the way through it to the tackroom in the rear. When they reached it, she opened the door for Seth to go in ahead of her.

And yes, when he did—even though she tried not to—her gaze dropped for a split second to his derriere. She hated herself for it, she really did. She silently berated and reprimanded and chastised herself. But still she enjoyed that glimpse of perfect male posterior.

"Yep, I remember that desk now," he said, as Lacey followed him into the room.

He took a closer look at it, hoisting one end to test the weight—probably with the thought of whether or not he could lift it himself. But when he did that the desk slid back several inches and something underneath it caught his eye.

"What do we have here?" he said, more to himself than to her.

He pushed the desk far enough out of the way to expose what appeared to be a hatch in the floorboards underneath it.

Seth hunkered down and Lacey lost herself once again in staring at his thick thighs stretching the denim of his jeans, the pure breadth of his back, the way his dark hair curved to his nape. And when his biceps bulged with the force required to pull the hatch up, chills danced along Lacey's spine.

"Buried treasure?" she said when he yanked out an old trunk from a narrow compartment under the floor, her voice cracking and giving away the fact that she was watching him rather than what he was doing.

He didn't seem to notice, though.

"Kind of looks like a pirate's treasure chest, doesn't it?" he said, setting the trunk beside the hole in the floor. "But as far as I know the Camdens have always been pretty landlocked, and this isn't big enough for *too* much treasure."

It was about the size of two shoe boxes stacked on top of each other. Hammered silver corners sealed the distressed metal that it was made of, and it was closed tight with a rusted padlock hooked through the latch.

After palming the padlock, Seth said, "Wonder where the key to *that* is? Probably long gone. I'll have to saw it off to see what's in here."

"Gold doubloons?" Lacey suggested.

He picked the trunk up and shook it. But whatever was inside didn't sound like coins. It just made a thunking noise.

"I don't think so," Seth said. But beyond that he didn't seem overly curious as he stood again, balancing the trunk on his hip. "I might as well take this with me now and see if I can find a key that fits the lock. But the desk will have to wait. Want to show me the *farm equipment thingy?*"

He was smiling.

"It's through this other barn door," Lacey said, leading him from the tackroom through a door at the back that opened to the outside.

"Ah, that's just an old rotary hoe," Seth said the minute he saw it. "But you're right, it isn't going to be easy to get out of here. I'll need a different truck than I drove today so that I can hook up a trailer bed and haul this away."

"So another day for that, too," Lacey said, sounding cheery at that prospect. Despite the fact that she needed him to get his things moved, she was still happy to think that there would be another time when he'd come out here.

And again, she hated herself for that feeling.

"Any chance I can put off moving things until next Friday?" he asked, as they went from the barn to his truck to drop off the trunk and then on to the house for him to see what was in the attic. "The truck with the trailer hitch on it is having some work done and won't be back until then. And I'd like to do everything at once."

If she said that wasn't all right did that mean he'd have to make more than one trip?

It was tempting to find out. To see if she could get him out there twice. But that was where Lacey drew the line with herself. She was being silly and she knew it.

So she said, "Sure."

"You can let your guys start building the shelves in the tackroom—that desk is too battered already to be salvaged, so it doesn't matter if they bang it up some more before I get it out of there. I'll just use it for kindling anyway."

They'd reached the house by then. Lacey was ahead of Seth as they climbed the steps to the second floor. It didn't occur to her until they were already under way that her position in front of him put her own rear end at his eye level. It made her self-conscious and she suddenly wished she'd let him go first.

But she still hadn't thought of a way to switch places with him when they were at the foot of the four steps that led up to the attic from the second floor, so she had to take the lead on those, too. And when she stepped up into the attic itself and turned around, she caught him raising his eyes in a hurry so she knew what he'd been looking at.

But she did feel a hint of secret gratification in the fact that he had a small smile on his face.

The ceiling in the attic was high enough for them both to stand up—although Seth had to slouch as he took stock of what was there.

An old, rolled-up rug. Boxes filled with Christmas decorations, toys, books, clothing, bedding and various discards. An antique mirror. A rocking chair. And other stuck-in-storage odds and ends.

"Doesn't look like anybody got up here at all," Seth commented. "Apparently it's been overlooked for quite a while. But I'll take care of it next week."

"Or whenever," Lacey heard herself say. "We need the space in the barn, but this stuff can stay as long as the house does—which will be until construction is finished. Then we'll demolish the house and the barn, and this whole area will be practice fields—which is actually why we need a different road…"

"I saw the model downstairs. Why don't you show me what we're talking about?" Seth proposed.

Lacey was pleased with herself for having remembered the road issue in the midst of her distractions. She was only too glad to take him back downstairs where the architect's model had been put on display in the living room of the farmhouse.

She was also only too happy to talk about the train-

ing center project once they got there. To explain all
that the center would encompass.

Referring to each toylike section of the model, she
pointed out the administration building, and the conditioning center and training facilities that would include locker rooms, hot and cold tubs, meeting rooms,
training areas, weight rooms, equipment rooms and a
video department.

She told Seth about the three full-sized practice
fields that were planned, one with synthetic grass, the
other two with natural grass—and that one of those
would be heated in order to maintain a year-round un-
frozen practice field.

She showed him where the living quarters and cafeteria would be, and talked about the two racquetball
courts that would be used both for training and for
leisure by the team and the staff.

"But a new, more concise survey told us that the
ground is flatter here, where the house and barn are—
which means that it's a better place for the practice
fields. The change can be easily accomplished at this
stage by just turning the whole compound around to
face the other direction," she concluded. "The only
problem is the road into the facility. We don't want that
to lead to the fields. We want it to lead to the administration building, because the administration building will be the main point of entry. It will house the
visitor's area, the media room for press conferences
and our trophy display area—for all the trophies the
team hopefully wins."

Lacey was afraid she'd gone on longer than she
should have, but since Seth didn't give any indication
that he was bored, she added, "And what that all boils

down to is that we need a new road that comes in off the highway right through there—" she drew the route through the model with her index finger "—which is your property…"

"I can see that," he said without committing to or refusing anything. Instead, he went from looking at the model to looking at her with interest. "So this is all your baby, huh?"

"With my father looking over my shoulder because this is the first time he's actually trusted me with anything important. But yes, it's all my project."

"What were you doing before this?"

Was he only trying to get her off the subject of the road, or was he actually curious about her?

Lacey couldn't tell for sure. Maybe it was only ego, but she thought he might actually be curious about her.

Going with that assumption, she said, "What was I doing before this? A little public relations, events planning, hiring some low-level personnel, decorating, office management."

What she didn't tell him was why she'd been given only those jobs. Then, possibly to avoid the subject, she heard herself mention something else that really was her *baby* and hers alone.

"A year and a half ago I also started a sideline of my own," she said, her voice slightly hushed, as if she shouldn't be talking about this, even though it was no secret.

"Your own football team?" he teased.

"No, but I've always wanted more involvement with the sports side of things, and it occurred to me that there are a lot of female sports fans out there. But the clothes with team logos on them are primarily aimed at male fans. So I started to design, manufacture and market a line of women's clothing using the colors and the emblems of major sports teams—some casual wear and some workout."

"Really?" Seth asked. He sounded genuinely interested.

"I've called it Lacey Kincaid Sportswear."

"How's that going?"

"It's actually taken off. I started with internet sales—which were good—but now my brother Hutch has placed some things in his stores, and he just told me the other day when I got to town that he can't keep them on the shelves. He wants to carry my entire line, and I'm going to have to increase production to keep up."

"On top of building the Monarchs' training center?" Seth said. When he put it like that, it seemed daunting.

"I know I should probably put the clothing line on hold—of course the training center is my number one priority. But—"

"You like the clothing line." His tone of voice suggested that he could tell just how important it was to her.

"I do," she confessed. To everyone else she acted as if Lacey Kincaid Sportswear was nothing more than a hobby that had flourished. She didn't understand why she was confiding in this man now.

But she was. And she continued to. "In a way," she went on, "the training center is my father's baby—as you say. And the sportswear is mine."

"So why take this on?" Seth asked with a nod at the

model of the facility. "Why not just go with the clothing line and let someone else have this headache?"

"Oh, I couldn't pass on this opportunity. I'm like a rookie player called up from the bench to show what I can do at the Super Bowl. *Nothing* could keep me from doing this. It's just that I don't want to give up the other, either."

"That makes for a very full plate."

"*Very* full. Especially if I step up production on the clothing line to meet the demands of Hutch's stores."

"But you're going to do that, right? You wouldn't want to pass up *that* opportunity, either."

"I put it into motion this morning. Between meetings for things here."

He studied her for a moment, and Lacey had no idea what was going through his mind.

Then he said, "Maybe I don't have any business saying this, but I can't help noticing that when you talk about the training center you seem kind of tense and... I don't know, like you're swimming upstream. But when you talk about your clothing line you actually smile and get into it, as if you're enjoying yourself more with that. Do you feel obligated to do the training center for your father?"

"Obligated? No! Seriously, this is the chance of a lifetime for me. The clothing line is just...for fun. It isn't as if it's important."

"Seems important to you."

"It's just a silly girl thing. Clothes. You know. But the training center—that's *huge*, and I'm lucky to get to do it."

"It *is* huge," he agreed, as if he didn't envy her the job.

"But I can handle it."

Why had she felt the need to assure him of that?

"If you say so. I'm just wondering, if it was a different situation, would you want to...?"

"Oh, I would. I do. I wouldn't pass this up for anything in the world."

Seth nodded—he seemed convinced. Then, pointing at the front door with his chin, he said, "Well, given that you are one very busy person, I probably shouldn't keep you."

It was on the tip of her tongue to tell him he could keep her all he wanted.

But she caught herself before she said it, and silently read herself the riot act for even thinking such a thing.

"We do need to discuss the road, though," she reminded him.

"I'm going to have to think about that," he said, as he headed for the door with Lacey tagging along.

"It's really only a strip of land—"

"Through one of my cornfields, which could cut down on quite a bit of yield. I'll have to do the calculations to know for sure what it would cost me."

As they went out into the late-afternoon heat and walked to his truck again Lacey persisted. "We'd be interested in buying that strip to add to what we've already purchased. So we would own the road, but you could retain the land on both sides of it." She knew that to merely lease access could get sticky in the future and become costlier than an outright sale. Not to mention that she'd learned in her class that any open-ended deal with the early Camdens had resulted in some form of takeover later on, and she didn't want to risk anything.

"We aren't in the habit of dividing our properties," Seth said.

But if the only road leading to the training center was owned by the Camdens, they could make demands under threat of cutting that road off and have the Kincaids at a disadvantage.

"Maybe you could make an exception..." Lacey said, wondering where that flirtatious tone had come from. And hating herself for it, both because that wasn't how she did business and because she should in no way be *flirting* with Seth Camden.

And yet it almost seemed to gain her some headway because it made him grin as he opened his truck door. And rather than hurrying to get into the truck, he hooked a boot heel on the runner, draped a long arm over the top of the open door and lowered those Camden blue eyes on her.

"I'll take a look at some things. Run some numbers. Study some property lines, and see what I can come up with," he said in a tone that might have had a bit of the flirt to it, too.

"I'd appreciate that," Lacey said, again more coyly than she should have.

"How much?" he countered with an attitude that told her they were venturing further and further from any sort of professionalism.

And yet she couldn't stop herself from smiling when she said, "How much would I appreciate it? A lot."

But that just made him laugh a laugh that sent ripples of something purely pleasant through her. "Are you just workin' me, *Ms.* Kincaid?"

Lacey laughed, too, because she couldn't help it. "Maybe a little," she admitted. "But I *would* be grateful."

He merely smiled at that while those blue, blue eyes of his gazed down at her as if he liked what he saw. "That might be enough," he said under his breath.

For no reason Lacey understood, her own gaze drifted from his eyes down to his mouth and she was suddenly thinking that there was an electricity between them that could easily lead to more than an exchange of banter. That could lead to kissing...

And what might it be like to be kissed by him? she found herself wondering.

Those supple lips eased into a lazy smile just then and made her wonder all the more. Made her actually wish he *would* kiss her. Just so she'd know...

Now *that* was unprofessional!

What was there about the Camden cowboy that kept getting to her?

Without an answer for that—and with even more self-rebuke just for what was going through her mind—Lacey was the first to break eye contact. To take a step back.

"I should get to work," she said in a voice that sounded like someone who had been thinking about something they shouldn't have been.

"Sure," he answered, pivoting around to climb behind the wheel. "I'll probably see you at home," he added as he closed the door.

Lacey nodded in confirmation even though she wasn't sure it was true, since she'd looked for him so many times this morning without catching a single glimpse of him.

Still, she hoped he was right.

Then he turned the key in his ignition and put the truck into gear, casting her one final glance and raising a big hand in a wave before he drove off.

And yet even then she didn't budge. She stayed where she was, keeping her eyes trained on the plume of dust his tires left until it had settled and he was long gone.

You have a training center to build, she pointed out to herself.

And she had a booming new business of her own, too.

But there she was, watching after a truck—and a man—she couldn't see anymore.

And trying not to acknowledge the part of her that was imagining herself sitting in that truck's passenger seat, driving off with Seth Camden.

The same part of her that continued to wonder what it might be like to have him kiss her.

And itching just a little for that, too…

Chapter 4

Lacey didn't get back to the guesthouse on Friday until almost midnight. There weren't any lights on in the main house. She had no way of knowing if that meant that Seth had gone to bed, if he was sleeping elsewhere, or even if he was sleeping in his own bed but not alone—those were the unwelcome and inappropriate thoughts she'd had as she'd let herself into the small bungalow.

One way or another, she had not gotten to see him again on Friday.

On Saturday she was up at 4:30 a.m. and out the guesthouse door by five. And again there was no sign of Seth.

It was after ten o'clock Saturday night when Lacey returned to the Camden ranch, and this time as she trudged wearily from her car and past the main house, the scent of Italian food drifted out to her through the open French doors that formed the kitchen's rear wall.

Who was cooking at ten o'clock on a Saturday night?

"Hey! Are you just getting home from work?"

It was Seth Camden's voice that called to her and before Lacey could make herself look for him, she thought, *Please don't let him be over there with a date....*

"I am," she answered, turning her head in the direction of the main house.

No one was in sight except Seth. He was standing at the kitchen sink, looking at her from the window over it.

Her first impression was that he was fresh from a shower—his hair was combed back and appeared to be slightly damp, and his face had a sort of just-scrubbed look to it. He also wasn't dressed for public display—he was wearing an ancient crewneck sweatshirt with the sleeves cut off and left ragged, and—from what she could see of his waistband—a pair of extremely faded jeans.

But he could have just had an evening of crazy-wild lovemaking that had left him and his partner hungry so they'd showered, thrown on just anything and decided to fix themselves a late supper.

That was the scenario Lacey imagined in a way that both titillated her with the fantasy of herself as the partner, and tormented her with the thought that there might be another woman in that role. Another woman who just wasn't in the kitchen at that moment. Because surely a Camden—and particularly one as gorgeous as Seth—would not be spending Saturday night alone...

"Hang on a minute," he said, turning to the stove to peer into a pot before he came back to the kitchen window.

"Are you cooking? At this hour?" Lacey ventured.

"Yep. Want to eat?"

He said that so easily. Seemingly without the kind of second thoughts that were already going through her mind about why she should say no.

But Lacey had had a cold hamburger for lunch and a protein bar out of her purse for dinner. Her options inside the guesthouse were crackers or cereal. And in that instant it seemed silly not to follow his lead and just say yes.

So that's what she did.

"I would *love* to eat! It smells wonderful and I'm starving."

Oh. But what if there *was* a date somewhere on the verge of making an appearance in the kitchen...

For one instant, she'd forgotten what she'd been fretting about. She really was tired...

"My pasta water isn't boiling yet," Seth was saying. "And I just started to put a salad together—I'm about fifteen or twenty minutes away from eating if you want to make a pit stop."

Lacey had no doubt she looked like something the cat had dragged in. Which added another reason she hoped some bombshell girlfriend wasn't going to appear. But it also occurred to her that she could use fatigue to rescind her acceptance, so she said, "Are you alone in there?"

Seth made a show of glancing over his shoulder

at the otherwise empty kitchen before he brought his blue eyes to her again. "Unless there's somebody here I don't know about," he said as if the question was odd.

So no date. No evening-long romp that had prompted a late supper. Just Seth.

And me....

"Do I have time for a quick shower? I'm kind of grungy," she said.

"Sure."

"Then I'll be right back," Lacey said with way more glee than she wanted there to be in her voice.

Renewed energy surged through her. She picked up speed as she rounded the pool and let herself into the guesthouse. The minute she'd closed the door behind herself she began a frantic unbuttoning of her blouse as she kicked off her shoes. Then down went her slacks to be flung onto the couch as she headed for the bathroom for the fastest shower in history.

After barely toweling off, she again opted for speed—and, taking Seth's lead, comfort, too—and put on her most comfortable undies and bra, a fresh pair of white shorts and a simple red V-neck T-shirt. Then she bent over to brush her hair from the bottom up, catching it at her crown in a rubber band, before she applied a little blush, a little mascara and some lip gloss. Then she slipped her feet into a pair of sandals and went out the guesthouse door, her fifteen-hour day a faint memory.

Seth was setting two places at one of the small poolside tables as she rounded the pool to join him.

"I was afraid I might be intruding on a date or something," Lacey said. Her two nights of wondering if he was with a woman spurred her to fish a little.

"Nope, no date. I don't do much of that, actually," he said, again as if he had no qualms about being perfectly honest.

And since that was the case, Lacey said, "So a girl-friend or a fiancée or a wife or someone isn't going to jump out of the bushes?"

"No girlfriend. No fiancée. Definitely no wife."

In other words, he was free as a bird...

Not that it mattered, Lacey told herself. She just hadn't wanted to come face-to-face with a woman who had claim to him. She didn't want to be the third wheel.

"What about you?" he countered. "Boyfriend? Fiancé? A husband lurking somewhere while you're out here in the boonies building a training center?"

"With my schedule?" she asked with a laugh. "I couldn't keep a houseplant alive, let alone a relationship."

"You *do* work a *lot*," he said.

Lacey didn't know why, but it sounded like he didn't approve of that so she skirted around the topic. "What about you? Why are you eating so late?"

He smiled as if she'd scored some sort of point. "I was working, too. But not by choice. I had a cow that needed help calving out—"

"*Calving out*—does that mean she was giving birth?"

"It does. And she needed help. I was doing that until about an hour ago. Then I came home, cleaned up and decided to go ahead and cook what I'd been planning to cook earlier."

"So you made what's causing those fabulous smells coming from inside?"

"All by my lonesome. And with tomatoes and onions and garlic and basil that I grew."

"I'm impressed."

He grinned. "Maybe you should reserve judgment until you taste it. But you can do that now—everything's ready, I just need to bring it out. And I recommend the wine I opened—the chef has already had a glass and tells me it's pretty good."

Lacey laughed. "So you're a glass ahead of me, is that what you're saying?"

"Just one."

"A glass of wine sounds great. Let me help carry things out."

He didn't refuse the offer, so Lacey followed him into the kitchen where together they managed to collect a bottle of wine and two glasses, a bowl of pasta, another of salad, and a basket of bread.

Outside at the table once again, Seth poured the wine and encouraged Lacey to help herself to the food. One bite of the thin strings of pasta with the sauce made from fresh produce and Lacey moaned her approval.

"That's wonderful!" she marveled when she'd swallowed. "And you made this?"

He smiled. "I take it you don't cook?"

"I can't even boil water," Lacey admitted. "Many attempts were made to teach me to cook because that's what girls are *supposed* to be able to do. But growing up, I refused to cooperate with anything that came with that stipulation. It was my blanket rule and I stuck to it—if my brothers didn't have to do it, I wasn't doing it."

"Just to make a point?"

"Just to make a point."

"Hmm. I don't know if I ever refused to do anything growing up just to make a point. Or if I would have gotten away with it if I had."

"I never did much of anything that *wasn't* to make a point. And then I got older and lost that freedom— in order to have any role in the Kincaid Corporation I had to do jobs my father considered *suited* to a woman. Until now." Lacey tasted the salad of butter lettuce, tomatoes, radishes, carrots and red onions—all of which Seth said he'd also grown. It was topped off with his own secret dressing that was vinegary with an herbal accent to it.

The fact that he'd made his own salad dressing, too, recharged Lacey's curiosity about him so she backed up the conversation a little and said, "I would be surprised if any man made this meal, but a *Camden?* Didn't you eat all of your meals with a silver spoon after they were prepared by your family's own personal chefs?"

He laughed, took a drink of his wine and said, "Oh, you haven't met my grandmother..."

"The one from Northbridge?"

"Actually, I really only knew one grandmother because my mother's parents died when I was too young to even remember them. But yeah, the one from Northbridge. We call her GiGi—her name is Georgianna, and Grandma Georgianna was a mouthful, so somewhere along the way it got shortened to GiGi. She raised us all—with the help of my great-grandfather and a husband-and-wife team who have worked for her forever. GiGi was unquestionably captain of the ship, but all four of them took care of my two brothers, Cade and Beau, my sister, January, and our cousins, Dane, Dylan, Derek, and the triplets, Lang, Lindie and Livi."

"There was a plane crash, wasn't there? That killed a big portion of your family at once?" Lacey said, recalling that from her college course.

"There was. When I was eleven. There was a trip planned for the adults—fishing for the men, shopping for the women, while the kids all stayed at home with the nannies—"

"So there *were* nannies," Lacey said. One of her assumptions of how the Camdens lived had just been confirmed.

"There were then. Before the plane crash we lived in our house with our parents, and our cousins lived in their house with their parents, and H.J.—our great-grandfather—had retired because of a heart condition and moved in with GiGi and Gramps. And Margaret and Louie—the married couple I told you about. They live above the garage. They—and Gigi, who's very hands-on—do most things or oversee what's hired out."

"And in your own houses with your own parents, there were nannies. And were there cooks and maids and butlers then, too?"

"My mother and my aunt were more into the high-society status than GiGi ever was, so yes to cooks and maids and housekeepers in our homes with our parents. But I don't remember a butler anywhere around, no."

She was teasing him and he seemed to know it—which Lacey appreciated. But the conversation was satisfying some of her curiosity about him.

"So your great-grandfather—H.J., the person who

had gotten the whole Camden ball rolling—retired at one point? I thought he worked right to the end of his life?"

"Information from your college course?" he assumed.

"Yes."

"H.J. had turned the running of Camden Incorporated over to Gramps, my dad and my uncle, and moved in with GiGi and Gramps about three months before the plane crash. He was still vital, just slowing down. Then, two days before everyone was set to go on the trip, H.J. fell and hurt his back. He ended up at home but in traction, and there was no way he could travel. GiGi says she didn't care about the shopping trip—if you knew her you'd understand that—so she volunteered to stay home to look after H.J.—"

"Ahh, so that's why your grandmother and H.J. weren't on the plane," Lacey said, as she finished her meal and settled back in her chair with her wine.

"But everyone else was," Seth said solemnly.

Lacey knew from her college class that there had been suspicions that the engines on the private plane had been tampered with, possibly by one of many people who resented the Camdens because they considered themselves wronged or cheated by them.

But the crash had been so devastating that there hadn't been enough of the plane left intact to prove anything. Which some people considered fitting since the underhanded maneuvers, manipulations and machinations that H.J. and his son, Hank, were suspected of had never been proven, either.

"You were just eleven—how old were the other kids left behind?" Lacey asked quietly, sympathetically.

"I was the oldest of the grandkids. The youngest were six—my sister Jani and the triplets. The other five kids were seven, eight and nine."

"Not babies but still, little kids."

"Yep," he said sadly. "Ten scared, freaked-out, upset kids."

"I know when my mother died—Hutch and Ian were twelve, I was ten—it was awful. No amount of money or status or anything made that any better. But at least we still had our dad. I can't imagine what it would have been like to lose him, too...."

"Well, we had GiGi. And H.J. and Margaret and Louie," Seth said. "GiGi brought us all to her house, let us know that from that minute on that's where we were going to live, that she loved each and every one of us, that we were hers and that there was no question that we were going to stick together—one big family. And that's just what we did. H.J. went back to work to stabilize the company and get people he trusted to keep things going under his supervision until we all grew up and could take over—so technically he went back to work but primarily in a supervisory role. He did his part in raising us, Margaret and Louie pitched in like surrogate parents and that was that."

"How old was your grandmother at the time, when she took this on?"

"She was fifty-five. H.J. was eighty-eight and GiGi went on looking out for him, too—making sure he ate well, that he took his medications, saw his doctors, that he didn't overdo it. Margaret and Louie were only forty, so that helped when H.J. and GiGi were a little outdated here and there—not to mention all the other ways they helped out. But we all lived in GiGi's house near the Denver Country Club in Cherry Creek. That's where H.J. died at ninety-six, overseeing Camden Incorporated until just the last few months of his life, when he had a stroke and was only lucid part of the time."

There was more sadness in Seth's tone. Lacey realized that regardless of the fact that she'd learned about the Camdens as if they were bigger-than-life, almost fictional characters, the founder of all of Camden Incorporated had just been family to Seth. His greatgrandfather. One of the people who had had a hand in raising him after his parents were killed. Someone he'd loved and lost.

But after a moment of solemn silence Lacey wanted to get the conversation back to something lighter, so she said, "And your grandmother took care of her father-in-law and raised ten grandchildren without someone else to do the cooking?"

Her attempt to brighten the tone worked because Seth laughed. "*Do not* discount Margaret—together with my grandmother they could run the country. But my grandmother alone is a little bitty lady with a core of steel and some ironclad views of things. One of those views is that family takes care of family, no matter what—which is why Margaret and Louie have always been considered family and why GiGi wouldn't even think about farming us out to anyone else or so much as sending any one of us to boarding school—"

"But you must have at least been in private school, for the sake of security," Lacey said, thinking about the rumor that the Camden plane had been tampered with to cause the crash. Surely safety must have been an issue after that if not before.

"We did all go to private school, yeah," Seth confirmed. "But other than that, my grandmother did not believe in spoiling us. We made our own beds, we cleaned our own rooms, and all the other chores were revolving. My grandmother worked right alongside Margaret and Louie and we were their assistants—we dusted, mopped, vacuumed, washed walls and windows, did yard work and anything and everything else. GiGi would never ask Margaret or Louie to do a job she wasn't in there doing with them. In fact, Margaret and Louie are still there and GiGi still works with them even now, when she's about to turn seventy-five and they're into their sixties."

"And when it came to cooking?" Lacey persisted, going back to the origins of this conversation.

"When it came to the cooking there was never anyone hired to do that. GiGi and Margaret fixed breakfast—and lunch on weekends and vacations. But Margaret and Louie went home to their own house at six sharp, and, with the exception of some prep work Margaret might leave behind, dinners were just us—GiGi and H.J., while he was with us, and ten kids in the kitchen, all with jobs to do. Then we sat down to eat together and there had to be a damn good excuse for anyone to miss that," he concluded with a wide smile that told Lacey he was fond of the memories.

"I never would have guessed that was how you were raised. I think *I* was more spoiled than you were," Lacey admitted.

"Like I said, GiGi has strong opinions on things— not the least of which is how kids should grow up. And that attitude has its roots right here in Northbridge."

"She raised you all as if you were living on a farm

in a small town rather than within spitting distance of the Denver Country Club?"

"She did. There's just no one like her. She's the salt of the earth, and I don't know anyone more universally loved than she is. She's practical and sensible and weathers every single storm with a stiff upper lip, a positive attitude, an eye for how things will work out for the best, and a determination to do anything she can to help—again, probably part of her small-town, everyone-lends-a-hand mentality. I've never known her not to have both feet on the ground, or heard of a problem she wasn't ready and willing to tackle—"

"After all, she took on *ten* grandchildren."

"She probably would have taken on twenty without blinking an eye."

"Am I wrong, or do you just adore her?" Lacey asked.

Seth smiled unashamedly. "We all do. Everybody who knows her does."

Seth had finished eating, too, and was lounging in his chair, his blue eyes honed in on Lacey.

"So," he said then, "nannies or no nannies for the Kincaid kids?"

"No nannies. My father also has very strong opinions about things and one of those is that a mother raises her own children—that's a woman's job along with running a household and taking care of her husband."

"But you lost your mother when you were ten."

Obviously he hadn't been simply content to talk about himself, he'd been listening to what she'd said, too.

"I did. But my father's sister—my aunt Janine—

had gotten divorced just before that, and without kids or much financial means of her own, she moved in. When my dad was away—which was a lot in the football years—Janine took care of the three of us. But whenever Dad was around—or if he could manage taking the boys with him—Dad thought it was his place to make sure Ian and Hutch were raised under his influence. Janine's real job was to take over my mother's role of teaching me how to be a *lady*. But I'm not sure how successful that turned out to be…"

It had gotten very late while they'd eaten and talked, though, too late for Lacey to get into her own childhood. So she stood and began to gather dishes. "Let me help you clean up. You must be tired from playing barnyard obstetrician, and I have to be up again in a few hours so I can get to the site and finish all of my work before—"

"Your brother's wedding—it just hit me that that's tomorrow night," Seth said.

He stood, and together they got everything inside. Once they had, Lacey set their plates in the sink and turned on the water.

"You didn't go to the rehearsal dinner tonight?" Seth asked then.

"No. Hutch is marrying Issa McKendrick—"

"I know. I'm invited. I know the McKendricks well."

"Then you probably also know that it's going to be a simple wedding, with only one of Issa's sisters as maid of honor and Ian as best man, so there wasn't anything I needed to be there for to rehearse."

"Still, it's your brother's wedding," he insisted as if he couldn't imagine her missing any part of that.

"I know, but I had work to catch up on, which is also true of tomorrow. And in fact, in order for me to get finished in time for the wedding, I need to start before dawn again."

"Wow, you just never quit. I'm surprised I could tie you down for a little while tonight."

"How could I resist the smell of your cooking?" she joked, even as she thought that she could have resisted that more easily than she could have denied herself the time she'd just spent with him.

Seth reached a muscular arm in front of her and turned off the water before she'd rinsed more than their plates. "I'll take care of that, I don't want to be blamed for bags under your eyes at your brother's wedding—go get some sleep."

"You're sure? I may not be able to cook, but I'm okay at doing dishes."

"That's what the dishwasher is for."

Kitchen clean-up *would* have bought her a little while longer with him but Lacey couldn't seem to convince him that she should stay. She finally had to concede his point and head for the French doors.

Seth went with her. Lacey stepped outside while Seth leaned against the doorjamb.

She turned to face him, intending to thank him for dinner, but before she could, he distracted her a little by hooking his thumbs into his jean pockets—looking too sexy to bear.

Then he said, "If we're both going to your brother's wedding tomorrow night it seems kind of silly to take two cars. Plus I'm thinking about you being exhausted behind the wheel after working from before dawn. What do you say you let me be your chauffeur?"

"A Camden as a chauffeur?" she teased.

"At your service," he said with a humble bow of his head.

Lacey had been dreading going to the wedding alone. And while Seth *was* only suggesting a carpool, if they arrived together they might stay together...

"That would be nice," Lacey heard herself say before the *shouldn'ts* kicked in.

"Do you need to go early?"

"No, like I said, it's a pretty casual thing." Lacey wasn't sure how many people knew that her soon-to-be sister-in-law was pregnant with a baby that wasn't Hutch's. Hutch had made it clear to the family that while he might not be the biological father, he considered Issa's baby his and he wasn't in the least disturbed by the circumstances, but the information seemed like Issa and Hutch's to let out. Still, as a result of the situation, they'd decided to keep their wedding simple.

"I'm just going as one of the guests," Lacey added, "so I don't need to get there any earlier than anyone else."

"Well, the wedding is at seven—I'll be ready and waiting for you anytime after six. Just come over and we'll go."

"Okay," Lacey said, suddenly looking forward to her brother's wedding more than she had been before. Much, much more...

But with that settled, there was nothing else to keep her so she said, "Thanks for dinner—it was really great. My compliments to the chef."

Seth grinned. "I'm glad you liked it. But everything tastes better when you have someone to eat with," he added in a voice that was quieter, his beautiful blue eyes peering thoughtfully into hers.

And suddenly, from out of nowhere, Lacey just wanted to kiss him. She wanted him to kiss her. And not in the vague way kissing had crossed her mind when they'd said goodbye at the construction site the day before. Tonight there was nothing vague about it.

In fact, the urge was strong enough for her to actually tip her chin slightly in invitation.

With Seth's shoulder still against the doorjamb he seemed to lean forward at about the same moment. Also just slightly. But enough so that Lacey thought it might actually happen. That he might actually be going to kiss her...

Until he drew back as if he'd caught himself and merely said, "Guess I'll see you tomorrow night, then."

"Tomorrow night," Lacey confirmed, hoping her extra-cheery tone concealed how let down she felt. "Thanks again for dinner." She took a deep breath and turned to walk around the swimming pool to the guesthouse, where she let herself in without a backward glance.

But once she was inside, the door closed behind her and the lights still off, she cautiously peeked through the gap between the wall and the curtains on the window beside the door.

There Seth was, continuing to lean against that doorjamb, his gaze on the guesthouse.

And that was when she knew that she hadn't imagined anything, that he had considered kissing her.

But whether or not he'd considered it, he hadn't done it.

Should I have? she wondered.

No. She shouldn't have taken the initiative and kissed him, she told herself.

Because while she hated to admit it, there was a tiny part of her that couldn't help believing that if any kissing would ever be done, he'd have to do it.

But that was just stupid. She silently chastised that part of her that clung to the ultratraditional, sexist views she'd been raised with.

But stupid or not, that was just the way it was.

So, disappointed, she stepped away from the gap in the curtain and headed for bed.

Knowing that if Seth never kissed her, it wouldn't ever happen.

But still hoping that at some point he might.

Because for no reason she understood, it was becoming a very big deal to her that he did...

Chapter 5

The wedding of Issa McKendrick to Hutch Kincaid was held on Sunday evening in Northbridge's Town Square at the juncture of Main and South Streets. The centerpiece of the square was an octagonal-shaped, whitewashed gazebo with a steep red roof.

For the occasion of the wedding, the entire gazebo had been adorned in tiny white lights and red roses. The ceremony itself was held at the top of the five steps that led up onto the gazebo. Guests sat on white wooden folding chairs on the manicured lawn below, beneath a canopy of more tiny white lights that draped out from the gazebo's eaves like a giant umbrella over that part of the square.

Lacey had never been to a wedding quite like it. When her brother had said he and his bride-to-be wanted it simple and casual and fun, Lacey had envisioned a backyard affair like others she'd attended that had claimed to be casual. In her experience, such events were every bit as formal as any other wedding—they would be held in backyards that were more like the rear portions of an estate. White tents would be in abundance, candles, linen and silver would still adorn every table. The only really casual part of these weddings was that they were held outdoors.

But her brother's wedding was more like a friendly, small-town festival with elements of a beautiful, gracious picnic.

The brief ceremony that united Hutch in his best black suit and a veil-free Issa in a white silk Empire-waist dress with a scalloped, calf-length hem, included Hutch's two-year-old son, Ash. Ash, who was Hutch's son with his late wife, stood proudly in front of the new couple in order to be included in the nuptials that made them all a family. Dressed in his own black suit, the toddler barely fidgeted at all, but he did very solemnly parrot both his father's "I do" and Issa's, making everyone laugh.

Afterward the reception was held on the Town Square lawn underneath the canopy of lights, where round tables were set amid a border of tall oak and pine trees all lit up in more tiny white lights.

The gazebo then became the bandstand for the four-piece band, while a buffet was set out and guests helped themselves to smoked meats drenched in barbecue sauce, potato and macaroni salads, corn on the cob, and mini-cheesecakes rather than wedding cake.

"Leave it to Hutch to have some kind of country hoedown wedding and not invite anyone who could do his business any good," Morgan Kincaid complained, as he walked up to Lacey and Seth. They'd just finished wishing the happy couple congratulations and left the receiving line.

After years of estrangement between Morgan and Hutch, father and son had reconciled in June. While tensions were lessening between them, Morgan could still be critical of Hutch. Of all of his children, actually.

Lacey knew there was no sense defending her brother. "Dad, you know Seth Camden," she said instead, fully aware that her father and Seth had met and trying to remind her father of his manners.

Morgan Kincaid instantly turned on the good-ol'-boy, football-celebrity charm and extended his hand to Seth to shake. "How are you, Seth?" the older man asked, as if they were long-lost friends.

Seth shook the outstretched hand. "I'm good, Morgan. You?"

"Great, great! Has my daughter talked to you about that little glitch with the road to the training center?"

"I told you we've been talking about it, Dad," Lacey interjected. She didn't appreciate her father interceding as if he could do a better job. Or talking business at the wedding.

"I'm looking things over," Seth assured him. "I don't see any reason why Lacey and I won't be able to come to some terms."

"Fantastic! The sooner the better," Morgan said pointedly. "And once we get this settled I'll make sure you have tickets to any Monarchs game you ever want to see—you *are* a football fan, aren't you?"

Seth shrugged apologetically. "I catch a game now

and then if I don't have anything else to do, but I wouldn't say I'm much of a *fan,* no."

Lacey had to fight not to flinch. There wasn't a worse thing Seth could have said to her father, or a faster way to turn Morgan Kincaid against him, no matter who he was. Not being a fan of the game that her father lived and breathed for was tantamount to criminal, and once he found that out, the other person ceased to exist for him. It was something Lacey had always known, but learned all over again not long ago. In a way that had struck much too close to home and might have affected her entire future if her relationship with that nonfootball fan had gone on.

Morgan Kincaid frowned as darkly as if Seth had just blatantly insulted him and turned so that his shoulder cut Seth out.

"I'll be at the site at seven sharp tomorrow morning," he said to Lacey. "You can bring me up to date on everything before the groundbreaking ceremony. You're on schedule, ready to go?"

There was nothing Lacey could do to bail Seth out, so she merely answered her father's question. "I'm on schedule for the ceremony. But our bulldozer was supposed to be here last week and didn't make it. The contractor says Thursday now, so—"

"And you let him get away with that when construction is set to start on Tuesday?"

Lacey's stomach clenched. "Things will still start on Tuesday. We just won't have a bulldozer until Thursday—"

"Which means that Thursday will be lost to unloading the thing, and it won't be in use until Friday and you'll be starting a full week late!"

"It's under control, Dad. It isn't as if everything is hinging on the bulldozer. Other things will still begin this week—materials are being delivered, other excavation can start, it'll be fine." Lacey was all too aware of her father's increasing ire and the fact that Seth was there listening.

"If you can't handle this—"

"I can handle this just fine," Lacey said firmly.

"Delays cost money, Lacey," her father said, as if that were news to her. "If you're soft you'll get run right over on this project. You have to let people know you're boss and you won't stand for screwups. If you can't do that—"

"I *am* doing that," Lacey said, forcing calm when what she really wanted to do was raise her voice.

"This isn't just fooling around, little girl. This is the NFL," Morgan Kincaid said, irking Lacey all the more by calling her *little girl*.

"You perform or you're out," he continued to rail. "That's the way it is. The way it was for me. The way it is for you when it comes to this. Don't forget what I'm trusting you with."

"I know what you're trusting me with and how important the Monarchs and this training center are to you, Dad. We'll have all day tomorrow before the groundbreaking ceremony to go over everything, and you'll see that I have it all taken care of, that I know what I'm doing."

Her father gave her the beady-eyed stare she and her brothers dreaded before he said, "I better not have made a mistake giving you this."

"You haven't."

After another dose of the stare, her father moved

off to talk to other wedding guests without saying more to Lacey or Seth.

A moment of silence passed while they both watched Morgan Kincaid go. Lacey used that moment to take a deep breath and try to regain some calm, to release the tension her father almost always raised in her.

"So that's your dad, huh?" Seth said when her father was well out of earshot.

"I'm not exactly sure what to apologize for first," Lacey responded. "He gets very dismissive whenever he finds out anyone isn't a football fan. And I'm sorry you had to overhear the whole training center thing. And he didn't even say goodbye to you…"

Seth waved it away. "No big deal for me. But are you okay?"

"Oh, sure," Lacey said with some resignation. "I'm used to him. And I'm going to prove that I'm up for this job, that I can do it. When he finally sees that, hopefully he'll relax—at least a little—about letting me head this project. Then in the end, he'll have his dream training center for his dream football team, and I will have earned my stripes."

Seth nodded, but there was a sort of perplexed frown pulling at his brows. His expression made her wonder what was going through his mind.

There was no time to investigate it, however, because just then Ian joined Lacey and Seth with his new wife, Jenna, and tiny Abby in tow. Abby was dressed in an adorably frilly dress that Lacey gushed over, and since Ian and Jenna greeted both Seth and Lacey warmly, it eased the brunt of what Morgan had left them with.

It also made Lacey glad that her brother was counteracting the sour impression of her family that Seth had to have been left with.

She knew that in her father's eyes, Seth Camden was now someone to be disregarded.

And that anytime she was with him, she would be in that same category.

"7:00 a.m.—*sharp!*"

"I'll be there long before that, Dad," Lacey assured her father. He had stopped by her chair on his way out of the wedding and leaned near her ear to remind her.

It was the only contact she'd had with him since their initial conversation right after the ceremony, but still it was a relief to her to watch him go.

He'd put a damper on the evening that she'd gotten to spend with Seth. Her hope that driving together might mean that they could sort of be at the wedding together had more than been met—Seth had stayed by her side the entire evening, and no one would have guessed that he wasn't her date for the occasion. But her father had set a bad tone at the start, and Lacey hadn't been able to enjoy much of the wedding or Seth's company.

Luckily he seemed to know everyone in the small town and consequently most everyone at the wedding, and there had been no shortage of people wanting to say hello, wanting to talk to him, wanting to meet her. They hadn't actually been alone, so Lacey didn't think it was obvious that she had been preoccupied.

But now it was after eleven, other guests were also beginning to leave, and with the removal of the stress her father had caused her, Lacey felt herself deflate.

Apparently it was noticeable because just then the elderly man who had come to their table to talk to Seth left, and the instant Seth turned his attention back to Lacey he laughed and said, "I was going to see if I could persuade you to dance just once, but you look worn-out all of a sudden."

"Just what every girl wants to hear," Lacey countered with a laugh of her own.

Still, she sat up straighter and pulled back her shoulders.

She was wearing a simple navy blue sheath with a crocheted short-sleeved shrug over it. The shrug barely concealed her shoulders and was tied between her breasts to make the dress fancier, camouflaging the front of the dress in the process. But still she didn't want it to gape open due to bad posture.

And she didn't want to appear as weary as she felt. Especially when Seth was still going strong and looking fabulous in the impeccably tailored gray suit, white shirt and maroon silk tie he was wearing.

He leaned forward and said in a voice for her ears only, "You're gorgeous. You just look tired. How about if we head home?"

He made that sound so couple-ish. So caring. And it sent a warmth through Lacey that she had no business feeling.

"Would you mind?" she asked him.

"Nah. I keep farmer's hours myself. I was just waiting for you to say the word."

With that, Seth stood and pulled her chair out for her, handing her the sequined clutch purse that she'd left on the table.

"I just want to say good-night and one more congratulations to Hutch and Issa," Lacey said.

Seth stayed by her side for that, too, so Lacey was sure he heard it when Hutch said, "Don't let Dad be too hard on you. You can always tell him to take that training center and shove it, you know."

"I know," Lacey assured her brother with a laugh.

Then she and Seth said their good-nights, and Seth took her back to the sports car they'd driven here.

He held the passenger door open for her, told her to buckle up once she was in the seat, then closed the door again.

As Lacey fastened her seat belt, she watched Seth round the front of the sports car, his height and broad shoulders dwarfing the low-riding vehicle.

He slipped in behind the wheel and started the engine.

"So..." he said, backing out of the parking spot on South Street. "Your dad... I know he had to be a pretty hard-hitter on the football field, but he doesn't seem to pull any punches with you, either."

The Camden property was fairly far outside of Northbridge proper, so Lacey knew she was in for about a half-hour drive. She slipped off her shoes, angled herself slightly to the right in the seat and let her head fall against the headrest.

"He's just like that," she told Seth. She drank in the sight of his profile, knowing that she must be overly tired when she found even his ear sexy.

Of course this was just a simple car pool, nothing more, and so it was silly to even think such a thing...

"My dad didn't get where he is by being an old

softy," she added. "Surely that must be true of your family, too…"

Seth cast her a smile. "When it came to business? Yeah. But I don't ever remember a time when any one of us kids was spoken to the way your father spoke to you tonight. Was he that tough on you growing up, too?"

"Oh, no. I was the little darling of the family. The baby and the girl. He was much harder on Ian and Hutch than on me. My earliest memories are of him drilling them for football, not letting up on them. But I was jealous of that," Lacey admitted with a laugh at how that sounded.

"You were the apple of your father's eye, and you were *jealous* of how hard he was on your brothers?"

"I guess it wasn't that I was jealous of how hard he was on them, but of the attention they got, of how much more important they seemed to him. He didn't just dismiss them, he took everything they were doing to heart."

"But he dismissed you?"

"With me it was always just a pat on the head and telling me I was pretty as he passed by. But the boys were his chance to keep the Kincaid legend going, to relive his glory days through them when his football career ended and they were just beginning to play. He was sure they would carry on for him in his business, too. They were *important*. It always seemed like I was adopted as my mother's consolation prize—a girl to keep her busy, to keep her company, to dress up and take shopping and have follow in *her* footsteps."

"You were adopted?" Seth asked with some surprise.

"All three of us were. Adopted and paraded out as the poster kids for adoption—it's one of my father's favorite causes. Ian and Hutch hated it, but it was the one way that I got to be included, so I was okay with it."

"You weren't *included* otherwise?"

"It wasn't as if my father ignored me, he just... Well, football, training the boys to be the next generation of football stars, building his corporation and indoctrinating them into taking that over someday, too—that was what my father was about. It always seemed as if a person only had any real value or worth or stature if they were involved in football or business pursuits with him. It's a great big boys' club. And I was The Girl. Just The Girl..."

Seth glanced at her with a grin. "Well, yeah, you are a girl," he said, approval in his voice.

Lacey laughed and delighted in that approval but didn't acknowledge it.

Instead she said, "I'm not saying that there's anything wrong with the way my father believes things should be if that's the way a woman wants it. My mother, my aunt and any number of women I know now are perfectly content and fulfilled doing what my father thinks women should do—my aunt Janine took over for my mother raising us kids and has always gone to tons of luncheons and committee meetings and charity fundraisers. She met and married one of my father's business associates five years ago, and she's really happy making a home for him, giving his parties, all of that."

"But it wasn't for you?"

"I was just so bored at fashion shows—"

"You have your own clothing line," he pointed out, finding a flaw in what she was saying.

"Not haute couture or even dresses—my stuff is sports-related. It gives women a way to *participate,* to be a part of things."

"Ah…"

"But when I was a kid, a teenager, sitting at fashion shows, going to etiquette classes, or luncheons or cotillions or being on dance committees—I felt like I was being forced into a straitjacket! Everything my father was encouraging and pushing and prodding and priming my brothers to do, that was what I wanted to do."

"You wanted to play football?" Seth asked with some amusement.

"If I could have, I would have! But it wasn't so much the playing as it was… I don't know—being denied access to what I wanted, if that makes any sense. It was like what my father was doing, what my brothers were getting to do, was more interesting, it was more of what I wanted to do than what I was *supposed* to be doing."

"Plus you felt left out…"

"As a kid, yes, I did. I *was* left out of a lot. But more than that, I just didn't want to sit on the sidelines. Okay, sure, that's where I had to stay during football games. But in every other way—in life, in the Kincaid Corporation—the sidelines were *not* where I wanted to be. And I certainly didn't want to be relegated to them for no better reason than that I wear dresses. That just didn't make any sense to me when I had the energy, the drive, the desire to be doing so much more."

Drive and desire…

There had been a hint of those things when she'd said good-night to him last night.

But Lacey didn't want to think about that. She didn't want to start thinking about kissing him again.

To start wanting him to kiss her and then have him not do it.

Again.

"So here you are," Seth said, interrupting her detoured thoughts. "Building your father's training center. Getting your chance to prove yourself."

"Finally! Yes," she confirmed. "So if my father is gruff with me, if he's putting the pressure on. I consider it my rite of passage."

"Okay," Seth said, as if he understood. "But I have to say, I'm glad I grew up a Camden and not a Kincaid. GiGi made sure we all knew that with the name and privilege came duties and responsibilities. She wanted us to be decent human beings, to give back, to do good wherever we could. But otherwise, I think we had it a lot easier than you all did. I know no one felt any more or less included or important—or as if they had to prove themselves—because they were born male or female. And I also know that if I'd been at the wedding of one of my brothers or my sister or one of my cousins tonight, we would have been drinking and dancing and toasting, and no one would've been riding anyone else about work."

"Dad just wants to be sure that everything is perfect. I understand that," Lacey said in her father's defense. "And I told you, this is my chance."

They'd reached the Camden ranch by then and as Seth pulled around the house and into one of the slots in the garage, he said, "I guess that explains why you're so happy to be working eighteen-hour days."

"Are you keeping tabs on me?" she challenged more flirtatiously than she'd meant to.

He shrugged, and her gaze rode along on those big, broad shoulders before she glanced at the smile that said she'd caught him at something.

"I wouldn't say I'm keeping *tabs* on you, no. But I've noticed when you're around or coming or going. When you're not around…"

Lacey never came or went or passed by a window in the guesthouse without glancing at the main house hoping for a glimpse of him. And there were innumerable times when she was home when she made a special trip to a window to look across the pool, too. Now she wondered if he was doing the same thing from his vantage point. Because it sounded like that might be the case.

She hid the satisfaction that gave her by finding her shoes on the car floor and putting them back on as she said, "Yes, I am happy to be working eighteen-hour days. Or more if I need to. I'll do whatever it takes."

"That's something I've heard before," he muttered to himself, as he turned off the ignition and got out.

Lacey didn't wait for him to come around. She let herself out and met him at the trunk of the car.

She wasn't sure what his muttering had meant but the way he'd said it didn't sound altogether favorable so she opted to let it go. Instead, as they walked out of the garage together, she said, "Will I see you at the groundbreaking tomorrow?"

"Rumor is it'll be quite a spread," Seth answered.

"Dad wants the whole town to be excited about

Northbridge being home to the Monarchs. The team and all the trainers and coaches and staff are coming, and with an open invitation to the town, we're expecting quite a turnout. After the ceremony there'll be food and drinks, and the model will be on display under its own tent where everyone can see the layout and the way it will all look. It seems only fitting that you should see the groundbreaking on the ground that used to be yours."

Not to mention that she really wanted him to be there just for her sake, that getting to see him in the process of doing her job somehow didn't seem as taboo as she kept telling herself things like tonight were.

"It's tomorrow evening?" Seth asked.

"Six o'clock. We wanted it to be at a time that wouldn't interfere with anyone's work—again, so more people would come."

"My day should be wrapped up by then, so yeah, I'll probably be there."

Not much of a commitment. He'd said it almost as if there was a part of him that was reluctant.

"Maybe you don't want to see the first step of your family's farm turned into something else," she said.

"No, I'm fine with that," he said.

She was confused as to why he might have dragged his feet. But she didn't pursue it. He'd said he would come and that was what mattered.

Lacey wasn't sure why, but he'd gone with her to the guesthouse door rather than parting ways when they'd reached the pool and going to the main house himself.

But in keeping with how the rest of the evening had seemed, it was very much as if he'd walked her to her door after a date. And it was on the tip of her tongue to invite him in...

Which of course she wasn't going to let herself do.

Even though she secretly wanted to...

What she did was unlock the door, open it and take a single step inside before she turned to face Seth.

"Thanks for tonight," she said. "For driving and for keeping me company through everything. It was nice having an insider to introduce everyone and fill me in on who was who."

"No thanks necessary. I enjoyed myself. Even if I never did get you to dance."

"I hated cotillions, remember?" she said.

But the truth was that she'd avoided dancing with him despite wanting to more than he could know. She'd been too afraid all evening of finding herself in his arms. Of using that opportunity to hold on tighter to him than she should. Of resting her head on his chest. Of moving in close and pressing herself to him. Of doing any of the things that would have given away to her father that she was attracted to this man. That would have made her father think that he shouldn't have given her the training center project because she was going to prove him right and put a man before her work.

"You could have danced with someone else," she told Seth. She hadn't suggested that, though, because he actually might have taken her up on it.

"I didn't want to dance with anyone else," he said then, his deep voice quiet, a small smile beaming down at her as his blue eyes peered into hers.

"Maybe next time," Lacey heard herself say wistfully, thinking that if only there could be a next time. *Without* her father around...

"I'll see you tomorrow, though?" she added then.

"You will," he confirmed.

But that was all he did. He didn't add a good-night. He didn't move from where he was standing tall and handsome in that dashing gray suit, looking nothing like a small-town rancher. He merely went on gazing down at her, studying her.

And yes, kissing was on Lacey's mind once more. On her mind and making every ounce of her long for it.

But she wouldn't be the one to kiss him first. She wouldn't. No matter how much she wanted to...

Then Seth reached a hand to either side of the door frame to brace his weight and leaned in across the threshold to do exactly what she wanted—to kiss her.

But too fast!

Almost before she saw it coming, before she could respond, before she could even close her eyes, it was over...

Fleetingly, she considered taking it from there and dealing out a second kiss herself. A longer, more lingering, better kiss that she could actually savor.

But she didn't do that.

She just tipped her chin a little to let him know she wouldn't hate it if he did it again.

Only he didn't.

He just said a simple good-night, pushed off the door frame, turned and headed for the house.

Lacey shut the door and closed her eyes for a moment, trying to relive that kiss, barely recalling the feel of his warm, supple lips. The scent of his cologne. His breath against her cheek…

He'd kissed her.

He *had* kissed her!

So it wasn't just a one-way attraction…

She opened her eyes, and there in the darkness of the guesthouse she smiled a secret smile.

Because while she knew this shouldn't be happening, while she didn't have the time or energy for it to happen, while she needed to put everything she had into the training center project and into proving herself to her father, while tonight she'd also seen for herself that Seth didn't fit in with her family—the same disastrous way that way Dominic hadn't—Seth *had* kissed her.

And something a little giddy went off inside of her just knowing that he'd wanted to.

That he was looking every day and night for signs of her the way she was looking for signs of him.

That he'd given in at the end and kissed her.

And no matter how brief that kiss had been, it had still been a kiss.

Chapter 6

Lacey Kincaid was a dynamo.

That was what Seth thought repeatedly throughout the groundbreaking ceremony on Monday evening.

The ceremony itself was held under a circus-sized white tent with a podium at one end, tables laden with food and drinks along the sides. Attendees filled the rest of the space.

For Seth it was almost impossible to concentrate on Morgan Kincaid's speech, on Morgan Kincaid introducing each member of the Monarchs team and staff, on the mayor's welcome-to-Northbridge speech and the Monarchs-as-a-boon-to-Northbridge talk that the head of the City Council gave. He didn't even spare more than a glance at the Monarchs cheerleaders when they performed.

But he was aware of where Lacey was every moment, of her every movement.

It was clear to him that she was orchestrating and overseeing the entire event despite the fact that after introducing her father at the start, she never took center stage again. But from the background she directed speakers on and off the podium, and made sure there was smooth transition from the speeches to the introductions to the entertainment. She also began the applause at the appropriate moments, encouraging it from the large crowd that had come out for the event, and deftly quieting it when it was time for whatever or whoever was next on the program.

Sometimes, when Seth was watching her, she slipped away, behind the rear curtain of the tent that kept them all out of the August sun. But she was always gone only for a moment before she returned.

And he was always glad when she did. For no reason he could figure out.

She repeatedly checked the clipboard she had with her, spoke into what appeared to be a walkie-talkie and was quietly consulted several times by other people sidling up behind her to whisper in her ear. But to anyone who wasn't paying particular attention to Lacey, it all appeared to be Morgan Kincaid's show— he was the star, he was the host, and he was the one who dug out the first shovelful of earth when that rear curtain was dramatically lifted and he stepped off the podium to actually break ground amid cheers that Lacey instigated.

At the meet and greet that followed the ceremony, Seth sauntered around. He socialized with other townsfolk, but never without a portion of his attention on Lacey. He tried not to be transfixed by her, but no matter where he was or who he was with, he was still watching her bustle around, tending to everything, seeming to be in her element juggling half a dozen things at once and keeping up a hectic pace to do it.

The longer things went on, the more he realized that he wasn't likely to be able to rein her in and get even a few minutes alone with her. Yet he still couldn't keep his eyes off of her.

She was dressed much like she'd been that first day they'd met, when she'd found him out fixing the fence—blue-gray, pencil-skirted business suit with a conservative white blouse underneath the jacket, and three-inch-high heeled pumps.

Her shiny, pale blond hair was pulled into a twist at the back of her head with some curly ends sprouting out the top at her crown. Her cheeks were pink, her eyes were bright and her lips...

He'd kissed those lips on Sunday night—he couldn't stop thinking about that—and every time he looked at her, he just wanted to kiss them again....

Which he told himself over and over was a damned dumb thing to keep thinking because he couldn't even catch up with her to say hello.

And he knew from experience that that was the way it was with dynamos.

High-energy, ambitious, determined, single-minded, driven—not only had Lacey described herself in those terms, Seth recognized it in her. Especially when he saw her in her element at the groundbreaking. She was a whirlwind.

And that wasn't him. It wasn't *for* him.

He liked small-town country living, farming and ranching, specifically because it allowed him the pace *he* thrived on. Sure, the work he did was hard—sometimes backbreaking—and it took time and required a seven-day-a-week schedule and frequent predawn days and even late-night hours if he had a sick animal or a storm to gauge or any number of other things that could happen.

But there wasn't the kind of pressure, the kind of demands and anxiety and competitiveness that went with the corporate world, the business world.

The kinds of things that Lacey seemed to thrive on.

Not that there was anything wrong with what it took for either of them to flourish and be happy, to meet their goals. It just made them two very different people who wanted very different things, who lived very different lives.

And when things—people—didn't mesh, they didn't mesh. He knew from experience that he would take a backseat to the kind of drive and determination that fueled Lacey. And worse still, that she could want and expect him to change.

Given that, he told himself, he should stop dragging his heels and go home. He should stop standing around hoping that Lacey might find a minute to do more than cast him the few glances, the small smiles, the scant waves she'd cast him throughout this evening.

That's as good as it's gonna get, he thought. He should just give up the ghost and go.

Finally listening to himself, he wove through the crowd to get to the buffet table and set down the lemonade he'd been nursing. He decided along the way that he wasn't even going to make an attempt to say goodbye to Lacey, that he was just going to leave.

And that was when he saw her excuse herself from talking to a group of football players and—keeping her green eyes honed on him to the exclusion of all else—she crossed to Seth.

"Can I ask a favor of you?" she said when she reached him, not seeming to realize there was no greeting in that.

"Anything," Seth answered. He could have kicked himself for how grateful he was that she was finally paying some attention to him, for the fact that the hours he'd spent at this event hoping for a little time with her suddenly seemed like less of a big deal now that she was standing right there in front of him.

"It looked like you might be ready to take off—"

"I was."

"I haven't had time for a single bite of food today," she continued. "And that isn't going to change while this is going on. If I ask the caterer to pack some of this before everything is gone, would you take it home with you so I'll have something to eat when I get there?"

I should have known...

But apparently he'd been hoping that she was going to ask him not to go because disappointment flooded him when she didn't.

Still, he said, "Sure," chafing at the fact that now that she'd finally sought him out there still wasn't anything personal being exchanged between them, that she was only engaging him because she'd thought of how he could be of service to her.

Because that's what backseats were good for...

"Thank you *so* much!" she said, as if he'd rescued her.

"Sure," he repeated with an edge he couldn't keep completely out of his voice. This felt much too much like déjà vu to him, too much like times with Charlotte.

"Lacey!" her father called to her from the other side of the tent, motioning with one hand for her to come.

"I'm sorry I don't have time to talk. But I really appreciate this!" she said then, dashing away without delay after giving the caterer his instructions.

And just like that Seth was alone and watching her from a distance again as she jumped back in.

"Can you pack that food up now?" he asked the caterer. "I'm done here."

And in that moment when he said it, he was thinking that he was finished with more than the groundbreaking event. That he was also finished with letting himself be in the grip of this attraction to Lacey.

And he meant it.

Until he had the food he'd agreed to take with him and he was on his way out of the tent.

Because that was when Lacey's eyes locked on him once more and she smiled a smile that seemed to be for him alone.

A smile that made everyone else around them, everyone that separated them, seem to fade away.

A smile that drew his gaze to those lips once more.

Those lips he'd kissed.

And despite everything, despite his best intentions—and hating himself for it—he still just wanted to kiss her again...

It was after ten o'clock when Lacey's day ended and she finally returned to the Camden guesthouse.

Lights were on in the main house—she never failed

to notice that whenever she was coming or going—but there was no sign of Seth.

She soon discovered that he'd left the food she'd asked him to bring home for her in the guesthouse's refrigerator. She was dizzy with hunger.

But the guesthouse seemed stuffy, so she opened windows, kicked off her shoes, tossed her jacket over the arm of the sofa, and went barefoot—food containers, a napkin, a glass of water, and a fork in hand—back out to eat at one of the half-dozen poolside tables.

Another glance at the main house told her nothing had changed—Seth was still nowhere to be seen. She faced in that direction anyway, sitting down to eat but keeping the French doors in her peripheral vision.

The containers held finger sandwiches, pulled pork glistening with barbecue sauce, tiny hot dogs wrapped in puff pastry, and pinwheels of flour tortillas rolled like jelly rolls around refried beans, guacamole, peppers, olives and cheese.

Lacey was so hungry she didn't know where to start. She popped one of the pinwheels into her mouth, then jabbed her fork into the pork with one hand and picked up a hot dog with the other.

And of course, just when she was the picture of gluttony, Seth appeared in the main house's kitchen and caught sight of her.

She could see through the French doors that he was barefoot, too.

Lacey didn't know why that was the first thing she noticed about him, but it was. Barefoot but dressed in faded jeans and a plain white T-shirt, his dark hair only finger-combed but looking sexily disheveled, his face beginning to show the faint shadow of beard.

When he saw her he hesitated, and Lacey had the impression that he was tempted to do nothing more than a neighborly wave before going on about his business.

But then he came as far as the French doors, opening a single set of them and stepping only to the threshold, where he leaned against the frame. He seemed intent on staying there, since he crossed one leg over the other and both arms over his chest. Keeping his distance, maybe...

"Another long day, another late night," he said, somehow sounding disapproving of that.

"I'm glad it's over!" Lacey responded after swallowing her food. But she was too hungry to resist the bite of barbecue before she held the hot dog aloft and said, "I'll share if you're feeling like a snack..."

What she really wanted was for him to stop keeping his distance and come closer, to join her.

"Not hungry," he answered, staying where he was and giving her the sense that he was purposely being standoffish.

"I kept hoping I'd get to talk to you at the groundbreaking—I'm sorry that didn't happen," she said, not because she thought it mattered to him. She'd seen him chatting and mingling and fitting right in with his fellow townsfolk, and she doubted that he'd missed her the way she'd missed having even a moment with him. "It looked like you were pretty well occupied, though."

"I was hoping I'd get to see a little of you, too," he said.

"How about now?"

The invitation went out purely as a reflex because she just wanted him to come and sit with her, to give her those few minutes she hadn't gotten to spend with him earlier.

But he didn't instantly accept the invitation. Instead he seemed to ponder it, not appearing eager to oblige her.

Then, almost reluctantly, he finally shoved off the doorjamb and came with a leisurely cowboy swagger around the pool to her table.

Lacey was just happy to have him there and couldn't help a small smile between bites of hot dog, more barbecue and another pinwheel.

"You saved my life with this food," she told him, as he sat on the chair across from her. "At home there are a dozen fast-food places I could choose from even late into the night, but things aren't that way in North-bridge. And I had to take care of everything else at the groundbreaking—there was no way to take care of me, too."

"You were running around."

"Like a crazy person! I was thinking that once the ceremony was over and people were just eating and drinking and talking, I could take some time for myself. I thought I'd maybe see if you wanted to sneak away with me and a couple of plates of food so I could just have a breather." She confessed this a bit quietly because she wasn't sure that was something he would have been interested in, and she didn't want to presume anything.

"That would have been nice. I would have liked it," Seth said, still with some reserve.

"But there was just no way. Every time I'd get a bead on you, say 'Excuse me' and take a step, someone or something else would have to be dealt with. And then I saw you set down that glass and I just knew you were leaving before I'd even gotten to say hello…"

"So you figured the next-best thing was to enlist me to bring home food?"

There was still something in his tone that said he wasn't particularly happy with her, but she didn't understand it. She pretended she hadn't heard it and said, "Definitely not the *next*-best thing, but I was desperate. And if you'd just have something to eat so I'm not the only one of us stuffing my face, this is *sort* of what I was aiming for earlier…."

He studied her for a moment, and Lacey thought that he was choosing whether or not to go on being stiff and standoffish with her. She still wasn't sure what was going on with him.

But then he shook his head as if in concession, sighed, took one of the pinwheels and popped it into his mouth.

He also sat slightly lower and more comfortably in the wrought-iron chair before he said, "Where *is* home for you when you aren't here—the place with all the fast-food restaurants you could want? I know your father is based out of Billings—he told me that at the closing on the land. But what about you?"

"I live in Billings, too. Where I grew up. In the carriage house at my dad's, actually."

"You still live with your father?"

"The carriage house is separate," Lacey explained. "And farther away from my dad's house than the guesthouse is from you. Plus it faces away from his house, so my front door is on the block behind his. We never know when the other has company or is coming or going or anything. I have to go out my back door and across tennis courts and his whole backyard just to get to the rear entrance of his place."

But yes, she *was* defensive about it because it sounded as if she'd never left the nest.

Which was why she added, "I lived at college for four years, shared an apartment with a girlfriend after that, then lived with someone else for two years—until two years ago—but then it was… I don't know…less lonely to go back home than to get an apartment or a house by myself."

"The *someone else* you lived with was a guy? A husband?"

"A fiancé. I've never been married," she said, unwilling to say more, so she went in another direction. "By then my friends from high school and college were all married and having kids. Almost everyone I work with is male except for the few women secretaries or assistants—and they don't relax around me enough to be friendly or to make friends outside of work—so I was really pretty isolated. The carriage house seemed like a way to maintain my independence but still not be as cut off as I felt at the time."

"And I'm betting that in the two years since you moved into your father's carriage house you've been too busy to make any new friends."

Busy—that word had an edge when he said it, but Lacey wasn't quite sure why, so again she ignored it.

"I have been too busy. Especially since that's about the time I started to work on my clothing line. Since then I've basically had two jobs."

"And now you have the biggest job yet."

"And now I have the biggest job yet," she confirmed.

"So no personal life? No social life?" he asked, frowning a bit at her.

"Not really. I get the occasional invitation but I usually have to turn it down unless it's for business. And I haven't had time for dating—so no, not much personal life or socializing."

"What about hobbies? Don't tell me work is all you ever do."

Lacey shrugged. "Okay, I won't tell you that, but it's the truth."

"How about movies or TV or skiing or sailing or hiking or knitting or gardening or... I don't know— kickboxing. Isn't there something you do to wind down?"

Lacey laughed. "Winding down—now that's a trick I haven't mastered. Tonight, for instance, I'm tired but I'll still have trouble sleeping—"

Of course Seth was part of that problem lately because she couldn't stop thinking about him. Thinking about what they'd talked about or done. Thinking about him being just a few yards away. Thinking about what he might be doing or if he was sleeping—and what he might be wearing if he was. Thinking about that kiss last night...

"And while I'm having trouble sleeping, it seems like a waste of time not to bring a little paperwork to bed with me, so I guess you could say that that's what I do to wind down—paperwork in bed."

Seth shook his head again. He let his blue eyes bore into her for a long moment, his expression showing disbelief.

Then he sat forward and said, "Are you done eating?"

She'd been eating all along, but had definitely slowed down. "One more thing…" she said, peering into the containers until she found the small cup of butter mints she'd asked for.

She offered them to Seth.

He took two and popped them into his mouth. She did the same.

"Okay, now I'm done."

Seth stood and began to gather the food containers as he gave instructions. "Go inside and change your clothes. Put on something old and comfortable that can be washed. And shoes that can get dirty. I'll throw this stuff away, get some shoes myself and meet you back here in a few minutes."

"For?"

"I'll show you one of the things *I* do to wind down."

The thoughts that went through her mind when he said that shocked her. It didn't involve a change of clothes; it involved *no* clothes…

There was just something about this guy that brought out a randy side of her that she hadn't even known she had.

She might not have taken his orders except that the standoffishness he'd been exhibiting before was gone and she was so glad that she didn't want to rock the boat. Plus she was curious about what he had up his sleeve and—as always—she was enjoying being with him and didn't want it to end.

Still, she said, "Am I going to hate this?"

"Maybe," he answered with some orneriness.

But then he took her food containers around the pool with him and headed inside of his house. "Go on, change," he called over his shoulder.

Lacey gave him a mock-stern look.

But, smiling to herself, she pivoted on her bare heels and did as she was told.

Twenty minutes later, dressed in a pair of old jeans and a T-shirt, with her most worn-out tennis shoes on her feet, Lacey found herself being led to one of the three warehouselike, state-of-the-art, two-story barns behind the garage. A place where she assumed animals were housed.

"I'm not crazy about getting too close to pets that are bigger than I am—if that's how you're thinking to get me to relax, it might not be the best idea," she warned, as Seth led her inside.

He merely smiled.

The structure was dimly lit until he flipped a switch, and then it was flooded with bright light. Lacey could see a horse looking out one of the stalls in the distance to the right of a wide center aisle. That was the only animal in sight.

"That's Bud, but he's not who we came to see," Seth informed her. "We're here for Bud's wife, Milly. She's a sweetheart. I brought an offer of friendship that will win her over, so there's nothing for you to be nervous about."

Lacey had noticed that Seth was carrying an apple, but she'd thought maybe he was going to eat it himself.

"It's a little smelly in here," she observed, peering into empty stall after empty stall as they went up the center aisle.

"Smells like a barn. Since most of the animals are out in the paddocks, this is nothing."

As they reached Bud's stall, the big, black horse raised his head as if in greeting, and Seth patted his nose.

"Sorry to bother you, Bud," he apologized, pausing to take what appeared to be sugar cubes out of his pocket with his free hand and feeding them to the horse before they moved on to the next stall.

As they approached it, he said, "Milly, you have company."

A brown face with a white blaze down the nose appeared over the stall's half door in answer.

"Bud's wife, Milly?" Lacey asked with a laugh.

"Milly and Bud are my oldest horses—they've been here since we were all foals—after a lot of begging, my grandfather made them my seventh birthday present. They were a few months short of turning one. They were bought together, and they've been inseparable ever since."

"That's why they're the only two horses in here?" Lacey asked.

"They're fairly old for horses, and they don't do as well in the high heat or the coldest cold, so they spend a lot of time in the barn year-round, where it's climate-controlled. Bud can be a little more cantankerous, but Milly is as gentle a horse as I've ever known."

Seth handed Lacey the apple. "Just hold it out to her in the palm of your hand. She'll take it."

"And my hand with it?" Lacey asked, only half joking.

"Maybe just a finger or two," Seth said, grinning and obviously enjoying his own humor.

Lacey did as he'd instructed, holding the apple in the palm of her hand and tentatively offering it to the horse.

The animal took the fruit without Lacey feeling anything.

"Now rub her nose like this—" Seth demonstrated and Lacey followed suit.

"Okay, I'm relaxed already," she announced, implying this outing didn't need to go any further.

Seth chuckled at her and opened the stall door. "Stay with me to the side of her and keep a hand on her shoulder or her back so she knows you're there."

Again Lacey did as she was told and followed him into the stall.

"Milly loves to be brushed," he said, taking a brush from a bucket nearby. "Sometimes I think she almost purrs, she loves it so much, and if you let yourself, you start to feel as good about it as she does. This is how you do it."

Once more he demonstrated, showing Lacey how to smooth the brush over the horse's coat in the direction that the hair grew; how to take slow, soft, rhythmic strokes; advising her to clear her mind and just be at one with the animal and the simple task of grooming her.

Then he handed the brush to Lacey.

She again did what he'd showed her, and strangely enough she could feel how much the horse really did like the brushing. The animal seemed to almost lean slightly into each stroke, and several times she turned her head to that side as if to tell Lacey how much she liked it.

And yes, Lacey did find the repetitive motion surprisingly soothing. Although in truth she thought it had more to do with Seth standing so close by, his big body protectively hovering, his powerful hand resting on the horse's hindquarter as if to make sure Milly knew who was boss.

There was something comforting and arousing at the same time in his mere presence there. In his commanding, take-charge attitude. In how strong and capable he was. In his ability to be master to the huge animal.

"Okay, you're right, there *is* something about this that kind of lulls you—smells and all," she said.

Seth grinned down at her. "Don't insult Milly by saying she stinks."

Lacey laughed. "Sorry, Milly," she said without taking her eyes off of Seth.

Lacey brought the brush to a stop on the horse's back, not far from Seth's hand, and laid her own head atop her outstretched arm as if she were too tired to go on. "Maybe I should just sleep out here in the barn," she joked.

"Bud would get jealous," Seth said. "He shares Milly for a little grooming but that's about all."

"He's possessive..."

"Well, she does seem to belong to him and he really likes her. You can't blame a guy for that...."

Lacey had the impression that Seth wasn't talking about the horses alone. That just maybe he was talking about himself. Liking her...

She was just glad to be there with him. To be looking up into that oh-so-handsome, slightly scruffy face. Into those blue eyes that were peering into hers in a way that let her know that all the stiffness, all the standoffishness that she'd sensed in him earlier was gone. A way that reminded her of how he'd looked at her just before he'd kissed her the night before...

Then he leaned forward. Instinct brought Lacey's head up off her arm to meet him in a kiss.

Tonight it wasn't over in a flash.

No, tonight's kiss allowed their lips to meet lightly at first, then more firmly. It went on long enough for eyes to close and heads to tilt, naturally deepening all on its own.

It was a kiss that mingled his sweet breath with hers and let her know the full feel of his warm, supple, agile lips accompanied by just the slightest roughness of that shadow of his beard. The slightest roughness that she kind of liked…

Apparently, Milly didn't like being the leaning post that supported their kiss, because the horse whinnied and nudged at them to let them know she was still there.

And ended the kiss before Lacey was ready to have it end.

Long before…

But Seth broke away to stand straight again, leaving Lacey no choice but to do the same.

Seth translated Milly's neigh and nudge. "If there's nothing in it for her, we're just bothering her."

"I think I've sufficiently learned the value of brushing a horse," Lacey said, unwilling to go back to the chore when they'd moved on to something she liked so much better.

Seth took the brush from her and patted the horse's rump once before dropping the brush back into the bucket and motioning for Lacey to lead the way out of the stall.

"'Night, Milly. 'Night, Bud. You two sleep tight," Seth advised the horses as he and Lacey retraced their steps to the door. He turned the lights down to a dim glow again as they left the barn.

Lacey had to admit to herself that whatever happened in that barn *had* left her feeling more relaxed, though. More at peace. More uplifted. But whether it had been the horse brushing or the kiss was a question she wasn't sure she should answer.

"It *is* nice out here," she said as they walked back to the pool area, feeling under the influence of the night air. "Peaceful, quiet and clean-smelling."

That made him laugh. "Nothing like a little barn perfume to make you appreciate fresh air."

She was hoping that once they reached the pool they wouldn't split to go their separate ways. And they didn't—Seth walked with her to the guesthouse.

But that was all he did before he said, "Now you can shower off the horse hair and smell and go right to sleep—works for me every time."

"I *will* welcome the shower," Lacey said, even though she hadn't had enough to do with Milly to really need it.

Seth merely smiled down at her for a moment before he did what she wanted him to do—kissed her again. Another kiss that went on just long enough for her to be getting into it before it ended, even without the horse to interrupt them.

Then Seth said a simple good-night and left her. She went into the guesthouse and closed the door behind her, then stood there staring at it.

Staring at it and thinking about what she could do if only she didn't have to rush to bed in order to get up again before dawn and be at work hours ahead of the earliest of her construction crew.

Thinking about going back outside, suggesting to Seth that they open a bottle of wine to share.

Thinking about where the rest of the night might take them, if only she could let it.

She yearned for that so much that it was a fight not to give in.

But she didn't. Instead she reminded herself of all she had to do the next day.

And once again went the way of her goals.

Chapter 7

The first week of construction on the training center did not go well. In fact it was hellish for Lacey. Equipment still hadn't arrived. The wrong materials were delivered, had to be returned, reordered, and replacements were delayed. Her contractor had a family emergency and had to leave the state. Her construction foreman broke his wrist. A midweek windstorm blew down a power line.

To Lacey it seemed as if anything that could go wrong had. Plus she'd had problems with the fabric being used to make the bike shorts in her clothing line, there was a sudden increase in orders for hoodies that she wasn't sure she could meet, and three new vendors had gotten irate over a shipment mix-up.

By Friday she was exhausted from getting even less sleep than usual, frazzled from dealing with too many problems on both of her business ventures, and so ragged around the edges that it was showing in the lack of color in her face and the circles under her eyes, which she couldn't quite seem to conceal even when she had the time to try.

And on Friday morning she did make the time to try. That was the day Seth was due to clear out the Camden belongings from the attic and the barn.

She hadn't seen him at all since he'd left her at the guesthouse door on Monday night. She just hadn't spent enough time at home for it to happen. She regretted not seeing him, not getting to be with him. She'd still managed to be thinking about him more than she should have been, and daydreaming about him, and longing to hear his voice right in the midst of some of her worst crises at work.

So Friday—knowing that he was coming to the site—she sacrificed yet another half hour of sleep to get up early enough to make sure she could actually condition her hair, shape her eyebrows and work on covering up those dark circles before she added some color to her face with blush and applied mascara.

She also chose her clothing more carefully, opting for tan slacks that did a come-hither hug of her rear end, and a T-shirt adorned with a cluster of knit roses that cascaded from one shoulder diagonally across the front.

Then, rather than the simple ponytail that had been her quick and easy staple, she twisted her hair up the back of her head and left a geyser of curls at her crown so it was still out of her way but looked a little more done than the ponytail.

Unfortunately, Lacey was under fire when Seth arrived at the site Friday afternoon. She was in the middle of a phone call with her father, who was shouting at her. He claimed that if a man were in charge of the training center project, none of the disasters this week would have happened.

"Well, of course a man wouldn't have let any of it happen, Dad, because everyone knows that men have the ability to foresee the future and superpowers to keep the worst from happening!" Lacey retorted.

"Don't get smart with me, little girl. I saw you with Seth Camden at the wedding. He never left your side and you didn't seem to mind it too much. And you're living at his place—these things at the construction office better not be happening because you're paying more attention to him than to this job!"

"I'm staying in the guesthouse on the Camden ranch and I haven't even seen Seth since Monday night. I've been right here at the site for so many hours this week that I might as well have pitched a tent for myself. And nothing—*nothing*—that happened this week had *anything* to do with Seth Camden or could have been prevented or handled any differently by anyone else!" she insisted forcefully.

"Just make sure the training center is coming first."

It wasn't the first thing on her mind at that moment, when Lacey was all too aware that Seth was out at the barn and that she was hating that she wasn't out there with him. But still she said, "The training center *is* coming first. We just had a bad run after the groundbreaking but everything will be fine from here on."

Her father grumbled and groused some more before he finally let her off the phone. But that still didn't free Lacey to say hello to Seth, because as soon as she hung up with her father, the foreman came in to tell her that even when the crane arrived they wouldn't have an operator for it because the man they'd hired wasn't taking the job after all. And now Lacey needed to find them another one.

She was still in the middle of the new crisis when Seth left the barn and came into his family's former house to deal with the attic. All Lacey could do was wave to him when he poked his head into the dining room she used as her office, whisper for him to go ahead and do what he needed to do, and continue with the phone call she was in the middle of then.

At least as best she could when she kept losing her train of thought watching the big cowboy lug something out to his truck.

From her vantage point she couldn't see him until he got whatever he was taking out onto the front porch. But then, framed by the living room's picture window that she could see through from her desk because there was an open archway joining the dining room with the living room, she feasted on the sight of massively muscled arms beneath the short sleeves of his white T-shirt, thick thighs testing the denim of his jeans, broad shoulders flexed to their limit toting boxes stacked on top of boxes.

But just when she thought she might be able to get off the phone knowing that she had a new crane operator lined up, she saw Seth put what was apparently the last of his family's old belongings in the truck and raise the tailgate to lock it into place. Then he glanced back at the house, and when he saw through the window that she had her phone to her ear, he merely waved to signal that he was done and ready to leave.

And the only thing Lacey had been looking forward to all week—seeing Seth, getting to talk to him—wasn't going to happen.

"I'm sorry, I'm going to have to call you back," she said, cutting the call short so she could rush out the old house's front door to catch Seth.

"Hi!"

Okay, bursting out the door and saying that as breathlessly as she had was not how she'd planned to handle the situation. But it did stop Seth from getting behind the wheel and driving away without a word to her.

"Hey, stranger," he said with a forlorn sort of frown creasing his brow. He paused on the other side of the truck bed, leaning both of his arms on it and glancing at her. "Looked like you were busy—I didn't want to bother you…"

"'Busy' doesn't even cover it—I've been swamped all week."

He nodded, as if she wasn't telling him anything he hadn't already guessed. "Everything going okay?"

"No. It's been one disaster after another around here *and* with my sportswear business."

"Sorry to hear that," Seth said. But there seemed to be something removed and distant about him.

Lacey went down the porch steps and joined him on the other side of his truck bed, closing at least some of the physical distance between them. "Did you get everything?" she asked with a nod at the contents of his truck.

"I had one of my ranch hands follow me over in the truck with the trailer on it—he came in the back way. We got the rotary hoe—the farm equipment thingy, as you call it—loaded onto the trailer and Ross took it out of here after he helped me with the desk. He left a little while ago while I did the rest. But now I think you're free and clear—the place is all yours to do with as you please."

"Thanks."

Silence.

Lacey wondered why this seemed a little strained. A little awkward. Was it just because so much time had passed since they'd last seen each other?

Searching for something else to talk about in order to have a few more minutes of looking at that sharply drawn, sun-gilded face, she said, "What about that old trunk you found in the tackroom last week—did you have a key for the lock?"

"No key. I pried the lock off."

"What was inside?"

He gave a negligent shrug. "Nothing big. Some old journals. I barely looked at them. Sent them to my grandmother in Denver. You haven't run into anything else like that hidden away, have you?"

"No, I don't think so. Besides the groundbreaking, about the only work that got done around here this week was on the main part of the barn, getting it ready to store construction materials. I'm sure you saw that. But as far as I know no one found anything else that belonged to your family—"

"And you'd know if they did?"

Was this more important to him than he wanted to let on?

"I trust my crew, so yes, I'm sure if anyone found anything they would let me know."

"And then you'd let *me* know, right?"

"Well, sure. Are you missing something?"

"No," he was quick to say. "But we didn't know we'd left behind *this* stuff, either."

"If we come across anything more, I'll bring it to you or tell you. You don't have to worry about me playing finders keepers."

He didn't smile at her joke. He was being very serious today...

"I'd appreciate it. For my grandmother's sake, you know."

"Sure," Lacey said.

Seth changed the subject then. "You weren't kidding when you asked to use the guesthouse and said I wouldn't even know you were around, were you? I haven't seen you all week."

"Tell that to my father. He seems to think I'm more interested in you than in the training center."

Oh, she wished she wouldn't have said that! Even if it did finally make Seth smile.

"I'm running neck and neck with the training center when it comes to your interests?" he asked.

She definitely wished she hadn't said that. It might have been true, but she didn't want him to know it.

"It's something stupid that my father accused me of because he saw us together at the wedding."

"Ahh..." The smile disappeared.

Just then, one of her crew bosses came around the side of the house from the barn and called to her in an ominous tone, saying that he thought she better take a look at their brick delivery.

"I'll let you get to work," Seth said, pushing off of the side of his truck without delay and opening the driver's door.

"Maybe I'll see you later," she said, not meaning for it to sound as hopeful as it did. But she was unhappy with how this brief encounter had gone, and she wanted some indication that it was all in her imagination.

Seth gave a shrug of one of those big shoulders as if it didn't matter to him one way or another—which was not at all reassuring. "You know where I live," he said offhandedly.

That didn't sound good, either.

But the crew boss called to her again, insisting that he wasn't kidding, that she'd better take a look at their brick order.

And Lacey had no choice but to move on to her latest problem before Seth had even started his engine.

It was nine o'clock that night before Lacey finished work and went back to the Camden guesthouse. There were no lights on in the main house when she arrived home—and it was Friday night and not too late—so she assumed that Seth was out for the evening.

And yes, again she was wondering if he might be with a woman, on a date. He'd said he didn't date much, but that didn't necessarily mean he didn't date at all...

Lacey hated the thought.

She told herself it was none of her business and that she had no reason to feel one way or another about it.

But still, demoralized and down in the dumps, she took a long shower and tried to wash away the week.

Then she did an at-home facial, put a deep conditioning mask on her hair, and sat for a while with pads over her eyes, hoping these measures would make her look rested.

It was ten-thirty before she concluded her self-pampering, and even though she was exhausted it still seemed too early to go to bed.

And no, she told herself, it wasn't because the main house remained dark and she was inclined to staying up to see when Seth got home and if he was alone when he did.

She just didn't want to go to bed yet.

So she blew her hair dry, left it loose around her shoulders, put on a pair of silky white pajama pants and a bright red crewneck, cap-sleeved T-shirt.

After that, realizing that she hadn't had anything to eat since lunch, she took a box of crackers out of the cupboard and dumped a pile of them onto a plate. Then she sliced a brick of cheese and took her handiwork outside to sit at the poolside table nearest to the guesthouse.

Not to wait for Seth. Just for the fresh air.

She didn't have long to not-wait, though, because by the time she was on her second cracker she heard his sports car come around from the front of the house to the garage.

Please don't let him have a date, she beseeched the fates, fully aware that it wasn't anything she should be asking of any higher power. That it was something she had no right to request. That it was something that shouldn't matter to her.

But she listened intently to the sound of his engine turning off, the car door opening and closing, and then the garage door closing, as well.

What she didn't hear was a second car door or voices that would lead her to believe he wasn't alone.

And her hopes rose like tiny helium-filled balloons freed of their moorings. Even though she was fully aware that their last meeting hadn't gone well and that she had no right to expect him to do anything more than say hello as he went into his house.

Then he came into the backyard and approached the pool. He was by himself, dressed in khaki slacks and a yellow sport shirt, carrying a bottle of wine.

He caught sight of Lacey then and raised his chin at her, not smiling, merely acknowledging her.

"Hi," she said, forcing cheeriness.

"You're home. I'm amazed," he responded.

Lacey ignored that. "Night out?" she asked, trying to sound neutral.

"Dinner with friends."

"Didn't they like your wine selection?" she asked with a nod at the bottle he was carrying.

"They gave the wine to me. It was a thank-you for helping them move a couple of weeks ago."

"A *Camden* helped somebody move?" Lacey exclaimed as if it were unheard of, her anxieties over how he'd spent his evening and with whom lessening.

Seth did crack just a hint of a one-sided smile at that. "Believe it or not—last name notwithstanding—I can lift the end of a couch as well as the next guy. And it earned me a bottle of wine."

He seemed to hesitate a moment and Lacey was worried that a simple good-night was about to happen.

That was when—before she'd even thought about it—she heard herself say, "I have cheese and crackers. You have wine. We could combine our resources…"

"We could," he repeated noncommittally.

Lacey wasn't sure why it wasn't a simple yes or no. But it took him a moment before he seemed to concede and said, "Okay. I'll go in and open the wine and get glasses."

It would have been nice to see more enthusiasm, but still Lacey's energy level was instantly renewed, and the effects of her miserable week suddenly diminished as she watched Seth go to the house. After a few minutes, he returned to join her and pour the wine.

"You look unusually relaxed," he observed, as he handed her a glass and sat in the chair across from her.

Lacey slid the plate of cheese and crackers to the center of the small table. "I had a little winding-down time. It *didn't* involve a horse, but it was good anyway."

"You probably needed it. A couple of nights this week I wasn't sure if you made it home at all. You weren't here when I went to bed around midnight and you were gone again when I got up."

"There was just one night that I didn't make it home—I slept with my head on my desk. Luckily there's still a shower that works in the old house, and I keep a change of clothes in my car just in case."

"Just one night," he repeated. "And you keep a change of clothes in your car in case you don't get home from work because it happens often enough for you to need to be prepared?"

Lacey shrugged.

"But you honestly think that it's worth it—keeping this pace?" Seth asked, as if it were a concept he couldn't grasp.

"Wanting my work on the training center to make

my father's jaw drop—plus keeping up with my clothing line—has made the pace worse than it ordinarily is. But I've always worked long hours and gone the extra mile. I'm not sure I'd know what to do with myself at any other pace," she admitted after a taste of the mildly fruity-tasting wine.

Seth took a drink. "That's good," he judged. "Good wine. Tonight I was with good friends, had good company and a good meal—"

"Things you don't think I take time for." Lacey guessed that that where he was heading with this.

"Things you *said* you don't take time for," he retorted. "Instead you drive around with a change of clothes in case you can't even get home to sleep."

"This project is important—I told you that, too."

He nodded but his expression showed pity. "No project, no *job,* should be *that* important. You need a life, too."

Feeling defensive, Lacey decided to turn the tables on him. "Okay, maybe you have more of a *life* than I do. And more friends—"

"More fun."

"But here you are, in the middle of nowhere—you *live* in a place we chose specifically because there won't be a lot of distractions for the team while they're training. You're out in the country, isolated. None of your family is here. You have friends who invite you to dinner, but what else? There's nothing much to do *but* work around here. I mean, I'm facing a weekend when nothing is going to happen at the construction site, with only some paperwork to catch up on, and I have to tell you, I'm dreading that I *won't* have my *pace* to keep me as busy as usual, because I'm not sure what I'm going to do around here."

Something about that made him smile genuinely— albeit a bit mischievously.

"You have the weekend off?" he asked, intrigued.

"After this weekend I'll have part of the crew working on Saturdays, but this past week was bad and nothing really got started, so there's nothing that can be done tomorrow. Like I said, I have paperwork to do— for the training center and for my sportswear collection—but other than that—"

"Give it to me, then," he challenged.

Lacey laughed. "Give *what* to you?"

"This weekend. Give me this weekend to show you how nice things can be around here when you *aren't* doing what you do. To show you how nice it can be when you aren't running around like crazy, when you just take some time to relax, to enjoy yourself. When you don't have to think about proving that you can do the work of three men. Or prove anything, for that matter. Tell your father you're spending the weekend at a convent or camping or something where he can't reach you—"

"My father is at a sports conference this weekend where he's the keynote speaker and will be wined and dined and the center of attention—I won't hear from him until it's over on Monday."

"Great! Then just be Lacey this weekend—not Lacey the overachiever, not Lacey the underdog-because-she's-a-girl, not Lacey who-needs-to-show-her-old-man-she-can-be-the-third-son-he-never-had, not Lacey the wonder-businesswoman. Just Lacey."

"Who's she?" Lacey joked.

"I'm not sure, but I think she might be somewhere between the pretty little princess her father got for her mother to play with, and one of the boys. But I'd kind of like to find out…"

He said that last part more quietly, as if he were admitting something he didn't want to admit.

But rather than think too much about what was going on with him, Lacey considered what he was suggesting.

She really was worn-out. Two days of rest and relaxation might recharge her and make her that much more able to hit the next week head-on.

Except that it *was* two days with Seth.

Whom she shouldn't be spending concentrated periods of time with because she knew she was overly vulnerable to his looks, to his charm, to him.

But whom she really *wanted* to spend two days with.

"It's not as if I have the *whole* weekend free—I do have paperwork," she said.

"Hedging already!" he accused. "Then how about if I give you tomorrow morning to work? I have animals to feed and water, crops to check on. But after that, you've already said you don't know what you're going to do with yourself, remember?"

It *was* only two days and then she'd be back to business on all fronts, full throttle, she told herself.

"Can we talk about the new road I need?" she said.

Seth rolled his eyes. "No! You get tomorrow morning and that's it—the minute we're together there's no more work, no talk about work! Do you honestly not have any concept of what it is to take time off, to relax?"

"I need a road," she said.

"Okay, I'll make you a deal—this weekend in exchange for your damn road."

"Seriously?" she said hopefully.

"We will seriously come to terms on your road next week if you give me the next two days."

"Excluding mornings," she reminded.

"Excluding *tomorrow* morning," he qualified.

"Okay," Lacey said.

He offered a second glass of wine, but Lacey shook her head. "It's getting late," she pointed out, feeling fatigue creeping back in. "And I do have a lot of paperwork, so I'll have to get up early to make sure I can clear the afternoon."

"Whatever it takes," Seth said, putting the cork back in the bottle and getting up from the table when Lacey did.

But Lacey really was exhausted. As she stood she reached for the plate that held what remained of the cheese and crackers, but knocked it over, sending it crashing to the brick pavers that tiled the area surrounding the pool. The plate broke and the cheese and crackers went everywhere.

"And now you know that I get klutzy when I'm tired," she said.

"Better let me handle the broken glass, then." He came around the table to pick that up while Lacey retrieved the slices of cheese and the crackers. And stole a glance at Seth as he hunkered down on his heels, his thighs testing the fabric of his slacks.

Once they had the majority of the mess gathered up, they took the debris into the guesthouse to discard it. Then Lacey trailed Seth back to the door where they both stood straddling the threshold, spines against the opposite sides of the jamb so they could face each other.

"Will this weekend's portion of my lesson in relaxation involve hairy beasts?" Lacey asked at that point.

"Just me," he answered with a laugh.

He was hardly a hairy beast. Though his hair was really nice in its finger-combed, disheveled sort of way. And when it came to beastly he was anything but—that handsome face of his was all chiseled and gorgeous...

Lacey made herself concentrate on what he was saying.

"This is the weekend we celebrate Northbridge's Founder's Day. There's a parade and all kinds of things going on tomorrow. Sunday there's the Founder's Day picnic out at the old bridge that the town is named for. It'll give you a taste of what goes on around here and how nice it is to just be a part of it."

"And if I get bored out of my mind?" she joked.

"Oh, I'm not gonna let *that* happen," he answered with a touch of the devil in his voice.

Lacey laughed, but she realized that somehow in that instant the tone had changed between them altogether. That they'd gone from Seth being distant and her being desperate for him not to be, to sharing friendly banter and teasing and exchanging a few challenges, to the chemistry that was always just beneath the surface.

Now, standing in that doorway, Seth was looking down at her, his eyes, slightly hooded and mesmerizing, searching hers....

"What is there about you," he muttered, shaking his head.

What was there about *him*?

What was there that made her so sensitive to everything to do with him, so sensitive when something was off between them that nothing felt right until she was with him and things were okay again?

What was there about him that made everything else fade into insignificance, that lifted her spirits and restored her spent energies, that left her wanting nothing so much as him?

He brought a hand around to the back of her neck and up into her hair, and Lacey gave over control just that easily. She let him tilt her head as he leaned forward, not resisting at all when his mouth found hers, answering the parting of his lips by parting hers, too.

And why, in that instant, did she feel as if all really was right with the world again?

Her eyes closed and her head fell back into his big hand as she placed a palm lightly on his chest—feeling the hardness of muscle behind his shirt and absorbing the power and strength hidden there.

He urged her lips to part more still and when they did, he sent his tongue to tease hers.

Glittery sensations rained all through her at that bit of increased intimacy, at that kiss that deepened and went where she'd longed for their kiss in the barn to go.

Lacey's awareness of everything else fell away and it was the man alone, the kiss alone, that carried her beyond her own weariness, that infused her and lifted her at once and made her melt.

But just as other hungers began to awaken in her,

Seth brought the kiss to a slow conclusion, retreating, then roguishly returning only to retreat again before the kiss grew more sensual than sexy, then chaste and sweet, then ended altogether.

When it did, Lacey opened her eyes. His face was still very close to hers.

"Tomorrow. Noon. Then no more work," he said in a deep voice.

"Yeah, yeah, yeah, I remember," she said sassily, making him smile.

He let go of her, dipping his chin to kiss the top of her head, and then moved out of the doorway.

"Leave the rest of this mess out here, I'll sweep and hose it off tomorrow," he ordered, as he walked around the remnants of glass and crackers.

Lacey had forgotten all about that. She nodded and shut the door, letting her eyes drift closed again so she could go on savoring the lingering sensation, the lingering memory of that kiss for another moment.

Before she reminded herself that things like that shouldn't be going on between them.

And then went to bed longing for more anyway...

Chapter 8

"Hey, I just swung by the training center site hoping to catch you, and you weren't there."

"No, I'm not there," Lacey confirmed, feeling a sudden rush of panic. It was 10:00 a.m. on Saturday morning when her cell phone rang and she answered the call from her brother Ian. "Did Dad send you out to check on me?"

"No, no, nothing like that."

"I'm doing paperwork at home," she added. "It was a bad week—Dad knows that—and it wasn't cost-effective to have the crew come in this weekend when they couldn't accomplish anything substantial, so I'm catching up on—"

"Paperwork," her brother finished for her. "Honest, Lace, I'm not spying for Dad."

She had to work twice as hard, be twice as diligent

and worry twice as much that anyone would think she was slacking off—it came with the territory of proving to her father that she could do the work of a man, and Lacey was accustomed to it. But maybe she didn't have to be so worried when it came to her brother.

On the other hand, the training center project had been Ian's, and he might be hoping she would fail so he could take over again...

Lacey hated herself for that thought. Ian had never done anything to her that was backstabbing or cutthroat, and he didn't deserve that.

"I haven't seen or heard from you since the wedding, so I just wanted to check in," Ian explained. "Jenna and Abby and I are leaving town this afternoon—Jenna has a friend in Billings we're seeing this weekend—and I just thought I'd let you know, and make sure you didn't need anything before I go."

"You'll be gone this whole weekend?" Lacey asked, trying to keep her tone neutral. But it wasn't easy. With Ian gone, Hutch still on his honeymoon, and no chance that her father would show up, the sudden feeling of freedom was heady.

"The whole weekend, yeah," Ian confirmed. "We won't be back until Monday."

Lacey couldn't help but smile. "Thanks, but no, I don't need anything," she said, trying to keep from giving away her feelings.

"So how is everything going with you?" her brother asked. "Are you doing all right living at the Camden place?"

"It's just somewhere to drop when I finally leave work at night."

"Sure," Ian said as if he would expect nothing less.

"Did you know that Seth Camden told Dad that he wasn't a fan of football?"

Lacey wondered if Ian had suspicions that something was going on between her and Seth and was giving her fair warning. "Yes. I heard them at the wedding."

"Is it true?"

"I guess," Lacey answered.

"Even if he is a Camden, you know what that means to Dad—"

"If you're not a football fan, you're nothing." Her father had said it more times than she could count.

"I like Seth, though," Ian offered as if in consolation, making her think he definitely had suspicions about what was going on between them. "I've talked to him a dozen or so times since I've been here—at one function or another, or just meeting him on the street—and he seems like a good guy."

"He is," Lacey confirmed.

"Are you seeing much of him?"

She hoped this was about her brother's own curiosity and that he wasn't on a fishing expedition their father had sent him on.

"Our paths rarely cross," she said. Then, not wanting to talk about Seth, she changed the subject. "When are Hutch and Issa and Ash due back from their honeymoon?"

"Monday, I think. I hear your clothes are doing big things in his stores—are you trying to keep up with that on top of the training center?"

"I am," she said.

"Wow, you've got your hands full."

"I do. Plus I had three people working my supply

and distribution center, and my shippers quit. The two people left are going crazy, and I've had to let them try to find a replacement because I just can't get to Billings to do it myself."

"I should probably let you get back to work then." Lacey didn't argue. "Have a good trip."

"We will. I'll see you when we get back."

"Okay." They said goodbye and hung up.

Almost instantly her thoughts turned to Ian's comment about Seth not being a football fan.

Had her brother been making a point of it?

Seth had admitted that he could take football or leave it. Trying to fit that into the super-jock-live-and-breathe-football-club that was the Kincaids? Not likely.

It was just something that she kept telling herself she had to keep in mind when it came to resisting any attraction to Seth.

Intelligent, strong, interesting, funny, staggeringly handsome and sexy as he could possibly be—that all might be true of the man, but none of it could carry more weight than the things that she knew dictated that they stay apart.

Camden or not, he was all easygoing country boy and she was anything but a nature-loving girl, even if she had been born and raised in Montana.

And while Seth might be great to relax with, to wind down with, that laid-back thing he did so well was not Lacey. A slower pace would likely drive her crazy in the long run because she liked to be going and doing and working and as busy as she could keep herself.

Put it all together and it added up to her and Seth

being two people who couldn't be more wrong for each other.

And you'd better remember that! she told herself.

She'd better remember it all through today and tomorrow when she was with him, and not give in too much to that attraction.

Doing the Founder's Day festival with him was just a way to fill some time she had on her hands. She wouldn't let it become any more than that.

She wouldn't.

But could she pull that off?

That tiny whisper of doubt floated around the back of her mind.

No, she wasn't one hundred percent sure she could. In fact, she wasn't even one percent sure.

Saturday afternoon brought the Founder's Day parade. Many Northbridge natives dressed in historic costume, representing their ancestors by walking the parade route or, in some cases, riding in old buggies, horse-drawn wagons or carriages.

There were marching bands and placards with pictures of the town in its earliest incarnations, along with pictures of the original founders and other people thought to have brought expansion and progress to Northbridge. It was on one of those that an old photograph of H. J. Camden was displayed. As it went by, there were several *boo*s called from various spots in the crowd.

Uncomfortable with that, Lacey glanced up at Seth, who was standing by her side. He showed no indications of having heard the jeers and merely went on watching the parade.

When it ended they walked through the maze of booths in the Town Square to the gazebo. There they watched Miss Northbridge be crowned, sat through the dance performance of a troop of local eight-year-old girls and several songs sung by the local church choir and then the barbershop quartet. Then they listened to the speeches given by the mayor and two of the city councilmen.

Dinner was a potluck held under an enormous white tent, and Seth and Lacey ended up eating with a group of Seth's friends.

After that they strolled in the direction of the college campus, touring the display where the placards with the pictures of early Northbridge, its founders and its most important citizens had been put up.

Someone had hung a black shroudlike scarf over the portrait of Seth's great-grandfather.

Lacey took a sideways glance at Seth, who calmly strode up to the picture, removed the scarf to put in a nearby trash receptacle and stepped back to Lacey's side.

Before she'd thought of what to say about that, Seth said, "There's always two camps—the ones who think old H.J. brought progress and good, and the ones who say he made his way on the backs of other people."

"Even around here? In his hometown?" Lacey asked cautiously.

"Oh, sure. This is where H.J. started out. He was a scrappy guy, determined to make something of himself. The property you're turning into your training facility was originally a farm and a lumber mill operated in the barn—H.J.'s folks owned it."

"H.J.'s roots."

"Right. From the minute H.J. was old enough to work, he did, saving every penny until he could start buying up timberland outside of Northbridge. The timberland contained a gold mine that was thought to be played out—"

"That's right. I remember something from my class about him actually striking gold."

"Not a whole lot of it, but yeah, he managed to find a vein that gave him the money to make his next and most important purchase—a chunk of land that was rich in iron deposits. Of course it's been said that he knew that was the case before he bought the land for next to nothing and duped the previous owners who *didn't* know about the iron deposits. It's also been said that by reopening the gold mine and mining the iron, he put people to work and kept Northbridge going when farming wasn't paying—like I told you, two camps."

"Then he left Northbridge?"

"In his twenties, after he had enough of a bankroll. But he kept what he owned here, and when he wanted to use Northbridge as a retreat he came back, bought even more land. But he was always looking for the best deal, so he bought from people who were struggling and about to lose their farms, so there are those who say he capitalized on the misfortunes of others to build what we own now."

"If people needed to sell their property and he bought it, that's just business," Lacey said.

Seth smiled tentatively. "Sure. But then there are also the contentions that he manipulated things in his favor, that he had powerful people in his pocket, so water rights were redistributed, or property lines redrawn to his advantage."

"Is that true?"

He shrugged. "I couldn't tell you. My great-grandfather, my grandfather, my father and my uncle—they all kept the business far, far away from us when we were kids. I do know that my father and my uncle started the policy of giving back—of getting involved in charities and organizations that benefited other people. The negative side says that was just to clean up the Camden name and reputation, to put a better face on wrongdoings. I can tell you that from my standpoint—and my brothers' and sister's and cousins' standpoint—we're all vigilant about anything to do with Camden Incorporated being on the up-and-up now."

"I know that there can be sour grapes when it comes to success," Lacey said. "We run into it. Even during my dad's football career, there were players he beat out for starter position who claimed he didn't deserve it, that he played dirty or that he made it for some other reason. And of course in business it's been said that he's only gotten where he is on his name. To some extent, resentment is unavoidable and you just have to live with it."

"And hope it's unfounded," Seth said so quietly she wasn't sure she was meant to hear it. She thought better of responding.

Then, in a normal octave, he added, "But H.J. was always good to me and I loved the old coot, so here's to you, H.J." He tapped his temple with two fingers and gave the photograph a casual salute.

Then he turned to Lacey and said, "Now how about you and I go dancing?"

"So you do dance?" she said.

"Yep," he answered with a smile. "I can't promise that I'm the best you'll ever come across, but I know how. And it's Saturday night and I can hear the music starting up, and here we are—seems like we should… Unless you don't like to dance…you weren't in favor of it at your brother's wedding."

"That was different. I love to dance, I just rarely get to. But I'm not dressed for it," she said. For dancing she would have worn something less confining than her butt-hugging jeans and more supportive than the white chiffon tank top with its cascading frilly front and built-in bra. And she wouldn't have worn sandals.

"It's the Founder's Day dance in the Square. We don't need to be dressed up." Seth glanced down at his own Western shirt with the long sleeves rolled to his elbows, the jeans that he looked too good to be true in and his cowboy boots. "I could probably do some damage to your bare toes, but I promise to be extra careful not to step on them, if you're game."

She was. Carried away by that sense of freedom, Lacey didn't hesitate a moment more. "Okay," she said.

He reached down and took her hand. Then he put it in the crook of his arm and kept his own hand over hers, tucking her securely into his side, where she instantly got to come up against that big body of his.

She'd been having a good time up to that point; suddenly having physical contact with Seth just made it all the better.

And the thought that she was about to dance with

him left her almost giddy and feeling a little like someone who could throw everything else away just for the chance.

At least for tonight.

Lacey had to give Northbridge credit—the little town knew how to kick up its heels. The entire wooden dance floor at the steps of the gazebo was filled with couples, couples carrying kids, teenagers and even a few preteen girls, all dancing to the music played by a local band positioned in the gazebo itself. And nearly everyone was dressed as casually as she and Seth were.

Friendly, relaxed and fun—that was purely and simply what it was, and Lacey gave herself over to it and to the pleasure of being with Seth.

They danced almost every dance. He never once stepped on her toes, and while the joy and merriment all around them contributed to Lacey's good time, it was Seth she focused on to such an extent that she didn't even notice when the crowd was thinning or the hour was growing late. So the announcement of the last dance came as a surprise to her.

And as sorry as she was to hear it, she was at least grateful that the last dance was a slow one. Seth swung her into his arms, pulling her close before he clasped his hands at the small of her back.

"You underestimated yourself," she told him, her own hands on his shoulders, wanting to lay her cheek on his chest but peering up at him instead. "You're a great dancer."

"Or maybe it was just my partner who made me

look good," he countered. "You never missed a beat—
I'm thinking you must have had lessons."

"Years of them. We all did. Mom insisted on them
for Ian and Hutch because she wanted them doing
something—*anything*—that wasn't football. She'd gotten me started about a year before she died, but my
dad kept me going because he thought girls needed
to know how to dance."

"Did he let your brothers quit?"

"No, by then he'd decided that it helped their agil-
ity on the football field, so he kept them in the class,
too. What about you?" she said. "Lessons?"

"In high school—there was an extracurricular class
offered, and not only did my friends and I figure it
would be an easy A, we also got the idea that it was a
way to hook up with girls."

"Ahh," Lacey said with a laugh. "Was it?"

He grinned. "Oh yeah!"

Then he perched his chin on the top of her head
and talking didn't seem necessary. Instead it was just
nice to sway to the music. To be there with him. To
have his arms around her. And Lacey merely went
with the flow of it all, a little amazed by how well
they seemed to fit together, to move together, to do
everything together...

So yes, she was sorry to have that last song end.
And their last dance with it. But for a moment longer
Seth went on swaying, not letting her go, keeping his
chin to her head.

Only when the other dancers finished clapping and
whistling and thanking the band, and began to leave,
did he take a deep breath that made his chest rise and

fall very near to her face, sigh the breath out into her hair and release her.

But what softened the blow of that dance and the evening coming to an end was when he held her hand as they headed for his car.

"I had a really good time," she confided along the way. "Since high school I've hardly ever gotten to dance."

"You haven't dated dancers?" he joked.

"No. On the rare occasions when I've dated, dancing hasn't been on the menu."

"Rare occasions, huh?" he repeated with a sideways glance at her. "Let me guess—you've done more working than dating."

"Yep," she said, mimicking the clipped answer he frequently gave.

"But there *was* a fiancé," he reminded.

"There was," she confirmed. She'd told him that on Monday night after the groundbreaking, when they were sitting by the pool. And she knew he listened intently to what she said and recalled it all, so it only followed that he'd retained that bit of information.

"How did you get engaged to somebody if you didn't date?" Seth asked once they were settled in the car.

"I dated a little. But nothing long-term or serious. Until Dominic."

"Tell me about him—or is that off-limits?"

It wasn't a subject she *liked* talking about. But she did like that Seth was up front with his curiosity and not using any kind of subterfuge to get answers out of her.

"No, it's not off-limits," she said, deciding in the

moment that that was true. "Dominic Salvadi. He's a hotshot criminal defense attorney."

"I've heard of him. He's in the news. He seems to end up representing any high-profile case that comes up in Montana."

"Yes, he does."

"How did you meet him? Or did I miss that you were accused of committing a heinous crime that he defended you for?"

"I swear it wasn't me who murdered my last land-lord, and I don't know who did," Lacey said theatri-cally.

Seth laughed as he drove out of Northbridge proper and headed for his ranch. "That's a relief to *this* land-lord," he joked.

"I met Dominic at a party. We had a friend in com-mon."

"Love at first sight?"

"No, we just sort of hit it off. He asked me out and it went from there, the way those things do—first it was a dinner, then there was a concert a week later."

Although she didn't remember caring as much about going a week without seeing Dominic as she'd cared this last week about not seeing Seth...

"Anyway," she continued, shooing that thought out of her mind, "we dated for a year, then moved in to-gether. We lived together for two years and were en-gaged for the last six months of that time."

"But no marriage. What happened?"

Lacey shrugged, but they were driving through the dark countryside and she doubted that Seth had seen it. "I broke up with him."

"Just like that? Not a big deal—"

Is that how she'd made it sound?

"Breaking up *was* a big deal—we lived together, owned things together, had wedding plans, our future mapped out. It wasn't as easy as *I just don't want to see you again.*"

"But you seem nonchalant about it now."

"I didn't catch him in bed with someone or anything like that. I just…" Another shrug. "It was just *things…*"

"Things," Seth parroted, to prompt her to go on.

"Two things," Lacey said tentatively, unsure if her reasons ever seemed strong enough to other people when she shared them.

But after considering it a moment, she decided that it was not altogether bad to let Seth know what her reasons were.

"On the surface, the issue was that Dominic had absolutely no interest in football," she said then. "He hadn't seen a handful of games in his entire life, he was nearly football illiterate, and he couldn't have cared less about it."

"And that was a problem?"

"I didn't care so much about it—in fact, it was kind of a relief to get away from football sometimes. But my father *is* Kincaid Corporation, and he eats, sleeps, breathes, lives and dies for the game. I needed Dominic to show just a tiny bit of interest in it the way anyone would need the person they're with to show an interest in something their boss is obsessed with, the way you'd hope someone you're partnering with for life would do with your father."

"And this guy wouldn't?"

"Absolutely not. He would not be bothered. He

wasn't interested in football and that was it. End of story. Even though football is *everything* my family is about."

"Are you saying that it was something you specifically asked him to do for you?"

"Because it was important to me both for my job and to be a part of my family."

"And he flat-out refused."

"Flat-out," Lacey confirmed. "Which made my life more difficult with a father who also happens to be my boss. It was just one more step outside of the boys' club for me."

"And essentially you felt like the guy you were with was doing damage to your career because he wouldn't give a little."

"And just a little was all I was asking so he and I wouldn't be relegated to the sidelines when it came to my father. But like I said, that was just the surface issue, and what I started to see was that there was an even bigger problem with Dominic—like the fact that the longer things went on, the more Dominic showed signs of being *like* my father."

"Signs of being like your father?" Seth echoed her words. "And you *didn't* appreciate that?"

Lacey laughed wryly. "You think that someone who reminds me of my father would be more appealing to me?"

Seth shrugged. "Sometimes that happens."

Lacey laughed at the notion. "I'm not neurotic about my father. I want to be a major player in the Kincaid Corporation. I deserve to be. I have a rightful place in the business I cut my teeth on, and I've been denied any *real* opportunity until now solely because I'm not a man. If anything, it's just that I'm competitive and I'm determined to prove myself and earn the rank that got handed to my brothers on a silver platter."

"Seems like competition was probably ingrained in you from the minute Morgan Kincaid became your father."

Lacey couldn't refute that.

"So the bigger issue with this Dominic guy was that he reminded you of your dad," Seth prompted. "How so?"

"Dominic started to talk about how he didn't want me to work after we got married. How he could *provide* for me and he wanted me at home, taking care of *his* houses, *his* kids. And when it came to my *little* clothing line, he let me know he saw that as my hobby, but he didn't think that should be kept up, either."

"You hate it when your father calls you *little girl*— I saw you flinch. *Little* clothing line pushed that same button," Seth guessed, impressing her with his perception.

"It did. And Dominic's whole attitude, the whole male-superiority thing, just made me look at him and see my father, and it was a *huge* turnoff. There was no way I was getting into a marriage with someone who had the same view of women that my father has."

"You've already had to fight that for too long," Seth agreed as he pulled onto the road that led to his property.

"So that was it for me. I cared about him…" Her voice went quiet again. "I loved him, and it wasn't easy to call it off. But it's bad enough to have my father think what he's always thought of me. I didn't want to marry that same narrow-mindedness. I didn't want to fight it in a marriage, too, or have kids—potentially daughters—and raise them with a father like that."

"I think that was a really wise choice."

Lacey laughed as he drove around the main house and into the garage. "I don't know how wise I am. Stubborn—that's been said of me. But no one has ever called me wise before. At least not in a good way."

"But you've never killed a landlord, so how bad can you be?" he teased her, turning off the engine.

Getting out of the car laid that subject to a natural rest. They walked together to the guesthouse in a moment of silence.

Not until Lacey had unlocked and opened the door did Seth say, "Sooo…you made it. An entire afternoon and evening without working."

Again Lacey laughed. "And I didn't even miss it— maybe there *are* a few lazy bones in this body."

He glanced downward at the body in question and smiled appreciatively. "I definitely don't think we can say anything negative about the body," he muttered.

Lacey didn't respond. Instead she repeated what she'd said when they'd left the dance. "I did have a really good time, though."

"And there's still a day to go."

She made a face. "Yeah. Any chance we could do tomorrow the way we did today and I could have the morning to do paperwork again? I didn't get it all finished this morning."

"I suppose. But only because I have animals to feed and water, a field to check on—"

"Oh, I get it—it's okay if you need to work," she goaded.

"Hey, hey, hey, don't go trying to make me into

your old man or the lawyer. I'm not saying what I do is more important than what you do. I'm just saying that what you do, you do too much of. To the exclusion of everything else. There needs to be a balance."

He leaned a forearm high up on the door frame and switched his weight to one hip. The change of position brought him in closer to Lacey, who was standing in the threshold.

"I had a really good time, too," he admitted, his voice deeper, more intimate.

His bright cobalt-blue eyes peered so intensely into hers that the two of them, and that moment, were suddenly all there was. And after her taste of being in his arms in public, on the dance floor, Lacey nearly ached with wanting to be in his arms again now—without anyone else around.

It was that urge that brought her hand up to his cheek.

He covered that hand with his own, curving his fingers around it, pulling it down to hold at his chest—his broad, hard chest—freeing himself to lean forward and capture her mouth with his.

Lacey closed her eyes and let herself drift off toward what seemed like heaven.

There was a familiarity between them now. A familiarity that left few reservations. Their lips parted without hesitation, freeing the way for his tongue to make an almost instant appearance, which Lacey welcomed.

She let her other hand rest on his chest, too, moving in nearer, tilting her head more and presenting a better angle for their kiss.

Seth wrapped his arm around her to bring her up

against him as commandingly as when he'd led on the dance floor.

She slipped her hand out from under his in order to raise her arms up and over his shoulders, pressing her breasts against his chest—something she'd longed for all evening. Her nipples turned to steely little pebbles that craved even more.

She wondered if Seth could feel them. His shirt wasn't heavy, and her chiffon tank top wasn't much of a barrier, either—even with the built-in bra and even if it *did* seem to her like armor.

He might have been aware of what was going on with her because he moved in closer, holding her tighter and taking them both over the threshold and slightly into the guesthouse. His mouth opened even wider over hers, and his tongue began to play a sensuous game of cat and mouse.

He spun her around then—as if they were still dancing—and Lacey found herself with her back to the wall beside the door, trapped between it and Seth in the loveliest way.

One of his hands went up the side of her neck and into her hair, as both of hers did a survey of his expansive back—all the hills and valleys formed by muscles made of steel. She dug her fingers into them, wanting that shirt out of her way.

It came free of his jeans without much trouble, and that seemed like an invitation to her. So she slipped her hands underneath the shirt and savored her first contact with his warm, satiny skin.

Her hands glided over every inch of that back. She trailed her fingers along his spine. She fanned them out over his massive shoulders. She massaged the curve of his rib cage.

And he must have liked it, because their kiss turned hotter, sexier, more demanding with every stroke.

His hand began a descent from her hair, and hope erupted in Lacey.

Keep going... Keep going... Keep going...

He did, from her neck to her shoulder. From her shoulder to her upper arm. From her upper arm to the side of her waist.

Too far!

Her tongue gave his an impudent little jab that made him smile even as he gave as good as he got.

And then his hand rose up her side to the outer swell of her breast.

It was unintentional, but on their own her shoulders drew back and pushed her chest out, revealing what she wanted all too blatantly.

But still he took his time, continuing to kiss her into near oblivion, to hold her to him.

Then that hand at the very edge of her breast finally came around front, finally engulfed her and gave her nipple the curve of his palm to nestle into.

It felt so good. Too bad her tank top was in the way.

Lacey brought her own hands around to the front of his shirt, spending a moment enjoying the feel of his honed pectorals, of his taut male nipples, before she let her hands traipse down his flat belly.

Ooo, it was tempting to just keep going. Inside his waistband, behind his zipper...

But she stopped herself and instead finessed his shirttails from his jeans in front, then fanned her arms and in one outward motion unsnapped all the buttons of his shirt.

That elicited a rumbling sort of chuckle in his throat as Lacey's hands rose again to his chest and delivered the full hint that she wanted him to get past the barrier of her shirt, too.

A hint he wasted no time in acting on. He quickly slid his hand under her tank top, under the shelf of a bra, engulfing her very engorged flesh in the heat of his unfettered grasp.

The man could dance.

The man could kiss like no one she'd ever kissed before.

But oh, what he did with that hand!

There were wonders to be had at Seth's touch. Gentle and tender. Tougher, rougher just when she needed it to be. Teasing and toying and playful. He kneaded her breast, he massaged and rubbed, tickled and tugged, circled and subdued and altogether worked Lacey into a frenzy of desires that sprang to life throughout her body.

Her head was back against the wall, her mouth plundered by his even as she did some plundering of her own. Her spine was arched to press her breasts into his grasp. And as her body began to crave even more she kicked aside her sandal and let her bare foot climb slowly up his calf.

And before she knew it, she was partially straddling his thigh and on the verge of taking things further....

Which was oddly when—for no reason she understood—she remembered that this Founder's Day weekend was supposed to be just a way to fill some time, that she'd sworn to herself not to let it become more than that. With Seth. To keep in mind why she needed not to let it become more than a time-filler. With Seth.

And this—and where she wanted this to go from here—was more than a time-filler. Much, much more.

So much more that it suddenly sent a ripple of uneasiness through Lacey.

She could be risking everything to let this go any further...

"Okay, okay, okay—we have to stop," she said breathlessly after tearing away from their kiss.

"We do?" he asked in a raspy voice that enticed all by itself.

"We do," Lacey decreed before she could think twice about it. She knew that to hesitate was to give in to what her entire body, her entire being, was screaming for.

Still he gave it one more try, kissing her fervently but also sweetly and intriguingly at once, and giving her breast a deep, earnest press that made her wish that he'd never take his hand from there.

But that ripple of uneasiness continued to shimmy through her; she couldn't ignore it.

"No, I mean it, we really do have to stop..." she insisted when he ended their kiss a moment later.

One final, lingering press of her breast, and he slipped his hand out from under her shirt. Lacey couldn't help the moan of disappointment that went with it.

"You're sure?" he asked after he'd kissed her again, glancing down at her leg still wrapped around his, keeping him in place despite what she'd said.

Lacey gave a chagrined laugh. "Yeah," she said, taking her foot off his calf and nearly melting at the feel of his hand on the back of her thigh when he clasped it to help ease her leg down.

Another kiss—such a good, good kiss—and he backed away, putting distance she regretted between them.

"Guess I'll see you tomorrow, then."

Lacey could only manage to nod. He sidestepped to the open door of the guesthouse and went out.

She took a deep breath and told herself she'd done the right thing.

But she also turned so she could watch Seth walk around the pool.

He hadn't snapped the buttons on his shirt closed, or tucked in the tails she'd pulled free, and watching those shirttails flap around his hips, knowing that the front of his shirt was open, exposing that chest she'd felt but hadn't actually seen, only made her want to call to him. To get him to turn around so she could see it.

But before she'd done that he reached the main house and let himself in through the French doors.

Then she got her wish when he turned around to close the door. Through the glass she saw just a strip of that chest, of his flat belly and the treasure trail of dark hair that went from his navel to disappear behind the zipper of his low-slung jeans...

Oh, but the man was gorgeous, and Lacey nearly came away from leaning against that wall. She nearly shot out her own door to join him across the way, to leap into his arms, to put herself against that chest again and allow her body what it so much she craved so much she was in a private little misery all her own.

But in the end, reason prevailed. She knew she had

too much at stake, so she merely groaned, reached across the open doorway and put the door in a death grip to close it.

Then she shut her eyes and wondered if anything was worth feeling the unquenched desires and longings that were all she was left with...

Chapter 9

"Another early phone call, and this one on a Sunday—that doesn't speak well of your Saturday night or your social life," Seth goaded his brother Cade, who called at seven-thirty the next morning.

"Yeah, well, I don't hear a female voice in the background there, either, so my money is on you spending last night alone, too," Cade countered.

Alone and in near agony, Seth wanted Lacey so bad he'd been up half the night pacing and looking out at the guesthouse, willing her to change her mind and come to him.

Then he'd told himself all the reasons why she'd been right not to let things go any further than they had.

Seth decided to one-up his brother. "I *was* out with a woman last night. This is Northbridge's Founder's

Day weekend, and I took Lacey Kincaid to yesterday's events. We danced until after midnight." *And then came home to do more than dance...*

But he didn't say that. There was something about Lacey, about what was happening between them, that he didn't want to cheapen. That he wanted to keep private and *just* between the two of them.

Apparently Cade had more on his mind, though, because he let the brotherly bantering end there and said, "I had dinner with GiGi last night—she hasn't been herself since she got those journals you sent, and I thought it might do her some good to get out."

"Is something wrong with GiGi?" Seth asked, suddenly concerned for their grandmother's health.

"The journals are what's wrong with GiGi."

"Should I not have sent them?"

"No, it's not that. In fact she told me something last night that she hasn't told any of us, something that she said she's tried to forget about since H.J. died, but now the journals confirm it."

"What did she tell you?"

"Apparently during those last weeks with H.J.— when he was in and out of it, sometimes making sense and sometimes not—he told her about some things he'd done. Business things. How he'd wheeled and dealed to make things go his way. He talked about paying off politicians, tampering with a jury, driving people off land he wanted—"

"The worst of what's been said of him and of Gramps."

"GiGi said he also kept saying something about a record of things or maybe a record book—"

"So he told her about the journals?"

"That isn't what he called them, and she thought he was talking more about there being a record of his life—like a religious kind of thing that might affect his afterlife or something. You know how H.J. was at the end—he was rambling and confused, he was seeing things and people who weren't there, talking crazy a lot of the time and not making sense. GiGi said she didn't pay any attention to the record-book talk, and she just hoped the more serious things he was saying weren't true."

"But they were," Seth said direly.

"She's only just scratched the surface of the journals, but she showed me a couple of things in what she's read so far," Cade said. Then, as if he were admitting something he didn't want to admit, he added, "It isn't good, Seth. In fact, it might be worse than what everyone's always said about us."

Seth didn't want to believe that. "You're kidding."

"I wish I was. But apparently the old man—and Gramps, too—didn't let anything or anyone get in their way."

"And Dad and Uncle Mitchum?"

"I don't know yet. But what I do know is that just from the little I read last night, if anything in those journals ever got out, donations and charity work and funding wings in hospitals and buildings for colleges and the fact that our practices now are strictly on the straight and narrow wouldn't be enough."

"Geez…"

"Yeah. The guys we knew our great-grandfather and grandfather to be, might really—*really*—not have been the same guys they were when it came to building Camden Incorporated."

"So we can't let anything in those journals get out," Seth said, going back to his brother's earlier comment.

"No, we can't," Cade agreed. "But I'm not sure GiGi is going to let it go, either."

"What does that mean?"

"She's rocked by this. She said she never paid much attention to the negative things that were said about us, that she chose to believe that what H.J. was confiding in her at the end wasn't true. But now the blinders are off and some things might need to be made right."

"What *things?*" Seth asked, new concerns rising in him.

"She wouldn't say. She said she's going to make sure she's read through everything by her birthday and we'll talk about it then."

"How shook up is she?" Seth said. "This isn't going to cause *her* to stroke out or something, is it? I mean, I know she seems to be in good health, but she *is* going to be seventy-five and we can't let old sins that weren't even hers take a toll on her."

"I tried to get her to give me the journals, to stop reading them. I told her I'd go through them and just give her the Cliff Notes. But she wouldn't even consider it. You know GiGi—"

"Stubborn and probably thinking to protect us. So she'll read the journals, try to filter out the worst and only give us the Cliff Notes."

Cade laughed. "Right. But beyond her being quiet and preoccupied—and showing the kind of determination she showed when she took us all in after the plane crash—I didn't see any signs that this was taking a toll on her health. Her cheeks were still rosy, she spotted a loose button on my jacket that she had to sew and she'd baked me cookies to take home with me—"

"Chocolate chip or oatmeal raisin?"

"Oatmeal raisin."

"Damn you! I haven't had GiGi's oatmeal raisin cookies in a year!"

"That's what you get for living in Montana," Cade said in a gloating tone. "Anyway, I think she's okay, but I'll keep an eye on her. I just thought I'd let you know that we dodged a bullet by finding those journals ourselves, and if anyone else knows we did—"

"Lacey asked if there was anything in the trunk and I told her the truth. But I didn't make the journals sound interesting at all. She's probably forgotten by now. And no one but me saw them."

"Lacey Kincaid again. Huh…"

"She's was with me when I found the trunk," Seth explained, a little annoyed by his brother's suspicious tone.

"Well, from here on we'd better keep it plenty quiet that those journals exist," Cade said. "Even when it comes to Lacey Kincaid."

"No problem," Seth assured.

And that was the truth. When he was with Lacey the last thing on his mind was an old trunk, the journals that were inside of it, or what those journals might reveal about the sins of his forefathers.

"And be warned," Cade said. "When you come for GiGi's birthday we'll probably have to deal with this."

"Sure. In the meantime, don't let GiGi get upset over any of it. Make sure she knows that we'll take care of it."

"I'm doing the best I can, but she's all up in arms

already. Last night she said H.J. and Gramps should be glad they're dead, because if they weren't she might kill them herself. Something in the journals hit her too close to home. She said there was one thing that was personal, and she doesn't know how she's going to live with it now that she knows about it."

"What could that be?"

"Your guess is as good as mine. She wouldn't elaborate. She pursed her lips together that way she does when she's so mad she's afraid of what she might say, and I know better than to push her when she does that."

"Her birthday ought to be interesting, then—is that what you're telling me?"

"I'd bet on it."

After working all of Sunday morning in raggedy shorts and a tank top for the Founder's Day picnic, Lacey showered and shampooed her hair, and changed into a lightweight, mid-calf-length black halter dress with a bright paisley print.

She wasn't sure about wearing the dress. Not only did it leave her arms and shoulders bare, it had an Empire waist with a neckline that dipped to within two inches of the band that ran just below her breasts. She wondered if it might be a little risqué for a small-town family picnic.

But she loved the dress. It kept her cool, the skirt was flowy and it made her feel feminine and about as far from work and business suits or construction-site jeans as she could get. And since the goal of the weekend was to escape work mode, she decided to wear it.

She also left her hair to fall free around her shoulders—the way she never, ever wore it on the job—and applied a touch more blush and mascara than usual.

"Holy cow! Look at you!" Seth said when he showed up at the guesthouse with picnic basket in hand, ready to go.

"Too much?" she asked, gratified by his response but worrying again that she'd overdone it.

"Too much of what? You look great!" he assured her, his eyes going up and down her body as if he couldn't get enough.

And because of that Lacey opted to stay just the way she was.

The Founder's Day picnic festivities were held at the old covered bridge that was the town's namesake. It had been recently refurbished, and the entire area around it developed into a lush park.

There were games galore for the many kids in attendance and some for the adults, too. There were stands selling hot dogs, ice cream, snow cones, cotton candy, pretzels, funnel cakes and a number of other treats. There was a raffle for a motorcycle, a craft fair, and contests for the best the local cooks had to offer in the way of cakes, pies, and home-pickling of everything imaginable.

After a full afternoon taking it all in, Seth and Lacey did what everyone else did—they claimed a spot for themselves on the grassy knoll, spread out the blanket they'd brought and settled in to eat the picnic supper Seth had packed. Cold fried chicken and potato salad helped occupy them while they waited for darkness to fall and the fireworks display that promised to be more elaborate than the one on the Fourth of July had been.

"I can see why my brothers both love this town," Lacey told Seth, as they each sipped a glass of the wine he'd brought. "It's like one big family here, isn't it?"

"Yep," Seth confirmed.

"Lots of couples, though."

"Yep," he repeated.

"Cuts down on the possibilities of finding someone yourself if you're single, doesn't it?"

Lacey watched Seth's handsome face stretch into a slow, knowing grin. "Are you headed somewhere with this, Kincaid?"

She was, and since he'd been straightforward with his questions about her history with men the night before, Lacey shouldn't have been surprised that he would call her on her own beating around the bush.

But her curiosity had gotten the better of her, and she couldn't help it—the man was gorgeous, personable, fun to be with, sexy, successful, intelligent, kind and caring and even more, and she couldn't help wondering why he was single.

So she asked him point-blank.

"How come you're not married or engaged or with someone?"

"I'm right here with you," he said, as if she were missing the obvious, teasing her.

"You know what I mean."

Stretched out on his side on the blanket, dressed in jeans and a white Henley T-shirt, he was the very picture of relaxation. Before answering her he sat up, leaning most of his weight on one hip, his elbow braced on top of an upraised knee.

Then he shrugged a shoulder that filled out the

Henley impeccably and looked her in the eye to answer. "You're right, small-town living isn't the best for dating—everybody knows everybody, if you haven't hit it off with anyone by the time you've been around the block a few times, you aren't going to find a whole lot more prospects in the pool."

"So you have dated people here?"

"Sure," he said. "Some really terrific women. Just not *the One*."

"And outside of Northbridge?" Lacey persisted.

"Sure," he repeated. "I've dated outside of Northbridge, too."

"And the One wasn't in either place?"

"Actually, the one I *thought* was the One was in both places—we met in Denver but I didn't date her there. Then I *did* start dating her when she came to Northbridge to get my computer network set up so I could run and monitor our other farms and ranches across the country from here."

Now they were getting somewhere...

"She was a computer techie?" Lacey asked.

"She was when I met her the first time in Denver. Two years later when she came here, she was the head of our whole computer division."

"She went from mere techie to head of the whole division in only two years?"

"She was smart. And ambitious. Driven," he said emphatically. Lacey knew he was saying that she and this Charlotte person were alike in that way.

But it didn't seem like a compliment.

"Charlotte and I met when I was still working and living in Denver. A hacker got into my system and she had to come in to work on it. She and I had a few late nights working, sort of had a good time together, but that was it. Then I came here and needed a much bigger system set up. She said that when she saw the order, she decided to do it herself—even though by then she could have just sent another low-level techie."

"She came herself because she *liked* you," Lacey said, hoping to hide the flash of jealousy that had suddenly come out of nowhere.

"Yeah, that was pretty much what she said. But I liked her, too—we'd joked around and talked a lot when we were working together before. We had some things in common. But she *worked* for me, and you know how dicey that can be, so before she came here I'd figured I better not get into anything personal with her."

"Something here made it less dicey?"

"No, I knew it was still dicey. But… I don't know, things here seemed different somehow. More casual. Not so restricted. And Charlotte and I still had the same… I suppose you could say chemistry…that we'd had the first time around."

"So the second time the two of you crossed paths one thing led to another," Lacey said for him.

"Charlotte actually instigated things, so I sort of lost sight of the risks of getting involved with an employee and, yeah, one thing led to another."

"Don't tell me she ended up suing you for harassment or something."

"No, that wasn't Charlotte's style. But she definitely saw an opportunity to become part of the Camden family, and she wasn't about to let it pass her by."

"She became part of the family? You married her?"

Lacey said with some shock. She'd never asked if he was divorced.

"No, it didn't get *that* far. She spent a lot of time here getting my system in working order and connecting it to what was being set up on each of the other farms around the country. By the time she'd finished, we were pretty hot and heavy, so we decided to try to keep it going long-distance. We did, for about eight months. Then we got engaged," he explained. "It was after that that things took a turn."

"How?"

Seth drank some of his wine, studied the glass for a moment and then said, "I knew Charlotte worked a lot—that was how she rose through the ranks as fast as she did. And I knew she was working a lot while she was in Denver and I was here, but I was under the impression that that was just how she kept herself busy because we weren't together."

"But it was more than that."

"Work was her priority. Everything—and *everyone*—took a backseat to that. And," he added in a voice filled with regret, "she wanted me to be more like that. More driven. More ambitious. More like she was. It didn't come out until after we were engaged, but she hated Northbridge, she hated country life. And she really, really hated that I'd handed over the CEO seat to Cade—"

"You were the CEO of Camden Incorporated and you handed it over to someone else?"

"My younger brother Cade," Seth confirmed. "As the oldest of the kids I stepped into it initially just by virtue of being the first of us to fully get on board with the company after college—it was how H.J. had it set up. He was determined that Camden Incorporated stay a family business. He arranged for us to have mentors he trusted, people to help us, advise us, but as each of us finished school and went to work, we went to work in a position of power. I was first, so I went in as head of everything."

"Only you didn't want that particular position of power—CEO."

"Right. I didn't want in on the business end of things—at least not any more than I have to be with the agricultural part of Camden Incorporated. Even though I knew I'd have to deal with business, I wanted that to be secondary to my working the ranch. So when Cade got his MBA and was ready to come on board, it just made more sense for him to become CEO so I could move here and do what I do."

"But Charlotte didn't approve of what you do?"

"She wanted me to *kick it into gear*—that's what she said. She figured my *rightful place* was as CEO, that together we could—and should—head the company."

"She was ambitious," Lacey marveled.

"Ambitious. She worked all the time. And I wasn't about to stage some sort of coup in my own family or become the business titan she thought I should become—which was really the only way she could respect me, she said. What it boiled down to was that the One was the Wrong One, and I broke it off with her."

"Oh, those *engagements*," Lacey said, making a joke to lighten the dour tone that had developed. "Sometimes they bring out the worst in people."

Seth smiled, going along with her attempt at humor. "I guess we should be glad it was the engagements that brought out the worst in Charlotte and Dominic, and that we didn't end up married to them before we saw it."

"That would have been *much* worse," Lacey agreed.

"So that's how come I'm not married or engaged or with someone," he summed up.

"And why you're trying to corrupt my work ethic?" she teased.

He laughed and gave her a wicked wiggle of his eyebrows. "Yes. Ever since Charlotte I'm determined to corrupt every overworked girl I come across by forcing them to take a day off."

"Two days," she reminded.

"Two *half* days—that equals one day."

"Still, it's corrupting me because I'm not looking forward to going back to work tomorrow."

"Then don't," he enticed.

Lacey laughed. "The training center won't build itself."

Dusk had fallen as they'd talked. On the other side of the creek running below the bridge, music suddenly blared from a loudspeaker, accompanied by a voice that announced, "The Founder's Day Light Show!"

Which Lacey thought was good timing, because clearly talking about how the One had turned into the Wrong One for Seth was a subject better left in the dust.

Except for one more small thing she was curious about.

As he moved to sit beside her so he could see the fireworks, she swayed in his direction and whispered, "Where is Charlotte now?"

"Long gone—she left for a bigger and better job with a software company in New Zealand."

New Zealand.

Far, far away, Lacey thought.

And for some reason that made her particularly happy.

"I can see a clock that's stopped from here—looks like the power has been out since about half an hour after we left this afternoon," Seth said, as he unlocked one set of the French doors on the main house. Then he opened them and a gust of hot air flooded out. "Woo! Feels like it, too! It's a blast furnace in there!"

They'd both noticed as they'd neared his ranch on the drive home that the streetlights weren't lit. None of the outdoor lights around the houses, the pool and the garage were on when they drove around to park in front of the garage door that wouldn't operate without the electric garage door opener. And now it was clear that the houses that were ordinarily air-conditioned had retained the August heat through the entire afternoon and evening.

Seth took out his cell phone and called the utility company in town. After a few minutes of listening, he reported to Lacey that the power would be out until approximately eleven.

"Why don't we open windows to let some of the heat out," he suggested, "and meet back here to sit by the pool while we wait for the air to come on again? That bottle of wine we started is still pretty full."

It *was* barely ten o'clock, and Lacey knew she wouldn't be able to sleep until the guesthouse was cool again. Not to mention that she wasn't about to pass up any excuse to extend her time with Seth.

"No, I guess we shouldn't let that wine go to waste," she said by way of agreement.

Seth smiled at her. "I'll meet you back here then," he repeated.

As Seth went into the main house Lacey rounded the pool and unlocked the door to the swelteringly hot guesthouse.

She made a quick tour of the place to throw open every window, then took a fast look in the bathroom mirror to see how her appearance had fared through the day.

There had been a breeze most of the time that had diffused the heat while they were out, so she hadn't done too badly: her mascara had kept its promise and not smudged or smeared, her blush might have been gone but her cheeks were sun-kissed and now had a healthy, more natural look to them.

She did brush her hair to make it fluffy and full again, reapply lip gloss and kick off her sandals so she could be in bare feet. But her sundress still looked fresh as a daisy, the fabric was light and filmy, and the halter top with its plunging neckline left her as cool as anything she could change into, so she let the dress stay, too.

Then she hurried out of the hot house and back into the cooler evening air.

Seth wasn't there yet. The clean, clear water of the pool beckoned, so she bunched up the skirt of her dress to hold high on her thighs, sat poolside and dangled her feet into the water.

"We could swim."

The sound of Seth's voice made her smile. She glanced up to see him coming out of the main house with the wine and two glasses in hand.

He'd stayed in his jeans and Henley T-shirt but now his feet were bare, too—free of the cowboy boots he'd been wearing before.

"I thought about swimming," Lacey admitted. "But I was just feeling too lazy."

He'd shaved. She didn't notice that until he smiled, but he'd grown a bit scruffy as the day and evening had gone on and now that scruff was gone, replaced by smooth, whisker-free skin and the scent of his cologne.

He joined her after pouring the wine, handed her one of the glasses then sat beside her. Not so his feet could go into the water, though. He sat facing her, his legs crossed, his own wineglass held in both hands.

"You look a little lazy—I like it," he said after a sip.

"Corruption complete?"

"Are you going back to work tomorrow?" he challenged.

"Of course."

"Then you're not *completely* corrupted, are you?"

Lacey answered that with a smile. "Still, this has been really nice—this whole *winding down* thing you speak so highly of," she said, emphasizing the phrase as if it were a foreign concept.

"And you're good at it, too. I'm glad to see that—it means there's hope for you after all."

"I'm not sure what there's hope for, but I wouldn't want to be considered hopeless," Lacey said with a laugh after sipping her own wine.

"Hopeless—like Charlotte, for instance—would have involved you being on the internet or your phone every minute of these last two days and barely humoring me. But you didn't do that."

"I didn't think that was part of the deal."

"It wasn't. But that wouldn't have stopped Charlotte."

"Points for me, demerits for her."

Seth laughed as he drank more wine. "Nothin' but demerits for her. But you earned a lot of points," he said in a voice rife with insinuation.

"Enough points to buy a road?"

"Next week—we're not talking about that until you've given me the whole weekend. And there's two hours to go on that."

"I just have to fill two hours and then it's back to business?" she asked with some insinuation of her own, even though she wasn't sure where it had come from or what she was insinuating.

"Yep, two hours. Have anything in mind?"

She had something in mind instantly.

For Lacey, what had ignited between them at the end of the previous evening had been simmering just below the surface ever since. So certainly now, in the quiet of the night, sitting beside the pool with nothing but moonlight and the glimmer of stars reflected in the water, it didn't take more than insinuation for thoughts of kissing, of touching, of making love to spring back to life.

But she wasn't going to say that outright.

"Do you have anything in mind?" she countered, knowing she shouldn't bait him and yet suddenly also knowing exactly how she wanted this night, this weekend, this down time to end. Exactly what would be the perfect finish…

"Wasn't me who stopped things last night," Seth said. "Seems like it shouldn't be me who starts them up again."

But he did dip forward to kiss the very tip of her shoulder and while that seemed innocent, it was still enough to get things rolling for Lacey.

Why had she stopped them the night before? she asked herself.

Because she'd thought that if she hadn't stopped, she would have risked everything.

But now, in the peace and calm of the evening, after two days of relaxing and recharging, she wondered what was really at risk. Would she not go back to work tomorrow morning if she had this night with Seth? she reasoned. Would she not build the training facility?

Of course she would go back to work; of course she would build the center. One night wouldn't— couldn't—change that.

So there wasn't really anything at risk.

Last night had just been jitters, she thought. And tonight she wasn't feeling jittery. She was still feeling the way she had been when she'd put on that dress this morning—feminine and free to do as she pleased.

"Too hot inside," she said in a seductress's voice.

"Nice out here, though," he answered quietly.

"Where anyone could see?"

"There's not another soul for miles." He kissed her shoulder again, moving up an inch nearer to her neck and lingering a bit longer. "But it's up to you."

Lacey could feel her nipples tightening against the soft drape of the dress. And almost on its own, her free hand rose to the first button of his Henley shirt and unfastened it.

Seth looked down at her hand and as he got the message she was sending, he smiled again. "You sure?"

Lacey undid the second button and made him laugh.

"Hang on," he said, getting to his feet in one lithe movement and disappearing into the main house.

Nothing about him had changed when he returned scant minutes later. Lacey had taken her feet from the water to place them flat on the poolside tile and pulled the skirt of her dress over her upraised knees.

"If you went in to turn on a video camera this is a no-go," she warned.

He laughed as he sat back down. "Protection," he said simply. "Unless you're against it."

"No, protection is good," she said.

And so was the first meeting of his mouth and hers when he leaned forward to kiss her. Very good.

He stretched out his legs on either side of her, took her by the ankles and pulled her toward him, draping her thighs over his. He let his forearms rest on his calves as he continued kissing her.

They were off to a slow start, which was just the way it seemed like things should be. Lacey's eyes closed so she could drift completely into the simple joy of that kiss.

In no hurry at all, his lips parted; he waited for hers to catch up. Then his tongue, tempting and sweet, brought mischief into the game, turning the kiss playful and coy.

As their heads tilted, the kiss inched its way toward intensity. Seth raised the back of his hand to her cheek, smoothing her hair away from her face, then he rested that hand along the side of her neck.

And yet the leisurely pace didn't matter. Anticipation mounted in Lacey anyway, and she was again very aware of her breasts, her nipples, striving for his attention.

She unfastened the remaining three buttons of his shirt. And with that done, it seemed silly to leave it on, so she found the hem and rolled it up his broad back to pull over his head and off during a split-second break from that kiss.

She tossed his shirt aside and ran her flattened palms from his sides to his washboard belly, up to impeccable pectorals, across to biceps built from hard ranch work, and up and over massive shoulders to that back that was cut and carved and gave her a wealth of hills and valleys to explore.

Just the feel of him was enough to light sparks in her blood. He was honed and taut, silky-smooth and strong.

And he liked what she was doing to him. She knew because his mouth was open even wider over hers, their kisses becoming deeper and deeper with every slide of her hands, his tongue more assertive and demanding.

His hands came away from her face, from her neck. He bracketed her hips, pulling her closer—not quite against him, not quite into the very V of his legs, but near to it. And when he'd finished with that he reached around her neck to the bow that kept the halter dress in place and slowly untied it.

Lacey's dress slipped down to form mere clouds of fabric dangling from pebbled nipples, and she felt the breath of evening air tickle the very top curves of her areolas.

Seth began a trail of kisses down her neck and along her collarbone to the hollow in front of her shoulder. From there the trail led farther south until it was his lips only faintly, lightly kissing that upper shadow of nipple.

The feeling was powerful, and it caused her breasts to heave forward, sending one side of her dress to fall completely away.

It was that exposed breast that Seth covered with a big, warm hand before he recaptured her mouth with an all-new fervor in a kiss that was hungry and demanding.

What had come alive in Lacey the previous evening was nothing compared to what was awakening now. Every nerve ending seemed on the surface of her skin, feeding sensations like tinder to the flames beginning to burn inside of her.

She answered his kiss with an urgency of her own as her hands coursed across his back, his shoulders, his chest and belly all over again.

And when she reached the waistband of his jeans she didn't even pause before she unfastened the button and unzipped the zipper, freeing his own burgeoning desire.

With his arms around her, Seth eased her back on the tile and stretched out next to her.

The other side of her dress came away with that movement. Again he broke the kiss and dropped his head to the other breast.

He drew her into his hot, moist mouth. Lacey's spine arched in response as his tongue flicked the crystallized crest, circled and taunted it, idolized and adored it, and worked her into a frenzy of need greater than she was sure she could bear.

He rolled them both to their sides, then reached around to unzip her dress, finally ridding her of it. This left her in only lace bikini panties. He abandoned her for a moment to shed his jeans and whatever else he had on underneath them.

Her quick glimpse of him through the French doors Saturday night had not prepared her for the pure masculine beauty of his naked body in all its glory, and seeing it now lit even more flames inside of her.

Magnificent and all man—he was lean and tight and rippling with muscle—and once he'd removed her panties and quickly sheathed himself, she was only too happy to be able to greet naked flesh with naked flesh when he came to her again.

Their mouths met once more, as Seth retook her breasts with big, adept hands.

Lacey took something of his, too, reaching low and discovering just what a frenzy she could raise in him, as well.

A gravelly rumble of a groan sounded from his throat and he once again moved his mouth to her breast. Tongue and teeth did a delightful torment of her nipple, and his hand slid down her stomach and between her legs.

Her breath caught at that first touch, at the fabulous fingers that brought her close enough to the brink to make her nearly beg him for more.

And that was when he part-rolled, part-eased them both into the pool, into the shallow end where the water was as warm as a bath.

But swimming was not what he had in mind.

Before Lacey could say anything, his mouth was over hers again and with her back against the smooth tiles of the pool's sidewall, he brought her legs up to wrap them around his hips and entered her in one sublime slide that fitted them together as if that was how they were meant to be.

A small sneak preview of a climax rippled through Lacey at just that moment. Her head arched backward as a gust of breath was stolen from her.

Then he moved deeper into her and showed her that there was so much more to come.

Lacey held on as he pressed fully, completely, into her, as he pulled slightly out again. In and out. Again. And again, until together they devised a rhythm of meeting and parting, of flowing with the movement they were creating in the water, rising and falling with it, striving, striving, striving for that ultimate of peaks.

The climax that broke over the two of them at the same time had them holding tight to each other as he embedded himself so deeply within her that Lacey felt as if he truly was a part of her core, of her being, sealing them together with wave after wave of an ecstasy so divine she lost herself to it, in it.

Tiny sounds emitted from her throat, and she could do nothing but cling to him until little by little the pure glory of it ebbed, slowly, slowly draining her until she wilted against him and trusted that he would brace and support her there while he, too, came down from that pillar of pleasure.

Lacey's head fell to his chest. His face dropped to her hair. And she could feel his breath hot and heavy there as they stayed wrapped in the pure afterglow, his strong arms around her, keeping her braced as the surface of the water calmed to glass again.

"It never—*ever*—occurred to me that *this* might be the way I got into this pool for the first time," she whispered when she'd gathered her wits.

Seth laughed a raspy, ragged laugh. "Kinda nice, though, wasn't it?"

So much more than *kinda nice...*

"I'm not complaining," she assured him, tightening her legs around him and getting a tiny aftershock that reminded her just how nice it had been.

"How 'bout hurtin'—you aren't doing any of that, either, are you?"

"I'm definitely feeling no pain," she answered with a smile.

He lifted her then and came away from her, repositioning them so he could scoop her into his arms and carry her to the stairs at the corner of the pool.

Climbing the steps, he took her to one of the oversized loungers and laid her there. Then he joined her and pulled her to lie conformed to his side where the heat of his body, of his arms around her, chased away the slight chill of the night air on her bare, wet skin.

"Still no lights, so it's probably too hot to go inside," he said, sounding weighted and weary. "Guess we'll have to stay out here... Maybe take another dip in the pool in a little while..."

Lacey laughed, but she didn't contradict him. It was just too wonderful to be there with him, like that, under the canopy of stars.

And the possibility of doing again what they'd just

done was not something she could deny herself. Not when nothing had ever felt as good or as right as that had.

And not when there wasn't a single other thought in her head but being with this man....

Chapter 10

After the most amazing night Seth had ever had with anyone, he spent the next five days as nothing more than an unhappy spectator in Lacey's overworked week.

They'd had all of Sunday night together. When the power and air-conditioning had come back on they'd moved into his bedroom where they'd made love, slept, made love, slept, made love again. And again on Monday morning, when Lacey had been no more eager than he had been to leave his bed and rejoin the world.

But since then Seth had been relegated to watching her from the main house.

He saw her leave each morning when he was barely rolling out of bed at dawn. And despite the fact that he'd waited up and watched for her to come home each and every night, there had been another night like the one the week before when she hadn't made it home at all, and on the other three nights she'd dragged herself back so late and looking so tired that he'd thought the kindest thing he could do was just keep his distance and let her get to bed. Alone.

Twice he'd thought there was a chance to spend some time with her when her assistant had called to arrange for him to go to the construction site for a meeting about the road she wanted to put through his property.

Both times he'd imagined getting her alone for an hour, maybe sneaking up to the old house's attic.

But her assistant had called to reschedule the first appointment, and when he'd arrived at the site for the second one her assistant had apologized but said that Lacey had had to rush out to the scene of an accident that had caused an injury to one of her crew, canceling that meeting before it could happen, too.

What it all added up to, he told himself on Friday night as he showered after his own day's work, was to more and more proof of why he should just write this whole thing off. Why he should resist his attraction to her. It was evidence right there in front of him of just how driven she was, of what was most important to her, of how obsessed she was.

Just the way his own father had been.

Just the way Charlotte had been.

Work, work, work. First. Foremost. Forever.

And even worse with Lacey was the fact that for her it wasn't only about the work or the drive to succeed, the way it had been for Charlotte. For Lacey there was that personal element, that determination she had to prove something to her father. To compete with her brothers for Morgan Kincaid's respect.

So if he had any brains at all, Seth told himself, he would just forget about Lacey and get on with things the way they'd been before he'd ever set eyes on her.

But the truth was, he wanted her, and he wanted her bad.

He ached for her. He burned for her. He couldn't stop thinking about her. He couldn't stop reliving in his mind their night together. He couldn't stop plotting and planning and trying to figure out a way to have some time with her—hell, he'd lost hours and hours of sleep this week just to catch a glimpse of her out his window when she was coming or going.

And none of that had been true with Charlotte.

He'd been crazy about Charlotte. He had. But somehow his feelings for her hadn't had the same kind of intensity as the ones he had for Lacey. Maybe that was why things with Charlotte hadn't really popped when he'd first met her in Denver. Why it had been so easy for him to keep it strictly business until later, when she'd come here.

But with Lacey? Things had popped the day they'd first met, from the minute he'd seen her walking across that open field in her high heels.

Finished rinsing away the soap and shampoo, he turned off the spray of water, closed his eyes, hung his head and shook it in disbelief of himself, of what he was thinking, feeling.

He couldn't stop wanting her. Craving just a glance from those beautiful green eyes. The touch of her hand. The silkiness of her hair falling across his skin.

He couldn't stop the images of them sharing a future together. The images of her sharing his bed every night. Waking up with him every morning. Having his kids. Spending the rest of their lives together.

Opening his eyes again, he reached for the towel slung over the shower door and began to dry off, wondering as he did what the hell was wrong with him. Telling himself to just let everything with Lacey go. To get over her before it went any further.

But the first thing he did when he finally stepped out of the shower stall and opened the bathroom window to let the steam out was crane around to catch the sliver of a view he got of the guesthouse to see if she might have gotten home while he'd been showering.

No, no lights.

Of course not, he thought. It was only a little past nine. And so what if it was Friday night? To someone like Lacey, Friday was just another workday; it wasn't the end of the week. She was probably planning to work Saturday and Sunday, too. He probably wouldn't be able to get any time with her then, either.

Just give it up....

Except that even as he dispensed that bit of advice to himself, he knew he couldn't. Last weekend had hooked him.

Because last weekend had been great. Even before they'd ended up making love in the pool. And it was the ways that Lacey was unlike Charlotte that had really sucked him in.

Because unlike Charlotte, Lacey could—and had—left work behind completely once she'd had her mornings to accomplish something. She could—and had—slowed down and enjoyed things besides work. And when she did, when she had, he'd lost sight of the workaholic in her, lost sight of everything *but* her. And then he'd fallen for her.

So why, if she could do it last weekend, couldn't she do it on a regular basis? he thought.

After all, Charlotte couldn't—or wouldn't—have done last weekend the way Lacey had. If he was remembering right, his father wouldn't have, either. His father would have worked, too, and left Seth's mother to spend time with the kids.

But now Seth knew that there was a part of Lacey that *wasn't* a workaholic. Now he knew that she could be persuaded to set work aside. And that once she had, she could enjoy not working.

And as long as that part of her existed, couldn't he keep tapping into it?

Not without some effort, he knew.

But when the effort paid off it was so worth it, that maybe he was willing to keep doing whatever it took.

It wouldn't be easy under the overriding shadow of her father and that determination she had to prove herself. To have a position with the family business that was as important as his sons had held. But easy didn't matter as much to him as having Lacey did, he realized.

It also didn't help that he'd already relegated himself to some kind of nonentity because he wasn't a huge football fan, or that Lacey could be relegated to that same nonentity status if she was with him.

So what if he became a football fan? he asked himself, still trying to fix things so he could have her.

He knew the game. The teams. Enough about the major players. A little more in-depth reading of the sports page, a little studying up on the subject, a little updating himself on Morgan Kincaid's contribution, stats, history, and he'd be able to hold his own with the former football star.

That was something small that he was willing to do if it meant he wouldn't be a detriment to Lacey. If it meant that she could feel better about being with him.

And it wasn't something she'd asked of him—that occurred to him as he shaved. That he'd come up with it on his own was important.

Because also unlike Charlotte, Lacey didn't want him to be something he wasn't. She didn't want to change him. She didn't disapprove of him or think she should turn him into another version of her. So doing something like showing more interest in football for her sake—when it was his own decision, when it wasn't a demand she was making of him, when it didn't entail changing who he was—was no big deal.

But really, wasn't that how he was leaning all the way around? If they each could just bend a little—if Lacey could just back off of work slightly, if he could show more of an interest in the sport that drove her family, then couldn't they meet in the middle and have something together?

Maybe he was kidding himself, but in that moment when all he wanted was to find any way to be with her, to have her, when he wanted to see her, to hear her voice, to touch her and kiss her and take her in his arms so much it had him tied in knots, he thought they could.

And he knew he had to at least talk to her about it. Give it his best shot.

Because he wanted her too much not to.

And nothing he did, nothing he told himself, nothing at all, could shut that feeling down.

"Dad, are you hearing what you're saying?" Lacey couldn't believe she was sitting at her desk at ten on Friday night having this phone call with her father. "I've just told you that we made up half the work that didn't get done last week and that by the end of next week we will have made up the rest. That means that at the end of week three, we will be where we're scheduled to be even though we lost all of week one. And you're *still* not happy?"

"*Ahead* of schedule! What have I always said? Just being good enough isn't good enough! Under budget and ahead of schedule—that's what you should be shooting for."

"Well, it helps the budget that we're getting three weeks' worth of work done in two weeks—*without* paying overtime. Right now that's all I can tell you." And she'd foolishly thought that that might please him, which was why she'd called to report to him.

"Don't you go paying overtime without getting my okay!"

"We aren't paying overtime, Dad—that's what I said. You've already made your position clear on the subject—it isn't something I've forgotten." And oh boy, was she sorry she'd called him. "I won't keep you," she said then, to at least cut short her mistake. "I just thought I'd give you an update. I'll talk to you next week."

"Did you get that road worked out with Camden?" her father demanded instead of letting her off the phone.

Camden.

Seth.

Just his name sent a wave of longing through her.

"We haven't worked out the details yet. I tried to do that twice this last week but couldn't get to it. Maybe this weekend…"

"Don't tell me you're taking this weekend off to spend with him! If I can't get things done because you're being googly-eyed over some man—"

"I'm not taking this weekend off. And if I talk to Seth about the road, that's work, isn't it? It's what you just *told* me to get done." It was time to end this call before her father could tear into her any more. "It's late so I'm going to let you go. If anything happens with the road I'll call."

"Don't you let him pull any Camden shenanigans on us, little girl," her father said suspiciously.

"I won't," she assured him, rather than saying anything else that might prolong this. "Good night, Dad."

Her father finally said good-night, and Lacey got to hang up.

Then she let her head drop to her desk.

Would her father ever think she was good enough? Would any job she did meet his standards? She knew how hard he'd always been on Ian and Hutch, but somehow it seemed like he was being even more unreasonable with her.

Naturally she knew he would say that she thought he was being more unreasonable because—like all women—she was overly sensitive and couldn't take what a man could take…

She drew in a deep breath and sighed it out. Then she sat up again, intending to get back to work.

Which was when she thought she might be hallucinating. Looking through the archway that connected her dining-room office with the old house's living room and out the picture window, she thought she saw Seth's truck coming down the road.

She blinked and kept watching, trying not to get too excited, telling herself that it could be any one of a dozen people who drove to work out there every day in white trucks.

Except that no one would be coming back to work now.

The truck pulled up to the front of the house, and she could see Seth behind the wheel. That first sight of him wiped away her exhaustion.

Cowboy boots, jeans, a cream-colored dress shirt— that's what she saw him wearing as he got out of the truck once he'd stopped the engine.

Nothing and no one had ever looked so good to her.

Too good for her to care why he might be there or that her own tan twill slacks and red crewneck T-shirt were hardly alluring, or that her ponytail could have become lopsided during her long, long day.

The only thing that registered was that Seth was on his way up the porch steps.

Lacey stood and went around her desk, calling "Come in!" in answer to his knock on the front door. It was only when she met him in the entryway that it finally struck her that regardless of how intimate they'd been when she'd left him on Monday morning, she hadn't so much as caught a glimpse of him since then and maybe she should curb the inclination to throw herself into his arms.

As if she needed something to anchor her to keep

from doing that, she wrapped a nonchalant elbow around the newel post at the foot of the stairs to the second floor and said, "This is a surprise."

Seth didn't even say hello. He merely crossed the entry and did what she'd had in mind—he took her by the shoulders, pulled her to him and kissed her as if nothing had separated last weekend and now. Deeply, intensely, profoundly, soundly, thoroughly, he kissed her. And while Lacey attempted to keep up and give as good as she got, some of that kiss just swept her off her feet, leaving her slightly light-headed when he ended it, let go of her and took half a step backward.

Luckily Lacey still had hold of the newel post to keep herself on her feet.

"That was some kind of hello," she said with a laugh.

"It barely scratches the surface," he countered in a voice that was lower than usual, that seemed to mean business—although Lacey wasn't sure why that thought occurred to her.

"I've been watching you coming and going all week—when you actually *did* come and go," he said.

"Tuesday night I fell asleep at my desk again. It's still been crazy, but I gained a little ground to make up for our slow start, so—"

"Do not say it was worth it," he warned.

"I was going to say *so that was good*."

"That was the only good thing about this week, then," he muttered, then said, "That's why I'm here—I want to do something about it."

Lacey was confused, and it must have shown in her expression because he went on before she'd said anything, telling her about how he'd hoped each and every night that she might get home early enough to spend some time with him, how he'd hoped every morning that she might hang around long enough to come and have breakfast with him, how he'd even fantasized about the meetings she'd missed turning into more than business meetings.

"And after all that, I started out tonight telling myself to forget it," he said. "To forget last weekend. To forget any hope that we might have any portion of that again. To forget you."

Lacey was still glad to be holding the newel post because she'd begun to wonder if he'd come here to end whatever it was that was going on between them. And even though she didn't fully understand it, she was struck hard by that thought. Hard enough to need some support to go on facing him if that was what she was in store for.

"So what was that entrance you just made—one last kiss to say goodbye?" she asked, hating that her voice sounded so apprehensive.

He shook his head. "I just wanted you to remember what things are like between us before I say what I came to say."

Things between them were amazing. Remarkable. Incredible. She'd missed him and wanted him so much this past week that it had been awful never even seeing him. She'd relived every moment of their weekend together, of their night of lovemaking a million times in her mind. She'd wanted nothing more than to get home earlier each night and maybe spend it with him. She'd looked over at the main house on her way out every morning, tempted to delay her day, to have even a few minutes with him.

So the kiss had been great, but she hadn't needed it or anything else to remind her of this man.

"What did you come to say?" she asked hesitantly, worrying that he wanted her to know what she'd be missing when he told her they were through.

"That even though I told myself to forget you, I came out on the other end of that—not only can't I forget you, I think we have something, Lacey. Something I want. Something that I'm willing to work on to have."

"I'm not sure what that means—"

"I'll tell you what it means."

He did just that, telling her how much he'd missed her and wanted her. How much he wanted her to be a part of his life—not merely a passing-through part, but a very real, very permanent part. The primary part. He went on to say words that she began to hang on because the picture he painted of them together, of a future together, was so appealing.

"I'll even become the biggest football fan of them all," he said as he drew to a close. "In a room full of football players and fanatics, I'll make sure I'm the one your father wants to talk football with. I guarantee that I won't drag you down. I'll be your greatest asset, not the drawback that other guy was. All I want is for you to meet me halfway."

"I'll never get my father to tone down the football stuff even halfway, if that's what you mean. Football is what runs in his veins."

"That's not what I mean. I want you to meet me halfway by putting some limits on the work you do so your hours are reasonable and we can be together."

"Put some limits on work?" she repeated with a

facetious sort of chuckle. "Do you think I wouldn't have done that already if I could have? I'm putting in the hours I need to put in to get the jobs done—for the training center and the sportswear line. As it is, I'm barely keeping up. Doing the smallest amount less would put me behind."

"Then let's find a way to fix that," he said. "I've thought about it and I'm figuring there isn't much wiggle room with the clothing line. But when it comes to the training center, I think there are some options."

"You're kidding."

"I know what it means to you that your father gave you this project. But it's too much. What you're having to do by yourself is unreasonable. So what if you take another look at it? See if you can extend some deadlines—"

"That isn't possible. My father wants this facility open in the spring. Or earlier—he wants me *ahead* of schedule, not extending the schedule."

"Okay, then what about including Ian again, sharing the load?"

"My father took Ian *off* the project."

"Because your father was angry about what went on with the property issue—but surely by now he's cooled down. I saw him at the wedding, at the groundbreaking—he and Ian seem to be on fine terms. And now that the project is underway, now that all the problems with acquiring the property are ironed out—"

"Not *all* the property problems are ironed out. There's still the access road we need."

"Anything you need, Lacey—that's what I'll give you. Anything, any way you need it, if you'll just work with me on this. Your father doesn't seem at odds with

Ian now—negotiate getting Ian back on the project, doing it jointly with him."

"I might as well just buy a billboard that announces that I can't do the job."

"You *can* do the job, but do you want to do it at the expense of everything else? I'm just asking you to do it in more moderation so we can have a life, too. If you *choose* to share the load and make your father see that it's a choice, not a necessity, that it's something you're opting for in order to have a life of your own, isn't that a position you can take?"

"The only way I can prove that I can do the job is to do it. Myself. Without asking for concessions or help or extensions."

"Then what about just *not* doing it?" Seth said.

"Just *not* doing it?" she parroted in disbelief.

"What's the worst that would happen if you said *to hell* with it all, with proving your father wrong, *to hell* with whatever role your father put you in, *to hell* with everything but just doing what you want, what makes you happy? Because from where I'm sitting, I'm wondering why—if what you really enjoy doing is sportswear—why go on with this project at all? Why not hand it back to your father, focus on the clothing line, have a life with me and forget the rest."

"I'll tell you why!" Lacey said, her temper flaring in the face of what seemed like Seth discounting her goals the same way Dominic had. "The training center is my chance. The only chance I've been given to step up and do what *I* know I can do. To grab the brass ring, if that's how you want to look at it. That's first and foremost. I've worked for this opportunity, *fought* for it. I'm not just going to shrug my shoulders at it now, slip away and be *your* little woman!"

She had a full head of steam and she couldn't contain it.

"And besides that," she shouted, "to say that poor-little-me can't do the job would mean that my father won every fight I've ever had with him, that he was right—that no matter what a woman says, she ends up focusing on a man, a family, *clothes!* He'd say he was right not to trust me with anything important before this. Not to trust any woman with anything important because the minute a man comes on the scene, that's where she ends up."

"So what? So what if he says that? If he believes it? In the long run, what difference does it actually make? Is it better to prove a point than to be happy? I saw a new you last weekend, a relaxed Lacey, a happier Lacey when you were out from under your father's thumb for a while, and you can't tell me otherwise."

She could, but it wouldn't have been true. She *had* been a more relaxed version of herself with Seth last weekend. She had enjoyed it and felt good about it and hated having it come to an end.

But that one weekend didn't change the fact that now that she had this opportunity with Kincaid Corporation, she couldn't just throw it away. And to do anything but handle it all herself, all by herself, was to throw it away because she knew that to bring Ian in would mean Ian would get the credit.

"So you'll become a football fanatic, and in return for that you think I should give up building the training center," she said.

"All I'm asking," Seth said, interrupting her

thoughts, "is just that you go at a different pace. A more human pace. That you do whatever it takes to end your workday sometime before midnight, that you take weekends off, so we can have some time together."

"I can do my job, but at *your* pace, the way you want me to do it," she said, unable to see how this could end well.

He reached to take her arms again, but something in Lacey made her step backward, out of that reach.

"What I want," he said slowly, enunciating each word, "is you. Time *with* you. A life *with* you. And I want you to do what you want to do, but I think that this *pace* you keep and your determination to make this point with your father is keeping you from admitting what you *do* want—even to yourself. Because just maybe what you *do* want is what your father thought you might end up wanting."

"Really? Is that so?" she said sarcastically, hating that he was telling her about herself as if he knew more than she did, telling her that her father was right, pushed buttons he shouldn't push. "You're so convinced that what I want is you and being your *little* woman, and maybe doing some token job to keep me busy."

"No, that's not what I said. I want us to have a life together and for that to come first for us both. And no, I can't be sure that's what you want. I can only hope it might be. What I *am* saying is that maybe you can't be sure, either, because you're so intent on competing and proving your point that you haven't thought beyond the damn training center and making your damn point with your father. That even if it creeps in just slightly—like last weekend—you push aside what actually *does* make you happy, what you just might want, and go back to burying yourself under that drive to show your old man that you're as good as his sons."

"What I want," Lacey said, enunciating each word the way he had, "is what I'm doing."

He studied her for a long moment before he said, "This might be easier if I thought that was true. But I think you'd deny what you actually do want rather than let your father be right. And at the end of that you just lose, Lacey. You lose by your own hand and I'm not sure you see that." He shook his head, his voice went low and gravelly, and he added, "The trouble is, I lose, too. But you aren't going to let me do anything about that, are you?"

This was definitely falling apart, and inside, so was Lacey.

But she swallowed back the tears that filled her throat and whispered, "I guess not."

He shook his head again—this time in disgust—then he turned and went out the way he'd come in.

And Lacey stayed frozen where she was, chin high, hanging on for dear life to that newel post until she heard the sound of Seth's truck far in the distance.

Then she slid down the post, feeling the heat of salty tears sting her eyes and trail to her jawbone.

And she told herself that she'd just done the only thing she could have done.

No matter how bad it felt.

Chapter 11

Lacey just worked.

All of the weekend that followed her breakup with Seth, all of the next week, Saturday and Sunday of the weekend after that, and even until four in the afternoon on Labor Day, she threw herself more into work than she ever had before.

Day and night—overseeing every tiny detail of the construction of the Monarchs' training center, and managing every aspect of her clothing line's production, marketing, sales, distribution and website over the phone and via the Internet—she worked. She barely slept more than three or four hours a night, and she'd spent those three or four hours on an air mattress she put upstairs in the old house, near the functioning bathroom.

It was only on Labor Day that she took her first real

break. And she might not have done that except that Hutch was back from his honeymoon and both of her brothers had threatened to roll her in a rug and carry her if need be to Ian and Jenna's Labor Day barbecue.

So Lacey had a plan: if she was going to be forced to take time off, she was going to catch up on a few nonwork things that she'd let lapse.

She would attend the barbecue from four until seven or eight o'clock that evening.

Then she'd drop some things at the furnished apartment in the upper floor of the house-turned-duplex that Hutch owned—the apartment that she'd again arranged with Hutch to use after her falling-out with Seth, but had yet to manage to move into.

At the apartment she would take a hot shower—a luxury, since the ancient shower she'd been using at the old house-slash-office was rarely more than lukewarm.

She would also wash and condition her hair.

Then she would bide her time with more paperwork until 1:00 or 2:00 a.m., when she could be reasonably sure that Seth would be sound asleep.

During the middle of that first Friday night she'd gone to the Camden ranch, made sure there were no lights on in the main house, then slipped into the guesthouse to pack a bag with just enough to tide her over. She'd sent her assistant to pack up her business-related things during the following week. But there were still some personal things that needed to be retrieved. So, at 1:00 or 2:00 a.m. she would finish off her Labor Day hiatus by finally and completely clearing her things out of his guesthouse.

And after that she would go back to the office for

another night on the air mattress so she could start the next week at the crack of dawn.

Because working like a fiend was the only chance she had of outrunning the misery that overwhelmed her every time a thought of Seth crept in, so it was important that any window of time that opened up be planned, filled and kept a tight rein on.

Which was what she had every intention of doing with her first dreaded downtime since the Founder's Day weekend she'd spent so blissfully with Seth...

"Oh, my gosh, you look *awful!*"

Lacey could tell that her new sister-in-law hadn't meant to greet her like that when she first opened her front door, because Jenna turned a bright shade of red and quickly followed with "I'm sorry! That came out wrong. Of course you don't look *awful,* just tired. I can see why Ian and Hutch are worried about you. Come in, come in."

Lacey went into the farmhouse her brother Ian now shared with Jenna and Abby and waved a hello to her even newer sister-in-law, Issa, who was watching from the kitchen at the end of the hallway.

"Yacey!"

Lacey's nearly three-year-old nephew Ash couldn't pronounce her name. *Yacey* was his version, and he shouted it as he charged her to wrap his arms around her knees.

"Hi, babycakes. How's my guy?" Lacey greeted him, bending over to give him a hug.

"We gots marshallows to cook later," he confided.

"Marshmallows," Jenna translated. "For s'mores."

"I can't wait," Lacey said to them all, faking enthusiasm and energy she didn't have.

Then Ash let go of her knees and reached for her hand. "I'm s'posa bring you out the back," he said, as if he'd been given a very important mission.

"Ian and Hutch are out there," Jenna explained.

"Is there something I can do in here to help first?" Lacey offered.

Jenna shook her head as if it were unthinkable. "No, no, go with Ash."

Lacey had the sense that something was going on, but she gave in and let her nephew lead her through the farmhouse and out the back door, where her brothers were sitting on two of three folding chairs.

They greeted her as Ash drew her all the way to the third folding chair and ordered her to sit. Then Hutch said to his son, "Go play with Abby now, Ash."

"'Cuz you gotta talk to Yacey," Ash said, echoing something he'd heard.

"What is this, an intervention?" Lacey asked with a laugh when Ash trotted off in the direction of the sandbox.

"Sort of," Hutch answered with a laugh of his own.

"No, not sort of," Ian corrected. "This is definitely an intervention. We're worried about you."

Jenna had told her that. Apparently it was a subject of discussion.

"Nobody needs to worry about me, I'm fine," Lacey assured them in an airy tone that sounded fake even to her own ears.

"Oh, come on, Lace, that's not true," Hutch cajoled. "You said you didn't want to stay at the Camden ranch after all and wanted to use the apartment. But Issa and I are still living downstairs until we move next month, remember? I know you haven't been there a single night since you said that—"

"And my assistant talked to your assistant when she called to find out where the copy of that first land survey was," Ian interjected. "We know you're *sleeping* at the construction site."

Was that *all* they knew? Had they heard or pieced together anything about her and Seth?

It didn't seem as though they could have, so she said, "We've had a rough start and I've been trying to make up time. Plus I'm dealing with my sportswear, don't forget. Sleeping at the office is just a temporary thing for convenience. There were nights I didn't even make it back to the Camden guesthouse—that's why it seemed silly to pay rent and I bought the air mattress. I plan to move into your apartment when the barbecue is over tonight, Hutch, but there will still be nights when I'm sure I'll end up staying at the site, using the air mattress."

"You can't let him do this to you," Hutch said.

Maybe they did know about Seth and what had gone on with him. But how could they?

"If you let him, Dad will take your entire life and use it as his own," Ian added, letting her know that it wasn't Seth they were referring to.

"He's done it to both of us and now he's doing it to you with the training center," Hutch put in.

Her brothers went on to talk about how the bigger-than-life Morgan Kincaid might not be aware of just how much he demanded of his children, but that they'd both lost years and relationships and things that were important to them in the course of doing what their father wanted of them.

"There comes a time with him when you just have to stand up and say no," Hutch advised her. "Because if you don't, you don't get a life of your own."

"You know Hutch figured that out before I did," Ian contributed. "But I had to come to it myself with Jenna, with the land for the training facility. You've avoided his wrath before—"

"Because I'm the girl."

"Because you're the girl," Ian agreed. "But now that he's got you doing the center, we feel like we're watching you fall into the hole we had to fight our way out of."

"And we're hoping we can save you from it before it goes too far," Hutch put in.

"I'm fine," Lacey lied.

"No. You're doing a great job for him, but you're not fine," Hutch corrected. "Look in the mirror— you're pale as a ghost, there are circles under your eyes, I swear you look like you've lost ten pounds since the last time I saw you. And we had to double-team you and threaten you just to get you to come here today. You would have worked otherwise."

"The thing is," Ian said, "we just want you to learn from our mistakes. You have to draw the line with the old man because no matter how much you give, he'll want more."

"It's something we learned when he was drilling us for football when we were little kids. And no, it isn't easy to buck him, and he'll pull out all the stops to keep you doing what he wants."

"He'd say that I can't do the job. That he knew it all along."

"He would and he will," Ian confirmed. "But you

can't let that get to you. I let what he said get to me for too long. I tried to please him at any cost for too long. You can work with Dad, for Dad, but it has to be you who draws the line and sticks to it, because he never will. He'll take all you've got and just want more, and you won't be left with anything for yourself."

Jenna and Issa came out the back door then, carrying trays full of appetizers, drinks and food to be grilled, effectively ending the intervention that Lacey was sure now didn't have anything to do with Seth.

But she couldn't help making a connection between what her brothers had said and what Seth had said to her that last Friday night at the office.

And it didn't help that she was sitting in Ian's backyard, with Ian who now had Jenna and Abby, with Hutch who now had Issa and Ash.

Her brothers had families. Lives. They had weathered storms with their father and absorbed his disapproval, his disparagement, his belittling. They had weathered years of separation from Morgan Kincaid.

Hutch and Ian had withstood the worst their father had dished out and pushed through it, gone beyond it, to find and have what they wanted. What made them happy.

And maybe she was really, really tired—no, there was no question about it, she *was* really, really tired— but she suddenly started to see something in the message of her brothers' intervention that they hadn't intended to give.

No one escaped Morgan Kincaid's criticism. No one was totally free of his narrow-mindedness or his biases. And no one could please him or win his approval unconditionally or for all time.

Her brothers might not have had to deal with their father's sexism, but they'd had their own burdens to bear with Morgan's expectations of them on the football field, in business, in personal lives he'd tried to use to his advantage.

And her burden to bear was that she *the girl*. She was female. And Morgan Kincaid had archaic, macho opinions about what that meant. None of which were any more important than anything he'd said about Ian or Hutch along the way when they hadn't done what suited him.

But she was killing herself to change her father's mind. To prove he was wrong.

And worse than that, she was turning her back on what she'd found with Seth to do it.

Seth wasn't her father or Dominic. He hadn't asked her to stop doing what she was doing, he hadn't ignored what was important to her or expected her to fit some idea he had of what a woman should do or be. All he'd done was ask her to do what Ian and Hutch had just advised her to do: put work into perspective, not let it take up every minute of every day—and night. Not let it be all there was to her life.

Seth had asked her to explore what she *wanted*. What made her happiest.

And she'd been afraid of doing that because if what she wanted was him and a life with him and a family with him, then her father would ride in on his high horse and say that he'd been right all along.

But so what? So what if he rode that high horse into a life she had with Seth? Into a life that was always like Founder's Day weekend had been? Into a life as happy as what Hutch had found with Issa, as happy as what Ian had found with Jenna? Wasn't that happiness—feeling the way she felt when she was with Seth—the real victory? Not that she could prove her father wrong or make her point, but that she had Seth and all he was offering?

How could I have been so dumb? she asked herself.

Seth was amazing. He was gorgeous, he was smart, he was funny and sexy and strong. He was his own man, a man who had shunned expectations that had been placed on him as a Camden because he'd had the wisdom to know himself and what he needed in life in order to find his own way.

And she was empty without him.

She'd filled every single hour since ending things with him with work or fitful sleep. She'd frantically done anything she could to keep from even thinking about him. But the truth was that in spite of any of that there was a huge hole in her heart that she couldn't fill, that never went away.

She wanted Seth. She wanted to be with him. No job, no point to prove, no worry of an I-told-you-so, carried more weight than that. Nothing and no one carried more weight than that. She wanted him. She wanted a life with him. A future with him. Kids with him.

If she hadn't already lost any hope of that...

"I have to go!" she announced before she even knew she was going to say anything.

"Are you okay?"

"Are you sick?"

Lacey's laugh at her brothers' questions was slightly batty. She knew she really, really was tired.

But what she said was "You guys are right—in

more ways than you know. And I need to take care of something—if it isn't already too late. So I'm not going to stay for dinner."

Ian and Hutch both looked worried and along with Issa and Jenna, they all tried to persuade Lacey to stay.

But they couldn't.

Because she had something so, so much more important to do than to eat a hamburger and an ear of corn.

Chapter 12

Lacey was anxious and eager and scared and worried and in a rush to get to Seth as soon as she could. She didn't want to lose another moment and risk that he might meet someone else or decide he was better off without her.

But she also didn't want him to see her looking like she'd showered and shampooed her hair for the last ten days under a barely warm drizzle of water and slept on an air mattress for far fewer hours than she'd needed.

He was likely at one Labor Day function or another and not home anyway, she decided, so she could take a little time to spruce up.

When she reached Hutch's duplex, she used the key he'd given her to let herself in and go straight up the stairs to the upper-floor apartment with her suitcase in hand. She dropped the suitcase in the middle of the living-room floor as soon as she went into the apartment, opened it up and took out the only thing she had to wear that didn't look like it belonged at a construction site—a short yellow A-line crepe sundress that was plain, sleeveless and shapeless.

She knew it wouldn't be sex appeal that won the day with that, but it was her only choice.

She found a hanger in the closet in the bedroom, hung the dress on it and took it with her into the bathroom, hoping the steam from her shower would rid it of wrinkles.

Then she took her first good shower in days and washed her hair so thoroughly her scalp started to hurt before she rinsed it.

There was nothing to be done with her hair but to let it air-dry because she hadn't packed her hair dryer. But she counted herself lucky to have enough natural wave and body to still wear the blond mass down once it dried on its own.

Even though she hated the time it was taking, she was careful with her makeup, using concealer on the dark circles under her eyes, blush to add some color to her face, and just enough mascara to draw attention to her lashes and away from the evidence of her lack of sleep.

She didn't have the bra she needed to wear with the dress, and since the ones she had would have left the straps showing, she went without, wearing only lace bikini panties under the well-lined shift.

Then she did a couple of fierce shakes of the dress to rid it of any lingering wrinkles, judged it presentable, and put it on.

Once she'd slipped her sandals on, she was ready to go.

Taking with her so many butterflies in her stomach that she had to pause to breathe deeply in an effort to calm them before they made her sick.

Just go find him... Maybe it will be okay...

Or maybe it wouldn't. Maybe it was already too late...

No, she couldn't think that, she told herself.

She couldn't.

But still the thought lingered as she grabbed her keys, hurried out of the apartment and headed for the Camden ranch.

She'd had her assistant notify Seth of two things during the last week—one that she would have all of her belongings out of his guesthouse by Labor Day, and two, that she would appreciate it if he would give her specifics on what he was willing to do on the issue of the road she needed to put through his property.

She'd received Seth's response via a messenger of his own—the Camdens would sell her the strip of land that she required at a price that was reasonable enough to please even her father, and with no conditions, exceptions, exclusions or contingencies despite the fact that it would be bisecting a parcel of their property.

There had been no comment about Lacey vacating the guesthouse.

As she drove to the ranch, she worried that that had been because it suited Seth just fine for her to get out. And that it might be an indication that he wouldn't be so welcoming of her when she showed up.

It didn't occur to her until she turned onto the road

that led to Seth's house that he might be having a Labor Day barbecue of his own. An entire party that she might be crashing.

But since there were no cars to be seen when she approached the house, she decided that wasn't going to be a problem.

So she pulled around to the garages and parked where she'd parked when she'd been staying there, opting to take the rear route into the houses again now.

Not only wasn't there a party going on in back, around the pool, but there also wasn't a single sign of Seth anywhere. In fact, the main house was locked up tight, and she went back to thinking that he was probably spending the holiday with friends. Hopefully male friends.

She considered using the time while she waited for him to return to pack what remained of her belongings in the guesthouse. Certainly a case could be made for it—if this didn't go well, it would be good to have all of her things cleared out, loaded in her car and ready to take with her.

But something about that just seemed so defeatist that she couldn't make herself do it. Instead she sat on the nearest lounger and decided to try to get her nerves under control while she waited for Seth.

Initially, she sat perched on the side of the lounger, her feet planted flat on the pool tiles, her spine straight, her hands in her lap.

But time passed and she could feel herself beginning to slump, so she swung her legs onto the lounger and sat back, her head still high and held away from the chair.

Then somehow her head fell back, too, and she started to look at the calm, clear blue water of the pool.

Then her eyes were burning so she closed them...

For only a minute, she told herself. She would close them for only a minute.

Or maybe for two...

"Lacey?"

Seth...

The man was insatiable.

But that was okay, because she wanted him, too. This really had been the very best way to close out Founder's Day weekend...

"Lacey? Wake up."

Founder's Day weekend? The power was out. They'd made love.

But they'd gone inside. Why did it feel like she was still outside?

It wasn't Founder's Day weekend.

It was Labor Day.

She wasn't supposed to be asleep!

Lacey jolted awake, realizing that somehow it had gotten dark. Very dark. And it seemed really late. And she felt like she'd been asleep for hours and hours.

And Seth was there—she could see him through sleep-blurred vision, wearing a gray polo shirt and jeans, sitting a few feet to the side of the lounger. On a suitcase?

"Oh... What time is it?" she muttered, struggling to get her bearings and recalling suddenly all that had gone on and why she was there.

"3:00 a.m."

"It's three o'clock in the morning?" She'd slept a

long time. "And you're just coming home? With a suitcase?"

"I've been in Vegas with my brother and a couple of my cousins. They, uh… It's something we do for each other when it seems like there's a need…"

"A gambling need?"

"A need to get away to cheer one of us up…"

"Which one of you?" she asked artlessly, still fighting her way out of the heavy cloud of exhausted slumber.

"I think you know," he said somberly.

Lacey's vision finally came into focus and she took a closer look at Seth—disheveled hair, scruffy beard, circles under his blue eyes, too.

"What are you doing here?" he asked. Then, before she could answer, he said, "Oh, yeah, it was Labor Day, wasn't it? You said you'd get the rest of your stuff from the guesthouse. What did you do, sit down to catch your breath between loads and fall asleep?"

"No!" she said, sounding slightly panicked that he thought that, that he was so accepting of that explanation for why she was there. "That's not what I came for at all."

She'd raised her head from the back of the lounger when she'd come awake but now she sat up completely, realizing that her short skirt was high on her thigh.

She tugged at the hem to pull it down as she swung her feet to the tile, wondering where her sandals had gone even as she caught Seth's gaze dropping to her legs for a moment before he yanked it away.

"What did you come for?" he asked then, a deep frown pulling his brows toward each other.

"My brothers twisted my arm to get me to a barbe-cue at Ian's house today… Yesterday, I guess… And, well, it was eye-opening."

Seth didn't say anything to that. He merely went on watching her, giving no encouragement or even an indication that he was glad she was there. Instead the expression on his heartbreakingly handsome face was still dark, leery, distant.

But Lacey knew this was all her fault, that it was up to her to fix it, so she went on to tell him just how her eyes had been opened earlier and the realizations she'd come to.

"I don't want to turn around one day, alone, with nothing but some point I've proven. Seeing my broth-ers happy, with their new families—Dad not being a factor in any of that—made me know that I just want to have a life, my own life, too. That I should be able to."

"Where do the jobs fit in?" Seth asked with some skepticism coloring his tone.

"To tell you the truth, I'm not sure. I've been think-ing about you, about us, about having a future to-gether—"

"*Before* thinking about work?"

He was skeptical, all right.

"*Instead* of thinking about work," Lacey said. "I know I want to go on with the clothing line because I enjoy that—it's mine, it's all mine, and I want to keep doing that. But it's manageable. And when it comes to the training center? I already feel like I've been working on that for ten years. And I don't enjoy anything about it. I know my father will say that I couldn't handle it—"

"But you can because you have."

"That won't matter to him. He'll still say that construction isn't a woman's work. But I somehow reached a place where I don't care. It *isn't* a job for me because I don't want to do it. Maybe he'll give the project back to Ian—if Ian wants it. Or maybe he'll have to do it himself—he'll get to have his say over every nail and splinter and clod of dirt that has to be moved."

"So he might as well be there doing it himself."

"All I know is that it's you I want, Seth," Lacey said, her voice going quiet all of a sudden and catching in her throat as she watched him stand up. She worried that he might be fidgety because he was about to tell her it didn't matter anymore what she wanted.

And in response to that thought, she stood, too, as if that would make her position stronger.

"For the first time," she continued, "there's something that's only about the one person I care more about than anyone I've ever cared about before—you. There's something that's only about being with you. About what we have when we're together. I know that essentially what Dominic wanted—my full attention—"

"Except that he wanted you to give up everything else and I didn't ask that of you."

"I know. And that's a very big deal to me. But when I thought about basically having the kind of life with Dominic that I've been thinking about having with you, I didn't want it. He wasn't that important to me. I didn't have the same kind of feelings for him. But when I think about having that life with you… It's exactly what I want. It's *all* that I want. *You're* what I want. And *everything* else takes second place."

His hands were on his hips. He switched most of his weight onto one of them and stared at her. But again he didn't say anything, and Lacey's heart was beating fast and hard with the worry that he just couldn't accept what she was saying.

She stepped nearer to him, facing him, and looked up into his eyes. "And you don't have to become the biggest football fan ever," she told him. "It means a lot to me that you'd be willing to go to such lengths in order to fit into my family, but you don't have to. Because you and I are enough. For the first time, with you, I can see myself building something of my own. A family of my own. A life of my own. All my own. And it's more than enough—it's the way it should be."

Seth went on staring into her eyes for another long moment before he said, "I love you, Lacey."

"I love you, too," she said, still unsure if that was the segue to something.

"I don't want you to give up anything you don't want to give up. I just want you. And time with you."

"You can have all you want," she assured.

"I want you to marry me," he said as if it were a test.

"I want you to marry me," she countered, as relief began to seep in and she started to feel a little cocky.

"I want to have kids with you."

"I want to have kids with *you*," she said.

"I want to grow old with you."

"Go ahead, but I decided a long time ago that once

I hit thirty-five I was sticking with it from then on," she joked.

He finally cracked a smile, and it was the best thing Lacey had ever seen.

"I'll be eighty and you'll be my still-thirty-five-year-old bride?" he asked.

"And I'm going to have to count on you to look like December so I can pull off looking like May."

He laughed. A sound good enough to go with the smile. So good that for no reason Lacey could fathom, it brought tears to her eyes.

"I'll ask for extra wrinkles with every birthday from here on," he promised.

Then his arms came around her and he pulled her to him, so tightly that she had to turn her head. Her cheek was pressed to his chest as she hugged him back.

"I was afraid I wasn't going to get this," he said then in a grave voice. "And no amount of Vegas or my brother or my cousins could cheer me up."

"I'm sorry," Lacey whispered. "I'm sorry I was so stubborn and stupid and blind and slow."

He loosened his grip on her and veered back, looking down at her while she peered up at him. "Watch it, I don't let anybody say those kinds of things about my fiancée."

Lacey laughed a little at that, finally conquering that threat of tears as she looked up at him and saw what ravages her actions had wreaked.

"You look tired," she said.

This time his smile was devilish. "I had a nap on the plane, so I'm not too tired," he said before he kissed her a kiss that, at first, only said hello.

But then it went on to say so much more, to renew and rekindle, refresh and reawaken things in Lacey that she'd had to suppress for the last ten days in order to survive.

A kiss that reminded her of what she had with this man, of how much he stirred in her, of the fact that she only felt truly complete when she was with him.

Then he ended that kiss, stepped back and dipped a little. The next thing Lacey knew she was flung over one of those broad shoulders and watching his divine derriere from a very odd perspective while cool night air touched hers.

"Oh, this dress is short!" she screeched.

"I'll say," Seth agreed, patting her exposed rump as he sauntered around the pool to the main house, unlocked one set of the French doors and let them in.

He didn't so much as pause to turn on a light, taking her to his bedroom where he unceremoniously deposited her onto his big bed and then joined her there.

Cowboy boots were the first to come off, but after that clothes flew, mouths came together and hands reacquainted themselves with tender flesh.

Desire and arousal ran rampant through Lacey with Seth's every wondrous touch. Needs grew and made demands, and a hunger that had been simmering in her for ten days went to a full boil as she ran her own palms over that exquisitely masculine body that she could never have lived without.

They made wild, passionate love. Wild, passionate love that spoke of how much they'd missed it and each other, of all the glories yet to come for them in a lifetime of lovemaking.

Once their peaks had been reached, leaving them both sated and satiated and their reunion finally and firmly sealed, Seth collapsed with his back to the mattress and pulled Lacey to his side, offering his chest as her pillow, his arms as her blanket.

"I love you, Lacey," he said, pressing another kiss into her hair.

"I love you, Seth," she answered, kissing his chest.

"Will you come with me next weekend to Denver for my grandmother's birthday? Can we announce our wedding then?"

"I'm at your disposal," she said. "But is your family going to hate me for causing your need to be cheered up this weekend?"

"My family will see that you've made me the happiest guy on the planet and love you for it. The bigger problem might be getting us out of this bed in time to go…"

"You want to spend the next four days in bed?"

"What a great idea!"

Lacey laughed, but in truth, the thought of spending four days in bed with him suited her just fine.

She said, "Get some sleep and we'll talk about it. I might be persuaded to take tomorrow off…."

"Hmm… I'll have to think of a way…." he muttered. She could tell he was already drifting off.

That was all right, though, because she was perfectly content to lie in his arms and just bask in what she'd found with him.

A sense of home.

Of things being right.

Of being exactly where she belonged.

And of finally, once and for all, discovering what she wanted for herself that didn't have anything to do with her father or the Kincaid Corporation.

Finally, once and for all, discovering what she wanted for herself.

And getting it.

* * * * *

THE WORLD IS BETTER WITH

Romance

Harlequin has everything from contemporary, passionate and heartwarming to suspenseful and inspirational stories.

Whatever your mood,
we have a romance just for you!

Connect with us to find your next great read,
special offers and more.

f /HarlequinBooks

🐦 @HarlequinBooks

www.HarlequinBlog.com

www.Harlequin.com/Newsletters

H HARLEQUIN®

A *Romance* FOR EVERY MOOD™

www.Harlequin.com

HARLEQUIN®

A *Romance* FOR EVERY MOOD™

JUST CAN'T GET ENOUGH?

Join our social communities
and talk to us online.

You will have access to the latest
news on upcoming titles and special
promotions, but most importantly,
you can talk to other fans about your
favorite Harlequin reads.

Harlequin.com/Community

Facebook.com/HarlequinBooks

Twitter.com/HarlequinBooks

Pinterest.com/HarlequinBooks

HARLEQUIN®

A Romance FOR EVERY MOOD™

Love the Harlequin book you just read?

Your opinion matters.

Review this book on your favorite book site, review site, blog or your own social media properties and share your opinion with other readers!

Be sure to connect with us at:
Harlequin.com/Newsletters
Facebook.com/HarlequinBooks
Twitter.com/HarlequinBooks

HARLEQUIN®

A *Romance* FOR EVERY MOOD™

**Stay up-to-date on all your
romance-reading news with the
Harlequin Shopping Guide,
featuring bestselling authors, exciting new
miniseries, books to watch and more!**

The newest issue will be delivered right to you
with our compliments! There are 4 each year.

Signing up is easy.

EMAIL

ShoppingGuide@Harlequin.ca

WRITE TO US

HARLEQUIN BOOKS
Attention: Customer Service Department
P.O. Box 9057, Buffalo, NY 14269-9057

OR PHONE

1-800-873-8635 in the United States
1-888-343-9777 in Canada

Please allow 4-6 weeks for delivery of the first issue by mail.